★★★

This series is dedicated to all
U.S. military veterans of all branches
who served in times of peace or war,
for your families who stood by you,
for all of you now serving our country,
for all now waiting for a loved one to return,
and for those whose wait has ended in tragedy.
God's love is for you.
The Homeland Heroes Series is for you.

★★★

HOMELAND HEROES

✫

Book One

WOUNDED HEALER

DONNA FLEISHER

GRAND RAPIDS, MICHIGAN 49530 USA

ZONDERVAN™

Wounded Healer
Copyright © 2005 by Donna Fleisher

Requests for information should be addressed to:
Zondervan, *Grand Rapids, Michigan 49530*

Library of Congress Cataloging-in-Publication Data

Fleisher, Donna, 1965-
    Wounded healer / Donna Fleisher.
        p. cm.
    ISBN-10: 0-310-26394-8 (softcover)
    ISBN-13: 978-0-310-26394-4 (softcover)
    I. Title.
    PS3606.L454W68 2005
    813'.6—dc22
                                                              2005002987

Interior design by Michelle Espinoza

Printed in the United States of America

05 06 07 08 09 10 11 12 /❖ DCI/ 10 9 8 7 6 5 4 3 2 1

For Audra.

A little girl named Morgan,
a tape of *Land Before Time*,
homemade sourdough biscuits,
and gobs of warm honey butter.
One of my best Thanksgivings ever.

This story has always been for you.

ACKNOWLEDGMENTS

PRECIOUS LORD GOD, YOU HAVE a purpose for this story. You've humbled me by allowing me to be the one to tell it. Thank You so much. And thank You for all those who encouraged and strengthened me along the way. Especially . . .

✯✯✯

MOM AND DAD. THEY WERE patient as I climbed my steps of faith.

Chris and Thess. Always supportive. Always there for me.

Christine. She was the first to read my stuff. And she didn't laugh. Thank You, Lord, for my precious family.

And Mario too. Yes, he's just a dog, but he oozes unconditional love. Like You.

Lord, please bless Karen Ball and Diane Noble and everyone at Zondervan. They are all the best. Thank You for their hard work. Please accept our offering and do with it as You will.

Thank You for everyone at the 2004 Mount Hermon Christian Writers Conference. Your perfect timing put me there. Thank You for the way You use so many people at conferences to work out Your perfect plan.

And please bless everyone in Oregon Christian Writers. This group, Lord, means so much to me. Thank You for their encouragement and sound teaching all these years.

For Shannon and Susie and Vickie and Heather and Melisa and Trish and Steph and June and all their beautiful families, Lord, thank You so much. I love them all. Thank You for Maddie and Alisabeth. Keep their friendship strong. Thank You, Lord, for Brooke. And for Margaret Becker. And for Gayle Erwin.

And Lord? Thank You for everyone at the Sandcastle. You put me there. They have put up with me. Surround them with Your peace, and touch them with Your love. Thank You, Lord, for my home.

Oh, and one more thing. Please tell everyone at Fort Campbell, Kentucky, that yes, I do know their division has only three brigades. I took some liberties and expanded their design a bit to fit my needs. I hope they can forgive me. It was an incredible honor to borrow them for this story. For everything they did to ensure certain victory during Desert Storm (and for everything they are doing right now), please make sure they know how grateful I am. How grateful we all are. They are awesome. They are Airborne!

WOUNDED HEALER

JANUARY 1996

ONE

CHRISTINA MCINTYRE. GOOD. SHE STILL knew her own name.

Arms, legs, fingers, and— She wiggled her toes. Good. Still intact.

She opened her eyes slowly, blinking carefully, trying to focus.

The cabin. Timmons Trail. She knew where she was.

Why was she on the floor? She started to lift up but froze as a bolt of agony ripped through her front to back, top to bottom. Breath stuck in her throat as her eyes pinched shut; she fell back and for a full minute did not move.

This . . . is not a dream. I'm really hurt. How? What happened?

Cold darkness surrounded her. Night had fallen.

This . . . is not good. I am so late.

Her breath came in puffs. Sharp stabs knifed deep through her right side with each new breath, as fear trickled into her blood. Carefully, she brought her hands around to check the damage.

Her hands were bare. Both of them. Where were her gloves? Her fingers ached with cold. It didn't make any sense. So cold, all over. The long-sleeved thermal shirt she wore under her bright red San Juan Search and Rescue jacket usually kept her warm enough, even on the coldest nights.

Her jacket was gone.

Panic swelled inside her, stealing her breath, returning it only in short gasps. Pain split through her with every breath. She reached her left hand around to feel for damage. She winced. If ribs weren't broken inside her, they were cracked. She cautiously lifted her hand and felt the back of her head. The lump she found there triggered a rush of rote emergency procedure through her mind. *Blunt force trauma to the head—loss of consciousness, moderate duration—contusion, severe swelling, possible con—* She forced it all away, silently mumbling, *Yeah, yeah, yeah.* She lowered her hand. *I'll survive. Just ... breathe.*

Too cold. She needed her gloves, her jacket. How could they possibly be gone? She'd freeze if she didn't find them—she needed them; why would she take them off?

She needed her flashlight. In the deepening darkness, she could tell the door of the cabin was open wide. *Did I come through the door and fall? I tripped over the door stop?* One of the table chairs lay on its side by her feet. Did she knock it over as she fell? Did she fall on top of it? That could explain possible broken ribs. And then she hit her head on the floor and passed out? Had she always been this clumsy?

Closing her eyes, she wanted to sleep. She could have slept, if it wasn't for the nagging stabs in her side.

She needed help. This irritated her. She hated even the thought of it—the rescuer needed rescuing. Because she tripped over her own big feet. The guys would love this. They'd want to haul her out on a litter just to embarrass her. She cringed.

But tonight, and soon, if someone didn't help her down off this mountain, she didn't think she would make it home.

That's just great. And we were supposed to go out tonight. Mexican with Travis. Her stomach churned and she groaned. That would be the last straw, throwing up all over the floor of the cabin.

Get up and get to the radio. Nothing to it. Every cabin in the San Juan District Three Search and Rescue region had a radio. If she could just stand up. Maybe she should light the kerosene lamp first. She needed to find her jacket.

If she could just stand up.

Grunting, panting, squeezing tears from her eyes, hoping no one was watching or listening to her pathetic display, she forced herself up and steadied herself against the table. That was it for a few minutes; quelling the dizziness and drawing in simple breaths had become all she cared about in the world.

She breathed; the frozen air burned her lungs, then hushed out on clouds of steam. *Light the lamp first, find my jacket and gloves, then call for help*. Easy plan. As she made her way around the table to the other side of the cabin, the plan started to concern her. Maybe not so easy after all. The kerosene lamp hung from a hook that had been screwed into the ceiling. The cabin was small but, at five foot six, Chris would have to stand tiptoe to reach the lamp's metal hanger. As she reached her left hand up, her ribs twisted, and she almost fell to her knees. Grabbing the table, gasping again, the pain swirled around her; her mind seemed to be shutting her body down without her consent.

She waited. She was already late. Another minute or two wouldn't matter.

She tried again. Reached the lamp and lowered it to the table. Now all she needed was a match. Just that morning she had tucked matches safe and dry inside her jacket pocket. Her teeth ground as she carefully felt her way in the darkness to the supply cache along the cabin's back wall. She lugged open a heavy drawer and rummaged. Stumps of candles, string, a potato peeler, a deck of cards, a small plastic sewing kit. Matches had to be there. It was her job to supply them. She had brought up a new pack of fifty boxes wrapped in a Ziploc only the week before last. She couldn't find them.

Cursing, she gave up on lighting the lamp. She could work the cabin's radio in her sleep. She inched her way to it, feeling for the box, but jerked her hand back when her finger sliced across something sharp. The sudden movement froze the breath in her lungs, and again she waited, sucking at the blood that welled up from the cut.

Broken glass was not a good thing. A sick sense of dread flooded her stomach. The radio was old—vintage Vietnam era—but it worked fine. Once a month she swapped out its battery, replacing old with new. Once a month she put out a radio check. Every month it checked out loud and clear. Encased in a box with a glass top and aligned only to be heard by San Juan District Three radios, it was available to anyone who needed it in an emergency. Carefully avoiding the shards of glass, Chris felt for the radio's microphone. She couldn't find it. Against the side of the radio itself, she felt where the mike's cord came out of the box. The cord was there, and she followed it out until it abruptly ended. It had been cut.

The fear that had been trickling through her gushed into a torrent; she backed away from the smashed radio case so quickly she hit the table, nearly losing her balance and crashing to the floor.

Standing there, steadying herself against the table, gasping for air and wincing at the agony of it, sick to her stomach and weary beyond belief, she tried to focus on what had become her reality.

One more radio. And her flashlight. Out at the snowmobile. And, she hoped, her jacket. And her gloves. She headed outside. Keeping her right arm pinned against her ribs, she eased herself down the stairs and across the slippery snow-packed ground to her snow machine. She clicked on the snowmobile's headlights and winced at the sudden brightness. She reached for the radio microphone. Without tethered resistance, the mike felt weightless. Terror seized her. Her knees gave out, and she turned just in time to sit on the snowmobile's wide seat.

The radio mike cord had been cut. She dropped the useless mike into the snow, then reached back into the storage compartment. The flashlight, flares, and solar blanket—all gone. Even the small chain saw she carried to clear blowdown was gone. The snowmobile's keys were in her jacket pocket. Her jacket was nowhere to be found. She couldn't even find one glove.

She sat still, silent. Eyes wide. *Breathe. Focus. Think!*

Perfect silence filled the night—loud, ear-ringing silence. Faint swirls of fine, floating snowy powder caught her eye as a light breeze carried them across the headlight beams. Mesmerized, she watched. Her eyelids felt laden with sand. She desperately wanted to sleep.

So quiet. So peaceful. Pain and terror and numbing cold cancelled each other out as she simply sat there, watching the night. In the distance, an owl hooted. Her lips almost smiled.

The silence felt oppressive. Nothing moved. Only the breeze. Until she heard a pop. Very faint. The kind of pop a knuckle makes. Or an ankle bone. Her entire being froze, strained to hear more, to see through the shadows.

Someone was out there. Someone was watching her.

She listened, barely breathed. Reached up and clicked the snow-mobile's headlights off. Darkness fell so quickly, so completely, it stunned her. *Just wait*, she told herself. *Don't panic.* There was just enough waning twilight left that if she could wait and let her eyes adjust, she would be able to see.

She saw something, to her left; she looked, just as that something exploded with light—the beam of a powerful flashlight pointed directly at her face. She turned away, eyes pinched shut.

"Not how I was hoping this night would go."

Did she hear the words? A man's voice. And what he said? She almost laughed, thinking, *You can say that again.* Her eyes opened slowly, but she could tell the beam was still pointed directly at her. "Do you mind?" came out before she realized it.

"Oh. Sorry." The beam of light fell to the snow between them.

Chris turned her head—a man stood about fifty feet away. In the faint light reflecting back over him, she saw the brilliant red of a San Juan Search and Rescue jacket. "Oh, well, sure. That explains it. Thanks a lot."

"What?" He sounded concerned.

"Fits you well. But I'd like it back."

"Oh." The flashlight beam shook as the man shuffled from foot to foot for a second. "Yeah. Well, I needed it more than you did. The stuff I was wearing got wet."

"Sorry to hear that."

The man was quiet.

Chris stared at his shadowy form. As the beam of light cut across her view, her headache spiked. She missed what the man said. "What?"

"Back to the cabin. I'll build a fire. We both need to get warm. Right?"

Well, one of us anyway. The man was wearing her gloves too.

"Let's go. In the cabin."

Chris looked up but couldn't summon the strength to move.

"Now. Let's go. In the cabin." The flashlight's beam swung to point the way.

As Chris sat there, a strange warmth seeped into her bones with every pump of her heart—coursing pumps of pure, building rage. Just who did this lunatic think he was?

"I said *now*. Get up and get back into the cabin. I'm not kidding."

She glared. Not only was the man a vandal and a thief, he was rude as well.

He started toward her, switching the flashlight to his left hand as he walked and then pulling off the glove on his right hand with his teeth. Spitting the glove away, he reached into the pocket of Chris's jacket and pulled out something that glimmered in the light.

He stopped a few feet from her. Chris saw what he now held in his right hand.

"Get in the cabin *now*. I'm not going to tell you again."

A 9mm handgun. Police issue. Or military. She glanced up, into the man's eyes. What she saw shattered her rage, laid bare her underlying terror.

The man slowly raised the pistol and pointed it at Chris's head. She pushed herself up and trudged back to the cabin.

✯✯✯

HIS DAY OFF AND HE was back at the station. Travis Novak still smiled. In a few minutes, Chris would be off work and they would share a corner table at Buen Tiempo, munching on chips and salsa and sipping cold drinks. Chris always sipped a margarita. She didn't hassle Travis that he didn't drink. He would savor his perfectly sweetened, perfectly lemoned iced tea. And then the chimichangas would arrive. He could hardly wait.

Only a few minutes after four thirty—ten, to be exact—but Chris usually met him in the parking lot right at four thirty so Travis headed inside to see what was holding her up. He made his way down the familiar halls to the locker rooms, but instead of turning right, he turned left. He barely opened the door and yelled inside, "Come on, Chris, our chimichangas are a callin'!"

Samantha Jeffries yelled back, "Stop it, Travis, you're making me hungry!"

He laughed. "Is Chris in there?"

"Nope. Just me and Mandy."

"Have you seen her?" He resisted the juvenile urge to look for himself.

"Nope. Not since roll call."

"Okay. Thanks." He pulled the door closed and headed down the hall to the main office of the San Juan District Three Search and Rescue station. Once inside, he leaned against the chest-high counter and said a quick hello to Carla Crawley before going to the wall beside Carla's cubicle to reach for the crew locator clipboard.

"Hey, Travis," Carla said without getting up. "What are you doing here on your day off?"

"Have you seen Chris?" Travis looked over the list of names and times on the locator.

"Not since this morning. She's out checking Tri-Lake and Timmons."

He didn't like what he saw. "She hasn't come back yet?"

"What?" Carla stood up and reached over the counter for the clipboard.

Travis handed it to her. "She put her ETA as three. But it's almost five."

"Now, that's strange."

"You haven't heard from her? When's the last time her unit's radio was checked?"

Carla handed the locator clipboard back to Travis and looked through her stack of incident reports yet to be filed. "She did a radio check as she left, let's see . . . eleven twenty. Sounded fine then. And she checked in when she left Tri-Lake."

"But you haven't heard from her since?"

"It's been crazy today, Travis. Staties keep sending us alerts about one thing or another. I haven't had a chance to check the rosters yet."

Travis frowned. He wasn't blaming Carla, but it was her job . . . and checking in would be the first thing Chris would do when she got back.

He heard Carla's voice working the radio. "San Juan Three calling twenty-twenty-four. Twenty-twenty-four, come in please." They waited. Listened. Travis tagged the clipboard back up on the wall and leaned against the counter. Still no response. Carla keyed the mike. "San Juan Three calling twenty-twenty-four. Please respond."

Nothing but silence.

A thread of fear began to lace itself around Travis's heart. "Try her again."

Carla keyed the mike and repeated the call. They waited. Nothing.

"This can't be right." Travis moved around behind the counter and pulled the mike out of Carla's hand. He reached over her to the radio, spun the squelch, then reset it to where he thought it should be and keyed the mike. "Chris? Chris? This is Travis." He ignored Carla's irritation. "Chris McIntyre, can you hear me? Come in. Please. Chris, please respond."

They waited. Travis reached over and cranked up the radio's volume.

Only light static hissed from the two speakers above them. Basic radio silence.

★★★

THE WALK UP THE STAIRS had been bad enough, but sitting in the freezing, hard chair was beyond bad. Careful not to bend forward or twist or even try to move her right arm, Chris squirmed in the chair. Her rage had melted, taking its warmth with it. As helplessness overtook her, she started to shiver, feeling the cold like never before. Usually she liked cold weather; she felt at home in the mountains of snow and ice. Right now she felt like ice, and the uncontrollable shivering did little to help.

The man stood across the table from her, leaning back against the wall of the cabin. He just stood there, watching her. He had put the gun back into the pocket of Chris's jacket and used one of her matches to light the kerosene lamp, but after that, he just stood and watched her.

Irritation shot through Chris's belly. She looked up at him as words shivered out of her mouth. "Are y—you g—going t—to light the f—fire?"

The man pulled out a cigarette and lit it with another of Chris's matches. After drawing in a deep drag, he said, "Nah. I don't think so. You can if you want."

Chris let out an exasperated breath and looked away. Tucking both hands under her armpits, she rode the fine line between wanting to live and not really caring anymore one way or the other. She let the shivering control her as she lowered her head, closed her eyes. Shutting everything else out, she focused only on helping her body reach down somewhere to find warmth.

A picture popped into her mind. A memory. She almost laughed. There was a time, a few years back, when she lay on an army cot in a parking garage in the middle of the world's busiest desert in nothing but shorts and a sleeveless T-shirt, drenched in her own sweat, panting like an old hound dog. Erin too, in the cot right next to her. It didn't matter that Erin was an officer; in Saudi, the miserable heat and humidity had everyone panting, officers and enlisted alike.

Lieutenant Erin Grayson.

That's just perfect. Think about her when I'm ready to die.

Chris heard movement. Raised her head and looked up.

The man had taken off her jacket and thrown it on the table. "There." He said nothing more.

Chris's jaw dropped. She couldn't think. But she wasted no more time. She reached out a trembling left hand, holding her breath as she did, and pulled the jacket back to her chest. It smelled like cigarette smoke, but she didn't care. It still held some of the man's warmth. She soaked in as much of it as she could. Then it hit her.

Somehow, she had to get the dumb thing on. She managed, right hand, right arm, reach back and around, gritting her teeth as deep bolts of shooting pain seemed to impale her. Her left hand in, her left arm. She pulled it around and fumbled at the zipper with numb, shivering fingers. After several tries, the zipper wouldn't cooperate.

"Don't expect me to help you."

"Nope," Chris said through clenched teeth as she worked. "Didn't expect that at all."

The man let out a breath of laughter and drew in another drag of his cigarette.

Fingers and zipper finally aligned, Chris quickly tugged the zipper up to her chin—still shivering, but immensely relieved. She loved this jacket. She looked up at the man. "D–Don't sup–pose you left the g–gun in the p–pocket?"

The man laughed out loud. Reaching around to the back of his waistband, he pulled the pistol out and displayed it to her, then tucked it back where it came from. He leaned against the wall and crossed his arms over his chest. The cigarette hung in his lips, a curl of smoke forcing him to squint one eye.

Chris gave him a sneer.

"You know, you weren't supposed to wake up until after I was gone."

She gave voice to her first thought. "You can g–go. I w–won't t–tell anyone."

The man drew in a deep breath. "If you just would've stayed down, there would be no need for all this."

She let out a disgusted grunt.

The man finished his cigarette and flicked the burning butt into the corner of the cabin.

I'm not ever picking that up, Chris thought, as her mind languished in its fog.

"I thought I hit you hard enough."

She looked at the man. "You d–did. Believe m–me."

"Then the way you went over that chair. I mean, ouch. You were down and out. And then, not even three hours later, you're up. Man."

A breath of laughter. "I hit guys in the joint that hard, they sleep for a week."

Nice to know . . . Chris closed her eyes for a second. *Just my luck. I have a hard head.*

"It won't be much longer now."

Did she hear what he just said? Maybe. "Yeah. It w—won't be long. Everyone w—where I w—work knows w—where I am. They'll be here any m—minute." She believed every word, but through her fear and trembling, did she sound convincing?

The man laughed as he lit another cigarette. "My friends will be here long before that."

His voice didn't tremble at all.

✯ ✯ ✯

Travis slowly handed the radio microphone back to Carla and sat on a corner of her desk. His mind spun. What could have happened? Something happened. Why else would Chris be this late? He reached for the telephone intercom. "Keep trying the radio, Carla," he said as he punched in the number for the shed on the telephone keypad. Pushing the handset tightly against his ear, he strained to hear the district's mechanic over Carla's voice as she worked the radio.

"Shop."

"Mike? Travis. Is Chris there by any chance?"

"Hey, Travis. You workin' on your day off?"

"Is Chris McIntyre there?"

"Chris? No. And, come to think of it, she's late. I need that sled she's ridin' to go up to snow camp tonight."

Travis could barely breathe. "Thanks, Mike." He hung up the phone. Carla looked at him, eyes wide with concern. For effect, she reached over to turn up the radio's volume.

"This is not good." Travis glanced up at the clock. Then out the window. "We should have caught this before it got dark."

"I'm sure nothing's wrong," Carla said softly. "Maybe she's just away from her snowmobile."

"Maybe."

"Maybe something happened to her radio."

Something happened, that's for sure. Desperation poured fuel into Travis's blood. "I'm going up there." He turned and headed for the hall.

"Wait! You're not even on duty! You'd better clear this with Sid first!"

He was halfway down the hall, almost to the door. "Show me code three, Carla," he yelled back at her. "And you clear it!"

★★★

IN FIVE MINUTES TRAVIS WAS suited up and ready to leave. It was a mile to the Timmons Trailhead, another six to the old Forest Service cabin on Uncompahgre Mountain. Half an hour. By then, darkness would be thick. He had to move quickly.

He rechecked his gear, verified a full fuel tank, then climbed aboard the station's slick new Ski-Doo, smiling a bit as he fired it up, hearing the powerful engine roar. He idled the engine down to a hum as he put out a quick radio check. Carla promptly told him he had better turn around; Travis took that for a "loud and clear" and signed off. He pulled on his helmet and gave Mike a thumbs-up as he revved the engine again. Then he settled in and let the snow machine carry him out of the staging area. It was hard not to feel exhilarated by the power and speed. But it quickly soured into pure fear.

He whispered a silent prayer as the machine slipped him into the falling darkness.

★★★

ON THE PHONE AGAIN WITH the Colorado State Police, the third time that day, Sid Thompson put his hand over the mouthpiece of the handset and whispered to Carla, who stood at the edge of his open door, "What is all the yelling out there?"

"Chris is late and Travis went up to Timmons to find her."

None of it made sense as the conference call in his ear rambled on. He grumbled, "This is useless," and hung up the phone. "They won't even know I'm gone; just sayin' the same things over and over." He looked up at Carla. "What's all this?"

"Chris McIntyre is late, and Travis is taking Unit One up to see if she's still at Timmons."

She always made it sound as if someone was in trouble. Sid drew in a deep breath and let it out slowly. As station commander, he knew all of his office manager's quirks. Travis was fully qualified to handle Unit One. But Chris late? That was cause for concern. "How late is she?"

"She gave an ETA of three."

Sid looked up at the clock on the wall. "Oh, Lord." He jumped up from his desk. "Where was her last reported twenty?"

"Leaving Tri-Lake for Timmons."

"You've been trying to reach her?"

"For the last ten minutes, yes."

Sid grabbed his hooded sweatshirt from the rack and rushed out the door of his office, forcing Carla to move hastily out of his way. "Get a four-pack together," he said as he headed for the hallway. "Meet at the shed in five minutes."

"Yes, sir, right away!" Carla hurried to her desk and grabbed the intercom to summon a four-party rescue unit for Timmons Trail.

✯✯✯

Panic shot through Chris, stunning her silent. Did she hear right?

Friends? On their way? Here?

An average-size man. Just standing there. Looking at her. Smoking his cigarette. Not too big. Armed. But what could she do? Her mind barely wanted to work, let alone formulate a plan of escape. That's what she'd been taught since childhood. Stay focused, find a way. Don't panic. Her dad taught her well. "Go for the nose," he would always say. "Make 'im bleed." Worked great when she was ten, but now? She'd be lucky if she could even raise her hand that high.

"Action is faster than reaction," he told her. "Keep 'im guessing." Great advice. But tonight, her actions wouldn't outwit a stick. *Don't panic . . . Don't panic . . .*

Friends. Just what did that mean? And what would happen when Sam and Craig and Liz showed up to rescue her? The man had a gun! She had to warn them somehow. How?

She couldn't tell now if she shivered from cold or panic.

Stop it. Listen. Focus. Think. Find a way to take him out. Go for the gun when he's unaware. Don't let this guy get out of hand.

And try not to get anyone dead in the process.

✯✯✯

TRAVIS KNEW THE WAY TO Timmons Cabin. In his eight years with San Juan Mountain Search and Rescue, he had traveled this trail probably a thousand times. In the summer, on horseback. Or mountain bike. Or ATV. Or on foot. In the winter, snowshoes or snowmobile. One time he transported out a state senator from Ohio after the man broke his ankle cross-country skiing. Once, he delivered a baby. What the mother-to-be was doing at the ten-thousand-foot level of southwestern Colorado's Uncompahgre Peak was a total mystery to him. But they brought a perfect little baby boy into the world that day, and the new mother named him Ethan right there on the spot. Travis Ethan Novak was stunned. As he was now, in a completely different way.

Something's wrong.

The snowmobile climbed and skittered through the packed snow; he leaned and twisted the machine around every tree and rock, along every crevice. His moves were automatic. He wasn't concentrating on the trail.

Please, God. Something's wrong. I feel it. She's never late. She calls in if she is. She would find a radio. She would call in! She's always prepared. Extra fuel, flares— He looked up quickly. *Keep an eye out, Novak. Watch for flares. Watch for stray tracks off trail . . . watch . . . Oh, please, Lord, be with her.*

He needed to concentrate on the trail. He couldn't. His mind held her there. Her eyes, dark and mysterious. Her smile. Her laughter. She didn't laugh nearly enough. She had such a terrific laugh. Fun. Full of life.

And sometimes, when she allowed herself to really let go and laugh, when she'd turn to look at him, her eyes seemed to reflect the most brilliant rays of the sun. Not always. Only when she would let them.

He liked her the moment they met, was intrigued. A young U.S. Army medic, she had just spent ten months in Saudi Arabia, in Operation Desert Storm. He knew nothing about her, but was drawn to her. She pushed him away, pushed everyone away. Had her own place in the world and wouldn't let anyone else in. Until that one night, two summers ago. Had it really been that long? Travis allowed the sweet memory to quiet his soul as he twisted the snowmobile around another sharp turn in the trail.

They had just hauled out a drunken fool. Had to carry him out on a wire litter, over a mile to the waiting rescue truck. The fool cussed at them, hollering the entire time, "Put me down! I can walk! Ain't nothin' wrong with me. Put me down!"

The man had compound fractures of both bones in his lower left leg. His six drunken friends stayed on the mountain to continue their party, offering no help at all. Because the district's helicopter was unavailable, Chris and Travis hauled the man all the way down as he tossed and jerked in the litter.

Afterward, as the rescue truck disappeared down the gravel road, Travis sat in an exhausted stupor, and Chris flopped backward into a patch of soft clover. She closed her eyes and, after a minute, started to laugh.

At the time, Travis had known her almost seven months. It was the first time he ever heard her laugh. He laughed with her; he couldn't help it. "What's so funny?"

She didn't move to respond. Didn't even open her eyes. "Can you believe they stayed up there? They didn't even care enough about their friend to follow him down."

Travis shook his head. "Some friends."

"I don't think I can get up."

He looked at her. She was drenched with sweat. Her nose was dirty, and her sun-bleached brown hair stuck out all over the place through her French braid.

Travis stretched out beside her, and for at least an hour, they both just stayed there. Talking. About nothing. About everything.

Later that night, showered and starving, they picked up sandwiches at the deli and drove out past Box Canyon to watch the sunset. Then they watched the stars. The night was fine.

Travis swallowed hard, forcing down the tightness in his throat. He was getting close, but the closer he got the more worried he became. No flares, no radio call, no wayward tracks, no overturned snowmobile. He shifted his weight back and forth on the seat of the Ski-Doo as it raced him up the narrow trail. His teeth clenched as fear worked his mind. *Two hours! Why didn't Carla call it in before it got dark?*

Reluctantly, he slowed the snowmobile to a stop and tried to raise Chris on the radio. No response. Sid called to tell him a four-pack was on the way. Travis was glad for the help. *Lord, please, don't let us be too late.*

Again on his way, he prayed for her. Now. Always. There was such pain in her eyes, something hidden deep inside she would not reveal. A memory. Something. Too much kept hidden. It seemed to eat at her. Weary her. But there were rare times, precious times, when she would relax around him, would just enjoy the moment they shared. Travis savored those moments. Allowed himself to be drawn in.

Her heart was hidden, yet tender. Her eyes were fierce, yet imploring. Her kiss . . .

He had to get there.

He prayed. He was five minutes away.

✳✳✳

EVERYTHING SHE THOUGHT OF SHE eliminated. In her present state, there was not one thing she could think of to prevent the night from turning plain ugly.

The man was too strong, too smart, and too quick. Maybe, outside, if she tripped him, got him down, she could kick him and get away. *Yeah. One kick on ice and down you go.* That plan did not hold promise.

This was the guy Sid had briefed them about that morning at roll call. Escaped prisoner from Arizona. They had no idea where the man was, only that he was "in the vicinity." Millions of square miles of uninhabitable landscape, and the man showed up at one of the two places Chris was scheduled to visit that day.

She only hoped his friends would arrive first; they would kill her, go away, and no one else would have to get hurt.

So this is how it ends.

She closed her eyes and gave in to her weariness.

Until she heard the distant hum of a snow machine. Her eyes popped open as panic flooded her heart.

The man heard it too. He quickly killed the light in the lamp, grabbed the flashlight, and stood in the cabin's doorway.

Chris couldn't move. Everything inside her felt rushed—breath, thought, hope. She focused on what she heard, waited for her eyes to work in the heavy darkness.

One snowmobile. A big one. Powerful, well-tuned engine.

The man cussing.

One snowmobile. That didn't fit into either of their plans. Would the man's friends ride only one snow machine? Sid never sent anyone on a rescue alone.

Still cussing, the man stormed down the stairs—out the door, Chris saw his long shadow thrown by the snowmobile's headlight beams. She pushed herself up and stepped carefully to the door.

"Shut it down! Shut it down," he screamed. "Shut it down right now!"

Who was here? Did the guy always yell at his friends like this?

"Shut it down! Or I swear I'll kill you, right here!"

The snowmobile fell silent.

Still the man yelled. "Get up. Get up! Now!"

No, not one of his friends. Good chance it was one of hers. Squinting into the snow machine's powerful beams of light, Chris struggled to see who it was. Then someone moved, backed away from the light, arms out to his side, a man . . . wearing a bright red jacket. His face! Chris's heart gave out inside her, as if she'd been kicked in the stomach.

Travis!

More yelling. "Get back! Back up. Hands up where I can see them!"

Oh, God, Chris prayed. Only she didn't know how to pray. Travis had tried to teach her. She didn't want to learn. Until now. "Oh, God," a whisper now, as breath barely found its way inside her, as she stumbled down the cabin's icy steps. *Travis, what are you doing here?*

The man fussed with Travis's snowmobile. Beams from his flashlight crisscrossed the trees to Chris's left. She picked her way toward Travis, blinking. Was it Mike standing there? Or maybe Danny? Had to be. It was Travis's day off. Wasn't it?

She heard his voice. "Chris! Are you all right?"

"Shut up!" came from the man before Chris could respond. He cursed now, loudly, and reached down into his boot.

Chris watched for a second, confused, then looked away and moved closer to Travis, drawn by the brilliant red of his jacket, by the warmth of his love.

A flash caught her eye. To her left, light glinted off something metallic, something the man now held in his hand.

A knife. A long one.

With one quick swipe, he cut the snowmobile's radio microphone cord. Chris stopped, gaped; her mind sputtered in the chaos. *Ahh, Mike is not going to be happy about that!*

She felt someone behind her, arms around her, softly surrounding her. Travis had moved in behind her. His touch melted Chris all the way down to nothingness. She leaned back into his chest, barely able to keep herself on her feet.

"No. Get back!" The man walked toward them, flitting the knife left and right in front of their faces. "Get back. Get away from her. Now!"

Chris felt Travis move away. No words were spoken.

"Get back! Keep walking!"

She couldn't move. Travis kept backing away, to his right, moving farther away from her. She watched him go. Wanted to cry.

"You and me, tough guy," Travis said, his voice soft, yet strained. "Let's settle this. Between us. Let her go."

The man seemed to consider the words, then turned and flashed the knife in Chris's face. "Get back to the cabin. Right now. Do not make me say it again."

"That's it. Go, Chris." Travis's soothing voice reached deep inside her. "Go on. The two of us are just gonna stay out here and have a little discussion."

She still couldn't move.

The man reached behind his back, pulled the gun out of his waistband, then thumped the barrel against Chris's forehead. "Go!" The gun clicked as he chambered a round.

"Chris! Go! Get out of here!"

Tears welled in her eyes. *Oh, God . . . please.* Whatever happened this night, someone was going to get hurt. With one last look at Travis, she turned and forced herself toward the cabin. One step, then another. Two more steps. Her foot slipped a little. Always careful on ice. Now she didn't care. Two more steps. Another.

And down she went.

Her world disintegrated into an explosion of agony, brilliant white light, rushing roaring in her ears, total breathlessness like she had never known before.

How long did she lay there? What brought her back?

Blinking deeply, weeping, coughing . . . curses, yelling, sounds of a fight. *No . . . God, no.*

Somehow, she turned. Gasping, she rubbed her eyes, trying to clear her head. Travis and the man were fighting, wrestling, throwing each other around in the snow, kicking, punching, growling . . .

Chris covered her face with her hands and crushed her eyes shut. Visions of swirling sand, the roar of a helicopter, yelling, screaming—her best friend hit, down, bleeding—*Erin down . . . bleeding!*

Cursing herself, cursing death and life, she stood. Staggering, she pushed herself as close to the men as she dared. In the beams of the snowmobile's headlights, one man would be spotlighted, then another. One second Travis was up, the next, he was down. Blood glazed his forehead, trickled down his chin. The man spun him and kicked him, but then Travis swung out, connected, and the man fell hard into the snow, only to leap up, swinging.

Chris could not move.

She had to do *something*.

The snow machine. Did Travis bring flares? She rushed to it. Set off all three. Did he bring a chain saw? No. Flashlight. She grabbed it. She stuffed the solar blanket into her jacket pocket. First aid kit, out where she could find it. Nothing else of use. She rushed to her snowmobile. Flicked on its headlights.

The two men still struggled and fought.

Chris could bring on some serious hurt with the flashlight, if nothing else. She'd throw herself on the man, give Travis time to—

A sickening sound stopped her, turned her stomach so quickly she gagged.

Both men were still. The man in the red jacket was down. The other struggled to his feet and stumbled back, swaying, breathing heavily, bleeding.

Travis was still down.

Chris fell to her knees in the snow.

The man doubled over and hung his head out over his knees, coughing, spitting, panting . . .

Travis didn't make a sound. His eyes hung wide open, frozen.

Chris covered her mouth. A deep, wrenching groan coursed through her as tears flooded her eyes. Crawling on hands and knees, staring at the man she loved, she reached him—and she knew. No pulse on his neck. Steam floating up from life pouring out of his chest.

It was done.

Life was dead. Hope. She floated in anguish. Everything in her universe pulled at her, pushed against her, crowded her on every side, squeezed the very breath from her soul.

Her head fell until her forehead touched his. Desperate weeping overtook her. Mired in it, she couldn't move or think or breathe or see . . .

Then barely, so very distant, she heard sounds.

No, God. Don't take me back.

Horrible sounds. Closer now. Louder.

God, please! Just take me now.

And louder. Only a few feet away, the man continued to cough and hack and spit.

She slowly raised her head as everything inside her started to turn. White-hot rage, pure and overpowering, pushed everything else from her mind. She forced herself up, cursed away her tears, stood.

Yes. She would settle things first. Then come back and die with Travis.

No matter what, tonight it would end.

She focused hard on the man's face. Saw a hint of wariness in his glare. She stepped away from Travis. Flexed her empty hands. Glanced at the man's right hand. Saw the long knife he still held. Saw the red. Looked away. Just for a second.

They stared at each other, until the man's eyes flicked to Chris's left. To her right. Down at the snow. Back to her. Right again. Left. Right.

Looking for the gun.

Chris spun around—found it first. She dove on it, then rolled, stood, just as he reached her, the knife raised. She stumbled backward a few steps, the freezing pistol in her right hand. She raised it, but had to use her left hand to keep it steady.

Both of them breathed heavily; the cold air burned Chris's lungs, strained her throat.

She forced her teeth to unclench. Aimed the pistol at the man's chest. Spoke clearly. "I'm gonna kill you."

Something flickered in the man's eyes. "Not if I kill you first," he said through a faint grin. "Come on. You don't wanna die, do you?"

Her teeth again clenched. She didn't mind. It kept her first thought from finding voice.

"No. Of course you don't. And I don't wanna kill you. Give me the gun. Walk away. I won't follow you."

"I don't think so. Throw the knife away." Chris tried to hold the pistol steady.

"Give me the gun."

She growled. "I am not giving you this gun."

The man spit into the snow. "My friends will be here any minute."

"I set off three flares. How long do you think it will take before *my* friends get here? Throw the knife away, and get on your knees."

The man waved the knife like a fan. "This little thing?"

Chris blinked to focus. The parley wasn't doing her any good. "Yes. Throw it away."

"Nope."

Her rage waned. Her strength. Pain seeped in, then bolted through her side as her arms started to shake. She glanced down at Travis. Her eyes pinched shut. She began to fall apart, piece by piece. Drew in a deep breath. "Throw it away and get down on your knees!" Screaming the words cost her too much. She started to cry.

"Ahh, lady." The man relaxed his stance. "You're strong; I'll give you that. Believe me. I never wanted any of this to happen."

"Shut up." Chris could only whimper the words. The gun shook so violently she squeezed hard to keep from dropping it.

"Just give me the gun."

Don't be afraid . . . slipped into her thoughts. *Today's a good day* . . . *to die.*

She blinked away her tears and looked into the man's eyes just to be sure.

Yes. He would kill her, given any chance.

No one would blame her if she killed this man. Right now. Pulled the trigger. Justifiable.

No one would mourn for her if he . . .

The gun came down. She had no strength left to keep it up. No desire anywhere inside her to kill another man.

No desire to stop him . . . from killing her.

She slowly looked away, started to turn. The man leaped at her, knife in the air, pointed down at her throat.

Chris raised the gun into his chest. And fired.

TWO

THE SETTING SUN PAINTED AN incredible sky. Pale yellow faded into soft pink into light, crystal-clear blue. Snow, brilliant white, clean and pure, buried the jagged mountain peaks that jutted into the gorgeous sky. The scene sparkled. The air was crisp and fresh.

Tucked under a thin canopy of firs and pines, a small two-room cabin overlooked the steep slopes of two stunning fourteen-thousand-foot peaks. The heart of Colorado's Uncompahgre National Forest.

Inside the cabin, warm and safe amid the cold and snow, she stood at the front picture window as night approached. Darkness would soon fall over this pristine scene. Engulf it. Blind its beauty. She hated the darkness.

She raised a large shot glass to her lips and sipped. The liquid burned her lips and tongue. Burned her mouth and throat. Burned her chest and stomach. Challenged the burn in her soul.

The whiskey was winning. She sipped again.

She stood, staring, seeing, half seeing. She blinked hard to focus, then studied every tree, every shade of color in the fading sunset, searched the landscape for movement, any sign of life. She saw none. Only her hand moved, bringing the glass to her lips. And the sky, fading to blackness.

She leaned forward and touched the side of her forehead to the window. Cold against her skin. She closed her eyes. A soft curl of hair fell over her shoulder and tickled her cheek.

Darkness descended upon the Rocky Mountains. Filled the small cabin. Dressed in black jeans and a heavy black wool sweater, she became part of the darkness. Joined it. Only the delicate gold chain around her neck still held some light.

She shivered, then sipped more of the poison from her glass. The burn chased off her chill. In one quick gulp, she finished the glass, then struggled to swallow.

The first two shots were easier to get down.

She hated to drink, hated the burn. Hated her weakness.

She hated her father when he drank, hated the monster he became afterward. She hated the sound of his voice, for the past four days, filling her mind. *You shoulda done something—anything! Didn't I teach you? You weren't aware when you first walked in, and you had the chance to end it when he stood at the door, watching Travis. You shoulda taken him out right there. The gun was right there, behind his back. You coulda grabbed it and taken him out the door. At least that woulda warned Travis. At least that woulda kept him from getting killed. So helpless. Always so helpless. My little Chrissy. You coulda stopped him from killing Travis. Coulda stopped him. But you were—*

Rage bolted through her. She pushed away from the window and threw the glass across the cabin. It shattered against the wall. She didn't hear it.

She doubled over and fell to her knees, clutching her right side. *You are so stupid! You're not healed yet! What's wrong with you?*

Beads of sweat broke out across her forehead as she struggled against the pain. Her entire body shook as she eased herself to the floor. Short breaths returned, and she choked them down, one by one.

It took so long . . . eventually she could pull air in. She broke down in violent, anguished sobs.

She lay there. In darkness. On the floor of her cabin. In the middle of the majestic Rocky Mountains. In the middle of a desperate misery she had known all her life.

A life she was ready to end.

✬✬✬

SHE HEARD A NOISE. SOMETHING loud. It woke her. Her heart thumped. She tried to open her eyes. It was difficult.

Where was she? On the couch? How did she . . . ? What time was it? The sun was low and bright, pouring in the front window, casting evening shadows. She blinked. The fog was in her head. She closed her eyes and relaxed. She wasn't going anywhere.

Her head ached. Throbbed. Her mouth felt dry and her throat raw, almost burned. Her side ached. Each breath reminded her; she wanted to forget everything. She wanted to sleep. Forever.

Four loud thumps on the door startled her so much she sat up straight and kicked her feet to the floor, knocking over her bottle of Jack Daniel's whiskey. She heard the clink of her boot hitting the glass, but saw nothing. The sudden terror, followed by the sudden movement, sucked her breath away. She sat still, eyes pinched shut, right arm down, pushing in against the pain, waiting for air.

Another loud series of thumps. And a holler. "Chriisss? Hey, Chriisss?"

Carla Crawley. Only Carla Crawley had that irritating voice.

"Hello? Chris? Are you home?"

She wanted to say, "Whaddaya want, Carla?" but as she opened her mouth, all that came out was a hoarse, "Whaaaat—!" She was satisfied.

"Chris? There's someone here to see you."

She blinked. Then used her left hand to rub her face, to rub away the fog, the swirl of the world. Everything swirled. Everything was fog. "Go away, Carla." Again a hoarse croak, but loud enough that the words almost blew out her eardrums and exploded her head.

"Chris?"

Another voice. Another woman. Definitely not Carla's nasally whine. Chris pushed her eyes open. Forced them to stay open. They fell. Down. To the bottle on the floor. The empty bottle. And not a drop spilled.

Did I drink the entire bottle?

She tried to stand but fell back into the couch. The fall hurt; she did not want to try again. She repeated the words, "Go away, Carla," as she again rubbed her eyes. She heard muffled voices on her porch. A truck door slam. A truck start up and drive away. Were they leaving? Good. She leaned her head back and closed her eyes.

"Chris?"

Her eyes popped open.

"Chris, it's just you and me now. And it's kinda cold. Could you, um . . . please?"

She could not breathe. Could not even think to try. What was she hearing? Was it possible? No way. Just another dream. That was it. That's all she did anymore anyway. Such horrible dreams.

She blinked deeply. Looked around the cabin. The log ceiling. Bright sunlight pouring in the large front window. She blinked again. She breathed. Was she dreaming?

That voice. She knew that voice. But it couldn't be . . .

She wasn't dreaming. The way her side hurt, this could only be her present reality.

And her head. Did she really drink the entire bottle? Why? What did she think that would accomplish? It didn't help before. It never helped. Only for a few hours, maybe. But never long enough to forget.

She heard a different noise. A muffled cough. Just outside her door. Someone was out there, standing on her porch, waiting. And the voice sounded so much like . . .

Chris leaned forward slowly and stood. But she couldn't get her feet to move. She looked down.

She still had on her funeral clothes: black jeans, black wool sweater, Travis's necklace, the matching earrings. She needed to change. Desperately. She was suddenly cold. She actually saw her breath. She blinked deeply. The last few clouds of lingering fog faded from the corners of the room.

The fire was out, the cabin was freezing, she was hungover, it was tomorrow night already, and someone was standing on her porch. Someone who sounded so much like—

She picked up her feet and moved them toward the door. A bit dizzy, she steadied herself against the easy chair. Almost there. Her right arm stayed in, pinned against her side. She made it to the door. Only ten steps, but it seemed like a hundred. She was suddenly exhausted. And suddenly very frightened. *What if it is? No. It couldn't be.* Still, her stomach had tied itself into a knot. She put her hand against the door latch, but then lowered her head to rest against the door frame. The latch clicked faintly.

"Chris?" The voice outside was quiet. Soft. "Chris . . ." A long pause. "It's me."

Her mouth fell open as her heart stopped. She opened the door. And saw Erin.

✹✹✹

ERIN MATHIS SLOWLY DREW IN a deep breath as her plane lifted off the runway at Portland's International Airport and climbed into the morning sky. She filled her lungs with air, laid her head back, and closed her eyes as the ascent softly crushed her into her seat. The plane leveled slightly, and she let the breath leak out through her pressed lips.

Lord . . . what am I doing?

Her stomach had started to burn yesterday when she heard the news. And this morning, in a ladies' restroom at PDX, she chewed and swallowed two Rolaids tablets. It still burned.

She breathed deeply again. And again.

A few hours and she would be there. She would see . . . what would she see? Who would be there when she got there? A friend she used to know? Or a shell of memories? Would memories be enough?

Lord, please help me relax. And forgive me. I know this is insane.

Yesterday, after hearing the news, her husband had all but begged her not to go. "You can't expect things to be like they were," he said.

Of course, he was right. Almost five years had passed. A long five years. *With no good-bye. And no word.* She had to force in a breath.

Turbulence. She hated turbulence. Especially when she couldn't breathe.

Yesterday afternoon, Scott had convinced her. She would stay home and pray for Chris. What more could she do? Last night's sleeplessness also convinced her. She needed to be on the first plane leaving Portland for Colorado.

Please, Lord . . . please help me. If this is wrong, please forgive me. Be with Scott. If You're in this, and I really think You are, please help him to understand.

Should she take two more Rolaids?

"Why are you packing?" Scott had asked that morning as soon as he stepped out of the bathroom after his shower. He smelled so good, looked so squeaky clean.

Erin continued stuffing an overnight bag with clothes. "I called the airport. There's a flight in an hour. I want to be on it."

"I thought we talked about this!"

"We did." She stopped packing and looked up. "I'm sorry, sweetheart, but I have to go."

His lips moved, yet it took a few seconds for him to get the words out. "You have to go?"

"Yes. Please try to hear me. I can't explain why I have to. I just know I do."

"I'm hearing you, Erin, but I'm not believing you."

She stepped around the bed and leaned into his embrace. "I don't believe it myself, love. I'm so sorry."

He squeezed her to his chest. Then drew in a sharp breath. "Why can't you just forget about the war? Forget about all of it! Even Chris." He pushed her to arm's length. "Especially Chris. From what you've told me, she's been nothing but trouble to you. She's why you got shot!" His eyes softened. "Please, Erin. It's been five years. I'm sure she's moved on. You need to move on too."

The words had sliced deeply through Erin's heart. How could she make her husband understand something she didn't understand herself?

Outside, below her, thick stratus clouds formed a pillowy white carpet over the world. Above her, wisps of high cirrus traced delicate patterns against the brilliant blue sky.

So beautiful, Lord. You are so big. So awesome. Thank You for that. Because right now . . . I really need You to be.

The plane leveled off. Cruising altitude. Erin breathed. And prayed no tears would fall.

Why was she doing this? Scott was wrong about Chris. But what if he was also right? What if Chris had completely forgotten about her?

Well, if that's the case, Lord, she's in for a shock. Because I remember her. And here I come.

Somehow, someday, she would make her husband understand. Too many times he had suggested she forget about the war; he didn't want to hear about any of it. Didn't want to be reminded of the danger she had faced, the madness of war. Any war. But Erin had to remember. Her memories and the pictures in her scrapbook were all she had left. She treasured every single picture. Six months of memories. Five years ago.

Six more hours. Then what would she see? From what little she had heard, she was afraid of what she might find. She didn't want to think about it. She didn't want to think about that last day, either. Five years ago. She wished this one memory would fade; it had played on the edges of her mind for so long. Of waiting, so desperate. Time had run out. The C-141 medical evacuation transport plane was ready to go. She had waited until the last possible second, frantically looking . . .

She's not even going to say good-bye?

With the words, "Let's go, Lieutenant! We're outta here!" Erin had taken one last hopeful look. It was a waste of time; in the rush of activity at Dhahran's airport, not one face looked familiar to her. Heartsick, she turned and climbed into the medevac plane and then settled in with her patients for the long ride to Germany. One stop. And then home.

Her work kept her occupied; happy faces warmed her heart, the joy of returning home, the war won.

After landing in Germany, she was told to escort a few of the ambulatory patients into Tent City. What she saw stunned her.

A city had been built almost overnight. Fifty-eight troop tents stood a few hundred meters from the Tarmac. Erin looked around, amazed. The tents held everything they could have possibly wanted: showers, a place to sleep, a place to pray.

Someone really cared.

The huge white USO tent was an awesome sight, longer and wider than any she'd ever seen. People clapped and cheered as she and her patients walked in. Banners hung from the ceiling. State flags. She found California's easily. Long yellow ribbons trailed each banner. Long white sheets hung down, all signed in a rainbow of colors, scribbles; schoolchildren from somewhere, from everywhere back home, welcoming the soldiers back. Home. From the Persian Gulf War.

And food! Tables of food, piled high. Everything they could have wanted.

Erin was starving, but not hungry at all. She picked up an apple.

Books. Magazines. TVs. Ping-Pong tables. And more scribbles on the sides of the tent. Messages, graffiti. Incoming troops; later, outgoing troops. Anxious soldiers, triumphant heroes. All had something to say. All had a message.

She bit into the apple, then shivered as a chill ran across her shoulders. Central Command had warned the homeward-bound troops to be prepared for a "unified display of gratitude and patriotism." This . . . was awesome.

The war was quick, massive, fought bravely, and won. The troops were homeward bound.

Army Lieutenant Erin Grayson sat on a bench outside the USO tent, her heart ached, and she wept.

Army Specialist Christina McIntyre was still in the desert.

And Erin was sure she would never see her again.

TURBULENCE.

She held her breath.

Why would a few bumps bother her? For six months she rode with the crew of a UH-1 Huey medevac helicopter as it raced into the desert to rescue fallen troops. More than a few wild rides. And she loved it. Now, she couldn't breathe. As her eyes pinched shut, a tear slipped down her cheek. She angrily wiped it away.

Lord God! Why am I doing this? Rushing to Colorado ... I'm six hours away from seeing someone who didn't even care enough to say good-bye! Am I just fooling myself? If she didn't care then, will she care at all now?

She signaled the steward and asked for a soda. Seven-Up to settle her stomach. Slowly sipped on it. And she prayed. To settle her heart.

OUT THE WINDOW, SHE STARED at the world below. Thirty-six thousand feet felt a little strange. She was used to about eighty. Eighty feet and not much more.

In Saudi Arabia, the Huey medevac helicopter buzzed the desert surface. So low. Less of a target that way. A full-tilt white-knuckle round-trip ticket to paradise.

She smiled and leaned away from the window, but not before hearing Teddy Brisbaine's voice in her heart.

"That's right, Lieutenant. She's our 'Ticket to Paradise.' So tell me. Be honest. Whaddaya think?"

I'll tell you what I think, Teddy. Erin closed her eyes and laid her head back. *I think I ... miss you, you big jerk.* She wanted to smile, but couldn't.

The day Teddy Brisbaine said those words, Erin stood on the helipad decked out in full flight gear. So hot, the gear so heavy, she stood there looking at a helicopter. A green one. With brilliant red crosses on its nose and both doors. "Nice," she said. With a little shrug.

"Nice?" Teddy Brisbaine flashed a to-die-for grin. "Lieutenant, let me introduce you to the sweetest, gentlest, purest ride you will ever know. She's been through the dirt for American soldiers since Vietnam, and Mr. Coffee here—"

A quick, "That's *Captain* to you, Staff Sergeant," was followed with a warm smile and softer words for Erin. "My friends call me Angelo. My handle's Nescafé. You, ma'am, may call me either."

Maybe it was the heat, but Erin blushed as she shook the Huey pilot's hand.

"Yeah, yeah, as I was sayin', Mr. Coffee here—I just love calling him that—is the best darn skipper you'll ever know. Treats us like a grade-A chauffeur. Cruisin' a limo. Right, skip?"

Angelo grinned at Erin. "Been trying for four years to toss this knucklehead crew chief off my Huey, but he's always strapped in."

Erin laughed.

"Your Huey? This is *my* Huey."

"Sorry, guys." U.S. Army Specialist and medevac medic Christina McIntyre arrived on the scene to promptly break up the argument. She tugged a pair of gloves from her flight vest pocket, then looked around the small group. An eyebrow went up. "But this here *limo* is bought and paid for by the taxpaying masses of our glorious country. God bless 'em. Every one."

Captain Angelo Coffee snapped to attention and flipped a rather brisk, yet terribly sarcastic salute toward the "taxpaying masses."

"Now let's go have us some fun with their machine." With that, Specialist McIntyre donned her flight helmet and headed for Ticket to Paradise.

They all climbed aboard. Angelo and his copilot, Warrant Officer Bobby Palmara, took them to eighty-five feet and held them there, hovering over the Tarmac.

"You ready, Lieutenant?"

Erin was not ready, but she looked at Chris McIntyre and smiled anyway. Then said into her mouth mike, her voice shaking as the

Huey thundered, "Guys, um . . . since we're going to be together in this for who knows how long, how about if you all call me Erin. That lieutenant tag is a little much."

And Specialist McIntyre flashed a wide, toothy grin. "Well, okay . . . Erin." She held her grin a second longer. "So. Eighty-five feet. Um, no sweat. Right? We'll get you set in the line, then just follow the rope down. Slow. Ease yourself down."

"You know, Chris? I, um . . . I've done this before."

"Oh."

And Staff Sergeant Edward Theodore Brisbaine laughed, more like howled, into his mouth mike and hollered, "But Chris here is our little repelling pro! Right, Mack? She just loves repelling out of Hueys."

Chris's response sounded like a growl. "Shut up, Teddy."

But the man did no such thing. He hollered, "Come on, Christina! Show the lieutenant how it's done!"

"Uh, guys?" came from copilot Bobby Palmara, "we're pulling in an audience here."

"Go on, McIntyre!" Teddy pushed Chris toward the helicopter's open bay door. "Show the luey here how we disembark ol' Ticket in a smokin'-hot LZ!"

The copilot said again, "Um . . . guys?" but everyone ignored him.

Chris blushed, glared at Teddy, shrugged, smiled awkwardly at Erin, tugged on her reinforced cotton gloves, slid to the helicopter's open side door, hopped backward, down onto the skid, unhooked, gave Erin one last look as she said, "On rope," paused a second, then fell backward, headfirst, off the skid.

Erin leaped so quickly to the open door her restraint strap snapped tight, the only thing keeping her from sliding out. On hands and knees, gasping in shock, hearing Teddy's howls of laughter, she stared wide-eyed at Christina McIntyre, who fell headfirst, feet flying, down at least two-thirds of the way in a free fall. Chris tightened her grip on the rope, her feet swung around, and as Teddy laughed and hollered, "Hit the ground runnin', sis-tah!" that was exactly what she did. A few steps were all it took, the last few a sashay. Chris released the rope, turned her head upward, beamed a smile, and flipped a wave to the occupants of Ticket to Paradise.

It was then, still on her hands and knees, that Erin spotted the Humvee parked on the Tarmac, recognized the skinny subordinate lieutenant storming his way in a beeline toward Chris; recognized his superior, Colonel Benjamin D. Connelly, commanding officer of the 101st Airborne's 4th Brigade, of which this medevac crew was assigned, standing by the Humvee, shielding his eyes with his hand. This was not good.

The skinny lieutenant was not a happy man. He returned Chris's salute, looked up and, after much hand waving and signaling, convinced Captain Angelo Coffee that he should descend and land the Huey immediately. Angelo softly cussed through everyone's headphones and obeyed the command, gently lowering the helicopter to the ground. He cut the engines, and the crew lumbered out, then double-timed it to where the lieutenant and Chris stood, Chris at stark attention, her flight helmet off and in her left hand. Her remaining crew members aligned themselves in formation and assumed the same position, Bobby and Teddy popping smart salutes at the lieutenant who awkwardly returned them. Erin stood beside Angelo, who outranked the lieutenant by more than a few lifetimes, and simply waited for the inevitable.

Erin snuck a quick peek at Colonel Connelly. Was that a smirk on his face?

"I want to know what you all call what I just saw!" The lieutenant almost screamed the words, then didn't wait for anyone to answer; he turned and moved into Chris's face, close enough for his bursts of breath to fluff the hair sprouting out of her French braid. "Just what was that, soldier? Were you trying to impress someone?" In a lame attempt at sarcasm, he looked around the field. "Is General Schwarzkopf here? Maybe our supreme commander in chief?"

Is this guy for real?

Erin heard Teddy Brisbaine, to her left, still standing at attention, squelch a burst of laughter in his throat.

Chris remained at attention as the lieutenant again got right in her face. "Sir, no sir!" she barked. "Just you . . . and the colonel, sir!"

"And do you think he was impressed, soldier? Because I certainly wasn't!"

"Sir, no sir! I am sure he was *not* impressed!"

Now it was Erin who squelched a burst of laughter. She squinted toward the Humvee and definitely saw a smirk on the colonel's face.

The lieutenant wasn't finished. "You're female, soldier?"

He framed the statement like a question, so Chris barked out, "Sir, yes sir!" at which Teddy did laugh but covered it with a cough.

The lieutenant's voice reached a higher octave. "So, I suppose you really think you're God's gift to this army!"

Chris's eyes widened. "Oh, no, sir!"

"The war hasn't even begun yet, soldier! And already you're out here risking your life? What happens later? Huh? When the war starts and some fighter pilot needs your medical assistance, but you can't go 'cause you're dead! And he dies!"

Erin wanted to punch the man in the nose.

Chris didn't have a chance to respond.

"And what do I say to your loving parents? Huh, soldier? Your mommy and daddy, who love you so . . . when mortuary affairs are out here scraping up your butt with a spoon! What do I tell them, soldier? Sorry, uhh—" he glanced down at Chris's name tag on her flight suit—"Mr. and Mrs. McIntyre, but your daughter is dead 'cause she was stupid! Got herself killed before the war even started?"

As Erin stood there, rage, red and hot, swept through her.

The uneasy silence lingered.

"Don't have anything to say, Specialist McIntyre?"

Chris's voice was almost a whisper. "No, sir."

"Get out of my sight, soldier!" And without waiting for her to salute, the lieutenant spun around and started for the Humvee.

Erin watched him go, seething at his command. *That's right, you get out of hers.*

Chris stood there for a few seconds, then turned abruptly and stormed toward the helicopter. Teddy followed, laughing and harassing her. Bobby gathered up the repelling rope, and Angelo gave Erin an exasperated grin as he turned and headed back to the helicopter. Erin stood there as the skinny lieutenant and the colonel climbed back in the Humvee, then she turned and followed Angelo. Her second day in Saudi and already there was abundant excitement.

Back on board the Huey, with everyone situated and waiting for her, Erin strapped herself in, then snuck a glance at Chris. The woman was grinding her teeth; her cheeks flashed brilliant red against her dark gray flight helmet and her dark eyes drilled holes through her crew chief. Her upper lip curled in a vicious, trembling sneer. When the silence dragged on, she turned her head toward the cockpit, opened her mouth, and said, basically, "Let us promptly leave the area."

Her actual words could have been used to strip the paint off a brand-new Cadillac.

✵✵✵

ERIN LAUGHED, THEN OPENED HER eyes and looked out the window. The plane had started its descent into Salt Lake City. Then a quick hop on to Grand Junction in one of the rubber-band planes. And then a two-hour drive to Ouray. And then . . .

She leaned back in the seat. Turbulence. She hated turbulence. Her husband's words drifted into her mind. She hated leaving him, knowing he was unhappy, knowing he was right, in a way, that all of this was insane. But she really hated the thought of what she might find in Ouray, Colorado.

She pulled the Rolaids out of her carry-on and chewed two more. Swallowed. Closed her eyes. And prayed.

✶✶✶

IN GRAND JUNCTION, ONE OF Chris's coworkers, Liz Caswell, met her at the gate. In ten minutes they were in a Forest Service Jeep Grand Cherokee heading south on Route 50.

Erin had knots in her stomach.

"So. How long have you guys been friends?" Liz steered the Jeep around a pothole.

"We met in Saudi, during Desert Shield." Erin's voice was weak. It took a concentrated effort for her to speak. Tiny knots from her stomach were finding their way into her throat.

"She's never said much about that. Hope you guys were okay over there. I know that was quite a time."

Erin smiled. "Yes, it certainly was."

In the silence that followed, Erin glanced at Liz, saw her bottom lip working a pout. Liz looked about forty, maybe. Dark brown skin, glistening jet-black hair pulled back and tied, five-nine, maybe. Tall and lean. She reminded Erin of Bettema. Same tall, lanky leanness. She wondered if Chris thought that too. She thought of Chris and had to swallow down a knot.

"Then again," Liz continued, her bottom lip still working that pout, "Chris never says much about anything." She looked at Erin. "Really keeps to herself."

"Yeah, I know." The words quivered. Erin did know. Very well. "How is she dealing with . . . ?"

"Oh. Well, okay, I guess. How much do you know, Erin?"

"Not much. My employer tried to tell me what little he knew, but all I could think about was getting here. Guess I didn't really listen."

"It's weird, huh." Liz reached down to adjust a heater vent. "How your boss knows your good friend's boss."

"And we didn't even know it."

"When's the last time you and Chris talked?"

Erin sighed and looked out her window. "It's been since Saudi."

Liz was silent. The Cherokee slipped through the town of Delta.

Erin stared at Colorado. Marveled. The mountains. The snow.
Beautiful. Small mining towns. And the mountains. She saw it all.
But, in her heart, she prayed.

Liz finally answered Erin's question. "Well, you know, things
could be better. We were all stunned by . . . everything."

Erin forced a small smile.

"Travis was a special guy. He was great. Quiet, considerate. He
was a handsome man. Had all the summer temp girls pantin' over
him." A pause. "He was close to Chris. No one else could get close.
Or wanted to, I guess."

"Do you get along with her?"

"Sure. I mean, we're not that close. We're friends. She works
harder than anyone, and I respect that. We go to Raymond's sometimes. Hang out. Kick back some margaritas at Buen Tiempo. You
know. We like going to Mesa State games."

When Liz shot her a quick look, Erin gave her a smile.

"We've got a runnin' game of hoops goin'." Liz laughed. "Three
twelve to two ninety-eight. I think. Well, I do know it's to five hundred. And I'm gonna get there first."

Erin laughed quietly and enjoyed the memory of hot desert basketball games, of nine sweaty guys and one sweaty lady, Specialist
McIntyre, holding her own. They played for hours. Sometimes Erin
would play. Mostly she liked to watch them.

"You know she was in the hospital."

The memory evaporated. "What? Oh, yes. How long did she
stay?"

"One night was it. They wanted to keep her longer. Get her to
talk to a shrink. She wouldn't do it. As soon as the police were done
talking to her, she made me take her to get her truck so she could
go home."

"Has she been there . . . alone?"

"Sid went up once. Took some groceries. Said she didn't say
much. Said he didn't feel . . . welcome."

Erin cringed. She had heard only the details: escaped convict, coworker killed, Chris injured, convict killed. She needed to know. "Liz, how badly was she hurt?"

The woman winced. "Well, by the time we got up there, she was unconscious in the snow. In shock, mainly. Lying beside Travis. Looked like there was a pretty messy fight."

Erin waited as Liz seemed to be choosing her words carefully.

"The doctors were concerned about the severity of her concussion, and her hypothermia. She also had some broken ribs."

"Some?"

"Well, one for sure. At least a few more cracked. She was bruised up somethin' awful."

Dear Lord . . .

"They set her up in her own room thinking she'd stay three or four days. She was out after fifteen hours."

Fifteen hours? When they wanted her to stay four days?

Liz squirmed. And cleared her throat. She looked out her side window, then stared at the road. She started to speak but stopped, then started again. "Did you, um . . . did you know about . . . ?" She glanced over but said nothing more.

Erin's stomach lurched. She looked out her side window but quickly closed her eyes. *Oh, dear God . . .*

"Oh well," Liz said. "Never mind."

Never mind. Lord, if it were only that easy to forget it.

Erin did know. She had seen it too. Only once. Just a glimpse. But she would never forget it. She was glad to see Liz wasn't a gossiper.

"They had a memorial service for Travis yesterday. Chris was there, but she looked . . . well, not good." Liz glanced again at Erin, caught the look Erin gave her, and added, "But hey, you know her better than I do. She'll come back from this. She's got something in her. A fight, you know?"

More like a war. Erin quickly wiped her eyes so Liz wouldn't see her tears. She drew in a slow, deep breath and said, "Yeah."

They rode in silence for a long while.

A radio call startled them both. Liz was needed back at the station, something about reports, so Sid volunteered Carla Crawley to escort Erin the rest of the way up to Chris's cabin. Liz signed off and gave Erin an apologetic look. "I was hoping to see Chris today."

"I'll tell her you're thinking about her."

"I'd appreciate that," Liz said with a smile.

✷✷✷

CARLA CRAWLEY WAS A VERY helpful woman, and she could sure handle a four-wheel-drive Chevy S-10 Blazer. With chains. Erin had wondered when Sid Thompson said, "Take the Blazer. It's already chained." Now she knew why. The road looked like a solid sheet of ice, yet they hardly slipped at all. She settled back into the seat and tried to relax as they bumped along.

The Blazer's heater puffed weakly, and Erin shivered. Nervousness still churned in her stomach, but the scenery held her in a constant state of awe. Breathing deeply, she looked out the window and listened to Carla Crawley's insightful commentary about the events of the past week.

"A convict. Can you believe that? Escaped from a place in Arizona. They think he was working his way to Denver. Taking the hard way, I'd say." Carla fussed with the defrost vents. "Pretty exciting night. FBI, Staties . . . and then all the media. Holy good night. Never seen so many cameras. All over the place. Big news."

The Blazer left the main road. Erin held on.

"It gets a little rough from here on out," Carla said. "It's about another six miles to the cabin."

"Six miles?"

"Yep. Travis, God rest his soul, his grandpa rents the place out. Chris prefers her privacy."

Erin's response sounded almost like a grunt. She held on as the Blazer slid and crunched through the snow.

"I don't really know Chris, but I think she's pretty amazing." Carla glanced at Erin. "If it was me up there on that mountain, I would've died just from fright." She downshifted and cussed when the Blazer slid sideways.

Erin's breath stuck in her throat.

"She took care of that killer." Carla seemed unaffected by the Blazer's slip. "Took him out after what he did to her and Travis. Amazing."

They turned off onto another road. Lined with pines and firs. And in the distance, a stunning, jagged, snow-covered mountain peak. It looked like they were heading straight for it.

They were.

Simply incredible. Erin's heart swelled with wonder and praise. Mount Hood near Portland was spectacular, but this . . . Chris had truly found heaven.

The Blazer slid sideways again, but Carla quickly corrected. Clumps of snow flew away from the tires as the chains gripped the road.

"How long you gonna stay? Be sure and go into Ouray. Oh, of course, Chris will take you in. It's beautiful. And Box Canyon is nice this time of year."

Erin heard the words, heard the woman's slightly nasal voice, but didn't really hear. She stared through the window, but couldn't really see. Sid Thompson's words came back to her. "I'm glad you're here," he had said as they stood in the district's office waiting for Carla to warm up the Blazer. "I couldn't believe it when Ben called."

"I'm glad *you're* here," Erin said. "Ben told me you two go way back."

"Way back." Sid's gentle laugh reached his eyes. It faded quickly. "Chris needs someone. We've all tried, somehow, but . . ."

Erin reached up and simply touched his arm. "I know," she said, her voice a whisper.

"I'm glad you're here," he had said. "You're an answer to prayer."

The Blazer slid as Carla turned onto another road. A narrower road, less traveled. Erin pulled in another deep breath to try to settle her stomach. She didn't feel like an answer to prayer. She felt terrified.

Five years. And she's killed. Again. She'll be devastated. Or . . . will she? What am I going to find, Lord? Please help me, Lord Jesus.

She closed her eyes and prayed until she heard Carla say, "Here we are!"

She looked up and saw a clearing in the trees. A small, rustic cabin. A dirty dark blue Ford Explorer, four-wheel drive, tires chained. She laughed out loud. Chris had found herself a piece of heaven to call her own.

And Erin had just found a long-lost friend.

✯✯✯

SHE STOOD ON THE PORCH, waiting, freezing. She was glad to be alone. Carla Crawley was helpful, but enough was enough.

She was here.

Waiting.

Just like that day . . . No, this was different. Chris was inside. Erin could wait as long as it took for that door to open.

No, she couldn't. She was freezing. She coughed as the frigid air caught in her throat. She closed her eyes and enjoyed the evening sun's light touch of warmth on her face.

Movement, from inside. Finally. She listened. Steps on a hardwood floor. A faint click of the door latch. Her heart pumped about six beats' worth of blood at once, flooding her entire body.

The friend she once knew, the friend she had prayed for all these years, cried for, wondered about, raged over, was just inside that door. She had touched the door latch. But the door wasn't opening.

Erin moved closer and said, just loud enough to be heard through the thick door, "Chris?" A pause. "Chris . . ."

That was it for a second. She swallowed, forced in a shaky breath, and said, simply, "It's me."

The door opened slowly.

Erin took one look. And she smiled.

THREE

SHE DIDN'T CRY. THAT WAS the one thing she did not want to do. But she wanted to. Terribly. The sight before her broke her heart.

Erin saw the dark brown eyes, the light brown hair, the smooth, straight nose. She recognized this person, but she didn't know who this person was.

Same five foot six. Erin was still an inch taller. Nothing else looked the same. The hair was longer, thicker, and looked like a brush hadn't passed through it in days. Those eyes, so dark, though wide with surprise, looked dull and weary.

Erin didn't let her smile fade as she waited, praying for words to say. She wasn't sure how Chris would react after all this time. And what did she think she would find? Just a shell of memories?

The surprise in Chris's eyes slowly faded into a state of simple nothingness, but then were touched with a faint hint of a smile.

Erin had no idea what to say. After a few seconds, she simply whispered, "Hi."

The happy smile that burst across Chris's face carried a hint of embarrassment. Relief flooded Erin's entire being.

Chris didn't cuss her out and slam the door in her face—two reactions that had crossed Erin's mind. She just stood there. Staring.

Erin shivered. She couldn't help it. She was freezing. Portland's weather was mild with rain. Heaven's weather was just a bit too nippy for a Portland jacket.

Chris backed up and swung the door open wide. She didn't, or maybe couldn't—Erin suspected the latter—say a word.

Erin grabbed her bag and walked through the door. And gaped.

The cabin, though small and sparsely furnished, was absolutely charming. Log beam walls. Huge couch, huge picture window illuminating the entire front room with brilliant evening sun, glider rocker and ottoman, old easy chair, coffee table . . . She took it all in. Bookshelf filled with books and trinkets, a walk-through kitchen leading to what appeared to be Chris's bedroom. A huge wood-burning cookstove stood in the kitchen, smack-dab in the middle of the cabin. She wondered what was wrong with it. The cabin was just as nippy as the great outdoors. She looked at Chris.

Chris pushed the door closed and just stood there, staring at Erin. She glanced at the stove. Words suddenly stumbled out of her mouth. "Oh. Oh, yeah. I'm so stupid. I'm sorry. I let the fire die. Sit down. No, here." She hurried into the bedroom, came back with two colorful fleece blankets, handed one to Erin, then threw the other over the couch. "Um . . . yeah. Sit. Wrap up. Get warm. I'll build a fire."

"Thanks." Erin wrapped the blanket around her shoulders and stood at the window, allowing her heart to scream out for guidance, to beg and plead. Low beams of sun sparkled off every single flake of snow. The sight stole her breath. *Oh . . . Lord . . .* Like grains of sand in a desert, how many flakes of snow? *How many stars? Quabozillions. At least.*

"Can't believe I let this die. I, uh . . . fell asleep on the couch."

Erin turned to look at Chris. *Asleep on the couch? With no blanket?* Still unsure of what to say, she glanced down, then noticed an overturned bottle of Jack Daniel's whiskey on the floor by the couch. She watched Chris crumple up newspapers and lay out kindling inside the stove.

Yes, okay. No big deal. Chris drank; Erin knew that. If the ban on liquor had not been in place during the operations in Saudi Arabia, things might have gone a little better for Saddam Hussein. But, to comply with conditions set by the honorable King Fahd, the ban was firmly in place. The entire operation, bone dry. The fighting men and women had missed it, but they pressed on. Chris had missed it; Erin could tell. Real life had no ban on liquor. And five days ago, from what Erin heard, Chris fought an enemy just as dangerous as any ever faced in any war.

She was hungover.

But still functioning. Erin wanted to laugh. *Lord, how's that for optimism?*

A flash. Flame. Chris's dark eyes reflected bright orange flickers. Erin watched. And smiled.

Chris grinned sheepishly. "Okay. Give it half an hour. We'll be toasty." She stood, but had to reach out to steady herself against the kitchen counter.

Erin quickly turned to look out the window. "This place is gorgeous, Chris. I bet you love it here." She pretended not to notice as Chris picked up the empty whiskey bottle and took it to the kitchen where she threw it under the sink, into the garbage. But she watched through the faint reflection in the glass. And said, "I love the ocean, but this is unbelievable."

Chris moved in beside her. "Yeah. I was lucky to get this place."

"I, uh . . . didn't notice any power lines."

Chris grinned. "That's 'cause there's no power."

"Oh."

"Yep. Hope you didn't bring your curling iron."

Funny. Erin's hair curled naturally, and Chris knew it. "Outhouse?"

Chris laughed, blinking heavy eyelids. "No. We got the real thing. You gotta go?" She looked at Erin expectantly.

Erin's heart tugged. She saw no life in Chris's eyes at all. She wondered if there was life anywhere inside her. "No. Not yet." She forced a smile.

"It's back through the bedroom, if you've got to . . . you know . . . later. Help yourself." Chris turned to point over her shoulder. "That's the food cache. It's stocked pretty well. You can help yourself there too. Whatever you want. Oh, about the can. There's a hand pump in there—do you want me to show you? In the winter I've got to haul water, but you still use the pump. You've got to, like, pump it three times to fill the bowl. Then it's just like the real thing."

"What. No foot pads and a hole in the ground?"

Chris laughed. "Pul-lease," she said, shaking her head, "don't remind me."

Erin grinned. "Such a rich place, and they didn't even have decent—"

"Water closets?"

They both laughed.

And Chris quickly pinned her right elbow into her side.

Erin's heart ached. How she wanted to throw her arms around this woman and tell her she was not alone. *Just reach out, Chris. You can trust me. Please, don't be afraid.* She passed a tremble off as a shiver.

"Are you still cold? Do you want—?" Chris started for the couch.

"No, I'm—" But the second blanket was being wrapped around Erin's shoulders even as the words came out.

She was going to cry. *No, Lord, I can't cry! I just got here!* She bit her lip, but could not stem the tears. She quickly turned, whispering, "Maybe I do need to use the bathroom." She lowered her head and hurried toward the bedroom.

✮✮✮

CHRIS WATCHED HER GO. AND then, when she was gone, almost fell into the glider rocker. She leaned forward over her knees and covered her face. Her hands shook. Her heart raced. *This can't be real. She's here! She's using my water closet. Right now! I can't believe this. I can't . . . What is she doing here? After all this time! How long . . . ? Oh, man. Five years. Five . . .*

Thoughts gave way to blurred images in her mind. An old army helicopter she called Ticket. Miles of flat sand. Chem gear. Brilliant stars on a pitch-black sky. That crazy deuce-and-a-half, a truck capable of two and a half tons, stuck up to its axles in sand. Outrageous.

Not knowing what else to do, she let the images continue. But then, as the back water pump squeaked, she saw an image that hurt like fire. Every day this image appeared in her mind, forced its way in; every day it cut to her soul. And now, with Erin Grayson right here, right now, the hurt overwhelmed her.

She stood up quickly; let her quick action pull away the hurt. Her head throbbed. A deep, shooting pain ripped through her side, freezing the breath in her throat. But she didn't care. The memory of a C-141 medical evacuation transport plane lifting off the runway, leaving Dhahran, Saudi Arabia, for home would not make her cry. Not this time.

She turned and went to check on the fire.

✷✷✷

WARMTH FROM A FULLY STOKED, fully engulfed full-sized wood cook-stove filled the small cabin like a soft, invisible fog. Erin basked in it, staring out the window. The sunset had simply been a gift from God. Long wisps of thin cirrus threaded brilliant pink across the stunning baby blue sky.

She absorbed the warmth and every inch of the view, sipping on a mug of sweet peppermint tea.

She knew she'd find peppermint tea in Chris's cupboard. Chris had so enjoyed it in the desert when Bettema had scrounged up a few packets for her. Or did Chris win them in a poker game? Either way, she had shared them with Erin. They sat in their tent that night, a miserably cold and damp winter night, slowly sipping tea, talking about nothing, just passing the time as they waited for war.

They did a lot of that. Hurry up and wait. Isn't that what defined war? Protracted periods of unbearable boredom interspersed with sudden moments of sheer terror.

Maybe that's it, Lord. Maybe Scott doesn't want to hear about the war because he knows he'd be bored to tears if I told him what we did. We were bored. Well, for the most part, anyway.

Bored, yet always on alert. Either way, in almost every way, Erin enjoyed her time in the desert. She made some great friends there, friends for life. A surgeon she met at the Air Force hospital in Dhahran still visited her in Portland every couple of months or so. Fellow soldiers Bettema Kinsley and Capriella Sanchez worked with her at the Kimberley Street Community Center. With that commanding officer full-bird-colonel now-retired Benjamin Connelly.

And his wife, Sonya. Great friends. All with the same Gulf War experiences. The hurry ups and waits. Melting in the heat, then freezing your tookis. Finding sand in the most amazing places. And choking down MREs. Yes, Meals Ready to Eat were three, three, three lies in one.

Erin couldn't help it. She laughed at herself and slowly shook her head.

The faint sound of splashing water coming from the back room ceased. She looked up. Looked around the cabin. She could hardly believe it. She was here. And the one person, the one friend who brought back the multitude of precious memories they shared in their Gulf War experience . . . just stepped into the same room, bringing glowing light with her as she carried a kerosene lamp.

"Whoa. Fire's kickin'."

Erin let her smile widen. "Feels good."

"Yeah, but I'm sweating." Chris left the lamp on the kitchen counter.

"The thawing-out process."

"Oh. Is that it?" She barely laughed. Then, wincing faintly, she wrapped a Scrunchie around her flowing brown hair.

Erin was suddenly warm. Too warm. Seeing Chris in bare feet, a T-shirt, and a pair of knee-length short-johns reminded her of warmer days. Warm, like a hundred and fifteen in the shade. And of the fact she still had on her jacket. She took it off and tossed it over her bag.

"That's it," Chris said with a laugh, making herself comfortable in the easy chair. "Now that you're here, take off your coat and stay awhile."

"I'd love to stay forever." Erin snuggled with the last of her tea into the couch.

"Okay."

She enjoyed Chris's silly grin. But it quickly faded.

"I can't believe you're here."

Erin looked down. "Thought I'd surprise you."

Chris's voice softened to a whisper. "Well, you certainly did."

An uneasy silence fell over them. Erin didn't know what to say.

After another minute, Chris let out a deep breath. "So. Since you're here, you've got to see some sights. Where do you want to go tomorrow? Telluride? Mesa Verde? Black Canyon?"

Erin looked up and smiled. "Carla Crawley said you need to take me to see Ouray."

Chris laughed. "She did, huh? Well, I think that can be arranged. It's only ten miles from here. What, did she think I wouldn't take you into town? It's beautiful. We'll go to Box Canyon and . . . everywhere."

"Okay." Erin grinned, then sipped her tea.

Chris fell silent for a long while. Serious. She started to squirm in the chair.

Erin tried not to look at her. Only sipped her tea. And prayed for words to say.

Chris was not comfortable. She was being nice, hospitable, but she was tense. Erin could tell. She stared at the brown liquid in her mug.

After another full minute of silence, Chris finally said, "So, how long are you going to stay?"

Erin kept her reply light. "As long as you'll have me."

Chris squirmed again. "Yeah. Okay. Sure. Um . . . you can have the bed. I'll—"

"Forget that, woman! I'll sleep right here."

"No, Erin, really. Take the bed. I'll sleep out here."

"Chris."

"What."

"I am not taking your bed."

Chris nodded. Looked down. And pouted. "Okay."

"Yeah, okay. This is the best couch. It'll be great."

"Well, if you get cold . . . here, I'll get you some more blankets." She was halfway to her bedroom before adding, "Pillows too. One or two, Erin? Do you want two?"

"Yes," Erin hollered as her heart screamed, *Please! Chris! Sit and relax.*

"These blankets are the best." Chris hurried back into the front room. "Three ought to do it. Here's a pillow."

Erin leaned forward and put her mug on the coffee table as Chris tossed her armload onto the couch. "Okay. Thanks."

"Do you want a sheet? I've got—"

"No. Thanks. The blankets will be fine. They're so soft."

"Yeah. Warm, too. But if you get cold, wake me up. I'll fix the fire up good before I go to bed."

"Chris."

"Yeah?"

"I'll be fine."

Chris stood by the bookshelf. Almost backing into it. As if she couldn't get far enough away. "Yeah. Okay." Her eyes would not look at Erin.

"Why don't you sit down."

Chris struggled for words, struggled with the moment. Her eyes moved around the cabin sheepishly. "Um . . . you know, Erin?" The struggle seemed to intensify. "I, um . . . I think I'm going to bed. I, like, got a major headache. You know?" She finally met Erin's gaze, but quickly looked away. "I'm . . . I'm really sorry. I mean, I know it's still early and all. And you came all this way . . . but . . ."

Erin wanted her words to come out softly. "It's okay." They did.

Chris frowned. "I'm sorry, Erin. Really. I, um . . . Oh, hey, did you get anything to eat? You need more than tea. Are you hungry? I'm sorry I didn't clean up the—I broke a glass over here, Erin." And Chris was over by the side window now, carefully tiptoeing around the glass.

"Chris?"

She turned around. "Yeah?"

Erin didn't know what to say.

"Oh. Yeah. Okay. Are you, um, are you sure you don't want anything else?"

"I'm not hungry. I'm fine." Erin smiled. "It's okay. Go to bed."

Uneasiness again fell over them.

Chris was embarrassed, and that was frustrating her; Erin could tell. A strange twinge of irritation came over her, but seeing the exhaustion in Chris's eyes, she didn't let it show, not at all. "Go on. It's all right. I'll be fine."

"If you want to brush your teeth or anything, go ahead. I mean ... don't worry about waking me."

"Okay."

Chris smiled, but it was thin and strained. "Um ... well ..."

"Good night, woman." Erin smiled easily as her irritation disappeared.

"Okay. I guess I'll ... see you in the morning."

"I'll be here."

"Oh, do you know how to turn down the light?"

"I'll figure it out."

"Yeah. Right. Okay. Well ... 'night."

"Good night."

And Chris was gone.

Erin's smile faded as Chris left the room. Her eyes closed. *Well, Lord, that could have gone better.* She leaned back into the soft corner of the couch. *Oh, Lord Jesus, please help this all ... be okay.*

✷✷✷

A FULL MOON DRAPED ITS eerie blanket of milky white over everything. Long, thick shadows of dark gray hid behind trees and jagged mountain peaks. The sky was so clear, each star sparkled like a diamond, and she wondered for the millionth time how her heavenly Father could possibly know exactly how many there were. Billions, she guessed. Including satellites. *Quabozillions. At least.*

Something scurried through the snow, under the protective reach of pine branches. Overhead she caught a glimpse of an owl, gliding effortlessly through the crystal sky. She marveled.

She shivered. She wasn't really cold, but she hugged herself tighter under one of the thick fleece blankets. It was so soft; in it she felt soft. She gazed out at the moonlit Rocky Mountain night, and smiled.

So beautiful. So peaceful. She thought about going out on the porch, maybe even going for a short walk. Just far enough out to see the entire sky. Away from the trees. Then she really shivered. *No, silly. It's probably ten below zero out there.* She laughed.

Chris had told her how much she loved watching the Northern Lights in Fairbanks. Middle of winter. Fairbanks, Alaska. Of course, it had to be a clear night, and clear meant cold . . .

Erin laughed again, imagining Chris McIntyre all bundled up in her army-issued arctic gear, standing, or as she liked to do in the desert to watch the stars, probably lying flat on her back on the hood of a Humvee, looking up, shivering, freezing to death, watching the Northern Lights.

Erin had never seen the Northern Lights. She wished again, as she often did, that someday she could see Alaska. Maybe, just maybe, Chris would go with her. Give her a guided tour of the Greatland.

She closed her eyes. She loved her husband dearly, but Scott would never want to go to Alaska. He talked of Cancun. Maui in the summertime. The night they married, Erin had no idea where he wanted to take her for their honeymoon. He had arranged everything, and told Erin nothing. They ended up in Cabo San Lucas. Yes, it was a glorious week of newlywedded bliss. She had no regrets.

No. When it came to Scott Alexander Mathis, she had no regrets.

Yet . . . deep in her heart, she missed her husband, and she prayed for him. She couldn't call him. She didn't know Chris wouldn't have a phone! He would be stewing in worry about now. There was nothing she could do. Except pray.

But, in a weird sort of way, she didn't want to call him. He had stated his position clearly. Voiced his concerns. As unfounded as they might have been, he had voiced them all. And she didn't want to hear them again.

Someday, Scott would understand. He would realize why she needed to make this insane trip. Someday, she would make him understand. That was all there was to it.

But . . . this night, this present moment, was not about him. And Erin didn't feel bad as that fact took hold inside her. No hard feelings. Nothing hurt. She'd stay in Colorado only as long as she needed. Not a day longer. She had made him that promise. And a promise was a promise.

Lord. Forgive me.

She had also promised her husband on their wedding night she would never take off the stunning diamond ring he gave her that day. She looked down at her bare hand. So much time had passed, it would be too much to tell Chris, too soon. Nervousness tore through her stomach. She sighed deeply.

It's not like I'm purposely breaking a promise. Or that I'm trying to keep my marriage a secret from Chris. I mean, Lord! You saw her! She looked like she was having a stroke when she saw me. I'll tell her. I can't wait to tell her. I'll tell her when things calm down a little. When the time is right. Oh, precious Lord . . .

Her hand slowly rubbed her belly, feeling the life inside. Still too small to show, still too precious to comprehend. Too wonderful in every unimaginable way.

Oh, Lord God, thank You. Thank You so much. For this child . . . Scott's child . . . Lord, please . . . now that I'm here, help me know what to do so I can return to him soon. I know he's being protective, but he was so angry. And he's wrong about Chris. Will he ever understand why I had to come here? Help him understand, Lord, because how can I ever explain it to him?

Just that morning, at the airport gate, their parting kiss had been deep and passionate. *Lord, he'll be all right. Help him work this out. When I get home, I'll just sit him down and make him understand. Oh, Lord, if only he could meet Chris. Dear Lord God, if only Chris . . . would believe in You. Please help her believe.*

Far away, faintly, an owl hooted. Gentle peace fell over Erin's soul. *Thank You, Lord. You know I can't worry about Scott. He's there.*

I'm here. Now's the time for me to worry about you-know-who. She let a tiny laugh escape her lips. *And . . . I'm worrying, Lord. Forgive me. I don't want to manipulate this. I really can't wait to tell Chris every-thing. Give us that quiet time. But first, Lord, help me figure out who she's become. Help me know if I even belong here. Help me to see her the way You see her. Your will be done. Whatever it takes.*

And please, Lord . . . hurry.

***

SHE WASN'T SLEEPY. NOT YET. It wasn't that late. Ten thirty, maybe. She didn't care. Somewhere, a clock ticked. Quiet and steady. The cabin felt peaceful. Warm. Erin stood at the window. Prayed. Counted stars. And she smiled.

But then . . . she heard it. She knew she would hear it. Yet, still, it broke her heart.

She had heard these sounds before, many times, in the desert. All the long nights of waiting for war. Fear. Fear made it worse.

She heard it again. Whimpers. Words. Mumbles. Tears filled her eyes as she debated what to do.

In the desert, after the first few nights, Erin woke Chris. Each time, waking up, Chris was embarrassed, and the following day would be extremely long. Chris would be distant, down, almost angry. Almost afraid. Erin would pray. And wait patiently. Go about her work as if nothing was wrong. And Chris would come around.

The other soldiers nearby learned to ignore it, to sleep right through it. Chris asked Erin to do the same. Erin couldn't. Eventu-ally, she would simply lie there, listening. The same sounds, the same words over and over. Every other night. Sometimes only once a week. Sometimes every night.

Mumbled words. Sometimes names. Tony. Sometimes Jeff. But, most of the time, Dad. Daddy. And the word *no. No. No. No.* Always that one simple word, always late at night, waking her from a fitful sleep, darkness heavy like a fog.

The word didn't terrify her; it was the way Chris said it. The way her voice became a tiny, sad sound. A child's wail. The sound of a terrified child saying, "*Nooo . . . nooo, please, nooo . . .*" And a name. And a sudden flood of pure anguish would rush Erin's heart.

She would pray hard, lying there on her cot. She would weep. And listen.

Chris wrestled with sleep, with her dreams. She flinched and her muscles twitched; she tossed her head from side to side, held her breath, then desperately gulped in air. She would wheeze sometimes, as if she couldn't get enough air, and then stop. Suddenly. And be still.

That moment always paralyzed Erin. She prayed for Chris to be still, to sleep, and then, when peace prevailed, Erin almost panicked. *Is she awake? Is she okay? Should I try to talk to her? Should I act like I'm sleeping?*

Chris would be still, then try to get comfortable. Then she'd fall back to sleep.

Sometimes, she would cry.

And Erin would pinch her eyes shut and pray with all her heart.

But what now? Should she go to her? Try to wake her? It had been a long time. Erin didn't exactly feel like a welcomed guest. Chris was embarrassed. She would be angry if Erin made a fuss after all this time.

Erin decided to wait. And pray. She swiped at the tears welled in her eyes. And listened.

The sounds continued. Chris was talking, pleading; her voice was soft, high-pitched, her words only mumbles. She tossed in the bed, but not violently. Relief trickled through Erin. This was good. The dream wasn't bad. Not like before. Not at its worst.

She suddenly felt exhausted. The long trip had taken its toll. She made her way to the couch, lay down in it, and covered up. It didn't take long to get comfortable; the couch was long and wide and soft. From where she lay she could see the needle-covered branches of the ponderosa pine and fir trees silhouetted against the moonlit sky. She smiled as the sounds from the back room diminished. And then, all was still. Only the clock ticked.

She heard another noise and her eyes popped open. Chris was up now, awake, moving to the bathroom. A few seconds later, Erin heard the pump squeak and a faint rush of water. She grinned. She heard Chris's footsteps back to bed, a deep sigh, a small cough, and then stillness.

Quiet and peaceful. Steady ticking. Silvery moonbeams.

Erin fell asleep.

She woke up, heart pounding against her chest—she heard something. What was it? She knew what it was. She could still hear it. *Oh, Chris*... She found her watch and pulled it close, trying to catch enough moonlight to reflect off the gold hands. Four? Was it already four? Hours had passed. She thought she had just closed her eyes.

The cabin was cold. Not freezing. Not toasty either. Her nose was cold. Under the blankets, nestled deeply in the couch, she was warm. Reminded her of the cold desert winter nights. Snug in her bug bag. Except for her nose.

In the back room, Chris was crying out. That one word. And then another. A word Erin hadn't heard in a long, long time. Years. Since . . . Saudi.

"Rinny . . . please . . . nooo . . . Rinny . . ."

She sat up quickly; her eyes searched the darkness. She heard the words. Didn't she? Was she dreaming?

Chris struggled now, thrashed in the bed.

Go to her, Erin thought. Then, *No. She'll be okay. What is she dreaming about? Oh, Lord! What else would it be!* She threw off the blankets and spun her feet to the floor. *But . . . I don't want to embarrass her. Don't want to baby her. She hates that. She might push me away!* Erin froze. Listening.

Chris drew in deep, sharp breaths. Quick gasps. Even across the cabin, each breath sounded loud, desperate. Not getting enough air—

Chris had a broken rib.

Erin leaped off the couch. She grabbed the kerosene lamp and lit it. Left it on the kitchen counter. In the bedroom, darkness was heavier, but not complete. The lamp threw out a warm glow, just enough light to see.

Chris had thrown her covers back, her T-shirt was drenched, sweat glistened her face, strands of hair stuck against her forehead and cheek. Her eyes were pinched shut; her mouth hung open, pulling in one frantic gulp of air after the other. Her entire body was stiff, as if the breathing—and the dream—was tearing her apart. Her arms held her sides, wrapped tightly around her chest.

Erin grabbed Chris's right hand, then sat beside her on the bed.

Chris sensed the touch immediately. "No! No!" Her face showed pure panic. "Don't! Bobby, don't take it off! Rinny!" She tried to pull her hand away, tried to push Erin away. "No, Bobby, let me do it! Don't touch her!" Chris started to cry. "No . . . Oh, God, please . . ."

Erin forced air into her lungs. Tears spilled down her cheeks, onto her arms, onto Chris's bed. She tried to speak, more than once, but couldn't. But she had to. She pushed the words out. "Chris, it's all right. I'm here. I'm safe."

Chris continued to cry. Tears mixed with drops of sweat and traced into her hair, onto her pillow. Still asleep, she was crying, moving her head slowly from side to side, saying, "Nooo . . . God help us. Please . . . Rinny . . ."

Erin had never seen anything like this before, never in her entire life. She didn't know what to say, what to do. Wake her quickly? Gently? Let her sleep? Her breathing still wasn't right. Erin had to wake her. She squeezed Chris's hand.

"Rinny . . . don't die. Please . . ."

Erin forced back a rush of agony. She spoke slowly; her voice shook. "I'm here, Chris."

"Nooo . . ."

"Chris, I'm here. Wake up. Come on, wake up."

Only anguished silence.

"Chris, please. Wake up. It's a dream. I'm here. I'm safe." She gently rubbed Chris's forehead, trying to soothe away the terror etching deep lines there.

"Rinny . . ."

"I'm here."

Chris, her eyes closed, still sleeping, still dreaming, relaxed. Her voice fell into a faint breath of a whisper. "Rinny . . ."

"I'm here."

Her head violently shook. "No. Rin—no!"

"Yes, I'm here. Right now. Listen to my voice. You have to wake up."

Silence.

"Open your eyes, Chris. Look at me."

"Nooo . . ." Her one word faded to nothingness. She shook her head, more slowly now.

"Chris, come on. I'm here. Look at me. Open your eyes."

The heavy silence lingered. Erin could feel Chris trembling. Chris opened her eyes. Slowly. Blinking. Not quite awake yet.

"I'm here. That's it. Look at me."

"R–Rin?" Chris's own voice now. Lower, scratchy, weary.

"I'm here. It's all right. You were dreaming."

Chris's eyes again closed. She pulled her hand away from Erin's and rubbed her face, her eyes. Lifting her arms, though, brought a groan of pain. She lowered them and rolled over onto her right side. Toward Erin.

Erin sniffed back tears and wiped her eyes on the sleeve of her sweatshirt.

The sudden movement startled Chris. She opened her eyes, then blinked slowly, deeply. "Rin?"

Erin gently smoothed the hair away from Chris's face. "I'm here. It's all right. It's me."

"What are you—?" Chris blinked a few more times. "Why are you—?"

"Shhh . . . Don't. It's all right. Can you go back to sleep?"

Chris struggled for an answer.

Erin sensed the building tension and pulled her hand away.

Chris closed her eyes. "What are you doing here?"

Erin wiped her wet cheeks, then gripped both her hands together and held them in her lap. "I'm here, Chris," she said quietly. "What's it matter why?"

"It's just . . . I . . ."

"Shhh. Just sleep." Erin leaned over and reached for the covers. She started to pull them over.

Chris tried to grab them. Her throat let out a squeak as her breath stuck there.

"Easy. Not so fast. Please, let me do it."

Holding her breath, Chris lowered her arm.

Erin pulled the covers up and tucked them in around Chris's back. "Your shirt's wet. You should change it."

"No. It's all right."

"Well, keep covered up or you'll freeze."

Chris started to rise up in the bed. Again her voice squeaked. "Fire's out. I need to—"

"Stay still. Chris?"

"But—"

"I'll take care of it later."

"But—!"

Erin gently pushed her back down to the pillow.

Chris held her breath the entire way down.

"Just be still." Erin waited. She didn't know how to ask. "Still kind of bad, huh?"

"What?" Chris pulled in an irritated breath, obviously refusing to reveal just how bad. "Oh. Yeah. I guess." She tried to get comfortable.

"Are you taking anything?" *Besides Jack Daniel's?* Erin wanted to say the words, but bit her lip to keep them inside.

"Tylenol."

"Do you want some?"

"No."

Erin sat there for a full minute, trying to decide what to do. She wanted to stay but didn't want to push it. She should probably go and let Chris sleep. Still, she decided to ask. "Do you want me to stay a little while? Until you fall back to sleep?"

"No."

Of course. What did you expect? She hasn't changed. Erin slowly started to get up. *She's all right. She'll sleep—* She stopped and quickly turned around.

Chris had reached up and grabbed the back of Erin's sweatshirt.

The pause was filled with tension. Erin waited, standing now, by the bed.

"Y–Yes."

She sat back down.

Chris closed her eyes. And reached out again.

Erin took Chris's hand. And squeezed it.

FOUR

SCRAMBLED EGGS, SAUSAGE, FRUIT COCKTAIL, orange juice, hot coffee, hot peppermint tea . . . and fresh baked biscuits. Bisquick. Easy. But smelling so good.

Maybe it was the biscuits, or maybe the sausage sizzling. Either Chris's nose or her ears. Something pulled her out of bed and dragged her to the kitchen.

As Erin worked, she hadn't said a word.

Chris sat on one of the two barstools at the kitchen counter, looked out over the spread of food, looked up at Erin, smiled, and said, "Wow."

"Eat up, before it gets cold." And Erin smiled.

Chris filled a plate and dug in.

Erin did the same—after a quick prayer of thanks.

She watched Chris as she ate, trying not to be obvious as she studied her, assessed her movements and actions, searching for something . . . even a simple spark in those dark brown eyes.

She saw the aftereffects of a long night. Puffiness. Sprouting hair refusing to be tamed by an obviously quick brushing. She saw color in those cheeks, and another forkful of eggs disappear into that mouth.

Erin couldn't help wondering how long it had been since Chris had eaten.

Chris's mouth was full, but she said, "This is great, Rin. Thanks."

"No problem." The cheddar cheese sprinkles over the scrambled eggs really did hit the spot.

A swallow. "You didn't have any trouble with the stove?"

"Nope. I figured it out."

Chris guided a chunk of sausage into her mouth. "Did you sleep okay?"

Erin paused her fork's progression just long enough to say, "Yep."

After a few seconds, Chris's eyes fell sad, increasingly serious. She sipped her coffee and stared out the window.

Erin spoke up quickly. "Your butter looked a little strange. Do you have any jelly or anything?"

Chris turned back, her eyes smiling again. "Did you taste it?"

"The butter? No. I wasn't sure—"

"Taste it."

"Why?" Erin almost laughed.

Reaching over to Erin's plate, Chris picked up her biscuit and split it open, then grabbed a knife and smeared a huge scoop of the butter on it. The biscuit was still warm. The butter melted beautifully. She handed it to Erin. "Here. Taste this."

Erin accepted the biscuit and took a small bite. And it melted in her mouth. She quickly took another bite.

"Good, huh?"

"Mmm!" Mouth full, she managed to swallow before adding, "Excellent! What is it? Sweet butter?"

"Honey butter. Isabella used to make this for her sourdough biscuits. Oh, man, they were good."

"Isabella . . . from Alaska?"

"I told you about her?"

"A little."

"Yeah. She's the best."

And they both ate another biscuit smothered with homemade honey butter.

They ate, stuffed themselves, sipped their coffee and tea, and watched chipmunks and chickadees out the side window, scurrying through the snow. They were quiet. Silent. Simply enjoying the morning.

At least Erin was. Until Chris stopped looking out the window. She stopped seeing. Her eyes turned dull as she stared at the wall below the window, stared, but didn't seem to see. She blinked, barely breathed. She held her mug in her hands, but Erin knew the last of the coffee had cooled.

Erin's breakfast soured in her belly. She drew in a deep breath. Didn't know what to say. What to think. What to do. She waited. Prayed.

Chris suddenly looked up at Erin. It took a moment for her eyes to focus, for her words to find voice. "Erin, what are you doing here?"

The question sent a shiver through Erin. She slowly lifted her tea and sipped. She prayed for a way to answer. And couldn't look at the one who had asked the question.

"Tell me! Who called you? How'd you find out?"

She swallowed deeply. "Nobody called me. Ben heard—"

"Ben? You mean Ben Connelly? *Colonel* Connelly?"

"Yes, Chris, you know who I mean. I know you got at least my first few letters."

"How'd *he* find out?"

"In the newspaper." Erin struggled to stay patient, to not let her building irritation show.

"Oh. I see. Ben reads the newspaper, tells you all about it, and so you decide to come on down here and—"

"I wanted to see you."

"Why, Erin? 'Cause I killed a man? You wanted to see where it all happened?" Chris slammed her coffee mug on the counter, then stood and moved into the living room.

"Chris . . . please. I—"

She spun around. "How did you find me?"

"We didn't even know it was you! We didn't put it together at first. Ben read about what happened in the paper." Erin hated to say it, but there was no other way. "He knows your base commander."

"Sid? Ben knows Sid?"

"Yes. They spent time in Vietnam together. In the army."

Chris grunted in disgust. "Oh, sure. Of course. I forgot. Ben Connelly knows *everyone*."

"Chris . . ."

"So he calls old Sid, and Sid tells him all about what happened, arranges everything . . . and here you are."

Erin did not want to continue this discussion. She closed her eyes and rubbed her forehead with a trembling hand.

"I asked you a question. Why are you here?"

"Come on, Chris!" Erin's hand slapped the counter as she looked up. "When we found out it was you . . . when I heard it was *you*! I—I couldn't believe it! I was worried about you!"

A disgusted laugh. "Oh. That's right. I must have forgotten that too. You do *so love* worrying about me."

"Don't be like that. You know I care about—"

"DON'T!" Chris raised her hand. "Don't say it."

Erin stood and started clearing the dishes. She desperately tried to keep from revealing anything. She wanted to lash out, to scream at Chris, to slap her upside the head and make her understand. She reached over to put the butter in the cache. The words she heard next stunned her, froze her solid.

"I don't want you here."

She turned and saw Chris standing at the front window.

Erin heard the words, but they were not powerful words. They were almost weak. "Why not?"

Chris didn't say anything.

But Erin knew why. She had seen too much, had gotten too close. Chris had let her guard down, had pulled down a wall or two, and made the mistake of letting Erin see a heart that was soft and sad and wounded and searching. Only the walls were hard. Walls glued together by fear.

She laughed. It startled her. Where the laugh came from, she had no idea. Yes, she did. She laughed again, then pushed her voice into a nasally whine. "But Carla Crawley said you'd take me to see Ouray."

And Chris laughed. She lowered her head, laughed again, then shook her head slowly.

Erin's heart swelled with relief, then quieted. Chris looked so broken, so completely exhausted. Her confidence, that hidden strength that pushed her hard, drove her, kept her going, was slipping away. It seemed to Erin that sometime soon it would be completely gone.

Chris pulled in a deep breath, turned around slowly, then glanced up at Erin. "Listen," she said softly as her eyes wandered, "Erin, I'm sorry. But please . . . don't—" The words ended. She clenched her teeth for a second. "Last night. Don't ever do that again."

Erin couldn't resist asking, "Do what?" She waited.

"You know what I'm talking about."

"I do?" This was new. Erin had never really challenged Chris before. Should she now? Maybe a little. "What did I do that was so bad?" All she did was sit there in silence, praying, until Chris fell back to sleep.

"Just drop it." Chris growled an indecipherable obscenity, pushed herself away from the window, and started for her bedroom. "You know exactly what I'm talking about. Don't do it again." She stopped at the stove, flipped the damper, whipped open the door, received a faceful of gray smoke, threw in a few pieces of wood, coughed, closed the door, flipped back the damper, then reached behind the stove and pulled the ropes lifting the thirty-gallon water box. "I'm gonna take a quick shower," she said as she yanked the ropes. "Don't worry. I won't use all the hot water." Biting her lip, she fussed with the ropes, locked the box in so it wouldn't fall, fussed with the outlet pipes, and then disappeared into her bedroom and closed the door.

Erin hollered, "I was really worried!"

She heard a grunt of laughter through the door for a response and was satisfied. She cleaned up the dishes and helped herself to another small glass of juice.

✷✷✷

OURAY, COLORADO, WAS UNLIKE ANYTHING Erin had ever seen. Nestled gently in the lap of the Rocky Mountain's San Juan Range and surrounded by a billion tons of snow, the small town of about seven hundred was a scene from long ago. Built in the late eighteen hundreds, the entire town, she was told, was listed in the National Register of Historic Districts.

Chris took her to Box Canyon, introduced her to a parka-laden lifeguard at the town's immense hot springs pool, then took her to Cascade Falls, which was actually a frozen river of falling ice, and they watched as a climber slowly, meticulously, inched his way up its face with pickaxes and crampons.

They stopped at a gift shop so Erin could browse, and then went to Bear Creek Falls. Finally, with stomachs growling, Chris took her to Raymond's.

Raymond Gordon was a master short-order cook. Made the best burgers in Colorado. In Chris's outspoken opinion, at least.

Erin felt at home the moment she walked into the out-of-the-way diner. She saw Raymond Gordon's bright, happy smile and heard his, "Well, hey there! Chrissy Mack!"

The huge smile that burst across Chris's face stunned Erin for a second. She hadn't seen that smile in a long time. And didn't Chris hate being called "Chrissy"? In the desert, she had snapped at anyone who even attempted to call her that. But not now. Raymond Gordon appeared to be getting away with it.

Chris parked herself on a stool at the counter. "Hey, Sarge! How's business?"

"Never better!" the old man hollered.

The diner was empty.

Chris laughed. "Sure looks it!"

Erin sat beside her at the counter.

Chris looked at Erin, then at Raymond. "Sarge, this is Erin Grayson. A good friend from Saudi. Rinny, this is Master Sergeant *Retired*, Raymond C. Gordon. Veteran of Korea, Vietnam, and over twenty-five years of slinging army hash."

Raymond extended his hand toward Erin. "A true honor to meet one of Chrissy's dear friends."

Erin shook the man's hand while absorbing every bit of his broad, gentle, and intensely warm smile. "Nice to meet you too, sir." She gave him one of her warmest smiles in return.

"So what am I fixin' for my dear friends this fine day?"

Chris slid a menu over to Erin and started listing recommendations.

Erin wasn't listening. Her mind swirled with the moment: Chris using Erin's maiden name, the oppressive heat of the diner mixed with the heat burning her cheeks, hearing Chris's joyous laughter, seeing the warmth of that smile. Raymond C. Gordon had captured her heart. She watched as he and Chris bantered over the menu. He was older, probably early seventies if she had to place a bet; his dark brown face sagged and beamed at the same time. Deep wrinkles had been grooved by a million wide smiles. His face was the face of a teddy bear: fuzzy with a day's growth of a faintly gray beard, dark brown eyes that shone brightly, framed by two huge ears, and crowned with short dark hair frosted with tiny curls of gray.

His smile . . . for him to smile so completely, was it a reflection of the pure joy radiating deep inside him?

His eyes . . . were now fixed on her. "And for you?" he asked.

Erin snapped out of her daze, grabbed the menu, and scanned it quickly. Had Chris said something about burgers? "Cheeseburger," she finally said.

"Should I burn it? Or just tickle it."

Erin laughed. "Not too pink, please."

"Fix 'er up good, Sarge," Chris added, so helpful.

"No onions!" Erin hollered as Raymond started for the kitchen.

"No weepers for the young lady!"

"Hey, Sarge," Chris called out, and then waited for him to look through the open wall above the kitchen counter. "This here 'young lady' was a U.S. Army officer. First Lieutenant when I knew her, then resigned as Captain. Right, Rinny?"

Erin smiled, glad to hear at least a few of her letters were read.

"Is that right?" Raymond dried his hands with a towel. "I tell dear Chrissy every time I see her. You all did one fine job against that nasty Saddam Hussein. He needed his clock cleaned. And y'all did exactly that!"

"And I keep telling you, Raymond, they let us do it right." Chris sipped a glass of ice water. "Not like they treated you guys."

"Well . . . y'all did a fine job."

"So did you."

The look Raymond gave Chris melted Erin's heart.

Chris tore open a pack of crackers. "You guys actually cooked back then, in the field, didn't you. No tray-packs floating around in boiling water."

"Well, now, we handed out our share of C-Rats." Raymond laughed as he worked on their burgers. "But we had our share of steaks too. Bakin' cookies in the field. Now that was somethin'!" He wiped his hands and moved to the soda machine. "Pepsi?"

"Of course." Chris grinned, then glanced at Erin.

"Do you have Seven-Up?"

"I most certainly do, my dear." Raymond filled two huge glasses with ice and soda and then slid them down the counter with style. Satisfied both glasses safely reached their intended targets, he returned to the kitchen.

Erin whispered, "He's great!"

Chris laughed quietly. "Yeah. I come here a lot."

"I love his smile."

"Me too."

They talked as they waited, then dove into the fattest, juiciest cheeseburgers Erin had ever seen. She ate every bite: burger, fries, and pie. She never laughed so hard; Raymond's stories were the best. They stayed and talked for almost two hours.

A small, older woman suddenly appeared in the kitchen, hollering, "Are you workin' hard, Raymond? Or hardly workin'?"

Raymond's wife. Same dark skin, same dark eyes, same bright, beaming smile. And a blushing husband. "Yes, my dear."

Chris asked, "Which of her questions are you answering, Sarge?"
The old man winked. "All of them, young Chrissy. All of them."

Before they finally decided it was time to leave, Chris made a quick trip to the restroom. Raymond watched her go, and then, when she was out of earshot, said to Erin, "Have you had a chance to talk to her yet?"

Erin didn't know what to say.

His voice took on a sincere softness. "I worry about her. She's been through so much." He slowly shook his head. "I pray for her. I'll pray for you too." He gave Erin a warm smile. "The Good Lord will take care of you both. He'll work things out."

Tears filled Erin's eyes—she couldn't hold them back. She had been right. This man was her brother. "Yes, please, Mr. Gordon, pray," she said softly. "Please. She needs the Lord. Desperately."

He looked back at the bathroom door as it opened and Chris walked out. "Yes. I'll pray for her. For her to find our Lord." His words ended in a whisper.

"Ready?" Chris said with a smile.

✱✱✱

The sun was setting as they left Raymond's and headed back into town. Chris glanced over at Erin. "I need to stop at the station quick to check the schedule. Then we'll get some ice cream. Sound like a plan?"

Erin grinned. "Like an excellent plan."

They commandeered the visitor's front parking space at the San Juan District Three Search and Rescue station. Chris led Erin through the front door.

Carla Crawley lit up like a Christmas tree. "Chris! Hello!"

"Hi, Carla. Can I get a copy of the schedule?"

Her face suddenly darkened. "I, um . . . Sid wants to see you about that. Hello, Erin."

"Why? What's up?"

She swallowed hard. "I better let him tell you."

Chris's eyes were filled with confusion. "Sure. Okay. Is he still here?"

"Yes." But Carla Crawley was already busying herself with other things.

Chris headed for the base commander's office without another word. Erin looked around, then studied the huge district map displayed on the wall. The front office was quiet. Carla responded to a radio call—someone with a code of twenty-fifteen calling in a completed supply check at Conner Creek. Somewhere down the hall, country music played. Somewhere down the hall, loud voices exploded.

"You don't need to do this, Sid!"

"Yes, I do."

"That's crazy! I'm fine! What am I gonna do for two more weeks?"

"Just take the time, McIntyre! I don't want to see you around here!"

A door slammed. Seconds later, Chris appeared. Her face was hard and burned with anger. Her voice, Erin was surprised, was soft as she said, "Let's go, Rin."

They left the station. They made three stops. One at the gas station for a fill-up, one at the Callahan Restaurant for a half gallon of their premium homemade mint chocolate chip and a half gallon of their premium homemade deluxe butter pecan.

The third stop was at the liquor store for a bottle of Jack Daniel's.

★★★

CHRIS SIPPED THE WHISKEY AS she stood at the front window of her cabin, staring out into a moonlit night. Not knowing what to say or what else to do, Erin picked up Chris's scrapbook and spread it out on her lap, then slowly worked her way through it, taking in every picture, slowly savoring every common memory.

Chris kept few reminders of her past. The small trinkets on her bookshelf, Erin noticed, were mostly shot glasses from Alaska and Germany. There were no pictures anywhere, except in the scrapbook. Here, they were carefully placed; the book itself was worn from use.

But no baby pictures. No pictures of Chris's early childhood. A few from her teenage years. In one, Chris actually smiled.

There were army pictures. Basic training. A group shot of buck privates hamming it up. A few landscapes of Landstuhl, Germany. Pictures of Alaska. Lots of them. Smiling faces, people laughing. Chris enjoyed her time in Alaska; Erin could tell. She studied a picture of a large Native Alaskan woman standing behind a long, polished bar under a beautifully etched mirror displaying the word— the bar's and owner's name—*Isabella's*. The woman was laughing, facing slightly away from the camera. But it was her expression that captured Erin's attention. Even through thick plastic-rimmed glasses, Isabella's eyes sparkled with joy. Erin had seen the same expression earlier that day, in an out-of-the-way diner. She hoped in her heart, maybe there was a chance Isabella believed . . . *But she owns a bar! There's no way* . . . She grinned. God worked in mysterious ways. Who was she to doubt?

She turned the page. There it was. Ticket to Paradise. UH-1 Huey 1207. In all her glory. Snowcapped mountains behind, four grinning, fully uniformed and fully entwined crew members in front; Erin laughed and pulled the book closer to her eyes. In the picture, Chris had to stand on tiptoes to get her arms around Teddy Brisbaine's and Bobby Palmara's shoulders. They looked like they were holding her up. And Angelo. What a cutie.

Her eyes fell closed. A strange hum flowed through her; she didn't just see the usual flood of mental pictures, of memories, faces, the sand; she felt the flood rush through her. She remembered what it was like to be part of something special: 4th Brigade's Wild Card. In their finest hour.

She opened her eyes, turned the page, and once again took in the images, real photographs of the places, the faces . . . and the sand.

Ugh. So much sand. Hundreds, thousands of miles of it. Fine, gritty sand. Rocky sand. Blowing sand. Sand in her boots. Sand in her hair. Sand in her stethoscope. Sand where sand should not be.

And so, so hot. How did we ever survive? One picture made her laugh out loud. Specialist McIntyre in a sweat-dripping-wet brown

T-shirt, sleeves rolled away to nonexistence, dark sunglasses, a floppy booney hat on her head, a wide, happy smile on her face. She had never seen this picture before.

Still at the window, Chris turned around. "Find something amusing?"

Erin glanced up, then lifted the book toward Chris. "When was this picture taken?"

Chris's face remained firm and cold, but she leaned forward to look. "We were setting up the Air Force hospital."

"In Dhahran?"

"Yeah." Chris turned back to the window. Lifted the glass in her hand for another drink of whiskey.

Erin lowered the book to her lap. "Do you ever miss the desert?"

"What?" Chris gruffed out a laugh. "No."

"Not at all?"

"Not at all, Rin."

"Didn't you have any fun at all?"

Chris turned around and leaned against the window, her right shoulder against it, her right hand holding her drink. "It was war, Erin."

"Yeah, I know. I was there, remember?" Erin again studied the photographs. "But it was a special time."

"We did our job."

Okay. Enough of this. Irritation swept through her. She closed the book and put it on the coffee table. "Want some ice cream now?"

Chris stared at the glass in her hand, then turned again to the window. "No."

"Well, I'm gonna have some more." Erin stood and headed for the cache. A few seconds later, she asked, "What do you do around here for fun?" as she dipped out a huge scoop of mint chocolate chip.

"I'm usually working," was Chris's growl of a reply.

"You've got some great books." Another scoop.

"I read. That's my fun."

"I'd go nuts without a stereo."

Chris said nothing. Just stared through the window.

But Erin remembered. Chris was one of the few soldiers in Saudi who didn't have a Walkman. No cassettes, no music at all. Erin had asked her about it; Chris had said she didn't like most music. Didn't like a heavy beat or lame, repeated lyrics. Which pretty much eliminated most of rock-and-roll and country.

She was curious. "What kind of music do you listen to?" She put the ice cream back in the cache, picked up her bowl, and savored a mouthful. Then browsed over to Chris's bookshelf. There were a few cassettes on a shelf next to a small tape player and headphones. She read down the labels. Journey. Moody Blues. Pat Benatar. *Phil Keaggy?* Erin could hardly believe it. "You have Phil Keaggy?"

Chris didn't turn around. She lifted her glass for a slow sip of her drink, then said, "Great guitar player."

"He's a Christian. Did you know that?"

Chris took another, longer, drink. After she swallowed and her grimace eased, she said, "Travis gave it to me."

Erin's heart hit the floor.

Chris finished her drink and went into the kitchen to pour another.

✯✯✯

SHE HATED TO DRINK. ESPECIALLY now, in front of Erin. She poured the liquor into her glass and tightened the cap on the bottle. She needed one more. So she drank.

She hated the burn, but the burn would fade. And, with it, her world. It was worth it.

She swallowed a long drink, then sat gingerly on the easy chair in her living room. Propping her feet up on the coffee table, she pushed herself into a lazy slouch and, for Erin's sake, tried to relax. *You can do this. Just . . . relax.*

Erin still stood at the bookshelf. "You've got a lot of paperbacks. Mysteries, huh?"

"Yep." Chris sipped her whiskey.

"Anna Pigeon. She's something else."

Trying to swallow, she almost choked. "You've read Nevada Barr?"

"Sure. Why not?"

She didn't know why. She shrugged and looked away.

Erin sat on the couch, pulled the scrapbook over her lap, and again studied the pictures as she worked on her ice cream.

Chris laid her head back against the soft chair and closed her eyes. Silence filled the cabin.

Oh, how she could have slept, right then and there. She was so tired . . . always so tired . . . so sick of always being so tired. She wasn't up for socializing. Wasn't up for anything life demanded. She heard Erin laugh again and, just for spite, pulled the glass to her lips and drew in a loud sip. Then regretted it as she swallowed.

"You could really handle military vehicles." Erin said the words through a mouthful of ice cream. "Angelo told me you could drive anything that had wheels."

He did? Chris didn't know what to say, even what to think.

"You sure got that one stuck, though. Big time."

She laughed; she couldn't help it. And grumbled, "That was a stupid truck."

"Didn't it take a tank to pull it out of there?"

How lucky was she that no one else found out about that? That she didn't lose a stripe, at the very least!

Erin laughed, but then groaned. "That place was so filthy."

"The Land of Sand."

"No, I mean the garbage. It was as if they just didn't care."

"Well, they didn't."

"They had everything they could ever ask for, and lived in a garbage dump."

"Yep."

"And the oil fires. And spills."

"Could we talk about something else, please?" Chris lifted her glass for another sip. Swallowed. Waited for Erin to change the subject. It took a few seconds.

"What about Teddy's birthday party? I know you had fun that night."

Chris remembered the night, and smiled. "Yeah, that was a wild night."

"See, you can have fun without booze."

She chose to ignore that.

Silence again fell.

Erin's voice, when she finally spoke, was soft. "Were you two ever friends? I mean, I saw how he treated you most of the time."

Chris opened her eyes as her mind brought the man up, like a computer search found. She didn't really like what she saw. "We were friends. It's a long story."

A pause. "Do you miss him?"

Did she? "No. But . . . I'm sorry he's dead." She sipped. The glass shook in her hand.

"Will you . . . ? Please? Chris? Tell me about Travis."

Chris glared at Erin, then quickly looked away. "There's nothing to tell."

"You liked him."

Loved him! Oh, Travis! She closed her eyes. The word shook. "No."

"Come on, I know you did. Liz said—"

Her eyes flew open as she sat up quickly. "Liz? When did you talk to Liz about me and Travis?"

Erin's face reflected instant regret. But, with a small sigh, she answered the question. "She picked me up at Grand Junction."

"You've got to be kidding!" Chris gaped for a second, then stood and went into the kitchen. "Are you serious? Are you—? Oh. That's just great. You two talked about me the whole way back from Grand Junction? Two hours?"

"Get off it, Chris. We didn't talk about you the entire time. I asked her about what happened. She's concerned about you. She wanted me to tell you that."

"Yeah. Right. I'm sure she is." Another grunt of a laugh. "And did *Carla* tell you all about *me and Travis* too? We were *in love*, you know."

She waited for a response. Heard nothing. Until the scrapbook slapped shut. She sat on a barstool, facing the side window. Against the darkness she saw her own reflection. She hated what she saw. She got up and walked closer, until she stood inches from the glass. Outside, the ponderosas rose majestically into a blue-black sky; milky white moonlight bathed everything.

Such beauty, such pure magnificence. Colorado's Rocky Mountains. The only place she had ever really found peace. The jagged peaks, the snow, the trees, the streams, the wildlife . . . just last week she watched a pair of bald eagles gracefully riding the cold winter currents; they flew . . . majestic, awesome, oblivious to everything. At peace with their world.

Peace was a fantasy. A hopeless dream. She thought she had found it—she *had* found it. It died in a heartbeat. Bled out. Dead and gone.

It would never be the same. She would never again look at these mountains, or spend the night in another trail cabin, or ride another snowmobile without thinking of him, without seeing . . . Travis. Bleeding. Dead and gone. Everything was lost. Again. Any flicker of hope renewed . . . now lay dead. Again.

Oh, God . . . Travis . . . I'm so sorry . . .

She swallowed the whiskey in her glass in one huge gulp.

✯✯✯

ERIN WAITED, AND SHE PRAYED. Had she ever prayed so hard? Part of her screamed, *Get out of here! This is ridiculous! You've got better things to do.* Another part, deep in her soul screamed, *Please, Lord God, help her. Give me the words to say. Oh, Lord, she needs You so much!*

Chris left her glass on the counter and sank back into the easy chair. She propped her feet back up, laid her head back again, but turned her head slowly toward Erin.

Erin looked her in the eye. She saw a hint of repentance. Heard those sad and weary eyes say, *I'm sorry, Rinny.* Erin gave her a small smile that said, *I know.*

Chris stared off at nothing, then closed her eyes.

They sat in silence. The clock ticked in the bedroom. The fire in the stove cracked and snapped. The flames in the two kerosene lamps hissed. Erin picked at a piece of fuzz on the arm of the couch. Until a thought crossed her mind. She almost laughed. A crazy thought. Yes. Just what she needed at this point. She lifted up a prayer for strength so she could get the words out. She pressed her lips, quietly cleared her throat, and said, "Chris, will you come back with me?"

Chris lifted her head and looked at Erin. Her eyebrow raised. "What?"

"Come back with me. To Kimberley."

She grunted a laugh. "Oh. You mean the house that Ben built?"

Erin almost groaned. "Please. Come and see it for yourself before you judge."

"Nah." Chris's head fell back again as her eyes closed.

"Come on. I hear you've got some time on your hands. Two weeks, was it?" She got no response so she tried a different tactic. "Chris . . . Tema's there now. And—"

Chris's head lifted as her eyes flew open. "Tee?"

"Yeah. And—"

"Bettema Kinsley is at Ben's—excuse me, at *Colonel* Benjamin Connelly's—little *amusement park*."

"You can call it whatever you want, but we have a good thing there. We . . . *he* . . . bought a huge building down the street, and Tee's been—"

"Buys whatever he wants, does he?"

"Tee's been helping him set it up as a gym." Erin paused, watching for Chris's reaction. Was that a spark?

"A gym."

"Yeah. The place is huge. It's awesome. Big enough for basketball and volleyball. They're setting up locker rooms and—"

"And ol' Ben suckered Tee."

"Chris."

"Oops, sorry. Guess he suckered you too, huh." Chris laughed, then relaxed in the chair.

Erin said simply, "I have a home there."

"Yeah, well, mine is here."

"Yeah, and so what. I'm not asking you to move in with us, just come and see it. You could use a—" The words ended.

"A what. A vacation?"

"Well . . . yeah."

"Yeah." The word was a snarl.

Erin's heart pounded. *Lord, You've got to make this work! Chris should come to live with us at Kimberley! Work with us!* But it sounded impossible, even as hope started to build within her. *Just keep going, Erin . . .* "All right, a change of scenery, then? The beach is only two hours away. Astoria . . . We can hit the shops on the bay front, go down to Seaside . . . maybe a little horseback riding on the beach."

"Woo. How charming."

Impossible. Yes. Of course it is. Erin sighed, loud and long. She lifted the scrapbook off her lap and dropped it on the coffee table. The spoon in her empty ice cream bowl rattled. Chris's eyes widened, but Erin ignored her. "I'm tired. I'm going to bed." She stood and headed for the bathroom.

She changed into her sweats and brushed her teeth. Splashed water on her face. Stared at her image in the mirror. *You are such a fool! This is insane! Why are you here? What did you think would happen? You'd come down here and save the day? You should have listened to Scott. You shouldn't have hurt him to do this.* She studied her sad, droopy, light blue eyes. The soft curls of brown hair. *Ahh, I could use a long, hot bath.* She glanced at the cramped shower stall and almost cringed. Her house in Portland had a huge old-fashioned claw-foot bathtub. She loved to fill it to the brim. Rich, creamy, coconut bubbles . . . water so hot it seeped into her bones.

She stared into the mirror. She wasn't sleepy, but she was tired. Bone tired. Of dealing with Christina McIntyre. Tired of caring about someone who simply wanted to be forgotten. Someone who didn't think she deserved to be cared about, let alone loved. Not then, and obviously not now. Chris hadn't changed one bit.

"Hey, woman! You fall in?"

Erin closed her eyes and laughed. "Gurgle, gurgle, gurgle."

"You're not sleepy. Not yet. Come on out and grab my jacket. I'm gonna warm up the truck."

Her eyes popped open. "What?" She rubbed her face with a towel and quickly headed for the kitchen. "Chris?"

No response. Chris was already outside.

"What are you—? Chris?" Erin stood there for a moment, staring out the cabin's open door. *Now what, Lord? What is this?* Another second later, she growled and gave in, pulled Chris's spare parka around her. Sliding into Chris's Sorrels, she grumbled, almost decided to forget the entire idea—hadn't Chris been drinking? And now she wanted to drive? But, Erin headed out the door—just as Chris headed back in.

"Need towels," was all the woman said.

And Erin's jaw almost dropped to the floor.

✳ ✳ ✳

CHRIS DROVE RESPONSIBLY, CAREFULLY, FOR the most part. The Explorer slid and bounced up the terrible snow-covered gravel road behind Chris's cabin for what seemed like an hour. Erin held her breath most of the way.

"Four-wheelin's a rush, huh."

"Huh." And Erin held on.

It was well past ten. Fresh snow had fallen earlier in the day, but now the night had cleared, the bright moon, the stars . . . stunning.

Erin allowed herself to relax. If Chris was drunk, she still handled the glorified full-sized snow machine like a pro. The moon seemed to wink at them through the truck's frosty side window. Erin smiled. And held on.

Not much later, Chris stopped the truck, climbed out, stretched, groaned, then gave Erin a wide grin.

"What are we doing here?" Erin crossed carefully around the front of the Explorer, her flashlight piercing the darkness with a thin beam of light.

"Come on." Chris grabbed her pack out of the truck, turned, and headed up a worn path. Not too worn, at least not since the morning's half-inch snowfall. But trodden.

Lord? This just keeps getting better and better! What is going on? Still, Erin followed. Grumbling. She trudged forward. "Where are we going? Tell me!"

"You'll see," was all Chris said as her boots crunched through the snow.

"Well, if you're trying to freeze me, woman, you're doing a great job."

"Good. It's better that way."

"Huh?" Erin tripped on a rock.

"You okay?"

"No, Chris, I'm not okay. Where are we going?"

"We're almost there."

Something smelled terrible. Erin looked up—she had been staring at her feet, illuminating the path with the largely inadequate beam from her flashlight. "Chris, answer me! Where are we going! And what is that smell?"

"Relax, Rin."

"Don't tell me to relax!"

Erin stopped and squinted through the darkness. Chris had led her to a shack at the top of a small hill. Erin stood there, her mouth open, as Chris lowered her shoulder against the shack's door and pushed a few times to force it open. She went inside and threw her pack down on the floor. Then popped her head back out the door. "Coming in?"

Erin couldn't move.

"Suit yourself."

Irritation crossed over into pure impatience. "What is going on? Why did you bring me here? Are we going camping? Wasn't your cabin sufficient enough for that?"

She heard Chris laugh, then thump and stomp inside the shack. Other curious sounds followed: a squeak, crackling paper, heavy clunks, the sandy scrape of a match being lit.

And something really smelled putrid.

Light from a flame. Snaps and cracks of dry kindling catching. A fire.

Erin stepped to the shack's door. Chris had lit a fire in a small pot-bellied stove. She stood there, watching the flames, grinning like a fool. "Okay. By the time we're done, it'll be toasty in here." She looked up at Erin, her grin never fading. "And no, silly, I'm not trying to freeze ya."

Trying to kill me then? Erin bit her lip to keep her nasty thought inside. *Patience, now. But Lord, this is absurd! I'm sorry I ever came here. I want to go home.*

Chris pulled off her parka. Then her sweatshirt. Kicked off her loosely laced mukluks. Then wriggled out of her jeans. Short-johns. A T-shirt. In twelve degrees.

Erin still couldn't move, could not even breathe.

Shivering now, but still grinning, in stocking feet, Chris moved past Erin, out the door, up the trail a little ways, then disappeared into the darkness.

Erin could only blink, watching her go.

FIVE

"CHRIS! WHERE ARE YOU?"

"Come on, Rinny. Water's fine."

Water? Erin carefully stepped up the trail toward Chris's voice. "Chris, stop this. You're scaring me. You're going to freeze!"

"Trust me, will ya? Get on down here. Watch your step."

Trust you? Famous last words. She swung her flashlight left and right but saw only snow, trees, and steam. And the smell . . .

"You're not trusting me, Rinny."

"How am I supposed to trust you when I can't even see you? Where are you?"

"Keep coming."

Erin heard a faint splash. "What are you doing? And what is that smell?"

"You've been in the city too long."

"Don't ch—change the subject." She rubbed her arms to warm them.

"Rinny, listen to me. Go back to the shack, take off your parka and sweats, grab a pair of shorts out of the pack and put them on, leave the boots, make sure the door is closed, and get on in here. You'll love it. You've got to trust me."

The debate raged inside her. Chris didn't sound drunk . . . Scott definitely would not approve of any of this . . . Water? In the middle of the frozen Rocky Mount—?

It hit her like a lightning bolt. How dense could she be? The stink was sulfur, the warm shack was for later, the water was . . .

In thirty seconds she was down to her T-shirt and Chris's short-johns, immersing herself in the most luxurious hot spring pool she ever could have imagined. Not too hot, no. Just right.

"Now. Didn't I tell ya?"

Joyous laughter bubbled out of her.

"Trust me, I said. And did ya? Nooo."

She could only hum in ecstasy.

"Did you find the right rock there? Sit on it and lean back."

Felt like a divine hand had lovingly carved a perfect sitting place in the solid rock.

"Kinda slimy, I know, but don't worry. It's not toxic or anything."

Erin still had not yet uttered a discernible syllable.

"Kinda stinky too. But you'll get used to it."

"It's . . . perrr-fect."

Chris laughed and grinned.

"Oh, you lucky dog. How often do you come here?"

"Every chance I get."

"This entire place is pure heaven."

"Well, if heaven exists, I hope it's just like this. It's better, though, when it's snowing."

"Snowing?"

"Best time. Or raining. I love to hear the rain falling through the trees."

The softly spoken words stole Erin's breath for a second. "Ahh, yes. Me too. Very much." She waited another second before asking, "How did you find this place?"

It took a long time for Chris to answer. Her voice was barely loud enough to be heard. "Travis brought me here. The night he helped me move into the cabin."

Erin didn't know what to say. She waited, then said, "Tell me about him." She gentled her voice. "What was he like?"

Chris barely smiled; her eyes softened. "He was . . . sweet."

Erin saw a sadness in Chris's expression that wrenched her heart. But no tears. Did she have any left to let fall? Erin tried to smile. "Was he . . . romantic?"

"He was . . . adorable. He used to say we were meant for each other. Mack and Novak." Chris smiled. "He was easy to talk to." After a slight pause, she looked down and added, "He was a good friend."

Erin's heart tugged. Had Chris opened up? To Travis? And now he was—?

"You're like him."

"Me?"

"Yeah."

She waited for more, then gently prodded, "Why?"

"He believed in heaven too." A whisper. "I hope he's there."

Erin prayed for the right words, closed her eyes and let the soothing water calm her spirit. She looked at Chris and said, "He gave you a Phil Keaggy tape?"

"Yeah. I told him I liked the guitar."

"Travis . . . was a Christian?"

"He believed in God."

"Did he talk to you about God?"

"Yeah. Some."

She could sense the subject was closing. She wanted to get her last thought in before it was too late. "Chris, if he truly believed, and loved Jesus as his Lord, he's in heaven. Right now."

Chris glanced at Erin for just a second, her lips pressed into a weary smile.

The subject was closed.

✯✯✯

HOW COULD THE NIGHT HAVE turned so quickly? From impossible to positively perfect in twenty short minutes. *Just like You to work this out, Lord. Thanks.*

Erin basked in the warmth, in the moment. Yet, still, she struggled for words to say. Struggled to know what any of it meant. Her purpose for rushing here . . . to this place. She could only pray. Then marvel at what the Lord provided. Small talk. *Just enjoy the quiet of this place*, she almost heard Him say. *And trust Me.* So she let her mind wander back to that time both she and Chris shared, and remembered the dumb stuff. Stuff that would make Chris laugh. Like MREs.

Just saying the words did the trick. Chris laughed.

"You know, they weren't so bad," Erin said with forced optimism.

"Are you for real?"

"Okay. I'll admit it. The orange nut cake thingies almost made me gag."

"Oh, no doubt. Seriously. They were disgusting."

"Still, the best dehydrated peaches I ever ate came from an MRE."

"Reconstituted, of course."

"Well, naturally." Erin tilted her head as she grinned.

A sweet silence fell. Lingered. Erin let it. Until, "All right, Chris. I'm sorry to bring this up again, but you've got to tell me how you got that truck so stuck."

Another burst of laughter came from Chris. "Rinny, come on! Trucks were getting stuck all over the place!"

"So, shouldn't that have been a deterrent to you?"

"I was just trying to see what it could do."

"You're just lucky there was a Bradley in the area."

"Oh, man. No kidding. Talk about unauthorized use of a tank!"

"You should have been busted back to private."

"No kidding, Rinny. Don't I know it."

Erin could only laugh. Again the sweet silence fell. Until, "And what were your intentions when you repelled? Were you purposefully trying to give me a coronary?"

"What, did I scare you?"

"You just disappeared! I didn't even see you hook on to the rope!"

"Well, that's the trick."

"I couldn't believe it. I still can't believe it! All I saw were your feet flying!"

"I was so stupid for doing it."

"Teddy put you up to it."

"Do you remember Bobby trying to warn us?"

"Headfirst out an airborne Huey, with our commanding officer and his inept sidekick only twenty-five meters away." Erin shook her head. "It couldn't have been set up more perfectly."

Chris didn't laugh. "Erin, I never told anyone this."

"What."

"Never. I mean it."

"What!" Breathless, Erin waited.

"The first time I repelled in Alaska? I mean, I'd repelled before, you know, lots of times. In flight. Off the tower at tech school. But this time, at Wainwright? With everyone watching?"

"Yeah?"

"That was the first time I went down headfirst."

She shook her head again. Slowly. "Amazing."

"I didn't exactly do it on purpose, Rinny."

Erin's eyes bulged.

"Thank God it was just off a tower, but I got tripped up in the lines and lost my balance backwards."

Her mouth fell open.

"Thought I was gonna die."

A breath of laughter.

"By the time I got situated, I was down. Perfect landing. Every-one was cheering."

"No way."

"I'm telling you, I almost puked up my biscuits, right then and there. But I heard everyone hoopin' it up, making a big deal, so I just pretended like I meant to do it like that. Gave them all a big wave."

Erin burst into raucous laughter.

"From then on, every time we repelled, I had to go headfirst. No one would let me go down the old-fashioned way."

More laughter.

"Especially Teddy. He saw the whole thing. And Collier. He was Teddy's medic then. I was with a different crew."

Erin didn't hear the last part; she broke into a coughing fit as her uncontrollable laughter tangled with the freezing, sulfury air in her throat.

Chris gave her plenty of time to recover. She just sat there, eyes closed, her chin barely breaking the surface of the steaming water, a faint smile on her face.

"I can't believe that story," Erin said as soon as she could breathe.

"Believe it."

In the distance, an eerie sound filtered toward them.

Chris's eyes opened wide. "Hear that?"

"Owl?"

"So cool."

Erin smiled.

"Heard a great gray the other night."

"Great gray?"

"Rare bird."

"What'd he sound like?"

"Now, Rin, it could've been a she . . ."

"Okay, what'd *she* sound like?"

"Cool."

Erin let out a laugh.

The owl hooted again. Chris jerked her chin up, listening.

"What kind?" Erin whispered.

"Great horned."

"What. Are all owls great?"

Chris grinned at her. "Yep."

Erin returned Chris's grin with one of her own. Then, after a few seconds, she settled against the rock and drew in a long, contented breath. She felt a stirring deep in her belly, a fluttering—her hands instantly went there—the breath stuck in her throat as her mouth hung open.

"You okay?"

"Huh?" She didn't realize she had made a sound.

Chris looked at her.

Deep, cleansing, overwhelming peace flooded Erin's entire being. Tears filled her eyes as her soul almost burst in adoration to her Lord.

"Rinny?"

Awash in the moment, her eyes slowly found Chris. "There's something I need to tell you," she said softly. "I'm sorry I haven't told you sooner. I didn't want to overwhelm you."

A curious look.

Erin laughed as the tingly sensation of pure awe ebbed. She drew in a deep breath and felt the luxurious water all around her, felt her heartbeat slowly fall back to its normal patter.

Chris waited, eyes wide, concerned.

"Two things," Erin said. "And . . . I'm probably going to overwhelm you." A long pause. "It's not like I was keeping it a secret from you; I just wanted to wait until the right time. A quiet time to tell you. I hope that makes sense."

Chris said nothing, though her eyes questioned.

"I think this is that time." Erin lifted her hands and let the water sift through her fingers. "Chris . . . I'm married . . . and I'm pregnant." She slowly looked up at Chris.

What she saw melted her heart. Pure amazement on Chris's face, pure wonder, and joy. But no smile. Chris appeared too shocked to smile. Was she breathing?

"I, um . . . I promised Scott I'd never take off my wedding ring. Technically, I kept my promise." Erin reached to her neck and pulled the gold chain from under her shirt. In the steamy moonlight, the diamond sparkled. She smiled and breathed a self-conscious laugh, then tucked it safely back under her shirt.

Chris seemed to struggle with the news. "How far . . . along . . . are you?"

"Four months."

Her eyes widened.

"Made for a happy Christmas."

"Who . . . ?"

"Scott Mathis. He's a doctor at Good Sam, in Portland. I met him just after I moved to Kimberley. He helped us set up the clinic."

Chris still didn't look like she could breathe.

"We've been married just over two years."

She started to smile.

"I'm sorry to throw all this at you. Better now, I guess, than the moment I walked in the door."

"No kidding. It was shock enough just to see you."

"I had a feeling it would be."

"But this . . . this, Rinny . . . this is overwhelming."

Erin looked down. "Yeah. Sorry."

"In a totally unbelievably *awesome* sort of way."

She laughed. "I hope so."

"Completely . . . awesome. Congratulations. Wow!" Chris slowly began to sink into the steamy water as the word carried out on her last breath. She didn't stop. Her head went completely under.

Laughing, Erin reached out playfully to grab her and pull her up. Chris came out sputtering; their laughter echoed across the stillness and almost carried them away.

★★★

SHE ANSWERED ALL OF CHRIS'S questions. Yes, Scott was handsome, smart, and very good to her. No, they rarely fought. Yes, Erin loved him with all her heart. No, she had no regrets becoming Mrs. Scott Mathis.

"Erin *Mathis*. It's gonna take some time for me to get used to that."

Yes, they both were delighted about being parents. No, sitting in a hot springs pool in fifteen degree weather was not dangerous for the baby. Yes, she had felt the baby stir inside her, earlier, for the very first time. No, again, sitting in a hot springs pool in fifteen degree weather was not dangerous for the baby.

Chris did not look convinced. "You should have told me sooner, Erin."

"No. This is okay. Really. Just a nice, hot bath."

"I wouldn't have brought you up here if I had known."

"Don't be crazy."

"Rinny! What if you catch pneumonia or something? Slip on the ice getting out of here?"

"Chris."

"What?" Rather sharply spoken.

Erin gave her a stern, yet playful look.

"Well, you should've told me. I mean . . ."

Grinning faintly, Erin let the awkward silence play itself out. After a few seconds, it did.

Settling back on the rock, letting her head rest against it, she simply simmered, feeling warmth course through the marrow of her bones. So deep in the water, her earlobes lightly broke the surface. Breathing steadily, she looked over at Chris and was glad to see a small smile on her face, her eyes fixed on the starry night sky.

Erin's heart took her back to that place, the desert, where the stars were brighter than she had ever seen. Unbelievably beautiful, the sky glittered. Chris would climb up on the hood of a Humvee, or lay herself out on anything flat, and just stare at them. For hours. Sometimes Erin would join her. They would just lie there, staring into the night sky.

One cold night, Chris whimpered and turned in her sleeping bag, obviously struggling with her dreams. When she woke up, she laid still. Erin thought she had gone back to sleep, but a few minutes later Chris wriggled out of her sleeping bag, pulled on her combat boots, and in just her long john shorts and a long-sleeved top, left the tent.

Gots ta go, Erin had thought, with a tiny smile and a silent laugh.

But time passed, lots of time, and Chris didn't come back. Erin was curious and more than a little nervous. She slipped out of her cot, slipped into her boots, grabbed her field jacket, and went looking. She found Chris sitting on the steps of the mobile kitchen trailer, just sitting there, leaning back against the canvas cover, staring up at the night. At the stars.

Now, soaking in the hot springs pool, Erin savored the moment. She glanced over at Chris. Her eyes were closed, her head resting against the side of the pool. As soft and steady as her breathing sounded, Erin could tell she was entranced. She hoped Chris came here often. At least here, she seemed to find peace.

Erin laid her head back and closed her eyes. And remembered. Chris on the steps of the MKT.

"What are you doing here?" Erin had teased. "Waiting for breakfast?"

"Just look, Rin. Have you ever seen anything so beautiful?"

Erin sat beside her and leaned her head back. "Wow."

"Unbelievable."

"Have you been counting them?"

Chris laughed. "Nah. Just looking at 'em."

"Any shooters?"

"One, so far."

"Cool."

"Yeah."

In the distance, through the trees, away from the steaming water, the owl hooted. Eyes still closed, Erin smiled, but her heart took her back to that night. She thought often of that night, sitting on the steps of the MKT. She had listened to the whisper of the Holy Spirit that night, and obeyed.

"You know what's unbelievable, Chris?" she had asked, trying to keep her voice steady as her heart pounded nervously. "The very One who created each star, knows each one by sight, knows us too. Knows everything about us. And loves us. Cool, huh?"

Chris's long moment of silence brought Erin's eyes down from the stars. Through the desert darkness she saw a terrible sadness in her friend's eyes. Those eyes blinked slowly and looked down. And then, even more slowly, looked back up at the sparkly night. A few more seconds passed. A whispered word. "God?"

"Yeah. God. He knows how many stars there are, minus the one you said just fell," She laughed quietly when Chris smiled. "He knows how many grains of sand are in this desert. Can you believe that? There's probably a billion in my hair right now. And in my boots and in my pockets . . ."

Chris laughed. "And don't forget the *quabozillion* that always end up in dinner."

"At least. Ack. I hate chewing sand. I can't even chew clam chowder. Now everything crunches."

Chris shuddered. "I'm always afraid a filling fell out."

Erin laughed. She watched a moment as Chris's eyes continued to scan the night. Then turned her own toward heaven and prayed.

She was praying still, five years later, soaking in a hot mineral pool six thousand feet up in the Rocky Mountains. She watched the woman who soaked beside her, as her head rested back on a rock and her eyes remained closed, as darkness and mist obscured the sight, as her own heart ached and trembled.

That night in the desert, by the MKT, was the only time Erin had ever really talked to Chris about God. About knowing God, the Creator, personally. To know Almighty God. Unbelievable.

A star fell across the Saudi-Arabian sky.

"See that!" Chris gasped.

Erin marveled. "Oh yeah. Wow."

"Can you imagine? At that speed, across that distance?"

"Twinkling of an eye."

"Huh?"

"Oh, nothing."

"Whoa. That was awesome."

Erin turned to see the bright smile on Chris's still-upturned face. *Do it again, Lord,* she couldn't help thinking. Then she said, "There's one less for Him to count."

"Huh?" Chris frowned. "Who."

"God. A quabozillion . . . minus two now."

Chris looked at the ground; her hands clenched into tight fists.

"What is it?" Erin asked gently. "Don't you believe in God?" So gently. Her heart pumped blood so hard it throbbed in her ears.

"Oh yeah, Rinny, I believe in God. There's no way this—" Chris glanced up and lifted her hands slightly—"could have just *evolved.* No way."

"Then what? You don't believe . . ." Erin paused, but knew the answer to her own question. "You don't believe He loves you."

Even now, after all the time that had passed, sitting in a hot springs pool, Erin shivered, remembering Chris's response.

Chris had pushed her head back into the canvas, as if the words hurt her, as if her response brought real physical pain. "He doesn't love me."

Erin was stunned. "How can you say that? Of course He loves you. The Bible says He knows all about us and still loves us. All of us. You too, Chris. He loves you, and He wants you to know Him."

"I don't want to know Him."

Erin barely whispered, "Why?"

The pause was long and frightening. Chris leaned forward and stared at the ground. Her voice, when she finally did speak, was quiet and sad. "I'm afraid of Him."

Erin almost laughed. Almost, until she saw how repulsed Chris seemed by her own words. And she knew. In a split second she knew. If she had laughed, she would have lost this friend forever. She thanked the Lord for keeping it down. Then waited for words. They came slowly, tenderly. "Why . . . would you be afraid of God?"

Chris let out a breath of laughter. "Ahh, I don't know. Really."

"Afraid? Chris, I didn't think you were afraid of anything. You're so strong."

"Me? Strong? Rinny, I'm afraid of everything."

The words stunned Erin, and the compassion—pure and simple love—flooding out of her at that moment, overwhelmed her. She let the words, and Chris's voice, echo in her thoughts. Finally, she said, "Tell me why."

A long moment passed. Breathing deeply, Chris leaned back again, rested her head back against the canvas, and stared, again, at the stars. She laughed, one time, almost silently, sadly, and said, "I was born scared."

"Of what?" Erin let the question fade gently.

"Everything."

She wanted to say twenty things at once, but her heart told her to be still, patient. She listened. And waited. And prayed.

The night air was cold. Winter was moving over the desert. Days were still hot, nights were now cold. Miserable place. But right then, there was no place Erin Grayson would rather be. She sat on the steps of the mobile kitchen trailer, beside a person she had only known two months, in the dark, in the desert, waiting . . .

Chris McIntyre opened her heart, just a crack, a peek, to Erin Grayson that night and neither woman would ever again be the same.

Chris shook her head against the canvas and simply breathed the word again. "Everything."

"Tell me."

"You don't want to know."

Erin had to swallow; she didn't know what to say. "Tell me why you're afraid."

The response was quick. "I'm afraid of what He'll do to me next."

Erin's mouth fell open. Her lips started to form the word, "What?" but the word itself did not come out.

"I must have done something. I don't know. Something, to make Him hate me."

"No. Chris, that isn't true."

"I don't know." Chris laughed as if ready to dismiss the entire conversation.

Erin sensed it. She quickly said, "No, please, tell me why you feel this way."

Chris laughed again and started to get up.

Erin grabbed Chris's arm. But Chris gave her a look worse than a glare, a cold, harsh scowl that sent a shiver of fear through Erin's entire body. A look of instant anger. Rage.

Their eyes locked for a moment.

Then Chris relaxed. She sat back down and turned her head away as if embarrassed.

Erin gently released her arm.

Chris let out a deep breath as she again leaned back into the canvas and stared at the stars.

The night was quiet. In the distance, generators hummed. Voices could be heard. Insects. Trucks. Peaceful. Strange. For a land waiting for war.

The thought brought Erin's head up. "Are you afraid . . . being here?"

"Sure. Aren't you?"

"Oh, yeah."

"It'll be soon, Rin."

"I know." She lowered her head and closed her eyes. "Are you afraid something will happen?"

"Something always happens."

Erin looked up.

"It'll be war."

"But we'll do our part to save lives, not take them."

"Absolutely."

"We won't be involved in any real combat."

"Hopefully."

"We'll be back, right? Won't we? Behind the main advance."

"Not very far."

Erin paused, then said, "Well, at least we won't have to engage the enemy. We're medics."

"Unless we're engaged and have to defend ourselves."

"I know."

Chris pushed out a breath of laughter. "And let's hope that doesn't happen, because all we'll have is an M-16 and a couple of peashooters."

Erin sighed deeply. "Are you afraid . . . of dying?"

"No."

Too quick. Erin looked at her friend. "Then you're not afraid of everything."

Chris breathed out a laugh. "Guess not."

"Why aren't you afraid of death? Everyone else is."

"It'll end it."

"End what?"

Chris fell silent.

A thought hit Erin. She had to force the words out slowly. Carefully. "Chris, are you afraid of your dreams?"

A quick look. A cold glare. Chris turned her head away as her teeth crushed together.

Erin almost whispered the words, "What do you see . . . in your dreams?"

Chris laughed bitterly. "I see how much God hates me." She gave Erin a smirk, though it quickly soured into a snarl.

"What else do you see?"

The snarl vanished. Chris's anger seemed to melt. She opened her mouth to speak, then stopped.

"What do you see, Chris? Every night, I hear you. Something . . . what is it? Please tell me."

"Trust me, Erin, you don't want to know."

"Yes, I do."

"Why?"

"Because I care about you."

Chris was stunned; Erin could tell. The light was faint, the darkness heavy, but Erin could see a rush of emotion in Chris's eyes. Fear was there. Lots of it. Confusion. Anger. Disbelief. Wonder. And a faint hint of joy. Chris said, "You don't even know me."

"I want to."

"Why?"

Erin smiled, pulled back just a bit, and said, "'Cause I'm yer friend, silly."

And Chris laughed. The sound of it warmed Erin's heart.

"Now tell me."

A deep sigh. "Rin . . . please."

"Let me help you."

Chris looked up at Erin. "Will it help?"

A pause. And then, "Yeah."

Chris let her gaze drift away. It took a few seconds. Almost a full minute. She said it. "I see my dad."

And Erin's blood turned cold. She held her breath, waiting for more.

Chris shook her head.

Erin rejected her immediate thought. She didn't need to know about Chris's dad, or what he had done to her. Not right now. Instead, she asked, "Are you afraid of your dad?"

Chris closed her eyes. "Not anymore."

"But you still dream."

The whispered words shook. "It never stops."

For a second, Erin thought Chris might cry.

No way. It was pure rage that shook Chris's voice. "I see my step-mom; I see my step-brothers . . . Oh, man, I hated them. You would never—" The words stopped abruptly. The hatred in Chris's eyes gave way to overwhelming horror.

Erin reached out and touched Chris's arm.

"NO!" Chris took off down the stairs.

"Wait!" Erin jumped up and ran after her. "Chris! Please! Stop!" But Chris was already halfway to the tent.

A soldier appeared. Sentry. M-16 at the ready.

"Just us, Davey," Chris said as she walked, giving him a wave.

"Keep it down," he gruffed at Erin.

The words stung. Her response was cool. "Yes, *Private*. As you were."

The young sentry almost choked as he squinted at the officer's insignia on Erin's field jacket. With a touch of sweetness, he said, "Yes, ma'am. Y'all sleep well."

Chris was almost to the tent by the time Erin reached her. She grabbed Chris's arm. "Chris, please stop."

Chris stopped. "Is that an order, ma'am?"

Erin gasped. "What's that supposed to mean?"

"Are you ordering me to halt, Lieutenant Grayson?"

"Stop it, Chris. Stop it right now."

"I'm going to bed." She turned.

Erin tugged gently on her arm. "Chris, please. I'm sorry. I didn't want to push you. I just wanted you to talk—"

Chris pulled her arm away. "Oh, so you're branching out now, is that it? Adding psych to your medical expertise?"

Erin stood there, gaping. Where was this coming from? What was this woman hiding, burying so deeply inside herself, under so much rage? What had Erin found here? A den of snakes? Her mind raced. *Leave her alone. Forget her. Let her be. Too much. She's a time bomb! Forget her. You don't need this . . .*

In the darkness, the hum of generators, the swirl of thoughts, Erin missed the tears that filled Chris's eyes. All she saw was Chris angrily wiping them away. She heard a faint sniff, and then the words, "Erin, I'm sorry. I didn't mean that. I . . ."

Erin waited.

"I just . . . I'm tired. I'm going to bed." Chris turned and disappeared into the tent.

Erin stood there, unable to move. In silence. In faint orange darkness. Staring. She didn't know what to say. She didn't know what to do. She made her way back to the steps of the MKT, sat down, and cried. She cried, and then she prayed.

And still, she prayed. In her present moment, as the painful memory faded, she felt herself giving in to her weariness, and let herself slide down all the way under the hot, sulfury water. She stayed under, shocked by the heat on her face, eyes pinched shut, holding her breath as long as she could. She came up gasping for air.

"Hey, Rinny! Are you all right?"

Erin coughed as the air froze in her throat. "Yeah. Wanted to try it."

"Well, take it slow next time. And give me some warning."

Erin laughed, then swiped at the water coursing down her face. "How can anything smell so bad, yet feel so good?"

"Thera-peee-uuuu-tic." Chris was so low in the water she blew bubbles.

"Am I gonna smell like rotten eggs now?"

"Just for a day or two."

"You're kidding, right?"

More bubbles. And a smile.

"Well, if I'm going to stink, so are you."

"Nope. I'm sulfur tolerant."

"What?"

"Yep. No stink. It's genetic, I think." Chris held her serious look for a few seconds longer, then gave Erin a wide smile.

"Oh, har-har. You're so funny."

"I've got sulfur-removing soap back at the cabin. With a little steel wool, you'll be smellin' sweet as a rose in no time."

Erin shrieked with laughter and splashed the stinky water in Chris's face.

Retaliation came quickly and completely. When the dust settled, both women had dunked each other at least twice and sat coughing and spitting the foul water from their mouths, their laughter shattering the silence of the frozen landscape.

SIX

SHIVERING, THEY HURRIED OUT OF the pool and into the cozy shack, laughing at the long wisps of steam floating up from their arms and heads. They made it back to the cabin where they stoked up the fire and hung their wet clothes from every hook, nook, and cranny. They laughed and talked until at least three in the morning, then slept until noon. They left for another trip to Raymond's, for a steak this time, and a baked potato and corn on the cob and baked beans and cornbread with honey. They ate until they couldn't eat a bite more, then sipped fresh hot coffee. Outside, eight inches of snow had fallen.

Again wearing her wedding ring, Erin loved every minute of the day. She loved Colorado. Chris wanted to take her down the Million Dollar Highway, the San Juan Skyway to Durango, then across to Mesa Verde National Park, then to Cortez, north through Purgatory and Telluride, and then to Placerville and Ridgeway . . . a trip that would take a full day, at least.

"Maybe if we get an early start tomorrow." Chris worked a toothpick to dislodge a sliver of corn stuck between her bottom front teeth.

"Nah, Chrissy, I don't think so." Raymond slowly shook his head. "Red Mountain Pass will be rough going with this snow. I think y'all should give it another day or two. Miss Erin, how 'bout a nice piece of pie."

Erin moaned. She could barely breathe as it was. She wore a long, bulky sweatshirt, and was glad. Yes, she was eating for two, but she had already unfastened the top button of her jeans. Soon these jeans just would not do, pie or no pie.

"Yeah." Chris narrowed her eyes in thought, obviously considering her options. "Maybe Wednesday. If the weather breaks. Can't see anything if it's shrouded in clouds."

"You could go on up to Grand Junction. Take in a picture show."

"What do you think, Rin? Want to go up to Grand Junction?"

Was now the time to bring this up? Again? Did she dare, with Raymond right there? Maybe she could use Raymond. *Yeah. He'll think it's an excellent idea. Or will he? Sure he will. I hope.*

Erin's heart thumped as she blurted out, "Chris, I want you to drive us to the airport in Grand Junction and then fly with me to Portland. I'll buy you a ticket. Put it on my Visa card. Whaddaya say."

Chris did not say a word.

Raymond gave them a wide smile and said only one word. He stretched it out for a full, long, solid breath. "Heeeeyyyyy!" Then he added, in another equally long breath, "That sounds like an outstanding idea, young Chrissy! You should take some time off! Go to . . . Portland, was it? Fine town, Portland." He took another breath and finished with, "I hear you've got two weeks available."

Chris gaped; her lips moved but nothing came out. Until, "What? Raymond, I'm not going to Portland."

Erin stayed out of the argument and tried not to smile as it dragged on. She sipped her ice water. Sucked in a piece of ice and let it melt slowly in her mouth.

"Portland's a fine town, Chrissy. It'll be a nice change."

Chris's mouth still hung open. Her eyes were wide as she glanced at Erin, then quickly turned back to Raymond. "I am *not* going to Portland!"

"Why not?" The old man furrowed his brow. "Don't be stubborn, child. You'll enjoy it."

"Stubborn? Who's being stubborn? I'm just saying, I'm not going!"

"She said she'd pay your way."

They both looked at Erin—she smiled sweetly.

"It's not the money, Raymond; I just don't want to go."

"Stubborn. That's what you are."

"Raymond!"

"The beach is only an hour or so away. I bet she'd take you to the beach. Wouldn't you, Miss Erin."

"Absolutely." She snuck the word in without missing a beat.

"I don't want to go to the beach!"

"What? Why not, child? The Oregon Coast is beautiful! You'd love it."

"No, I wouldn't!"

"Now, Chrissy Mack, don't you go fibbin' to me here in my own establishment. If I know anything about you, I know you'd love to take a nice long walk on a beach. And besides, I heard you before, sittin' right here in this same spot, say exactly that not even one month ago. You remember? We was talkin' about surfin' and all that."

Chris blushed, and stammered, "I, uh . . ."

Erin entered the fray. "Come on, Chris. A week, if you want. A few days. Just come with me." She gave voice to a sudden thought. "Come see Tema. And Cappy."

Chris turned. Her eyes bulged. "Cappy?"

"Yeah. She's there too."

A blink. "Cappy *Sanchez*?"

"Yes, Chris."

"Cappy Sanchez . . . is working . . . in a *church* place?"

"For a couple of years now."

"No way."

"I'm not lying. She works with Isaiah, fixing everything in sight. They're putting up the electrical in the gym probably right now, even as we speak."

Chris lifted her hand. "Whoa, wait. Wait one minute. You're telling me, Capriella Sanchez, *the* Capriella Sanchez we both knew in Saudi, is working with Colonel Connelly . . . at his little church camp?"

Erin had to bite her lower lip to keep from bursting into laughter. The moment passed, burst unreleased, and she said, simply, "Yes."

Chris stared at Raymond. For a long while. She glanced away, shook her head in total disbelief, and then said, through the release of a deep sigh, "Man! This I gotta see!"

It took a second for the words to sink in. Then, Erin's heart leaped. A silly grin spread across her face.

"But we're not flyin'."

Her grin evaporated. She waited, not sure what to think.

"I've got two weeks, so . . . I'll give you twelve days, Rinny. It'll take us . . . what." Chris looked at Raymond. "Two, maybe three days to get there? Through Salt Lake and Boise. I'll stay four days. That's it."

Erin would have agreed to anything, but . . . did that equal twelve?

"And you're coming back with me."

"What?"

"You grew up in northern California, right? On the way back we'll travel the entire Oregon Coast, go through the Redwoods, then cut across to Shasta; you can show me around, then we'll hit Tahoe, cut through Nevada—" Chris looked at Raymond as a smile spread across her lips—"into Utah, down through Bryce, then up seventy right into Grand Junction." She looked at Erin. "And *then . . . I'll* put *you* on the plane back to Portland."

Erin stared.

"Hey, woman, if we're gonna do this, we're gonna do this right."

Erin still stared.

"My way or the highway."

Erin grinned. "When do we leave?"

And Raymond's hearty laughter rivaled sweet music as Erin watched Chris's face, and especially those dark brown eyes, soften . . . and smile.

✳ ✳ ✳

THE NEXT DAY, ON THE road heading north and west, they laughed and joked and talked and munched on chips and cashews, then on red licorice and green apples, stopping only for various fill-ups and bathroom breaks and dinner. Erin funded the trip to Portland; Chris would fund the trip back. They both had a Visa card. Chris's was Visa Gold.

Cautiously exuberant, Erin knew she had to be careful. So much joy flooded her, but she didn't want to drown Chris in it. She bit her tongue at times. Avoided certain, more difficult, subjects. Kept the conversation light. Raved about the scenery most of the way. Laughed about silly memories of the desert. Like the first time she got off the plane in Dhahran, Saudi Arabia. First steps in a desert land. "I thought we'd been hit with a jet wash. I kept looking around for the taxiing F-15!"

"You did? Me too! I couldn't believe it. It was just the heat!"

"Oh, man. I almost died."

"What was it, a hundred and thirty? And a hundred percent humidity?"

"I thought the desert was supposed to be dry."

"Dry heat. Hah. Not along the gulf."

"Oh . . . that was awful."

"Couldn't even touch Ticket's skin. It'd burn your hand!"

"Couldn't breathe . . ."

"Couldn't sleep . . ."

Just munching out and enjoying the ride, talking and laughing at silly memories. It went on like that from Salt Lake to Twin Falls.

The next morning, from Boise to Baker City, Erin snoozed against the frosty side window. She stirred as the Explorer slowed, coasting down the interstate off-ramp.

"Hey. Mornin', woman."

Erin rubbed her eyes. "Where are we?"

"Baker City. I'm hungry."

"Me too."

"Got the Blue Mountains coming up."

"Should be pretty. When did the sun come out?"

"Soon as we crossed into Oregon."

Erin smiled.

They found a Taco Bell near the off-ramp and enjoyed one of everything on the fifty-nine-cent side of the menu.

"We'll be there around eight tonight, I figure. Sooner, probably." Chris barely finished the words before chomping into her soft taco.

"We made good time." Erin squirted green chili sauce on her tostada.

"Not bad. Two solid days," Chris said, chewing.

"You tired?"

"Nope. This is great, Rinny. I'm glad you thought of it."

She enjoyed Chris's silly grin, but deep in her heart she heard the words, *Hope you still think so when we get there!*

✬✬✬

THE BLUE MOUNTAINS OF THE Wallowa-Whitman National Forest in northeastern Oregon were shrouded in snow. Blankets of snow. Trees were engulfed, signposts wore tall, furry, white caps. A brilliant blue sky and a shiny golden sun illuminated the splendor; everything sparkled. Clean, fresh, glittering and radiant, except for the dirty white band of Interstate 84 in front of them. And their filthy dark blue four-wheel-drive Ford Explorer creeping along at a safe speed as Erin and Chris gawked and talked.

It couldn't have been more perfect. Erin glanced at Chris from time to time, trying to sense if anything was amiss. But she saw nothing worrisome in her friend's eyes. Sensed nothing in her demeanor. Chris seemed to be having a good time. That was all Erin could hope for. Or pray for.

Along the way, Chris wanted to know more about Erin's husband. Erin told her about his background, about how they met and fell in love. She didn't mention how unhappy he was when she left for Colorado. Or how unhappy he sounded on the phone last night when he heard where she was and what she was doing. Or his misconstrued conclusions about what happened during the war. These were things Chris probably didn't need to know anyway.

Chris then asked about Ben Connelly's little "amusement park."

After giving her a smirk, Erin carefully chose her words. "Well, officially, it's called the Kimberley Street Community Center. That's what the media calls us."

"Media?"

"Yeah. We've been featured in the paper a few times."

"Under the police report?"

"Chris."

"Sorry." But she didn't look sorry.

"Under community events, or the Metro section. A Metro reporter for the *Oregonian* is a good friend of Ben's."

"Uh-huh. Of course. Go on."

"Anyway, we like to—everyone that works there—we call it Kimberley Square."

"Charming."

"Well, practical. We work extensively with a sixteen-block square in the northeastern part of the city."

"Rough neighborhood?"

"Not bad. There's a lot of great people there. Quite an eclectic bunch. All kinds of people."

"One big happy family."

"Something like that."

"So what all do you do? Tell me about your clinic."

Erin glanced across at Chris. "So you did get the letters I sent?" Chris grinned.

"I was hoping you did. I kept mailing them to Fort Wainwright, hoping they'd be forwarded."

"Straight to Isabella."

"Isabella?"

"Yep. She saved them for me."

Relief and gratitude filled Erin's heart for the woman named Isabella. "Tell me about her. What is she like?"

"You were telling me about your clinic."

"Oh. Yeah." Erin slouched in the seat and put her stocking feet up on the dashboard. She wouldn't be able to assume this position much longer; she felt the tightness and lovingly rubbed her belly. After just a second, she reached into the cooler between their seats for a can of Seven-Up, popped the top, took a sip, and said, "Well, it's not very big. The other half of my duplex."

"You guys live right next door?"

"Literally." She grinned. "The front room is a waiting and treatment area; there's a bathroom and a kitchen with a door that leads right into my own living room, and then a bedroom for private examinations and another for record storage. Upstairs is an apartment where Cappy lives. Tee used to live there too, but she moved out a few months ago."

"Does Scott run the clinic, or do you?"

"Scott sees patients there; in a way it's his own private practice. But he spends most of his time at Good Sam. There's a good friend of mine from Providence who sees patients too. Mostly the Hispanics. I'm still working on my Spanish."

"What. *La hablar pequeno Español?*"

"I didn't know—!"

"That's the extent of it. Unless you include enchilada, quesadilla, empanada ..."

"Stop, you're making me hungry."

"*Mucho dinero, hasta la vista ...*"

Erin laughed.

"So, what does Cappy do?"

"Oh, you know Cappy. First thing she did when she got there was change the oil in all the center's trucks. Said they needed—"

"Trucks?"

"Well, yeah. We've got a pickup, two big passenger vans, a small Blazer, and Ben's Explorer."

"Ben has an Explorer?"

"Just like this. But cleaner." Erin grinned.

Chris gave her a smirk. "Sounds like a regular little fleet."

"Yeah, I guess."

"So, old Cap's right at home."

"Absolutely." And Erin smiled. She noticed a flicker of chagrin on Chris's face after she said the word *home*. "Tema's set up an awesome computer center for the kids. They love it. Games, CD-ROMs, Internet access ... everything."

Chris looked amazed. "How in the world did they end up work-ing for Ben?"

"He recruited them."

"Recruited them?"

"Yep. As soon as Tee finished out her enlistment, Ben sent her a letter asking her to come and work at Kimberley. She told him about Cappy, and he sent her one too."

Chris faked a pout. "I never got any letter."

"If we would have had any idea where you were . . ."

"So," she said quickly, "what else? There's a church, obviously."

Erin laughed, then sipped her Seven-Up. "Yep. The Kimberley Street Community Church."

"Nice name. Original."

"Andy, Ben's son, is the pastor."

"All in the family."

"I guess you could say that. His wife, Sarah, has a day care in the basement of the church, along with a library and a clothing recy-cling shop, plus she also leads the choir and teaches voice."

"Busy woman."

"And she has three kids. One's only three months old."

"*Very* busy woman."

"Yep."

"What about Ben's wife?"

"Sonya? She's the best, Chris. You'll really like her. Anyway, Sonya and Kay Valleri and Maria Velasquez—"

"Thanks for sharing . . ."

"—run the senior lunch program, the canned-goods distribu-tion center, a small women's shelter, a larger low-rent shelter, and . . . what else. Something else. Anyway, they have a couple of cook-ing classes and Kay teaches a photography class and—"

"Regular little—"

"—and she also teaches self-defense, so don't give her any lip."

"Who. Me?"

Erin laughed.

"So." Chris let out a deep breath. "What does ol' Ben do?"

"Well, I guess he oversees the entire operation."

"The Great Overseer."

"Pul-lease."

"Has a command and control tent all set up in the backyard, does he?"

"Chris, the man—why am I defending him? All right, look. This is the deal." Erin sat up and put her soda in the cup holder. She turned as far as her seat belt would allow. "Chris, Ben Connelly has poured his heart into Kimberley Square. He has found ways—incredible ways—to finance the entire operation."

"Legal ways?"

"Including a few nice perks for Scott and me."

"Ahh. *Mucho dinero*. What. Does he slip you cash under the table?"

"No, he just charges us a ridiculously low rent, pays our utilities, allows me to use one of the center's trucks if I need it, and . . ."

Chris glanced at Erin. "And?"

"Every year we get a ten-game ticket package for the Portland Trailblazers."

"No way."

"Sincerely."

"No—absolute—way!"

Erin settled back in her seat and grabbed her soda. She chugged a huge gulp and swallowed, then didn't even hide the burp. She tried not to grin. She couldn't help it. She grinned. And said, "He's a sweet man, Chris. We do a lot of good. We don't do it for the money, or to get our names in the paper, or for all the glorious warm fuzzies. We just do it. Like Saudi. 'Cause it's our job."

Chris was silent.

Erin added her last thought. "We do it for our Lord."

Nothing more was said until they stopped five minutes later, in Pendleton, for a bathroom break.

✭✭✭

THEY PULLED INTO THE PRIVATE parking area behind the Kimberley Street Community Center's main house at 7:14 p.m. Colonel Connelly's house. Chris already hated it. It was raining. She sat in her truck.

Erin let out a huge sigh, opened her door, and started to get out, but stopped, turned around, then pulled the door closed again. "Are you all right?" she asked softly.

Hah. Very good question. Chris stared straight ahead into the rain-drenched darkness. *Am I all right? I don't think so. I should have my head examined. What am I doing here? Why did I ever agree to this?*

"Chris."

She turned her head.

"Come on. It's okay. I know you're tired. My place is just across the street. We'll get some dinner and maybe watch a movie or something."

Chris couldn't move.

"They're all at church, for the Wednesday night prayer meeting."

"Yeah?"

"Yeah." Erin's smile was so warm. "Come on. I'm sure Scott's got our dinner all ready but the heatin'."

After a few seconds, Chris gave her a small smile. Her stomach had just growled. If nothing else, she would eat well while she was here. She climbed out of the Explorer and took her first few steps into a brand-new world.

✳ ✳ ✳

ERIN READ THE NOTE LEFT with the tuna-noodle casserole on her kitchen counter. "'Welcome home, you two. We can't wait to see you.'" She grinned. "Sonya. Ben's wife. We're in for a treat."

A few minutes later, as the casserole spun on the microwave's tray, its aroma caused Chris's mouth to water. She ate two helpings and washed it down with a big glass of milk. Not long afterward, it made her as sleepy as a two-helping tranquilizer.

Erin took her upstairs and showed her to her room, the room that would soon be a nursery. The next morning, up and showered,

Chris sat on the bed, yet didn't want to move. She knew she couldn't hide all day, and already it was after nine. Her stomach quivered. She drew in a deep breath. Then slowly pushed herself off the bed and ventured downstairs.

Erin was sitting at the kitchen table reading a newspaper. She looked up and smiled. "Hey, lady. Good morning."

"Hi," was all Chris could muster.

"Coffee's fresh; mugs are in the cupboard above the microwave. Sonya brought over some of her famous orange cranberry muffins."

Chris found a mug and filled it to the brim with steaming black coffee. The muffins looked delicious, but her stomach wasn't quite ready for food. She carried her coffee to the table and sat down.

"It's supposed to clear up by this afternoon."

She sipped her coffee and gave Erin a quick smile. Rain had pattered off the roof of the house most of the night. A soothing sound. Especially since Chris had awakened lost in a trembling, cold sweat.

"You don't want a muffin? I already had one, but I'm seriously considering another."

"Not right now."

"We've got Golden Grahams too, if you'd rather have that. I could make you an omelet. Cheese, green peppers, mushrooms?"

"No, really. I'm not hungry. Thanks." She tried to give Erin another smile, but knew it was a poor attempt.

Erin got up and went into the kitchen. "Some toast? How 'bout a piece of toast."

A strange warmth filtered through Chris. "Yeah, okay. That sounds good." She hated being fussed over, but really did love being ... Raymond cared too. He would also make her eat something, just like Erin. "Can't have too much coffee on an empty stomach, Chrissy," he would say. The exact words obviously going through Erin's mind right now.

She cringed as regret sliced through her. She reached for her coffee and swallowed a scalding gulp. *Why do you ... care, Erin? After all this time. Why do you still care?*

"You've got to show me how to make honey butter. Is there a secret to it? Just add one to the other . . . and season to taste?" Erin carried a plate, a knife, butter, and a small jar of jelly to the table. "One of the ladies at church made this jelly. It's apple cinnamon."

Chris hummed her approval just as the toaster popped up.

A few minutes later, finished with toast, muffin, and coffee, they cleaned up the dishes and then shot each other *Now what?* expressions.

Chris looked away and fought off the nervousness in her belly.

Erin handed her a rain jacket, led her to the Explorer, and said, "You drive." They climbed in, headed downtown, and spent the entire day browsing a hundred shops and galleries, and the Washington Park Rose Gardens, and the Washington Park Zoo.

At noon, the sun broke out.

It was a good day.

✯✯✯

"You ready for this?"

Erin had a way of asking a question that could cut right to the bone. And this question? No. Chris wasn't ready. She tried to keep the terror she felt from reaching her eyes. "There, um . . . wouldn't, like, possibly be a Thursday night meeting they'd all have to go to?"

Erin let out a laugh. "Nope. I'm sure they're all waiting for us. They're dying to see you, Chris, and they have been patient."

"I know." Chris gripped the steering wheel of the Explorer and stared straight ahead. "Rinny, what is wrong with me?" As soon as the words left her lips, she regretted them.

"You're nervous! Is that an accurate diagnosis?"

"You should be a nurse."

"Come on, girl. It's time to conquer your fear. Ben Connelly will not bite."

"Maybe not, but Cappy will."

"Cappy?"

"I still owe her seventy-five bucks."

Erin's, "Whaaat?" came out as a silly laugh.

Chris turned to look. "She had three queens. Can you believe that?"

Erin still laughed. Then just shook her head.

Silence strained the moment. The question that rose in the back of Chris's mind burned, yet required an answer. Especially with what lay ahead. She forced it out. Regretted every word. "Why am I so afraid of him?"

Erin's response came slowly, when it seemed she wouldn't even answer at all. "Ben's a caring man. You don't want him to care about you."

"Well, why should he? What did I ever do for him?"

"Your job. Better than anyone."

"Oh, sure."

"He told me once he had complete confidence in us. In his Wild Card."

"Well, yeah, Rinny. Other than Doc Cornum's Blackhawk, we were the only medevac hauling an experienced trauma nurse."

"And you were the only medic who liked to repel in a free fall, upside down."

Chris grunted a laugh.

"We can't sit out here all night."

"Sure we can."

"Maybe Cappy forgot all about the money you owe her."

"Sure she did."

"Maybe we'll just go in, say, 'Hi,' see what happens, have a little ice cream, see what happens after that, and then see what happens after that."

"What. A one-day-at-a-time sort of thing?"

"Absolutely."

She took a deep breath. "Okay."

✯✯✯

THEY WALKED IN TO INSTANT pandemonium. Chris was overwhelmed. With pure and simple love. The absolute one thing that terrified her most. But she put on a brave smile, found the three faces that looked the most familiar, and waited to see what would happen next.

Bettema Kinsley's voice hit her like a blast from the past. "Hey, woman! Look at you! You are a sweet sight!"

She avoided the full force of Tema's hug by leaning sideways into it, only to be squished against her bony shoulder. Tema's chin dug into the top of Chris's head. The woman was not only a mischievous ex-Huey medevac copilot, she was a long-legged African American string bean as well.

Tema was a friend. Didn't matter. Chris hated hugs. She hated the entire concept. Hated being this close to anyone, hated when arms surrounded her, when hands touched her back. But as much as she wanted to push away, she didn't. Not for another second.

Strange . . . the thought that hit her when Bettema finally let her go . . . *Have I ever hugged Erin? Ever?* She missed half of Bettema's next sentence trying to answer that question.

" . . . you to meet. Baby, this is Chris. Outstanding medic, lousy poker player."

Chris laughed. She shook the man's hand and said hello. Tema's boyfriend. Too bad she missed hearing his name. She had the answer to that question now. Cappy was moving closer. Grinning. The answer was no.

"Hey, girl! You got my hundred and thirty-six bucks?"

Chris evaded Cappy's outstretched arms with the words, "What? Seventy-five!"

Cappy Sanchez dropped her arms, but smiled brightly. "*Interest,* Specialist McIntyre. A dollar a month. And it's been five long years."

"Not long enough," Chris grumbled through a fake scowl.

"Sixty-one months, girlfriend. Another year and I'll double my money."

"If you ever get it, *girlfriend.*"

"I can only hope."

"Well, keep on hoping."

Cappy burst into loud, happy laughter, then threw a playful soft-fisted punch that Chris quickly dodged.

Who was this woman? Was this really Cappy? The woman who cussed and spit, who always got in the last word? Until now? The body was Cappy. A little rounder. The face was Cappy. Those joy-filled eyes were not Cappy's. Where was the snarl? The glare that could melt a major's gold leaf from fifty meters?

Speaking of majors, Colonel Connelly was approaching. His hand out. A strange expression on his face. A hint of . . . fear? He looked strange, out of place, out of uniform. She had never seen the man in anything but the green camouflage or the khaki chocolate-chip Battle Dress Uniform. And a snappy matching cap. Flaunting a flapping full bird.

She resisted the sudden urge to salute.

"Chris." He smiled, his hand still extended. "It's good to see you again."

She took his hand and shook it firmly. "You too, sir," she said, her voice not quite as strong as she hoped. The colonel's handshake was a good one, official-like. His hand felt cold and clammy. She let it go.

Was Ben Connelly nervous too?

"Chris, I'd like for you to meet my wife, Sonya." The colonel motioned for his wife to join him.

Chris gaped. Kindness seemed to radiate out of Sonya Connelly. From her bright, pale green eyes to her bright blonde and gorgeously curled hair. She wore blue jeans over a lean waist and white sneakers over tiny feet. She stood next to her husband, and they seemed to blend into one. They belonged together. Chris stared into the woman's smiling eyes and heard a voice that tickled her ears. A soft hint of a southern drawl. So sweet.

"Hi, Chris. I'm glad you're fanally here."

"Me too," slipped out before she could think of anything different to say. This lady had grabbed her heart. And now her hand. Did she lift it? Must have. She smiled sheepishly. And enjoyed the warm handshake.

"May I introduce you to everyone?" Sonya moved closer, still holding Chris's hand. "Y'all, this is Christina McIntyre. Chris? Our son, Andrew, and his wife, Sarah. Our three precious grandchildren: Amanda, she's six; little Benjamin, all of four years old; and precious Kayley, born just three months ago."

Little Benjamin came forward for a closer look. Chris gave him a smile.

Sonya released Chris's hand and swept the boy up in a grandmotherly hug. "This little guy is why we came here, Christina. Why Kimberley Square is here." And the joyous giggles bubbling out of the child put smiles on everyone's face.

So many smiles. So many faces. Sonya's voice continued softly in Chris's ear, a few more names, Isaiah somebody. And his wife. Andrew was the preacher. Yes, Erin had said. Little Benny was why Big Benny retired after the war. So many smiles, handshakes ... pure and sincere ... Sarah had boxes of baby clothes to haul over to Erin's. Loud laughter. Isaiah still had a collection of kittens if anyone wanted one.

Erin. Standing back by the huge fireplace. Smiling. Standing beside a handsome man ... *Wow.*

"Have you met Scott?" Sonya's voice. "Has she met Scott yet, Erin?"

Erin barely shook her head. "Not yet, Sonya."

"Oh, my. Well ..."

Sonya stepped back as Erin beckoned Chris closer. "Come here and meet the man who stole my heart." Her bright smile wavered a bit.

Moving closer, Chris looked at Scott Mathis, took in his strong features, his thick brown hair, his light brown eyes. A hint of annoyance flickered in them—Chris's heart fell so hard her blood turned cold as it shot through her veins.

"Hi, Chris. Erin's ... told me a lot about you." His hand extended toward her. His smile seemed forced. Fake.

I'm sure she has, swept through Chris's mind. She glanced at Erin, then shook Scott's hand. "Hi," was all she dared to say. She tried to smile.

She heard six-year-old Amanda ask, "Grammy, can we have ice cream now?" and Sonya's response, "Why, of course, sweetheart. Ice cream for everyone!" The energy in the room intensified.

Chris tried to release her handshake, but Scott firmly held on, giving her hand one more solid shake before releasing it.

So. Whatever this man's problem was, the line had been drawn. Yes, it was a subtle line. But a line, nonetheless. And Chris swore in her heart, for Erin's sake, it was one line she would never cross.

✷✷✷

SHE ATE TWO BIG BOWLS of orange sherbet mixed with vanilla ice cream. In the overwhelming stuffiness of the crowded room, it felt so good sliding down, the sweet chill calming the storm brewing in her soul.

She couldn't go back for a third bowl.

Too many people. Too many voices. Little Benny laughing and running around. Little Amanda asking, "Were you with Auntie Erin? And Pappy? In the *war?*"

"Yes, sweetie, I was." *Now please, go away.*

Music played in the background, softly, but a strong beat was constant, and sounded too much like—

Just for a second, she closed her eyes. She wanted to keep them closed, but knew she couldn't.

What was happening? The air in the room seemed thinner now. She couldn't get enough. She smiled when Bettema said, "The rain is doing your Explorer good. It looked like it needed a bath." She couldn't think of a response. Her mind swirled. She only smiled. And tried not to gulp the air in.

She needed air.

She politely excused herself and headed for the back door.

Outside, on the long wooden deck, the cool air was an incredible relief. She pulled in one long breath after another. Her ears were ringing. *Light-headed? What in the world?*

She needed a drink.

She needed to get out of here.

Why? Couldn't she hold it together for a few more lousy days? She promised Erin she would stay four days. Was she going to blow it now?

A sudden presence startled her so much she jumped and spun around, hands up and ready.

"Whoa. Easy, Chris . . ."

Erin. Chris dropped her hands and hung her head.

"A little much, huh."

She barely smiled.

"It's a beautiful night. Not raining, at least. Well, not at the moment." A pause and a smile. "Wonder what Raymond's up to."

Chris pulled in a deep breath and let it out as a laugh. "Probably sitting around fretting about us."

"He's a sweet man, Chris."

"Yeah."

Sounds of the city filled the night air. They listened for another moment, then Erin whispered, "Are you okay?"

Chris leaned over the deck railing. "Yeah."

"It's not usually like this."

"Like what?"

"So many people. Andy and Isaiah wanted to meet you."

"Um, Rin? How much do they know about me?"

It took a second for Erin to respond. "Well, everything that was in the paper. And then what Sid told Ben."

"That I killed that guy?"

"Yeah. They know."

Great. Chris drew in a deep breath and let it out slowly.

"We're all glad you're here."

"Rin?"

"Yeah?"

"I think I almost had a panic attack."

Erin looked like she wanted to laugh. "Feeling dizzy?"

"Yep."

"Ears ringing? Shortness of breath? Heart palpitations?"

"Yep, yep, yep."

"I think you're right. You didn't run out kicking and screaming, so your 'almost' is accurate."

"Thank you, Nurse Mathis."

"No charge."

"So, now, tell me this. Why? Rinny . . . why am I like this?" Chris immediately regretted asking the question, but a part of her truly wanted to know. She glanced at Erin. Saw the hesitation.

"Chris, please. Don't be afraid." So very slowly, Erin moved closer as she said the words.

Chris took a step backward.

"Please, Chris. You once asked me to trust you; trust me now." Erin slowly reached down and took Chris's hand.

Chris tensed. Why? She trusted Erin. Didn't she? Who else had proved to be a more trustworthy friend? Still, she tried to pull her hand away. Erin held on. Chris looked up at her.

Erin spoke so very softly. "I don't want to crowd you, Chris. Try to hear me out. This is just a simple touch. It's just a way to show you that I care about you. You know I do. And you know I'd never hurt you."

The words grated against her like sandpaper. "I know, Rinny." That didn't stop her from trying to pull her hand away. Erin held on, using both hands now. Panic swelled inside Chris. "Please, Erin. Don't. Let go."

"You're not trusting me, Chris."

"Is that supposed to be funny?"

"No. I'm sorry. But . . . please, can you close your eyes?"

"Huh?"

"Try to relax. Close your eyes. Please. Listen to me. Hear me."

Chris met Erin's gaze, saw only concern. She allowed her eyes to close.

"You're trembling."

Yes, she was. Why was she trembling?

"Please, Chris. Don't be afraid. Keep your eyes closed. Tell me what you're feeling."

"What I'm . . . feeling?" How could she even begin to describe it?

"Can you tell me? Why are you trembling?"

Her eyes opened. "I don't know, Rinny. I can't—I can't explain it."

"Just a simple touch. You trust me, yet it's too much, isn't it? You know me, Chris. I don't want to push you. I want to understand."

Chris stared at the ground. "Yeah. I know." The whispered words shook.

"Please tell me why that scares you so much."

Her heart thumped as she struggled for words.

"I wish I could read your mind."

"Wouldn't do you any good."

Erin barely shook her head. Barely smiled. "Please don't be afraid."

"I'm not afraid."

"I know you are. I wish . . ."

Chris swallowed deeply against the tightness in her throat.

"I wish I could help you never be afraid again."

"Rinny . . . please . . . stop this."

"I wish you'd trust me. I wish you'd talk to me."

"I can't—" She pulled her hand out of Erin's grip, yet Erin still stood too close. She tried to back away from her, but hit the deck's side railing. Trapped in the corner, she couldn't take it. Looking up at Erin, seeing the look in her eyes, the concern, her heart screamed, *But this is Rinny! You know her! You trust her! She's just trying to show you how much she—* A deeper scream wrenched its way out of her, "ERIN, STOP IT!" She shoved Erin away.

Erin stumbled backward but caught her balance to keep from falling. She looked up, slowly raised her own trembling hands, then whispered, "It's all right, Chris. It's okay."

No, it was not okay. Nothing was *okay.* Deep inside, Chris's heart raged; huge pumps of blood throbbed through her entire body. Her mouth fell open and she blinked deeply, trying to understand, trying to focus. *Rinny? Did I—Did I just almost push you down?* She stared at her, unable to say a word.

Tears filling her eyes, Erin was saying, "I'm sorry, Chris. I'm so sorry . . ."

Why was she sorry? For trying to help? Trying to reach out? For a simple touch of friendship? *She wasn't trying to hurt you. She cares about you! She loves—!*

"NO!"

Erin gasped, her face reflecting pure terror.

No . . . No, Rinny, this is all wrong. Why did I push you like that? What if you had fallen? Oh, God . . . Chris slowly worked her way down the deck railing to the short flight of stairs, the words repeating in her mind, *I am so sorry, Rinny . . . I am so sorry.* Slowly, still looking at Erin, wanting to stay, wanting to say the words aloud, she backed down the stairs to the gravel walk.

Erin took a few steps toward her. "Please, Chris, don't go. Stay. Please. Sit here with me. We don't have to talk. Please . . ."

In silence, in anguished confusion, slowly at first, then more determined, Chris turned and walked into the darkness. She heard Erin call her name and stopped to look back, saw Sonya slip through the back door to stand beside Erin, looked up at the light pouring through the doorway—and saw Scott Mathis standing there, staring at her, as if he could clearly see her in the darkness.

Chris turned and ran away.

SEVEN

Yes, the porch lights are on. How many times are you going to look? Why won't you just come to bed? Are you going to sit down here all night? Waiting?

Scott Mathis felt a check in his soul. *I know, I know, Lord. Trust. But she's my wife! And she's carrying my child. This whole thing is messed up.* He drew in a deep breath and held it a second before letting it out.

"Sweetheart, why don't you go on up to bed? You've got a big day tomorrow."

"Only if you'll join me."

"I can't, Scott. Please try to understand."

"I'm trying, Erin, but you're making it difficult."

Irritation flashed in his wife's eyes. "*I'm* making it difficult? You've made this difficult for me from the first minute."

He sat on the love seat across from the couch, where Erin sat. "What do you want from me? Chris is dangerous. And if you can't see that, I've got to see it for you."

Erin blew out a breath of laughter. "Dangerous?"

Scott clenched his teeth to keep from stating the obvious. Chris was nothing like Erin. Erin could never kill a man.

"You think she's dangerous to me? That she'd intentionally hurt me?"

"You tell me. You obviously know her better than I do. Or . . . do you? You've said you don't know all that much about her."

"She's my friend, Scott. That's all I need to know."

He grunted. "Fine. Stay down here. I'm going to bed." He stood abruptly.

"Scott . . ."

"She's done nothing but hurt you, Erin. You told me that yourself."

"I never said that."

"You didn't have to say the words for me to know."

Erin stayed silent.

Scott's heart ached. "Erin . . ." He moved in to kneel beside her. "Sweetheart, I don't want to make this difficult for you. I want to trust you on this. But please, be honest with yourself. How much do you really know about her? She's obviously unstable."

"And who wouldn't be, in her situation?"

"I saw the look in her eye tonight."

"When. On the porch?"

"Sonya and I heard a shout. We went to the door together. I saw the way Chris looked at you. I saw the look in your eyes too, Erin. You were terrified."

"I wasn't—"

"Chris is not well, and if she needs professional help, that's what we should get her. I'm not blaming her. I know she's been through a lot."

"She needs Christ, Scott."

He looked down. "Of course, she does, Erin. I know that."

"The pain she lives with runs so deeply inside her . . ."

"Maybe she should talk to Andy. Or Ben."

Erin pushed herself off the couch and walked into the kitchen. "You don't understand, Scott, because you don't want to understand. I know you're being protective of me, of our baby, and I love you for it, but with this, you've got to back off. I mean it."

Scott stood but didn't go into the kitchen. "You would put Chris before your own safety? The safety of our child?"

"You're forgetting it was Chris who saved my life."

That stunned him.

"You told me to forget the war; you told me to forget Chris. You won't even look at the pictures in my scrapbook anymore. Fine.

But hear me, Scott. Hear me well. There is no way I will ever forget. And there is no way I am going to abandon Chris now, when she needs me the most."

He moved closer, so close he reached out and caressed her face with his hands. "Erin, *I* need you."

Her eyes glistened with tears. "I know."

"Our little one needs you."

Her tears spilled, breaking Scott's heart in two. He gently kissed her salty cheek, her closed eyes, her forehead, the tip of her nose, then full on her lips. Her arms came around him, and he pulled her into a strong, yet tender embrace.

"I'm sorry," was just a breath.

"Don't be," Scott whispered. "Come upstairs with me. Please. She probably won't even come back tonight."

"Where would she go?"

Erin started to pull out of the embrace, but Scott held on. "She'll be all right, Erin. She's a big girl."

"I should've tried to find her."

He released her. Then gazed into her eyes. "Erin, I'm going to bed. Come with me. Please."

The anguish on her face cut him to the bone. "I can't. I'm sorry."

He slowly nodded, turned, and started for the stairs. He stopped and looked back. "I'll be waiting for you. Okay?" He couldn't sleep now anyway.

She nodded. Her smile barely lifted her lips. Scott continued up the stairs to bed.

✦✦✦

JUST AFTER 2:00 A.M., ERIN sat in the corner of the couch, curled up under a blanket, worried and afraid. She didn't cry. She prayed. And sipped lukewarm water from a glass.

The front door was unlocked; the porch lights burned brightly. This also made her a little nervous. It wasn't smart to leave a door unlocked on Kimberley Street.

It wasn't smart to be out alone in the middle of the night, either. If Scott hadn't stopped her, Erin would be out there, searching. *Please, dear Lord, keep her safe. Where would she go? Please, bring her back here. To me.*

She heard a car pull up outside, the sounds of laughter, a car door slamming, then thumps on her porch. Her heart swelled. The door squeaked open, then quietly closed. She knew Chris stood behind her, just inside the door, but she didn't turn around.

Slow boot steps on the hardwood floor. Chris appeared beside Erin, to her left, standing there, swaying a little.

Chris was drunk.

She flopped down on the love seat, then winced, holding her right side.

Erin stared at her. She ached with concern, then rejoiced, then raged. The strong stench of alcohol and cigarette smoke turned her stomach. Her voice was firm. "Are you all right? What happened to you?"

Chris blinked. Focused. Said, "Huh?"

"You're drunk."

"Just a wee . . . bit."

"Where did you go?"

"Don't really know . . ."

"Uh-huh. But you knew how to get home."

"Am I home?"

Erin smiled. Her rage was melting. "Yes, Chris. You're home."

"Rinny?"

"Yes?"

"Oh. So this isn't, like, home-home."

"Chris . . ."

"More like . . . *your* home. And . . . *Scott's*."

"Your home too."

"Nah. Not really." Those dark eyes studied the ceiling now.

Erin wondered if what she was about to say would do any good. "Chris, I want you to stay."

"Barney's."

"What?"

"I ended up at . . . hoo-yeah. What a place. Barney's." A laugh. "Hey, Rin, you ever been to Barney's?"

Erin took in every bit of Chris's face. Especially those eyes. Dark, dark brown. And very, very red. Wasted.

"Stompin' place. Barney's."

"How did you get home?"

"Billy."

"Who?"

"Great . . ." Chris seemed to savor something as she lifted her hands into the air. She peeked at Erin and grinned. " . . . intellect."

"Uh-huh."

"Like Scott." Chris's grin widened with a giggle.

"What?"

"Scott can sure fill out a pair of Levi's, Rinny. Wow. In a good way, of course."

Of course. But Erin didn't give voice to her thought.

"Billy. Yeah. Bought me shooters all night long."

She didn't want to cry.

Chris looked at her. Continued to gaze at her.

Erin picked at some fuzz on her blanket. And prayed no tears would fall.

"Hey. Rin."

"What."

"You okay?"

"Sure." *Why wouldn't I be?*

"Hey, let's get Tema and Crappy and—oops! I mean . . ." Chris's eyes pinched shut as she wheezed out a huge breath of laughter. And then the rest of the laugh hit her, and filled the room. "Oh, man, if she heard me say that! *Cappy!* Cappy. Shoot, that little burrito would kick my—"

More laughter. Drunken joy. Erin knew Scott could hear it. Her heart welled with unbearable sadness.

"Cappy. Yeah. What was I saying?"

"I don't know, Chris."

Chris's face grew serious. She leaned forward. "Rinny? You sure you're okay?" She tilted her head.

"Yeah. I'm fine."

"You don't look it."

"I'm fine, Chris."

"You look like I feel."

"Oh? And how's that."

"Lousy."

"Your own dumb fault."

"No, no, I don't mean that—" Chris waved a hand that almost caused her to fall out of the love seat. "Whoa!" She caught herself on the coffee table.

"Go on upstairs and sleep it off."

She pushed herself back up, was silent, still, and again suddenly serious. "Erin, are you mad at me?"

"No. I'm not mad at you."

Those eyes blinked to maintain their focus. And focused hard on Erin Mathis. "Yep. You're mad at me."

"Chris . . ."

"I can tell, Rinny. Don't deny it."

"I'm not mad." Irritated, maybe.

"Dis-pointed, then."

Erin was silent.

"Sure. Say it. You're dis-pointed in me." Chris leaned back. "You should be. I'm sorry, Rinny."

"Don't be sorry."

"I lost it."

"You did not."

"Freaked out."

"Chris . . ."

"I can't take it, Rinny."

Erin was cautious. "Take what, Chris?"

"Being here."

And her heart prepared itself for a major fall. "Why not?"

"I don't belong here."

"Sure you do."

"No." And Chris's eyes closed.

Erin pushed the blanket away, leaned forward, and asked softly, "Where *do* you belong?"

A long moment passed before Chris said, "I don't know."

"You belong here. With me." The words slipped out. Erin could hardly believe it.

Chris's eyes flew open and found Erin quickly. "What?"

"You heard me."

"No, Rinny." She again closed her eyes, then raised a hand to cover her face.

"Why not?"

"Because."

"Because why?"

"Because ... people die."

Erin's breath caught. What was this? "What do you mean, Chris?"

"Nothing." Chris started to get up, but lost her balance and fell into the seat. Growling, she leaned back and covered her face with both hands.

"Say it. Tell me what you're thinking."

"I'm not thinkin' nothin'."

Erin bit her lower lip. She didn't know what to do. Chris was drunk. Would she remember any of this conversation? Could Erin push, just a little, to draw out some of the answers to the question of Christina McIntyre? Should she? She ventured ahead very, very slowly. Backtracking. "Where do you belong, Chris? Tell me."

The silence turned heavy. Until, "Nowhere."

"That's a very lonely place."

"It's safe there."

"Safe?"

"For you."

Erin didn't give in to her confusion. "Maybe I don't want to be safe."

Chris uncovered frightened eyes.

"Maybe I want to be with you."

"No."

"Why not?"

"Because you . . ." And nothing more.

"What, Chris."

Silence.

"I'm perfectly safe around you," Erin said. "You saved my life."

"I did not. I'm why you got shot."

Erin's jaw dropped. She had to remind herself Chris was drunk. But was this how Chris felt? Did she really blame herself? Erin pressed her lips, then asked, "Why would you say that?"

"I shoulda listened to Teddy and left that dumb ring."

"What would that have done?"

"Saved Teddy's life."

Erin's mind raced to keep up. The events of that day were terrifying; she relived them in a terrifying split second. "He didn't have to follow you to the wreck."

"It wasn't his fault."

"What wasn't his fault?"

Silence.

Erin waited.

"It shoulda been me, Rin."

She gasped. "Don't say that."

"He died; you almost—"

"No. Chris? Because of you? That's what you think?"

Silence.

"Come on. What you did for Archie—"

"Almost got you killed!"

"Come on! You didn't even know Archie, yet you were willing to risk your life in an act of compassion. You did what needed to be done. Teddy wouldn't have done it. I wouldn't have done it."

"It was stupid."

"It was courageous."

"Stupid! I shoulda died. Not him."

"No one should have died, Chris."

Those dark eyes looked up, filled with hurt.

Erin wiped her tears. Scott was listening; she could almost feel his presence. He didn't need to hear all of this. It would just make him worry more, would just confuse him. At this point, Erin didn't care. He would just have to deal with it. This moment was too important. She drew in a deep breath. "Chris, you know I couldn't have taken it. If you would have died ..."

She waited for anything from Chris, but there was only silence.

"You know how it feels. Don't you."

More silence.

"To lose someone you really care about."

"I didn't care about Teddy," Chris said, her voice a growl.

"You cared about Travis."

And tears rimmed Chris's dark, bloodshot eyes.

Erin was afraid to follow this new direction, frightened of what it would reveal. She pressed on. Slowly. Gently. "But, you know, Chris, I did lose a friend in the war."

Chris swiped at her eyes and blinked deeply.

Erin waited to be sure Chris was with her. She retraced and added a step to give Chris more time. "I found a good friend ... and lost a good friend. Weird, huh."

Confusion. Chris stared. Then barely mouthed the word, "What?"

"I only knew you six months. But in that time, you became my friend. One of the best friends I've ever had."

Confusion gave way to disbelief, then to reluctant acceptance.

"I loved to watch the way you cared for them. Especially after ..." Erin's strength was seeping away.

"After what?" was a whisper.

"After we hauled out Seth and Marcus. Marcus should have died, Chris. There's no doubt in my mind."

"Nah, Rinny, he wasn't that bad."

"You were so sure of everything, moving so quickly. You were . . . precision. Vitals, IV, putting the chest tube in, constantly talking to him. You talked him right out of dying. Screaming. I remember it. You screamed at him. Right in his ear. He heard you. And held on."

"He owed me fifty bucks, which I never got." Chris laughed. "I needed it to pay off Cap—" And the laughter overwhelmed her.

Erin listened, but knew, deep down, Chris wasn't laughing. She waited.

The laughter died. And tears flooded those dark brown eyes. Chris closed them and whispered, "I know what you're tryin' to say, Rin."

"What am I trying to say?"

"But, Rin! I . . . I couldn't! You saw my—! Oh, God . . . Rinny." Chris covered her face as sobs choked her.

Erin bit her lip and closed her eyes. Tears fell, then slowly slid down her cheeks. So many tears, all these years, but she had made the trip, and survived. And brought Chris with her to that very moment . . . when all was lost.

"Rinny . . ." Chris whimpered the words through her hands. "I know you did. I could tell by . . . the look on—" The rest was washed away in racking sobs.

Erin's throat pinched shut. She forced air in, then one word out. One simple word. "Yes."

Yes.

Erin had seen.

Teddy, joking around. Stupid game of "beach" volleyball. In the Land of Sand. At least it wasn't raining, not too cold. February. Chris wore a khaki T-shirt tucked into her BDU pants. They wrestled in the sand. Why? Stupid Teddy. No wonder Chris . . .

He had her pinned on her belly in the sand. She was yelling, cursing, screaming at him. Teddy was laughing, rubbing the fine sand in her hair, in her face. In the struggle, Chris's shirt came up. Untucked. Teddy was laughing. He didn't see. Tim Boyd was laughing. He didn't see. Only Erin saw the scars. Long, thin lines laced across Chris's back. So many. So quick. Only a glimpse. That destroyed everything.

Erin shuddered, remembering the horror that flooded her, the look in Chris's eyes. She couldn't bear the memory, the sight of it, the thought of . . . the pain.

She couldn't bear to hear Chris crying, sobbing now, so desperately. And the sounds of the words, "Oh, God, Rinny . . . I never wanted you to see."

She had to swallow. Then cough to clear her throat. Still, her words stuck there. "I know you didn't, Chris. You wouldn't want anyone to see."

"Nooo . . ."

"It doesn't matter. Chris, I still—"

"NO!" Chris stood up so quickly, Erin flinched back into the couch.

Too quickly. Chris's eyes pinched shut as she fell back into the love seat. She rested her elbows on her knees and covered her face with her hands.

"It's okay, Chris."

"Nooo, Rin . . ."

"Just know that I do."

And Chris broke down into her hands.

Erin marveled. It was as if Chris could read her mind . . . and could not bear to hear she was loved. The very word triggered anger, pure and lightning quick. *But you are loved, Chris. Hear me. I love you.*

Erin moved closer to sit on the edge of the coffee table, just to be closer. She waited, so very patiently. Praying. So desperately. Waited, then heard the words, "He said he loved me."

Chris's voice was tiny, buried under her hands and choked by ragged gulps of air. Erin could barely make out the words.

"He didn't. He hated me."

Erin believed her. She saw the man's handiwork.

"Why did he take me? He never wanted me."

Chris kept her face hidden. Her voice remained a quiet, barely discernible wail. Erin struggled for words. Ways to reach out. To help. She was given nothing. She didn't force that. She waited, and didn't move. Barely breathed.

"I did everything he asked. And he said he'd take care of me! He said he loved me."

How could a father say that . . . and do what he did? Erin drew in a deep breath and held it, using it to force a raging scream down. She struggled to stay quiet and still.

"He wouldn't stop!" Chris trembled; her hands pressed hard into her face, against her eyes and forehead. Her sobs became violent; her words, so desperate. "Oh, God! He told me not to—I couldn't help it! I cried. I screamed! He wouldn't—! I couldn't move! My hands, he—! Oh, God help me! I couldn't—!"

Erin's scream escaped as a massive choking sob. She quickly covered her mouth with her hand.

But Chris heard; she felt Erin's sudden movement, pulled her hands away from her eyes, blinked to focus, and looked up. Her expression turned to pure terror. She stood and backed away so quickly the love seat slid back an inch or two. She stumbled, then stood there, gaping, staring, eyes wide.

Erin slowly stood but did not move closer. She raised both hands, though they trembled; she held them up, imploring, palms out, as if to say, *It's all right, Chris. It's okay.* Over and over, the words repeated in her mind. She prayed Chris would hear.

Those dark eyes flitted all over the living room. To Erin. And away. To the floor, the walls, the couch. She stared at her hands, then clenched them into fists and rubbed her eyes frantically. She looked at Erin, and finally saw her. She blinked. "Erin! What—? How did—? What—!" She glanced at the door.

Erin spoke quickly. "It's okay, Chris. You're all right."

Chris was going to bolt for the door; Erin could tell. The look in those eyes . . .

She spoke loudly. Clearly. "Focus. Chris? Look at me. Listen to me. It's all right."

Chris looked at her and blinked. Three times, deeply. And said, with a hint of surprise, "Rinny?"

Erin tried to smile. It was so hard at first, then it wasn't. She smiled, and said, "Yes. Chris, it's me. You're here. With me. You're safe."

The surprise disappeared. "No ..."

"Yes. Chris? Yes."

Fear took its place. "I can't stay here."

"Yes, you can."

"No! Rin ...?"

What she saw in those eyes about tore Erin's heart out of her chest. She tried to keep her hands up, using them to keep Chris from bolting. And said, gently, "You know? Chris? I'm, um ... I'm really sleepy. You know? How 'bout you? It is pretty late."

Those eyes softened so quickly, fear dissolved so instantly, Erin could not believe it. And the reply, "Yeah. Man. I'm really tired," pushed her lips into a smile.

"Come on. I'll, um ... walk you to your room." She had to bite her lip to keep from laughing.

"Gonna tuck me in?"

"Sure. Why not."

They slowly made their way up the stairs and down the hall to Chris's room. Chris went in. Erin waited at the door.

Chris headed back out, saying, "Gotta go, first."

Erin laughed quietly. She waited by the door until Chris came back. Praying. The entire time. Did she ever stop?

Chris returned and went into her room. Erin leaned on the door frame. After a few seconds, she said, "Okay? You set? Are you gonna be able to sleep?"

An "Oh, yeah," came out quickly.

"Okay. Well ... I'll see you in the morning." Erin started for her room.

"Rinny?"

"Yeah?" She peeked back inside Chris's room.

"I'm really not drunk, you know."

"Sure. I know."

"Only had a few." Chris couldn't get her boots off.

Erin almost laughed. Why not. She laughed. And said, "Need help there, cowgirl?"

And Chris's laughter fell over Erin like a cloud of warm fuzzies. Even drunken laughter, at this point, sounded wonderful.

The boots came off. Chris flopped backward on the bed and closed her eyes.

"Cover up."

She reached out with one hand and pulled the bedspread over her, without getting up or even opening her eyes.

"Night, woman."

"Uh-huh."

Erin was almost to her room when she heard her name, in that way only Chris said it. She stopped and smiled, then looked down at the floor and said, loud enough for Chris to hear, "Yeah?"

"Three more days. That's it."

Erin closed her eyes and had to steady herself against the wall.

✯✯✯

INSIDE THE BEDROOM SHE SHARED with her husband, wanting nothing more than to crawl into bed and sleep for a week, she stood at the door but could not move closer to the bed. She winced and squinted when Scott turned on the bedside light.

They stared at each other without speaking.

"So," he finally said. "She's back."

Erin nodded.

"And she's drunk."

She let her gaze drift away from him.

"Imagine that."

"Did you enjoy our conversation?" She tried to keep her voice low, the question neutral.

Scott didn't answer.

"I know you heard every word."

"Oh, about ninety-eight percent of it, anyway. There wasn't anything good on television." He gave her a goofy grin.

Erin almost smiled.

"Please. Come to bed. You're exhausted."

"I have to turn off the porch light and lock the door."

Scott threw off the blankets. "I'll do it."

"No!" The abrupt word stunned them both. "I'll do it. It's okay. Don't get up."

Silence and sudden tension hung over them.

"I'm . . . I'm going to stay down there for a little while," Erin said. "I really need . . . to pray."

"Can't you pray up here? With me?"

Would he ever even *try* to understand? "No. Sorry, babe. But not about this."

"Erin, you know I care about what happens to Chris."

"No, Scott, I don't know that. If you had your way, she'd be staying in the apartment with Cappy tonight." Erin sighed deeply. Tried to smile. "Please, sweetheart, be patient with me. Just a little while longer. Give Chris and me a few more days."

After a second, Scott flashed a warm smile. "I'll give you as long as you need. And I'll try to understand. I promise." His smile quickly faded. "But please, Erin, make me a promise." He waited.

She looked into his eyes. "Name it."

"Promise me . . . you'll be careful, *very* careful. Don't push her so hard that she snaps back at you. Like tonight. Please, love. Promise me."

She nodded slowly and turned to open the door.

"Say the words, Erin."

She pulled the door open.

"Erin?"

She turned her head, lifted her left hand, her wedding ring, to her lips, and kissed it. Her eyes smiled at her husband, but no words were spoken. She turned, pushed herself out the door, and closed it behind her.

EIGHT

BEN CONNELLY SLOWLY, ALMOST SILENTLY, slipped out of bed and into his sweatpants. The night was chilly, the big house drafty. He pulled on a sweatshirt, slipped into his slippers, then quietly, as his wife softly snored, headed out his bedroom door and eased it closed behind him.

It was well after two. Unable to sleep, he had heard a car pull up across the street, heard laughter, the car door close, then drive away. Obviously Chris sneaking home after disappearing earlier. Good. Now he hoped he could go back to sleep.

Not a chance. He padded downstairs, a tiny night-light faithfully illuminating his way. He walked into the dining room, then felt a hankerin' for a hot cup of coffee. He turned left and went into the kitchen where he flicked on the light and made himself a pot of dark Colombian. He stood at the counter while it brewed, smelling the aroma, breathing deeply of the peaceful silence in the house.

Patience had never been his virtue; he pushed the pot out of the way and let the stream of brown liquid fall straight into his mug. Sonya always scolded him for this. He'd clean up his mess. She would never have to know.

Replacing the pot, he carried his mug as he headed slowly across the living room to the huge front picture window. He pulled back the drapery and was washed in an orange glow of streetlights burning in the fog. Lights still shone across the street, at Erin and Scott's house, and he hoped in his heart that it was Chris he had heard, that she had made it safely home. *Please, Lord, let it be so.*

He pushed himself away from the window and padded to his favorite sitting place, the big recliner situated in the middle of the living room, facing away from the window, toward the fireplace. Ben loved Kimberley Street, but saw enough of it during the day. At night, relaxing at home with his wife and family, he liked to see a roaring fire, liked to watch his southern belle, his love of thirty-seven years, playing Candyland with the children at the big dining room table after one of their huge Sunday dinners.

He loved this big old house. Loved the raucous sounds of laughter that seemed to echo even in the silence of the night. Loved those two massive beanbags he, at first, hated, until he heard Amanda and Benny squeal with delight as they jumped in and were engulfed. He had yet to try one, but someday . . . maybe when he finally broke down and bought a cell phone. Then, at least, he could call 9-1-1 if he got stuck and needed help getting out of the crazy thing.

He reached up and turned on the light by his recliner. Slowly pulled his mug up and sipped the burning, bitter elixir. Slowly pulled out the worn book and his reading glasses from inside the table drawer next to where he sat. Opened the book, situated the thin plastic glasses on his nose, drew in another long sip of his brew, and began reading the familiar words in his favorite book.

The words calmed him, soothed him, filled him with peace, washed over him with cleansing, healing power.

He heard a noise, a soft rap on the back door. Startled, he held his breath, listening. He heard a woman's voice. "Ben? Sonya? It's Erin." He quickly pushed himself out of the recliner, left his mug, Bible, and glasses on the coffee table, and hurried to open the back door.

"Erin. Hi." He quickly stepped aside so she could enter.

"Hi, Ben. Saw the light. Do you mind . . . ?"

"Of course not. Come in." He waited, then pushed the door closed and locked it.

Erin stopped, lifted her head just a little, and slowly sniffed.

"Hot and fresh. Have some."

"Nah. Thanks. But it smells good."

"Some milk, maybe?" Ben raised his eyebrows.

"Builds strong teeth and gums." Erin laughed and headed for the kitchen.

Ben slowly followed. "I take it, Chris came home."

"Yep."

"In what condition?"

"Inebriated."

Suspicions confirmed. "She's all right?"

"Passed out."

"And Scott?"

Erin reached into the refrigerator, brought out the gallon of milk, and poured herself a glassful. She put it back, then turned to face Ben as she lifted her glass and took a long drink. Even after she swallowed, she didn't say anything.

"Ahh." Ben slowly nodded and gave her a small smile.

Erin returned it. She looked weary to her soul.

"Are you hungry? Want a muffin? Or crackers?"

She let out a breath of laughter. "No. Thanks. Haven't needed crackers in a while."

"Good." Morning sickness had brutalized the poor girl for weeks.

They made their way into the living room, both commandeering their favorite sitting places: Erin in the corner of the couch facing Ben and the front window, Ben in his recliner. Erin leaned over carefully, trying not to spill her milk, and looked to see where Ben had been reading.

He smiled. "'My peace I give to you; not as the world gives do I give to you.'"

Erin's face softened. "'Let not your heart be troubled.'"

"'Neither let it be afraid.'" The two friends basked in the peace for a moment, until Erin's eyes welled with tears. Ben's heart wrenched.

Erin leaned back into the couch and picked at a piece of fuzz on her sweatpants.

Ben reached for his mug and drew it to his lips for a long drink. He watched Erin the entire time, ached for her. A few small clicks as the last embers in the fireplace burned away, the persistent soft tick of Sonya's grandfather's old mantel clock, and the distant hum of the refrigerator were the only sounds.

Erin didn't say a word.

"Are you okay?" Ben asked, though he already knew the answer.

Erin lifted her glass of milk, sipped, swallowed, pressed open her lips, and whispered, "Yeah."

"Wish I could believe you."

Erin barely smiled, but it didn't last long.

"Can you tell me?"

As she closed her eyes, a tear fell down her cheek. She swiped it and sighed. "Too much to tell."

"Too much for you to bear alone."

And that brought more tears. Erin bit her lip, looked into the fireplace, and let them fall.

Ben watched her tenderly, praying for guidance. He hated the sight of anyone in pain, but this was Erin. He hated the thought of anyone hurting her. His voice carried a hint of disgust. "It's Chris. Isn't it."

Erin wiped away her tears and rubbed her nose. She sighed again, and whispered, "Yeah."

"She seems to make a definite impression on people."

"Yep, that she does."

"She's made quite an impression on Scott, I've noticed."

"He can't stand her."

"No, Erin, that's not true. He just doesn't know her yet."

"Do any of us really know her?"

Ben didn't answer. It was a question without an answer anyway.

"Excuse me a second." Erin pushed herself out of the couch and went into the bathroom for a tissue.

Ben sighed deeply. He wanted to understand, but he did not understand. Chris McIntyre was a complete mystery to him. Yes, he knew her file; it was interesting stuff. In Saudi Arabia, as her acting commanding officer, he had both opportunity and motive to study her file. He allowed himself both. Years later, with his photographic memory, he still remembered nearly every word.

Funny, how it all started with a favor for a friend. Command Sergeant Major Mitch Calegra, Ben's top noncommissioned officer assistant, had served in Panama with one particular medevac pilot named Angelo "Nescafé" Coffee. "Best Huey pilot in the army," CSM Calegra had said. "If we're going to war, we need 'im."

So Ben got him. The next day, orders were cut. In less than a week, Captain Angelo Coffee, his UH-1 Huey helicopter and his three-member medevac crew from Fort Wainwright, Alaska, sat on a C-5 transport plane crossing the Atlantic bound for Saudi Arabia and Operation Desert Shield. The day they arrived at King Fahd International Airport, Ben stood on the scorching Tarmac about to officially welcome his Airborne brigade's newest medevac crew to the Land of Sand.

He again perused the crew's roster. Four names, four Army 201 files tucked neatly into his attaché. He had studied them. He was prepared to meet the pilot, Captain Angelo Coffee; the copilot, Warrant Officer Shawn Skala; the crew chief, Staff Sergeant Edward Brisbaine; and the medic, Sergeant Curtis Collier. Four brave and dedicated men. Warriors all.

He met three brave and dedicated men that day, though the copilot was not Warrant Officer Shawn Skala, but Warrant Officer Robert Palmara. No mind. But then there was this female. The medic was not Sergeant Curtis Collier. The medic was a Specialist . . . a *female* . . . named Christina McIntyre.

He shook her hand. Welcomed her to Saudi Arabia and to the 4th Brigade of the 101st Airborne Air Assault Division. He looked at her. Tried to be nice. Yet couldn't completely hide his scowl.

Back in his office, the first thing he did was demand her 201 file. What it contained impressed him at first. Then angered him.

Name: Christina Renae McIntyre
HT: 5-6 **WT:** 124
DOB: 17 April 1967 **POB:** Denver, CO
DOE: 24 June 1985 **NOK:** None

Emergency Contact: Isabella Costas,
  Fairbanks, AK
HS Diploma: No **GED:** Yes
Medical Training: Fort Sam Houston,
  San Antonio, TX
Overseas Tour: Landstuhl RMC, Germany
CONUS Tour: Fort Wainwright, Fairbanks, AK
Commendations: Master Marksman 1985,
  1986, 1988, 1989
Good Conduct Medal 1988
Achievement Medal 1990
Disciplinary Action: 27 July 1990
Article 15: Suspicion of drug use.
Loss of noncommissioned officer status.
One step demotion with loss of pay.
Official permanent reprimand.
APR:1985-86: Exceptional. Much
  potential. Promote ahead of peers.
1986-87: Exceeds standards. Example of
  excellence.
1987-88: Promote to NCO immediately.
  Exemplary performance.
1988-89: Promote. Career material.
  Highest attention to detail.
1989-90: Do not demote this soldier.
  Promote. Wake up.

This last line caught Colonel Benjamin Connelly's attention. He despised even the faintest suspicion of drug use by the soldiers in his army. McIntyre should have been demoted, if not discharged. Yet someone, her immediate supervisor, a Major Walter P. Condisson, believed in her innocence.

Not enough. Ben needed to find out the truth. He immediately invited Captain Angelo Coffee to his office to explain his new medic's "suspicious drug use."

Captain Coffee replied, as he stood at stark attention, "Sir, with all due respect, that charge is hogwash. The investigators found evidence of cocaine in Sergeant—I mean, Specialist McIntyre's footlocker. On an anonymous tip, I might add. But they found no fingerprints, sir. Not on the bag, not on her footlocker, not on the padlock—that had been broken, sir—and none on the doorknobs of her door. None. There should have been *some*, sir. But they found none. The place had been wiped clean."

"Is Specialist McIntyre a clean freak, Captain?"

"Meticulous. Yes, sir. Except for one place."

"And that would be . . . ?"

"Her room. Sir."

"And how would you know that, Captain?"

"She, um, sir . . . consistently fails room inspections."

"Consistently?"

"Yes, sir. She, um, doesn't like to make her bed."

"Cause for demotion right there."

"Yes, sir." A hint of a smile crossed both men's lips.

"Captain Coffee, we're not on a bivouac here. There is going to be a war, and I need soldiers—medics included—who are one hundred percent tuned in to my frequency."

"Yes, sir. Point well taken, sir."

"Look me in the eye, Coffee. Tell me if Specialist McIntyre should be in my army."

Captain Angelo Coffee met his commanding officer's unwavering stare, raised his chin a notch, and without further hesitation, said, "Sir, Specialist McIntyre is a valuable member of my medevac crew, and an integral part of the army of the country we both love and serve."

Colonel Benjamin Connelly did not smile. But he nodded, snapped shut Specialist McIntyre's 201 file, stood, and held out his hand. "Outstanding. Welcome to Desert Shield, Captain Coffee. You will be my Wild Card, the medevac crew I'll be calling upon to serve the men and women in my brigade anywhere and at a moment's notice. Are you and your crew up for that?"

The men shook hands, then Captain Coffee snapped up his position of attention and barked a brisk, "Hoo-UHH, Colonel!" His face cracked into a huge smile.

Dismissed with a wave, Captain Coffee spun and marched out the door as Ben filed away Specialist McIntyre's 201. And he didn't give the woman another thought for three weeks, until he saw her repel out the door of an airborne Huey. Headfirst.

From that moment on, Ben Connelly stopped scowling. And that "suspicion of drug use" was tossed out of his mind like yesterday's garbage.

And now, he sat in the recliner, sipped his cooled coffee, and listened to the soft ticking of the old mantel clock.

He knew everything of what there was to know about the soldier, Specialist Christina McIntyre. But he knew nothing about the person. He knew the *what* and the *when*. He had no idea of the *why*. And the *whys* plagued him.

Why no next of kin? Who was Isabella Costas? Why a GED? Why were you set up at Fort Wainwright? Why were you even in Saudi? What happened to Collier? And Skala, for that matter? And . . . why did you refuse my nomination for the Bronze Star?

But the worse question, the one that twisted his gut, the question that angered him to the core: *How could you hurt Erin, so severely, so many times . . . again, now, after all these years?*

He pushed himself up and headed to the kitchen to refill his coffee cup.

✯✯✯

BACK IN HIS RECLINER, HE waited for Erin to return from the bathroom. She had tried to blow her nose quietly, but Ben heard. She sounded miserable. He had to draw in a deep breath to calm the rage in his gut.

He wanted to help, but just how should he proceed? How could he be any help to Erin on this night? He had no idea what to say, or even if he should say anything. He simply sat quietly, slightly rocking in the big chair, and he waited.

His first thought was a selfish one. That concerned him. But he couldn't shake it. Maybe he should just lay the question out and see what happened. "Erin?" he said softly, and then he paused, deciding just how to word such a selfish question. He decided to just blurt it out. "Does Chris hate me?"

Erin's eyes bulged.

Ben smiled in spite of himself.

"No, Ben. I'm sure she doesn't hate you."

"Oh? So, you mean, that's not a snarl I see on her face every time she looks at me?"

Erin laughed. A quick exhale of a silly grunt. That faded into a deep sigh. "Yes, that probably is what you see. But she doesn't hate you."

Ben slowly sipped his coffee, swallowed, then lifted his eyes, tilted his head, and said, "Okay. Let's cut to the chase. Erin . . . tell me about Christina McIntyre."

✰✰✰

ERIN LAUGHED AGAIN; THIS TIME she really laughed. She looked at Ben, the stalwart army commander, sitting there in his slippers, all comfortable, patiently waiting. She noticed his already slightly plump belly seemed plumper; his diet obviously wasn't keeping pace with . . . She laughed once more, pulled her feet under her, and leaned into the pillowy side of the couch. She lifted her glass of milk for a sip and then drew in a long, deep breath.

Christina McIntyre. She had no idea where to begin. "What do you want to know?"

"Everything."

Too quick. Did Ben even consider his answer? Erin squirmed. Did Ben really want to know everything? Should he know everything? Why not? He could handle it. Couldn't he? And, if he knew, maybe he could help. Help keep Chris . . . from leaving.

"Everything?"

"Everything."

"Might take awhile," she said, just for confirmation of Ben's intent.

"Fine. Can't sleep anyway."

Confirmation. Hesitantly, Erin proceeded. "Well, the truth is, we became friends during a war. I only knew her six months." She felt a bit foolish as her husband's words echoed in her mind. "Scott's right about one thing. I really don't know her that well at all."

"But you still care about her. Enough to not let go."

"Yeah." She pressed her lips into the faintest of smiles. "It's like I can't let go."

Ben slowly nodded. "I think I know what you mean."

"I hope so. Because I certainly can't explain it." Erin sighed deeply. "Anyway, well, I guess you should know how we met. You had something to do with it, I do believe."

"Completely unintentional."

A laugh spurted out of her. "I certainly don't blame you."

"And, right at the moment, you're not all that eager to thank me, are you."

She considered that for a second, then gave Ben a sheepish smile.

"I thought so. Now, please. Go on."

"All right. Well, let's see. I got off the plane in Dhahran—almost fainted from the heat. An hour later I was in a Humvee heading for King Fahd. Teddy and Bobby met me there and helped me in-process, then they took me to the garage."

"Ahh, yes. Home sweet home."

"You know, for a parking garage, it wasn't so bad. Sturdy, fairly clean."

"For a parking garage."

"Yeah. Not exactly first class, I guess. Anyway, when I finally convinced Bobby I didn't want to bunk with the other officers—"

"Wait a minute. Why not?"

"Why? Oh, I don't know. Commanders and such. You know." Erin suddenly blushed. Of course, Ben knew. "Most of the medical officers were assigned to the evac hospital. I guess I just wanted to stay close to the medics. The medevac people. You know."

Ben's lips were pushed into a smirk.

"I mean, I wasn't exactly a member of any unit; I didn't know anybody, didn't have anybody to command . . . and besides, I was the same age as Teddy, only two years older than Chris—"

"Erin."

"I just didn't want people treating me like . . ."

"An officer?"

"Well, yeah. Saluting and all that."

Definitely a smirk. "You know, Erin, you earned those silver bars."

She looked down. "I know."

"And you straight-up volunteered. Alone. That still impresses me."

"They put out the call for volunteers."

"And you answered it."

"Don't make it sound so dramatic, Ben. I was just due for a little excitement."

"And did you find it?"

Erin laughed heartily. "Yes, I guess you could say . . . I found it."

Ben gave her a wide smile.

"Well, so, anyway, Teddy took me to where the medics were set up. And he threw my gear down on a cot beside . . ."

✯✯✯

9 September 1990 1548 Hours
King Fahd International Airport, Saudi Arabia

"Well, here y'are, Lieutenant. Your very own piece of the Land of Sand."

Erin looked up and smiled at the handsome staff sergeant. Edward Brisbaine. Huey 1207's crew chief. Helpful young man. Considerate.

But then the considerate staff sergeant turned and gave the cot beside Erin's a vicious kick. A cot occupied by a young woman adorned in the desert Battle Dress Uniform, except for the long-sleeved overshirt that hung draped over a brown metal chair behind her. The khaki-colored T-shirt she wore was wet with sweat.

The sudden kick woke the woman with such a start she sat up in the cot blinking and cussing. Every nasty word in the book.

"Now, now, Chris*tina*," Sergeant Brisbaine said through a snide grin, "we've got an officer on deck."

The woman took one look at Erin and was about to stand, but Erin said, "No, please don't get up." She turned to the man beside her. "And thank you, Sergeant Brisbaine. You've been very helpful."

"Please, ma'am, call me Teddy. And, if you need anything else, just let me know. My cot is right over there." He turned and pointed.

How nice, Erin thought. *Which one, of the hundreds lined up in a row?* "Thank you, Teddy. I'm fine now."

The man bowed slightly in a weak imitation of a congenial waiter, smiled at Erin, then turned and growled at the woman who had settled back into her cot. "Don't forget your shift at the aid station starts in twenty minutes."

And Erin's mouth fell open as she heard the words the woman said to the handsome Teddy Brisbaine.

He walked away, laughing.

Erin said nothing.

The woman lay back on her cot and closed her eyes.

Erin tried to be quiet as she sorted through her meager belongings. Not much to call her own, but enough. She'd have to carry this stuff around for who knew how long; she packed light for a reason. But her Bible was a necessity. She hadn't been reading it enough lately; now she would need to more than ever.

She sat on her cot and peered through the open sides of the parking garage, out over mile after mile of flat, dusty landscape. Inside, her gaze followed the long rows of green canvas cots surrounding her on three sides. Small groups of sweating soldiers lounged here and there. Far down the line, someone had tied a sheet up, partitioning off some privacy. It wouldn't be too bad here, until it really started to fill up. But how long would she be here? How soon would the crisis escalate? Would Saddam Hussein back down? Would he give in to the United Nations' demands?

Not likely. War was inevitable. And here she was in the thick of it, assigned to a UH-1 Huey medevac helicopter, soon to be rushing into the middle of the war to pull out fallen soldiers. Women in combat? Definitely.

A twinge of fear struck her heart. She sighed deeply. She didn't realize she had sighed so hard, until she heard the words, "I resemble that emotion."

She turned to look at the woman who lay on the cot beside her. "Excuse me?"

"Kind of scary being here. Isn't it." The woman's eyes were still closed.

Erin said, "Yeah. A little."

The woman grinned. And said, "A lot." But she didn't look scared. She looked perfectly relaxed on her cot.

Erin took the opportunity to study her next-cot neighbor. Not tall, not short. Solid. No baby fat. Dusty khaki leather boots. Baggy, yet tightly belted desert BDU pants. Sweaty BDU T-shirt. Sweaty brownish blonde hair pulled back in a French braid. A soft, yet weather-beaten face, pinked with the heat. A small, straight, sunburned nose. Thin, dark eyebrows. Strong, deeply tanned arms. Small, smooth hands. No rings. No earrings. No jewelry of any kind. A pair of government-issue dark sunglasses lay on the floor under the woman's cot beside a water bottle, a holstered pistol, and a chemical gear face mask. All three, always out in the ready. A duffel bag lay beside the chair. On the chair sat a small satchel for personal items. Wrapped around the back of the chair hung the desert BDU long-sleeved shirt with specialist stripes on the lapel, sleeves rolled up properly to ensure instant protection in case of chemical attack. Looking around, Erin saw nothing more. No pictures. No Walkman. No cassettes. No books.

The woman opened her eyes and looked at Erin; such dark brown eyes, Erin wondered if they were black. *Hispanic heritage, maybe?* She saw a tiny smile.

"Um . . . ma'am? Are you my trauma nurse?"

Erin's head tilted an inch. "Are you . . . my medic?"

The woman sat up and offered Erin her hand. Erin reached out and accepted it. The woman smiled. A small, simple, yet amazingly warm smile. Erin felt stunned by it. The woman shook Erin's hand and said, almost timidly, "I'm Chris McIntyre."

And Erin smiled.

A few minutes later, after helping Erin set up her chemical gear, Chris asked, "Are you sure you want to sleep down here? You'd have a lot more room with the other officers. A whole parking space all to yourself."

"No. I'm fine here. Really." Erin gave her a smile. "They said the aid station is in a hangar? Will you take me with you when you have to go?"

"Sure. It's not far from here."

"Who all works there? How many medics are there?"

"Well, not including Doc Cornum, there's about six of us. We take turns."

"Make it seven. I'll take my turn."

Chris gave her a funny look. "You don't have to, ma'am."

Erin squirmed a little. "Sure I do. I'm just a glorified medic."

"With four years of college and a silver bar."

"Will that be a problem, Specialist?" Erin tried not to grin.

"Oh, no, ma'am." Now Chris squirmed. "No problem at all." She looked down at her dusty boots, then back up at Erin. She grinned sheepishly.

"All right then." And Erin laughed.

★ ★ ★

Over the next few weeks, Erin watched her medic. She liked what she saw. A genuine compassion. Pure, natural talent. Acute attention to detail. Eagerness to learn. Willingness to teach. The woman was elusive. Evasive. Always on the defensive. Adventurous and fun-loving. Yet a terrible recluse at times. Almost shy. Very deep. Yet extremely shallow. Lazy as a fat cat. As diligent and dedicated and hardworking as anyone Erin had ever known.

And something else.

One quiet, lazy, sweltering afternoon at the aid station, with Chris lying on her back on the examining table repeatedly tossing a wad of tape into the air and catching it, Erin leaned back in her chair and kicked her feet up on a box of IV equipment. Leaning over slightly, she used the heel of her hand to prop her head up. Then closed her eyes.

"You know I'm not used to this," Chris said, her voice carrying a hint of a whine.

"Who is?" Erin mumbled.

"The pukes from Florida. Or Hawaii. Or Texas. I'm sick of hearing them complain about the heat. They should be used to it. I have every right to complain."

Erin remembered Texas, remembered the fool in her officer's training school class, the same fool who took her to dinner that one night. Why would she think of him now? Texas. Sweltering . . . Chris's voice. *Want a little cheese to go with that whine?*

"Just eight short months ago it was forty below where I'm from."

Dinner was fine; Mexican food always was. But the man's arrogant rambling . . .

"I don't know how poor Ticket's gonna survive."

What was the man's name? Half asleep, Erin couldn't remember.

"Shoot, I don't even think *I'm* gonna survive."

Rodney? Roger? Something like that. After an hour of listening to his self-adoring monologue, Erin came up with another name for him. World-Class Idiot.

"You know why we're doing this, don't you, Erin?"

Hearing her name carried her out of her daze. Her eyes remained closed. "Huh?"

"You know why we're doing this."

"Doing what?"

"Broiling. We're broiling because of him."

"Who, Chris?"

"Sad Man."

"Who?" Her daze must have been deeper than she thought.

"Saddam Insane? Surely you've heard of him."

Erin laughed. Chris. Trying to be funny.

"World-Class Idiot."

And Erin's eyes popped open as her heart slammed to a stop inside her.

✯✯✯

THE ENTIRE TIME IT WAS like that. Where Erin was weak, Chris would be strong. When Erin needed company, there was Chris. When Erin needed space, Chris was nowhere to be found.

Something slipped into her heart those first few weeks. She learned to see through the rough exterior of her new friend, through the walls closely guarding her heart. Even that first week, Erin knew there were walls.

They would talk about dumb stuff, about anything that crossed their minds. Chris didn't talk to just anyone. Some days she would go hours without saying a single word to anyone. But she would always talk to Erin. Talk and laugh and joke and be serious.

How could Erin describe the joy of this simple new friendship? Her lieutenant's bars didn't intimidate; Chris respected Erin's rank, yet didn't treat her like an officer. Especially after that day of repelling practice. Erin's second day in Saudi Arabia; the day she met the rest of her crew. The day Chris took the quick way down.

Erin marveled at that day. Was the woman crazy? Did she have a death wish? But the way she treated the injured, the sick; she had great compassion, an honest kindness. Buried under that guarded exterior.

Chris liked to hang out and play poker with the guys. She laughed and joked with just about everyone. But with Erin, Chris was serious. Sincere. Erin saw genuine concern in Chris's dark brown eyes, almost as if Chris was looking out for her. Like that day in the Huey, hovering over the Tarmac. Erin repelled that day. With seventy-five feet of nothing but hot, blustery wind beneath her, her heart already taking a major beating that day, again pumped her chest like a way-too-cranked bass on a hyped-up car stereo. And it had just settled down from Chris's little "stunt."

Erin repelled, slowly, gingerly. She glanced up repeatedly, back into the helicopter, and saw the reassuring sight of Specialist McIntyre on her knees at the door with her hands out as if to say, *Not so fast, easy now, don't rush it.*

As Erin hung there, she almost laughed. How long did it take Chris to cover the eighty feet in her free fall?

But the sight spoke softly to Erin's fears, calming her heart, giving her the courage to continue all the way down to the ground. Angel-soft landing. Looking back up, she saw a wide, beaming smile on her medic's face, along with a pumping thumbs-up. She could have floated on the wind back up to that hovering helicopter.

But later that same day, after returning to the garage to stow their gear, Chris disappeared. It was late, well after midnight, when she quietly returned. Without a word to anyone about where she was. Or why.

Too many walls. Too much hidden behind them.

It was Erin's first sleepless night in the Land of Sand.

★★★

"You worry too much about her."

Erin drew in a deep breath and let it out slowly. "Yeah, I guess."

"It should feel good to be worried about."

"She didn't think so." A pause. "She still doesn't."

Ben was silent.

"You remember that day, I suspect."

"Which. The day Chris repelled?"

"Yeah." Erin smiled.

"Oh, yeah." And Ben laughed.

"Why was Gunderson such a jerk?"

"I guess he thought he had just cause."

"Well, maybe he did, but he certainly didn't have to go off like that."

"He probably thought he was earning points with me."

"Was he?" Erin's eyebrows lifted.

"Why do you think I shipped him over to Riyadh?"

"He took that as a promotion."

"I didn't care, as long as he was out of my hair."

Erin laughed.

The two fell quiet for a moment.

"Did he ever tell you about the guys putting pepper spray in his aftershave?"

Ben let out a laugh, then fell into an "Oooo . . ."

"You never heard about that?"

"No. But is that why he had that serious sunburn?" Ben slowly shook his head. "Guess it wasn't a sunburn."

"They were getting him back for what he did to Chris. But not because she wanted them to."

"Who did this?"

"Piper, mainly. And Quintair. And Hostettler. It was so hot that night. Especially suffocating. I'll never forget it. Chris and I were hanging out at the garage, just before dinner. It was like we couldn't move. We just lay there gasping in the heat. We were hungry, but didn't want to make the effort to go on down to the kitchen trailer. That's when Chris pulled out an MRE."

★★★

13 SEPTEMBER 1990 1753 HOURS
KING FAHD INTERNATIONAL AIRPORT, SAUDI ARABIA

Erin looked at her medic and cringed. "Girl, you must be tired, if you'll pass up real food for an MRE."

Chris struggled to open the ugly greenish-brown heavy plastic bag. "I'm not going anywhere the rest of the night. I'm down for the count."

Erin turned in her cot, onto her left side, and watched Chris tear the bag open with her teeth, then suck lukewarm beans and weenies out of it. She really cringed this time. But said nothing.

Chris chewed, grimaced, then threw the bag and its remains in the direction of the garbage barrel, all the way across six other cots. She tried to put proper spin on it but failed miserably. Beans-n-weenies splattered all over Private Craig Jamison's duffel bag.

"Hey!" hollered one of the lounging soldiers under the bag's flight path.

"Incoming!" yelled another.

"Oops," Chris said through a goofy grin. "I'll get that later, you guys. Don't anybody touch that. I'll get it."

Smooth Kenny Tyler, the stunningly handsome Blackhawk crew chief, sauntered over and picked up the mess. "Don't you worry, Little Doc," he said in a smooth, sultry tone, "I'll get your back." He threw the bag in the garbage.

Chris called out to him, "After this war's over, Ty, you be ready, 'cause I'm gonna take you home."

He continued sauntering down the long path between the rows of cots, but laughed and said, his deep voice easily carrying across the distance, "Meet me in Baghdad, my sweet. I'll be the one kicking Saddam's big hairy backside."

Erin winced at the sudden mental picture, then laughed as Chris flopped back on her cot, grinning like a fool.

"Just leave the mess on Jamison's bag, McIntyre," someone hollered. "He can suck it off later in the desert if he's ever desperate enough."

"Just may save his life," another soldier added.

Chris laughed as her eyes fell closed, her tongue pushing out the sides of her cheeks, inside her lips, obviously removing the remaining sticky goo from her teeth.

Erin rolled over onto her back and smiled, almost laughed. The perpetual pajama party. Without the pajamas. BDUs did come awfully close.

She closed her eyes, feeling a strange peace flow through her. She silently whispered a grateful prayer, washed in the simple silliness of the moment.

"Hey, McIntyre. Heard you had a go-round with Connelly's shadow."

Erin's eyes popped open.

"Yeah, heard he ripped you a new one," came from another direction.

"Just a minor setback, guys," Chris hollered. "I had it coming."

"Don't we have rights around here? Shouldn't we be allowed to take a dive if we want?"

"Depends on the dive, I guess. And who's watchin'."

Erin glanced at Chris, waiting for a response, but Chris lay still, her eyes closed.

"Are we Airborne, or what?"

"Hoo-uhh!" came from way down the line.

"So, what's it matter how the doc wants to fly? I say, let her fly!"

"Will you guys give it a rest?" Chris finally said. "Go get some dinner."

And half of the assorted group of young American soldiers did exactly that. One stopped briefly by Erin's cot to ask, "You comin', LT?"

"No, thanks," she said with a smile. "I'll just eat what's left of Chris's MRE."

"Be sure and save the beans for Jamison!" one baby-faced private hollered.

"And steer clear of anything looking like dog-food granola!" shouted another.

Erin relaxed in her cot, the laughter in her heart keeping the smile on her face for quite some time.

She must have dozed off. Whispers woke her, restrained laughter. She opened her eyes and saw a group of six soldiers huddled around a cot across the way. Rolling over onto her side, she pretended to sleep. Chris was with them. They were showing her something.

"No, you guys," she heard Chris say. "No way. Don't do it."

"Come on, McIntyre! This is perfect! And you know the man needs a wake-up call."

"He seriously needs something, that's for sure."

"No. Not like this. Absolutely not."

Curiosity burned inside her, but Erin remained quiet, just listening, pretending.

"This is for you, McIntyre!" Someone in the group hushed the speaker, and his next words were harder to make out. "He dissed you! In front of your entire crew! In front of the colonel! He didn't have to do it, but he did it!"

"Don't do this for me! I don't want you doing anything to him because of me."

"Hey, if anyone shoulda ripped you about your jump, it shoulda been your crew boss. Right? Not some stupid-talkin' second luey big mouth."

"Commander wannabe."

"No. Guys? Listen to me. I mean it. Dump that stuff. Don't mess with it."

"Hey, we could dump it in the john and blow up Outhouse Row!"

Erin snuck a peek, trying to see what bomb-making material the clowns had acquired since dinner.

"I'm serious. Forget it. Dump that stuff."

"We're gonna do it, McIntyre."

"No! Give it to me—!"

The sounds of a scuffle brought Erin up in her cot. Sitting there, now holding the attention of all seven lower enlisted U.S. Army personnel, Erin said, "Do we have a problem, people?"

"Oh, no, ma'am," one of the sergeants said.

Chris's face burned brilliant red in the heat.

"Specialist McIntyre? Is there a problem?" Erin noticed she held a small bottle of liquid in her hand.

"No, ma'am. No problem. Just something I've got to throw away."

"Okay. Go ahead. The rest of you stay put, please."

She noticed teeth grinding, eyes following Chris as she headed for the garbage barrel, the collective look of dismay as Chris opened the bottle and poured the liquid into the garbage.

"Nothing is going to explode, is it, Specialist McIntyre?"

"No, ma'am," came from Chris's direction.

"Good. How was dinner, gentlemen?"

She heard a grumble of comments, mumbles of, "Fine. Very good, ma'am. Good, ma'am, thank you."

"Did they have any fresh fruit tonight?"

More grumbles. "Apples, ma'am. Yes, ma'am, they had apples."

"Good. I think my medic and I will go get ourselves an apple. Carry on, gentlemen."

More various grumbles of, "Yes, ma'am," came from the dejected bunch.

Chris gave her a strange look as Erin walked up. "Come on, Little Doc," Erin said with a smile. "Let's go get us an apple. I might even buy you a Coke."

Chris grinned. "Make it a Pepsi, ma'am, and you've got yourself a deal."

✯✯✯

"BUT THEY STILL WENT AHEAD and did it," Ben said. "Incredible."

"Yep. Sergeant Piper was determined. When Chris found out, she just about went ballistic. She was absolutely furious."

"Shouldn't she have been glad they did it? They were getting him back for what he did to her."

Erin shook her head. "She said she deserved what she got from Gunderson."

A few seconds later, Ben seemed to be carefully choosing his words. "You and Chris were . . . close. What happened?"

Erin stared at the fireplace. "It's hard to explain."

"I couldn't believe it when she requested a transfer to the evac hospital. Basically asking to be grounded. Before the ground war even started."

Erin sighed. "Me neither."

"It had something to do with Sergeant Brisbaine's split lip, didn't it."

Erin let out a grunt. "He was lucky she didn't break his jaw."

NINE

"WOULD YOU MIND TELLING ME about it?" Ben asked gently. "You don't have to."

Erin didn't know what to say. She wanted to tell Ben, but did she have the right? But this wasn't just anyone. This was Ben. And she needed him to understand. She needed his help. "It's not something Chris wants people to know about."

"Oh. Okay. I understand."

"But I'm going to tell you anyway. I need you to know. Chris needs you to know. Even if she doesn't know it."

Ben nodded.

After a long sigh, Erin said, "A stupid game of volleyball." She stopped. She dreaded where this story would take her, knew her heart would suffer from it. Already, it pounded too hard, and her stomach ached. She sighed again. "Teddy and me. Chris and Tim Boyd. Two on two. A lousy waste of time."

"When was this?"

"At Rafha, after the weather broke. Early February. Things had dried out and slowed down a little. We were bored. We played for at least an hour. It was fun. Until Teddy missed one. Badly. It was hilarious."

★★★

5 FEBRUARY 1991 1417 HOURS
ALONG TAPLINE ROAD NEAR RAFHA, SAUDI ARABIA

Chris McIntyre never laughed so hard in her entire life. Her back to Edward Brisbaine, she fell to her knees, holding her belly as hysterical silliness engulfed her. The image of what just happened replayed in her mind, and she laughed until tears fell from her eyes.

She didn't hit the ball all that hard. Definitely not one of her better spikes. But placement? Perfect. Right off the top of Brisbaine's head. The ball *doinked* off his forehead, then bounced all the way over to roll under a Humvee. Tim Boyd immediately fell to the sand, howling; Chris could hear Erin's laughter—until something heavy hit her hard in the back and pushed her down into the dusty sand, crushing all breath inside her. Hissing curses, it was Teddy on top of her, pushing her face roughly into the sand, then tossing handfuls of sand into her hair. Sand stuck to her sweat, turned to mud in her hair; Chris instantly stopped laughing. Rage pushed her to the opposite end of hysteria. She struggled and fought against him with all her strength.

The jerk wouldn't budge. But he laughed in her ear, and hollered, "How's it feel, *Sergeant* McIntyre? Like that?"

She did not. Not at all. She tried to push up but could barely move. Sand stung her eyes and throat, made her cough and rasp. She tasted sand. Crunched it between screams.

Chris screamed. Rage gave way to a sudden, furious panic. She needed to get up. Now. She couldn't take this man against her, on top of her; playfully or not, he was crushing her, all his weight against her shoulders and back. Images burst through her mind, helpless, terrifying images. She felt unspeakable terror. She felt sand everywhere. She could not breathe. Each attempt only brought more sand into her throat, making her cough, making her desperately crazy. She pushed and struggled and fought.

But then she knew. Somehow, she knew. A sudden coolness, cold air across her lower back. Her T-shirt must have come loose, untucked out of her BDU pants. Exposing her back. Exposing—

She almost threw up, right there.

Such horror, panic, hysteria—screaming, she threw Teddy off with one massive push. He rolled away laughing, eyes pinched shut, arms flopping out from his side, completely pleased with himself.

Chris pushed herself up quickly, stood, spit and coughed uncontrollably, looked up at Erin—and instantly knew.

Erin had seen.

But how? Only a second, that far away . . . but the look on her face said there was no doubt.

Erin had seen.

Chris stood there.

It was done. Never to be erased. Erin would never again look at her the same way. There would be concern. Pity. She would question. Maybe not directly, but her eyes would question.

It was over.

Another friend. Lost.

Teddy managed to work his way up to one knee in the sand. He looked at Chris. Chris looked at him. He was still laughing. He didn't see. Tim Boyd was still laughing. He didn't see. Erin was not laughing.

Of all people, Erin had seen.

Chris stood there. Rage overwhelmed her. As tears fell from her eyes, she drew her fist back and hit Teddy on the mouth with everything she had.

✷✷✷

BEN SAT IN COMPLETE SILENCE. He saw Erin blinking back her tears. He heard every word she said. He sat there. Stunned.

Erin sniffed deeply. "Ever since that moment, she was a totally different person. It was as if I didn't even exist anymore. No." She looked up quickly at Ben. "It was as if *she* didn't exist anymore. I wasn't allowed to care about her anymore. I was just supposed to forget about her. Not look at her. Not—"

Ben waited. He didn't want to move.

"I couldn't talk to her; I couldn't be with her." Erin's voice strengthened. "She immediately had *new* friends. Amazing. Out of nowhere. Colter. Jamison. LeMay. Poker buddies. Oh, yeah." She let out a disgusted grunt. "And Bettema too. Did you know that? Chris got quite close to Tee. And Cappy. Since she played poker too." The strength left Erin's voice. She again sniffed back tears. "Ben, if it wasn't for you . . . and the meetings; you were just what I needed. I see that now. God gave me . . . you."

The words touched his soul. He tried to smile, but it quickly faded. Seeing Erin so shaken, so desperate, hurt him deeply. Hearing her weep, feeling the pain of what she had silently borne all these years; he looked up as Erin stood and excused herself. In the bathroom, she blew her nose and wiped her face with a towel. Ben closed his eyes.

There was one other time he had seen Erin this miserable. She lay on a hospital bed on board the USS *Mercy*, dark bruises around her eyes . . . the image shook him to his core. In such a sanitary, efficient war, it seemed Lieutenant Erin Grayson had paid a dear price. He heard her return from the bathroom; watched, heart aching, as she sat again in the couch and tried to get comfortable. She gave him a wan smile. He returned it with one of his own.

He hated to bring it up, hated even to think about that day. He hated taking Erin back to that place, but he had the feeling she was already there. He pushed open his lips to speak, reconsidered one last time, then pressed on. "Erin," he said softly, "please, if you can . . . please tell me what happened. What *really* happened that day . . . on Newmarket . . . during Dustoff Five."

$$\star\star\star$$

Newmarket. Dustoff Five. The words sent a violent chill through Erin's entire body. As Wild Card's commanding officer, Ben knew all the facts. He had read all the reports. Directed the follow-up investigation. Wrote the letter of condolence. And then filed the proper forms to ensure Dustoff Five's medic received the U.S. Army's Bronze Star.

But he hadn't been there.

Only Erin had been there. And Chris. Colonel Connelly's Wild Card. Twelve miles south of Cobra on the Main Supply Route Newmarket. Dustoff Five.

✯✯✯

25 February 1991 1011 Hours
Tactical Assembly Area Cobra, South-central Iraq

"Is this a war or what? I've been on fishing trips more exciting than this."

Lieutenant Erin Grayson wanted to laugh, wanted to state the obvious, but she didn't have to. Her medic said it for her.

"Shut up, Teddy. You're so stupid."

"Puts the term 'combat fishing' into a whole new light," Warrant Officer Bobby Palmara said. He looked at Erin. "That's a true Alaskan experience. Shoulder to shoulder with a thousand other guys all trying to reel in the same fish."

Erin smiled, then looked up as Captain Angelo Coffee approached. "Let's ride, folks," he said to his crew. "More of the same awaits."

Teddy grumbled and led the way to the old Huey medevac helicopter her crew had affectionately nicknamed Ticket to Paradise. Full of fuel and raring to go, 4th Brigade's Wild Card lifted off from Tactical Assembly Area Cobra, the huge logistics base that had sprung up overnight in south-central Iraq, for another long, somewhat less-than-exciting patrol up and down the endless convoy of U.S. Army vehicles snaking their way north along the main supply route CentCom dubbed MSR Newmarket. Not really a road, just an ancient pilgrim's path, but in less than twenty-four hours U.S. Army engineers had cleared almost one hundred miles of it, preparing the way for the supply convoy. The first trucks bringing troops, food, equipment, water, and fuel arrived in Cobra late the previous night. The last trucks in the convoy had yet to leave Saudi Arabia. The logistical enormity of it all staggered Erin's mind.

Sitting quietly in the trap seat behind Angelo, she rode out the Huey's thunder, watching the barren Iraqi desert flash beneath her, watching her medic sit at the Huey's open side door, dangling her feet out into the abyss, waving occasionally at a Chinook helicopter or a fellow soldier below. Truck after truck crept along almost bumper to bumper in a line of army green and brown trailing as far as Erin could see. From time to time, she saw a burned-out enemy tank, smoldering bunkers, evidence of the war that had raged only hours before.

The war they apparently missed.

Was it really supposed to be this easy? Predictions before the war spoke of thousands of possible allied casualties. So far, twenty-nine hours into the ground war, Wild Card had yet to medevac anyone. When Teddy heard that another medevac crew hauled out a soldier with an upper respiratory infection, he almost threw a fit.

Erin whispered thanks in her heart to God for boredom, for simple upper respiratory infections, for a medevac crew in a war with nothing to do.

"Ladies and Gentlemen, the 101st has just reached the Euphrates River Valley."

Hearing Angelo's deep, soft voice through the headphones imbedded inside her flight helmet, Erin turned to look over his shoulder out the front window of the Huey.

"How long until they set up operations and take Highway Eight?" Teddy's voice carried a hint of a whine at being left out of the festivities.

"With this weather, it's hard to tell," Angelo said. "But I'm sure as soon as Third Armored Cav can get there, they'll run 'em straight on down to Basra."

Teddy let out a few joyous curses.

In days, not weeks, considering what little resistance Iraq could muster, this war would be over. It was unthinkable. Amazing. A powerful sense of awe, of pride, of belonging, swept through Erin's heart. Down on the ground or up in the air, from all directions in every imaginable way, Iraq didn't stand a chance against Erin's fellow soldiers, men and women just like her, scared, courageous, just doing their job, and doing it well. All branches of the world's strongest military working together to achieve one goal.

Hoo-uhh. Seriously. She smiled.

She heard Angelo's voice again. "All right, folks, this is it. Are you awake back there, Specialist McIntyre? Hold on, we're doublin' back."

Erin quickly turned in her seat, held her breath, and then held on as the Huey turned on a dime at eighty-five feet. Her mouth fell open; her medic was standing on the helicopter's skid leaning out as far as her restraint strap would allow, arms out to her side, riding out the full force of the turn with every fiber of her being.

Oh, Lord . . . whispered up from Erin's soul.

The turn quickly faded as the Huey raced ahead. Teddy moved forward to sit in the trap seat behind Bobby Palmara, asking, as he did, "What do we got, skip?"

"Dustoff," Angelo replied, at which Erin's heart quickened.

"Vehicle accident," Bobby said. "Back toward Cobra."

"How many wounded?" Erin asked.

"Two. They're still trying to extract the driver," Angelo said.

As the Huey raced northward up the convoy, Erin watched Chris, who sat back down on the floor of the Huey. Her heart flip-flopped inside her. She closed her eyes and whispered a prayer, then drew in a deep breath, trying to relax. The Huey thundered on.

A few minutes later, Angelo said, "We've got issues, people. Listen up. We've got a Humvee thinkin' it wants to be a tanker. And a tanker just not havin' it."

"Tanker?" Chris asked. "As in . . . ?"

"Diesel. Fully loaded. Leaking."

"Great."

"LZ's clear, but we've got to get in and get out in a heartbeat. They're bringing up fire so they can foam it out. They can't have the convoy stopped, not even for a minute."

"Understood," Teddy said. "You got that, McIntyre?"

Erin's teeth clenched. Chris's mood lately had been dismal, and Teddy's attitude and constant badgering did nothing to help. "Update on injuries?" Erin asked quickly, hoping to focus Chris's mind back on what waited ahead.

"Minor head and shoulder injuries for one; the driver they still haven't extracted."

"What's the holdup?" Teddy asked.

"Look for yourself," Chris growled.

Outside, below them, as the break in the convoy widened, two U.S. Army vehicles had fused into one. As the Huey closed in on the scene, out the side door looking forward, Erin could see the crumpled Humvee, three men carrying a wounded soldier up the road away from the accident, and heaps of two burned-out Iraqi tanks just off the side of the road. She pushed herself back into her seat just as the Huey, and then her stomach, lurched to a stop.

"Set us down sweet, bro!" Teddy hollered.

"Like a fallin' featha!" Angelo joyously shouted.

Teddy, Chris, and Erin all unhooked and grudgingly replaced their cozy flight helmets with Kevlar combat helmets. Grabbing her gear, standing on the skid, Chris jumped off and ran even before the Huey touched down.

Dustoff.

With dust flying everywhere, squinting her eyes, carrying her own gear and trying to hear the men yelling over the whupping helicopter blades, Erin ran down the road to where the injured soldier lay. Chris had already ensured an open airway and was grabbing the cervical collar out of her bag.

Erin helped her stabilize the wounded soldier's neck, then needlessly said, "Get a line in." Chris didn't seem to mind. The two women worked smoothly, quickly, professionally, sharing vital information in succinct exchanges. Erin assessed the soldier's badly broken right leg as Chris cut through his field jacket to insert the IV into his left arm. Erin heard Chris's voice, raised to a shout to carry over the roar of the Huey, through the haze of shock and pain engulfing the soldier.

"So. Danielson, is it? You got a first name? I bet you do! Everyone does!"

Erin wanted to smile, even as the severity of injury to the leg she worked on made her cringe.

The young corporal laboriously said the word, "Arch-ie."

"Archie? Okay, Archie. So. Tell me." Chris said to Erin, "IV in and up." She handed the IV bag to Teddy. "Archie? Huh? Were you rubberneckin', big guy?"

The soldier barely smiled; Erin's heart swelled. She said to Chris, "He's got multiple compound fractures. Let's get him out of here."

Chris quickly stood and assessed, then slapped a compress on the other soldier's forehead laceration, then tried to assess his shoulder injury, but seeing how the sergeant kept swinging his arm around, Erin wasn't too concerned.

"Let's go!" Teddy hollered, handing the IV bag to the sergeant and quickly moving in opposite Erin to help lift Corporal Danielson onto the stretcher. "They're pulling everyone out of the trucks and moving them back. We gotta go, now!" He looked up at Chris. "Grab the litter, McIntyre!"

As Chris moved in to help, Danielson immediately jolted to life, screaming, "No! No, wait! Please! WAIT!"

Chris grabbed the young man's arm and shouted, "Archie! Hey! Relax! We're getting you outta here!"

"No! Please!" The young man's frenzy bordered hysteria as he fought against Chris. "My ring! Franklin! Where's my boot? Where's my boot!"

Sergeant Franklin, still holding the IV bag and rubbing his shoulder, shouted, "Man, forget it! Your boot's a permanent part of the Humvee!"

"No! No, please!" Strength failed the hurting young soldier. He clawed at the thick cervical collar around his neck. "Please, you don't understand. I can't leave it. Inside . . . the pouch . . . please. I need it. Please!"

"What's he talking about?" Teddy hollered. "Forget it, man! We gotta go! This whole place could blow!"

Danielson would not be convinced. Sudden hysteria shot adrenalin through him, giving him incredible strength. Arms flailing, as Erin moved in to help, he pushed her away so hard she sprawled backward onto the road, the weight of her Kevlar helmet snapping her head back. The young soldier pulled off the collar around his neck and started to lift himself out of the stretcher—

"NO!" Teddy almost jumped on him. "We gotta go, man! Forget it! It's gone!"

Falling back into the stretcher, Danielson started to cry. "Please," he wailed. "You don't understand. I promised her—my ring—I can't lose it! My boot. Just inside my boot."

Franklin turned and looked sadly at the Humvee.

"Where."

That one word, Chris's voice—boiling terror spilled into Erin's stomach.

Teddy screamed, "No, McIntyre!"

"Where!" Chris stood now, staring at Sergeant Franklin.

"Chris . . ." Erin couldn't say anything else. Over the roar of the Huey, she didn't think Chris heard her anyway.

"Under the dash," Franklin said. "They had to cut it to get his foot out."

"NO!" Teddy took two steps around the litter and gave Chris a shove. "Grab the litter, McIntyre! We're outta here!"

Danielson screamed in desperation, "Noooo!"

"One minute," Chris shouted at Teddy. "Get him loaded. I'll be right back!"

"NO!"

For a second, Erin thought Teddy might swing out and hit Chris. Erin stepped up, shouting, "No, please, Chris! You can't!"

"RIGHT NOW, McINTYRE! GRAB THE LITTER."

Chris looked at Teddy, then at Erin, then at Danielson, then took off running down the road toward the wreck.

Erin stood paralyzed, watching her go.

Teddy ripped off about a dozen obscenities, then slapped Erin on the shoulder. She ran for the front of the stretcher as Teddy stormed to his place at Danielson's head. They grabbed the stretcher, lifted it quickly, and headed for the Huey.

Chris ran down the road toward the crumpled Humvee wedged under thousands of gallons of leaking diesel fuel.

✯✯✯

Ben blew out the huge breath he didn't know he was holding. He had tried to imagine what it must have been like during Dustoff Five. Many of his most harrowing memories of Vietnam had faded. Sometimes, though, the horror of his worst memories flooded back over him. Like right now, because of one tiny ring. He said it. "One tiny ring."

Erin pressed her lips. "Fourteen-carat gold. Archie was a devoted newlywed."

Ben shook his head slowly. "And she found it."

Erin whispered, "Yep." And then, after a long, silent pause, added, "I knew she would. Or die trying."

✯✯✯

25 February 1991 1349 Hours
Twelve Miles South of TAC Cobra on MSR Newmarket, South-central Iraq

Chris wasn't purposely trying to make this particular Dustoff more exciting. The sharp stench of diesel fuel burned her nose as her boots splashed through the mud, as she lifted off her Kevlar helmet and set it on the mangled Humvee's hood, as she squeezed inside the mangled cab. She tried to slide close enough to reach Archie's crushed boot but had to stretch full out on her belly, reaching with her left hand through the twisted metal debris. She was amazed Corporal Archie Danielson still had his right foot.

Feeling inside the torn leather boot, she found a small sewn-in pouch. She searched desperately for an opening, felt the ring inside, but couldn't figure out how to get it out. She grabbed the entire pouch and pulled, cussing as her knuckles raked across jagged metal.

She pulled again. The pouch started to tear away. "*Ay caramba*, Danielson," she said aloud. "Where'd you learn to sew?"

She felt a presence behind her, outside the Humvee. Blood froze in her veins. She heard Teddy's voice. "Just what are you trying to prove, McIntyre?"

One more vicious pull tore the pouch away from Archie's boot. An instant rush of joy and rage swept through her. "I am sick of you, Brisbaine!" she hollered. "Help me get out of here." She clenched the pouch in her bleeding left hand, feeling the ring inside dig into her palm.

She felt Teddy grab the back of her survival vest and start to pull. Heard him start to say, "Do you—?" Then heard loud, smart blasts hit the Humvee with such force, even wedged under the tanker, the truck shook. Again and again and again thumps smacked into the Humvee. She heard a different, sickening thump, and another, heard breath whoosh out of Teddy as if he'd been hit in the gut with a baseball bat.

The man fell heavily on top of where she lay, still stretched across the driver's seat. She lost all ability to breathe, to think. The thumps continued. She remembered the diesel in puddles directly under them.

"Teddy! We gotta—!"

He didn't move.

"Teddy! Quit it! We gotta—!" She pushed him up and back, until she could free herself from under the steering wheel, continued to push, grunting, pushing Teddy back and up—the man felt like dead weight on top of her.

No. No, no, no, no, no . . . She pushed him up enough to turn and guide him down to the ground. They fell, landing in a heap. Chris looked—two jagged holes in Teddy's chest wept brilliant red blood. Massive exit wounds from large-caliber bullets.

No. It couldn't be. The stupid jerk was playing a joke on her. Bored to tears earlier, he had concocted this harebrained scheme . . . More loud thumps smacked the side of the Humvee, and dawning awareness pushed away her doubt. She fell on top of Teddy, trying to shield him . . . from what? Who was shooting at them?

No more thumps. She looked up, to her left. The side panels of the Humvee had turned into Swiss cheese. She looked right. Out over the desert. Saw two Iraqi burned-out tanks. Over the turret of one hung a body. A very dead Iraqi soldier. On the top of the other tank, behind what looked like a mounted machine gun, stood another Iraqi soldier. And this Iraqi soldier was not dead. This Iraqi soldier angrily worked the gun, shaking it, aiming it at Chris.

Stunned, she looked down at Staff Sergeant Edward Theodore Brisbaine.

Screams. Piercing, from deep in her soul, from the fibers of her being. *No, Teddy! Stop this! You jerk! Enough! Wake up!* She felt his neck for a pulse, then shook him, screaming, "Please! Teddy!" Screams. "Noooo!" Screams. Faint. Over the distant roar of the helicopter. Listening, Chris heard screams. She looked up, blinked tears from her eyes, looked out at the tank. Saw the Iraqi soldier turning the machine gun toward the helicopter, saw him shake it and hit it. Heard more screams, a woman's scream . . . Erin's scream.

Chris looked back, behind her, up the road, toward the Huey, tried to focus . . .

ERIN!

"ONE LONE IRAQI."

Drawing in a deep, ragged breath, Ben Connelly held it a second, then blew it out slowly. "On a T-72 already hit at least twice by Apache fire. Unbelievable."

"We never saw him," Erin said. "Nobody did. I didn't see him. Didn't even know he was there."

"How many rounds hit the Humvee? Without igniting the fuel?"

"It was a miracle."

"And still . . . you ran."

Erin seemed to consider that for a few seconds. "I saw Chris and Teddy down, by the Humvee. That's all I saw."

Ben knew the rest. It tore at his gut. He looked at Erin, but could tell by her expression she was back in the desert, running desperately toward the one person in the world she could not bear to see fall.

✷✷✷

25 FEBRUARY 1991 1354 HOURS
TWELVE MILES SOUTH OF TAC COBRA ON MSR NEWMARKET,
SOUTH-CENTRAL IRAQ

What was happening? Why was Erin—?

"Noooo!" Chris pushed herself off Teddy and quickly started for Erin, hoping to reach her before the Iraqi fired again.

Too late.

Erin's head snapped to the side. She fell hard and out of control, only twenty feet away. Chris screamed and dove onto the road, then crawled on her stomach the rest of the way. She wriggled up beside her. Erin was on her side, a wide crease in her helmet; her unseeing eyes hung open for just a second, then slowly closed as she lost consciousness.

Chris screamed at her, screamed her name, screamed in blinding pain as something sliced across the side of her leg, heard faint pops of machine gun fire through the continuous roar of the helicopter. She threw herself on top of Erin, angry heat coursing through her.

No more pops. Chris pushed herself up and felt for a pulse against the side of Erin's neck. Her hands shook too violently. She tried again. A pulse. Strong. Relief did not dampen her rage. She turned to check her leg. Saw a ragged tear through her BDU pants, a long, bleeding gash across the side of her thigh.

She looked out at the tank. Saw the Iraqi soldier shaking the big machine gun, pointing it at the helicopter, smacking the top of the gun with his open hand, shaking it, pointing it . . .

Chris stood. Slowly. Stared out at the tank, gritting her teeth in pain, then in overwhelming rage. She reached down, unholstered her 9mm pistol, lifted it, flicked off the safety, then aimed it across the desert. At the Iraqi tank. At the Iraqi soldier.

Holding it steady with both hands, she started to walk. Across the packed dirt road. Over the small berm to the desert floor. Across the scrubby dirt, closer . . .

The big gun swung her direction. She stopped, watching. The soldier desperately worked to force the jammed gun to fire.

Their eyes met. Just for a moment. Chris squinted. Pulled up her hand to rub her eyes. Blinked.

The man was gone.

Her stomach lurched. Staring over the top of her 9mm, she started again toward the tank, slowly, deliberately, hearing nothing but the Huey's constant thunder. The Iraqi soldier appeared to the right of the tank, on the ground, walking out, then just standing there, a few feet away from the ruined heap of blackened metal.

Chris stopped. Aimed her pistol at the soldier's head. Again their eyes met. Locked. Dark-haired, bearded, thin. Unmistakably unfriendly. Her enemy. Standing before her, face-to-face, only forty, maybe fifty feet away.

Chris froze. Aimed the pistol. Steadied it. Ready to do it. Ready to shoot. Ready to kill.

Something stopped her. Not the man's dark, imploring eyes. Not fear. Not human compassion.

Her enemy carried no weapon.

She carefully searched the man with her eyes. Searched the ground around him. Found no weapons of any kind. The gun he had fired was permanently mounted onto the tank. She looked at the man. Then saw him slowly start to lift his hands.

Her mind short-circuited. She blinked. She could not register the scene before her. Was she now expected to accept this man's innocent surrender? After he killed Teddy? And possibly her best friend?

The pistol shook in her hands; she squeezed it tighter, desperately trying to keep it steady, keep it trained on the man's head. She tried, but slowly, so very slowly, it fell to her side. Strength gone, hands trembling, she almost dropped it. She looked away. Wanted to turn away. But something caught her eye. The man, holding his hands up, held his right hand differently than his left.

His eyes no longer implored; the scene suddenly became clear. Chris lifted her pistol, aimed at the man's chest, and pulled the trigger. Five times.

Then turned and ran.

The grenade in the Iraqi's hand blew up as he hit the ground, pelting Chris with chunks of rock and dirt, kicking up dust and sand into the helicopter's rotor wash.

Chris kept running, stumbled over the berm, fell onto the road, dropped her pistol, falling there, beside Erin, crawling closer, gasping, horrified by what she had just done—she stopped and groaned, seeing what she feared most.

Blood. Under Erin's Kevlar combat helmet.

Her head fell into her hands as black light crowded the fringes of her mind. Noises swirled together into nothingness inside her. But she heard Bobby Palmara's voice shouting at her, felt hands touching her shoulders, saw him move around behind Erin, acting as if he wanted to take off Erin's helmet—Chris jumped up and pushed him away, screaming, "No! Don't, Bobby! Don't take it off! DON'T TOUCH IT!" She pushed him again, keeping him away. "Go get the backboard! And my kit! Now!"

She paid no attention to the flurry of activity around her, men running, shouting; she saw only Erin, her closed eyelids, the bright red blood falling in a line down her bruised forehead. Chris worked instinctively, gently releasing the helmet's straps under Erin's chin, carefully supporting Erin's neck as she wept, "No ... Oh, God, please ... Rinny ..."

She directed the men who helped her as they slowly and carefully eased Erin onto the backboard and secured her tightly to it. Chris triple-checked the brace around Erin's head and neck, then ran alongside as the men carried Erin to the helicopter. She tore through her pack as the Huey's rotors thundered, inserted the IV needle as the Huey lifted.

When they had almost reached the combat support hospital—after Chris had done everything possible for Erin and Archie—she reached into the pocket of her survival vest and pulled out the tiny pouch. She tucked it into the front pocket of Archie's field jacket, then gave it a gentle pat. Slowly, she turned her eyes to look at him. She barely nodded. Then gave the ring another pat.

Tears spilled down the young man's anguished face as he closed his eyes, his trembling lips lifting in a smile.

★★★

"YOU WERE OUT FOR SOME time."

"Two days."

"Serious concussion. Et cetera."

Erin gave Ben a wry grin.

He gentled his voice. "How did she react? Afterward. Did you ever find out?"

Silence fell heavily. The refrigerator kicked on in the kitchen. The soft hum helped lift some of the weight.

"Teddy was dead."

Ben drew in a breath and let it out in a rush, with the word, "Yeah."

"Angelo told me later the trip back was ... quiet. He said he'd never heard Chris cry before."

"She thought you were ... well, she thought you at least broke your neck."

"I guess I wasn't very graceful when I fell."

"You were hit by a two-and-a-half-inch bullet, Erin."

She smirked.

"And you were bleeding. No wonder Chris thought you were ..."
Ben couldn't finish his thought.

"I guess seeing blood under an industrial-strength dented Kevlar
helmet would be a tiny cause for concern."

He smiled. "Palmara's report said, when he got to you, you were
down and bleeding profusely."

"Scalp wound. You know how they bleed."

"Took ... what." Ben paused for effect. "Fifteen stitches to close
up your little 'scalp wound'? And how long for the baseball-sized
lump to finally go away?"

Erin scowled and rubbed the corner of her forehead. "Part of it
still remains."

Ben let out a faint laugh, shook his head, then grew serious. The
images of the words; Erin's words; Palmara's report; the image of
Chris kneeling over Erin's body, weeping. He closed his eyes for a
moment, then looked up at Erin. "Correct me if I'm wrong, but
didn't you say Chris didn't care about you anymore? I mean, that's
how she treated you, isn't it? After you saw ... " He frowned. "And
then she sat by your bed on the *Mercy* for two days?"

Erin's lips pressed into a grin. "Yep, that's exactly what she did."

Ben tried to understand, but none of it made any sense. "And
then she just disappeared? After you woke up? Why would she do
that?"

A pause. "She said she had orders."

That struck him. "I never gave her orders."

"I know."

Ben waited.

"She needed to be sure I was okay. Then she needed to leave."

He slowly shook his head. "And I didn't do much to alleviate
the situation, huh. Trying to pin a Star on her chest."

Erin smiled. "No, Ben, you didn't."

"But she deserved it. From everything I heard, from all the reports I read, if that Iraqi would have thrown that grenade anywhere near that tanker, the resulting explosion would have taken out ..." He couldn't even imagine it. " ... everything. All of you, the Huey, the MSR, at least five of the other trucks ..."

Erin nodded.

"The guys standing there would not have been able to stop it. Only Chris saw the grenade."

She stared at the coffee table.

Ben sighed again, deeply, then looked at Erin. "Why did Brisbaine leave the helicopter?"

Erin's head lifted quickly. "What?"

"Why did Brisbaine leave his responsibilities at the helicopter and go down to the wreck?"

She pondered that.

"Did Coffee command him to go?"

"No."

"Then why? He had no business going down that road."

"He wanted to give Chris a hard time, I guess. Make her feel stupid."

Ben growled. Then was softened by another thought. "Why did you leave the helicopter?" He barely smiled.

Again, Erin's head quickly lifted.

"Did Coffee order you to go?"

Her eyes flickered.

"Do you know why you did it? Weren't you afraid?"

"Yeah. I mean ... I guess I didn't even think about it. When I saw them both down ..."

"You had to save Chris."

She looked directly at Ben. "Yeah."

"And you did." He chuckled. "In a roundabout way, of course."

She seemed to struggle with that.

"Maybe I should have requested the Star for you."

Her eyes widened. "No way, Ben." She smiled and shook her head. "No way."

"What's the deal with the poor Bronze Star? Nobody wants it anymore."

They both laughed.

"I sure tried to pin it on Chris," Ben eventually said.

"You tried to do the right thing."

"But I blew it."

"Only in Chris's mind."

"You don't think I blew it?"

"I think what you tried to do was . . . sweet."

Ben laughed, then drew in one more long, refreshing deep breath. He relaxed in his recliner. "And the war ended."

"Yep."

His eyes closed for a second as his heart whispered, *Thank You, Lord, for a very short war.* He looked at Erin. "When I saw you on the *Mercy*, you were doing better. Where did you go after that?"

"Doctor Cayman was able to get me on a transport out of Dhahran later that week, and I was back home at Fort Lewis three days after that."

"Quite a reception, huh."

A smiled beamed across Erin's face.

"Did you know I was invited to ride with Schwarzkopf in the parade at Times Square? Not beside him, mind you. A few cars back."

Erin's eyes widened.

"I turned it down. We had more than our fair share of parades at Campbell."

Her eyes turned sad. "Chris stayed."

Ben pressed his lips. "I know."

"Can I ask you . . . now? With respect, Ben, but why did you allow her to stay? Why did you clear her . . . to stay?"

His defenses rose before he could stop them. "I couldn't order her to return home, Erin. That was up to her CO at Wainwright. She was so close to the end of her enlistment anyway, he told her she could stay. I ordered her to suspend offensive operations, like everyone else, but she volunteered to stay and help clean up, to help with Provide Comfort, and there was nothing I could say or do to change her mind. Believe me, after our little 'Bronze Star' discussion, I tried to get her to come home. She wasn't interested."

Erin's eyes welled with tears. "She didn't want to be a hero in a parade."

Stunned, Ben said, "Why not? She deserved it. You all did."

"Teddy died."

"That wasn't her fault."

"Doesn't matter."

"She saved your life. The lives of your entire crew. Danielson's, Franklin's . . . and who knows how many others."

"Wasn't enough."

Frustrated, Ben growled, then leaned forward in his recliner, resting his forearms on his knees. They had just spent almost three hours talking about the war, about a time both of them would rather forget but never would, about friendship and fear and courage . . . and Chris McIntyre. And, after all this time, he still didn't understand her. Not at all.

He rubbed his face roughly with both hands, then stared at his mug on the coffee table. "Erin," he said wearily, "I'm sorry. But I don't understand. I still don't understand."

"Me neither."

That stunned him. In many ways. Why did Erin still care? He remembered the shock he felt, then the shock on Erin's face when he passed along Sid Thompson's message about Chris only last week. Erin still loved Chris deeply. Chris obviously didn't want to be loved. Erin still cared. Chris pushed her away. Erin stayed. Chris ignored her, shut her out, abandoned her.

But Ben knew why. It was because of Christ Jesus, her Lord and Savior. Because of His love.

God wouldn't let Erin give up on Chris. Because He would not give up on Chris. That was His plan, and it was playing out right in front of Ben's eyes.

His heart overflowed. *How can I help, Lord? What can I do? How can I share Your love . . . with Chris? And with Erin? Your pure love, broken and spilled out, cleansing, redeeming, remaining forever. Oh, please let me be a part of this. And please help Erin.*

Her swollen eyes had again flooded with tears. He quietly cleared his throat, then waited for her to look at him. "Will you please be sure to come to me if there's anything I can do to help?" He swallowed down the lump in his throat. "I mean, I want to help. If there's anything I can do."

Her words barely carried to him. "You are helping, Ben. More than you know."

He pressed his lips and nodded slowly. "Can I pray with you?"

Tears dripped down Erin's cheeks. "I'd like that very much."

The two of them knelt together over the couch, buried their faces in their hands, and prayed. They prayed for each other, for those hurt by the war, for strength . . . for the one who lay sleeping across the way, sleeping off a trip to Barney's.

For her to know the living Christ, to allow His love to save her, His peace to heal her wounded life. For hope and joy and life everlasting.

They prayed. For Chris.

TEN

IF THE RED IN HER eyes didn't tell the tale, the dark circles around her eyes sure did. Dark, puffy circles. But Erin didn't mind. She knew she had them too. It was a long night. At least she didn't have the obvious headache. Chris looked terrible.

"Hi," was a mumble, almost a hoarse whisper, as Chris passed by the dining room table on her way to the coffeemaker on the kitchen counter. Erin, sitting at the table, heard her rummaging through the cupboard, probably for a mug. Chris would probably fill that mug to the brim. Straight and black. Fuel for weary bones. And a gray, rainy day. Erin swallowed another sip of her own coffee, though even with decaffeinated, she knew she had long since had enough. She hated coffee overload. And she was overloaded.

A new day lay ahead. And all Erin wanted to do was go back to bed. But she read her paper. Friday morning's edition of the *Oregonian*. Not really reading. More like scanning the headlines. And the pictures. But acting fully engrossed.

Chris sat at the table next to her, not lifting her head or saying a word. She silently sipped her coffee. Erin silently "read" the paper. Not a word was spoken. For several minutes.

Until . . . a whisper. "Rin?"

A murmur. "Mm-hmm?"

Another whisper. Slightly stronger than the first. "Rin . . . I'm, um . . ."

Erin lowered the paper. She saw humiliation in Chris's eyes. Frustration. Deep, hard exhaustion. And a longing, a loneliness that seemed to cut to Chris's very soul. Erin's heart ached as she waited.

Chris stared at her steaming coffee and whispered, "I'm sorry, Rin. About running off last night."

Erin picked up her paper. Why should she let Chris off the hook so easily? Why should she continue to let this woman wreak utter chaos in her otherwise quiet and normal life? She turned the page. Scanned the headlines. Said to Chris, simply, "Don't worry about it."

She hoped Chris got the hint. And why not a little indignation along with it? The woman crossed a big line last night, running off and getting drunk. What could she say that would make up for it?

But, as Erin sat there, pretending to be reading a story about Bosnia, her flimsy resolve caved in on her. No matter how much chaos Chris McIntyre wreaked in Erin's life, it would be worth it. If Chris would only believe.

You've got to hurry and work this out, Lord. I can't give up on her. And I won't. But I don't know how much more of this I can take.

A split second later, in an instant, Chris pushed herself away from the table and, without a word, headed for the stairs.

Startled, Erin looked up. "Where're you going?"

"Home," was all Chris said.

Erin jumped up and caught Chris by the shirtsleeve at the foot of the stairs. "What? Hey, come on!"

Chris stopped and slowly turned around.

Their eyes locked. Then Chris hung her head.

Oh, Lord . . . Erin wanted to smile even as she wanted to weep. With gentle peace filling her, she knew this was the moment she had waited for, hoped for, prayed for, all these years.

She took a small step forward and wrapped Chris in a gentle embrace. Careful at first, not too fast. She felt Chris tense, heard the catch in her breath. But then her head fell to the top of Erin's shoulder and softly rested there. She felt Chris's arms slowly come around to return the hug, felt her own hand tremble as she gently placed it on Chris's back. She held it there for a moment, then pulled Chris in as tight as she could.

It only took a few seconds. In her shame, her exhaustion, Chris broke down. Erin held her and quietly wept as her heart whispered, *Precious Lord Jesus, let her feel Your love, and from this moment on* . . . *embrace her with Your love.*

The words sifted sweetly through her as the moment lingered. When Chris finally pulled away, both women looked at each other and smiled, almost laughed, embarrassed, at the same time they swiped at their tears.

"You know what I'd really like to do?" Erin said a few seconds later.

Still wiping her tears, Chris shook her head.

"Go on upstairs, crawl back into bed, and sleep for a week. Sound like a plan?"

And Chris smiled.

★★★

ERIN SLEPT UNTIL HALF PAST two, when Scott called to check on her. Trying not to reveal her grogginess, she told him all was well. For the first time in a long time, she almost believed it.

Through her large bedroom window, a brilliant golden sun poured long beams of warmth through the slats of the vertical blinds. Peeking through, squinting, she let out a sigh of relief. The rain was gone. The night was gone. It was a new day. And she was now finally ready to face it. In the bathroom, she washed her face and brushed her hair, then headed downstairs to fix some lunch. Grilled cheese sandwiches. And tomato soup. Can't have one without the other.

Chris came downstairs as the sandwiches grilled. They sat at the dining room table, gobbled up two of the golden-brown delicacies, from time to time dunking them into their tomato soup, then as Erin loaded the dishwasher, Chris snuck upstairs for a quick shower. When she returned a few minutes later, Erin hardly recognized her. Along with her jeans, sneakers, and white San Juan Search and Rescue hooded sweatshirt, Chris wore a small, simply stunning smile.

★★★

"ARE YOU, BY ANY CHANCE, ready for a tour of Kimberley Square?"

Chris pulled her smile into a smirk. "Well, I guess. If I have to." She ducked away, but not before Erin playfully slapped her on the shoulder.

"Come on, woman. First stop? My clinic."

"Are we taking the long way? Or the short cut."

Erin grabbed her jacket and led Chris out her front door. "Yes, I'll admit, this way is longer, but it's definitely more scenic."

Chris laughed and followed her out to the porch that ran the entire length of the house. Squinting into the harsh sunlight, she lifted her head and breathed the cool, fresh air, letting the moment carry away the last remaining traces of her hangover. Erin stood at the porch's edge, eyes closed, her face tilted toward the bright sunlight. Chris smiled at the sight.

"I love it after a rain." Erin grinned as she put on her jacket. "Which, around here, basically means I love it all the time."

Chris looked out over Kimberley Street, across the street to the Connelly's big house, to the huge, majestic church on the corner. As she took it all in, she felt comfortable here, safe. For the moment. Tiny wisps of steam floated up from the street. The air, for a city, smelled clean, almost sweet. She marveled at the lush green grass. Back in her world, she'd be shoveling snow right now. Here, and soon, someone would have to mow grass.

Erin headed for the door to the clinic, so Chris turned as well, just as it swung open and two young children—black-haired, brown-skinned twin brothers—burst through and bounded down the stairs, slamming the door behind them. "Hi, Nurse Erin!" they hollered as they ran, and before Erin could say, "Hi, Tyrone! Hi, Tyrell!" the two boys were halfway down the street.

Erin's eyes flashed with joy. "Did you see that? No bandages. Cool."

Chris only noticed both boys firmly gripped a lollypop in each hand.

"Tyrell needed care for some serious cuts and scrapes last week," Erin said as the boys raced around the corner. "I put eleven stitches in the palm of his left hand alone." Erin grinned at Chris. "So. Shall we try again?"

"Maybe we should knock this time."

Erin let out a laugh, pushed the door open, and waved Chris inside.

Chris took three steps into the front room of the Kimberley Street Community Clinic and stopped. She could only stare. She had tried to peek inside before, but all the blinds had been pulled. Now, with the large room filled with light, she stood there, gaping. She had tried to imagine Erin's clinic. Now, she realized she knew Erin better than she thought. It was just as she had pictured.

A big bouncy couch lined the far wall. Flowering planters hung from the ceiling. Dozens of toys—hundreds maybe, counting the Legos—lay spread out all over the floor in front of the big picture window. Coloring books, a Little Tikes dollhouse, a child-sized basketball hoop and balls. Lots of balls. And dolls and trucks and teddy bears. Chris resisted the urge to fall to the floor and grab one of the Tonka ambulances. When she was a kid, she and the neighbor boy wore out the knees of their jeans pushing Tonka trucks from one end of the neighbor's backyard to the other. She didn't fall to the floor, but she did laugh.

She felt Erin beside her. Heard Erin's voice. "You can come on in, you know. It's not like I'm gonna put you to work."

Chris wanted to laugh but was startled when a round, bald-headed man appeared from behind a curtained-off back room. He wiped his hands on a paper towel as he strode toward them. "Hey! Erin!" He shot them both a wide smile. "Great to see you back! Did you see the boys? They didn't run you down on their escape out of here, did they?" He gave Erin a quick hug and a kiss on the cheek.

Erin turned to Chris. "This is Kyle, my friend from Providence. Kyle, this is Chris. Chris McIntyre. My friend from Colorado."

"Well, hey there, Chris. Nice to meet-cha."

Chris shook the portly doctor's hand and said a friendly hello.

"So, how is Tyrone?" Erin asked. "Did you take out his stitches?"

"He didn't even cry. What a trooper. It's amazing there wasn't any muscle damage."

"Ahh, that's great. They both looked so happy."

"Especially with those suckers you gave them." Chris gave the doctor a smirk.

Guilty as charged, Kyle grinned at Chris. "One for each hand!"

As Kyle talked shop with Erin, catching her up on some of the clinic's happenings from the past few days, Chris listened for a moment, then became lost in her own thoughts as she studied the rest of the room.

A bookshelf lined with all shapes and sizes of various waiting-room material stood in the far left corner of the room. Houseplants cascaded from small wall-mounted shelves between the two big side windows. Smaller potted plants sat on sills beneath the windows where construction-paper snowflakes had been taped. *Probably the only snowflakes these people will ever see!* Looking around Erin's clinic, Chris slowly shook her head. A hint of envy trickled into her heart. She enjoyed the feeling.

"Let's go see Velda, Chris. She is so sweet. Did you hear? Kyle said she hasn't been feeling well." Erin turned back to Kyle. "Thanks for keeping an eye on things while I was gone."

"No problem at all," he said. "I'm just glad you're back."

Chris gave him a smile, then followed Erin through the clinic to the back door, down the stairs, and across the gorgeous backyard. Again she marveled. Towering fir trees guarded the entire Kimberley Street community. Douglas fir, she noticed. The Northwest's cash crop. The clinic's backyard sported two of the trees. And a large, freshly tilled garden spot. She drew in a long, deep breath. The air tasted wonderful.

To the end of the rickety wooden fence, through the rickety old gate, Erin led the way to Velda Jackson's house. Down the sidewalk of a car-lined street, through puddles of winter rain, over the massive buried roots of the massive trees above them. A dog barked from a distant backyard. Bare maple and elm trees, bare apple and pear trees. The place was an inner-city jungle.

Passing cars splashed water at their feet. Sirens wailed in the distance. Chris pushed her fists into the front pocket of her sweatshirt. She was glad she had burned her bright red San Juan Rescue jacket. As pleasant as this neighborhood was, wearing bright red on the streets could prove to be deadly.

A rush of terror, of grief and regret swept through her as she walked. Her teeth clenched as she shivered. And not from the cold.

Far away, she heard a shout. A mother shouting for her child? Sounded like it. No. A mother shouting *at* her child. Her stomach lurched. She heard Erin's voice.

"Next street over yet. Not far."

Chris glanced at her and smiled. But the smile faded too quickly. She drew in another deep breath and tried to relax, tried to quiet the sudden storm in her soul. She looked up when she heard another sound. Over the noise of the occasional passing car, there it was. Faint. Distant. Yet distinct. She knew of several sounds so instantly identifiable: the sizzle of bacon, the *whup-whup* of a Huey, the bounce of a basketball. Somewhere, someone, out in this inner-city jungle, dribbled a basketball.

A steady bounce, then quicker, then steady again. Chris strained to hear as she walked beside Erin. The sound continued. Quick bounce, steady bounce, quick bounce. *Aren't they ever going to stop to shoot?*

Erin laughed. "You hear it, don't you? It's Alaina."

"Who?"

She stopped at the street corner and pointed down the side street toward a small vacant lot sandwiched between two abandoned storefronts. Chris looked for movement, but saw none. She heard the bounce of the basketball, then a rush of familiar words representing severe disappointment. The bouncing stopped, and a basketball rolled down the sidewalk and across the street, then lodged itself under a parked car.

Two blocks north of Kimberley Street, and the jungle here had nothing to do with trees or lush green grass. This was an urban jungle, complete with spray-painted graffiti and smashed windows. Beat-up cars lined both sides of the street. Far in the distance, a car alarm sounded. Halfway down the street, a young boy walked out to retrieve his basketball.

Chris's mouth fell open.

Not a young boy, a young *girl*. A child. Nine, maybe ten. Curly blonde hair pulled up in a ponytail, she skipped across the street and hunkered down under the car.

Chris heard a shout. "Hey! Get away from my car!" She heard the child say, "Relax, old man! I'm just getting my ball!" The return, "I'll give you something else if you don't get away from my car!"

She immediately took a step toward the girl, but Erin reached out and stopped her. "It's okay, Chris," she said softly. "Mr. Potts is old and grouchy, rather obnoxious, but otherwise harmless."

The girl crawled out from under the car, turned her head toward the window above her, and shouted, "See! I didn't touch yer stinkin' car!"

In the third-story window of a square, concrete apartment building, a bulky figure moved away. Then the young girl turned and, after a few seconds, spit on the driver's side window of the car. After that, she skipped back across the street, carrying her basketball. Dribbling soon resumed; Chris heard the bounce of the ball and, otherwise, relative quiet. She turned and looked wide-eyed at Erin.

"Alaina Walker," Erin said as she smiled. "Sweetest kid you'll ever meet." And then, after a slight pause, she grabbed Chris's arm. "Let's go meet her."

Chris had no time to object, no time to even think about objecting. Before she knew it, she stood in front of one of the abandoned stores.

Erin leaned around the building and peered into the vacant lot. "Come here, Chris," she whispered. "Look at this."

Chris slowly peeked around Erin's shoulder; her heart fell at the sight.

Alaina Walker dribbled the basketball on a cracked and beaten concrete surface no bigger than a truck. There was no hoop anywhere, only cracked concrete and an old shopping cart pushed over into the corner of the enclosed lot. Long stalks of grass poked through the cracks, but only in the places where the young girl hadn't trampled them down.

Chris stared, unable to believe her eyes.

Alaina Walker could flat out play the game. Nine, twenty-nine, it didn't matter. Pure, natural ability. She stood there, feet apart, dribbling the ball in a figure-eight pattern around her feet, carefully avoiding the folds of her baggy sweatpants. Right-handed dribbles around her right foot, left-handed dribbles around her left foot. Around a tiny pair of terribly worn-out high-tops, tightly tied, excess lace encircling the ankle.

Around and around and around.

Chris looked at Erin. Erin smiled. Chris only gaped.

Who was this kid? Who would play basketball in a cold, concrete hole . . . without a hoop? She grabbed Erin's wrist to check her watch. 3:15. School must have just let out. This child rushed home after school and came here? Just to dribble a basketball?

Where did this child live? In this urban jungle?

Chris pulled away and leaned against the front window of the vacant store. She had to breathe deeply to calm her raging heartbeat. Such a sweet kid. Tiny, blonde-haired, ponytailed . . . and this was her playground?

"What are you thinking?" Erin whispered.

Chris turned her head. "I . . . I'm not sure."

"Don't you want to say 'hi'?"

Chris swallowed. "N–No."

"Why not? She won't bite."

"She might spit on me."

And they both tried not to laugh. Erin looked over her shoulder at the line of goo streaming down Mr. Potts's car window. She cringed. And whispered, "Man. That is really gross."

"She won't—"

Erin looked at Chris. "Won't what?"

"He won't get her in trouble for that. Will he?"

Erin waited before saying, "Because she spit on his car? I doubt it."

"You doubt it?"

"He probably won't even notice. He never drives it anyway."

"I'm gonna wipe it off." And Chris started for the car.

Erin grabbed her. "Hey, I don't think that's necessary. Look, it's gonna rain again, anyway. Besides, I wouldn't go near it." She made a face and shuddered.

Chris smiled. Then laughed. They both heard another hushed cuss, and peeked around the edge of the storefront. They stood there silently watching for almost five minutes. Until it started to rain.

They left for Velda's. But Chris heard the bounce of the basketball all the way down the street, until it blended into the other sounds of the bustling city and disappeared.

✫✫✫

SWEET VELDA JACKSON. PORTLY DOCTOR Kyle. Little Tyrone. Little Tyrell. Little Benny. Big Benny. Sonya. Andy and Sarah and Amanda and Kayley. Isaiah and his kittens. Kay Valleri. Capriella Sanchez. Bettema Kinsley.

Erin Grayson Mathis. And Scott.

Alaina Walker.

A mother shouting at her child.

An obnoxious old man threatening a small girl.

Chris rolled over onto her belly and closed her eyes. She was so tired, but she wasn't sleepy; it was only 6:45 p.m. She was supposed to be getting ready, changing her clothes. Mr. Benjamin Connelly wanted to treat everyone to dinner. A deluxe table at Shenanigans, overlooking Portland's beautiful downtown waterfront.

Chris could hardly wait.

Eyes closed, she ran her fingertips along the beautifully stitched quilt on her bed. Somebody had worked hard on this. The fibers felt warm and soft on her cheek. She didn't care if she fell asleep on this warm, soft quilt and never woke up.

But her eyes would not stay closed. Through the peaceful sounds of the house, the murmurs of Erin and Scott as they dressed for dinner, she could hear only the shouts of an angry old man: *I'll give you something else if you don't get away . . .*

Alaina! she wanted to scream, *Where are you now? Are you safe? Are you home? With your parents? Do they love you? Will they protect you?*

Stop cryin', Chrissy. Didn't I teach you? Defend yourself! Don't take nothin' off nobody! Next time Tony comes around, let 'im have it. And quit your cryin'. I can't stand it when you cry!

She quickly rolled over, silently cursed away the familiar terror. She stared at the ceiling, but couldn't stop her dad's voice from filling her mind, his face from appearing on the ceiling.

Don't cry. Stop that! I'll give you something to cry about if you don't shut up!

Block the jab with your arm. Stick it out. Like this.

She closed her eyes. A quivering sneer barely curled her upper lip.

Protect your face. See it coming! Anticipate it. Duck! Then counter with a jab to the gut. Like this. Duck, pow! Right in the gut. That's it!

Her sneer widened. Slowly, still lying on her back on the bed, she raised her right hand, crushed it into a tight fist, and punched it into the air. "Duck, pow!" she whispered, eyes still closed, ignoring the sudden pain shooting through her side. "Anticipate! Stop being so helpless!" A pause. "Thanks, Dad."

Her hand fell with a thud, intensifying the shooting pains, freezing her breath inside her. She lay still, waiting, but as the pain eased and breath returned, another face appeared in her mind, a tender smile, eyes welled with laughter . . . and concern. She brought her left hand around and pushed against her hurting ribs. *I am so sorry, Travis. I'm so sorry. Please . . . forgive me.*

See it coming! Anticipate! Counter!

Travis . . .

And don't cry. I hate it when you cry!

Sitting up quickly, blinking deeply, she waited again for the pain to ease, for breath, then pushed herself up and headed for the bathroom.

***

She never did develop a taste for oysters. But the steak? Not bad. Not as tasty as Raymond's, of course. Nothing could compare to Raymond's right off the grill—

"So, Christina, Erin told me you met our Alaina."

Chris almost choked. Sonya Connelly's sweet southern drawl carried the young girl's name like a song. She swallowed her chunk of steak, more like forced it down, and smiled. "Yeah. Yes. I mean, I guess. We didn't really . . . meet."

Bettema said, "Can you imagine how thrilled that kid's gonna be when we get the gym finished?"

Chris swallowed a sip of her iced tea. Her smile came easily. "Man, if she shoots anything like she dribbles."

"What about Jazzy?" Cappy leaned in. "And Jen White? She plays just like a little Michael Jordan. What would that be? A Michelle Jordan?"

"What a wonderful opportunity we have," Sonya said. "That gym will be their very own safe place to play. Basketball, volleyball, and Kay can't wait to expand her classes. We are so fortunate to have acquired the building."

Cappy grabbed her glass of Pepsi and grumbled, "Maybe now those little Bandolero creeps will leave Alaina alone."

"What?" Chris quickly asked.

"Couple of—" Cappy glanced at Sonya—"*degenerates* gave her a rough time a few months back."

Gaping, Chris glanced at Erin.

"Didn't you notice the poor kid didn't have anything to shoot at?" Chris turned to Cappy. "How could I not notice?"

"We all went over there a few months back, and put up a hoop for her. Not a brand-new one; we weren't that stupid. But a nice one. It was up for what, six hours? Until the Bandoleros found it. They had it trashed in less than five minutes."

"Who? How? What do you mean?"

"They flooded the place. About ten of them. They stole her ball and pushed her around."

Chris stared, then turned to Erin. "Why didn't you tell me?"

Erin met Chris's gaze, but didn't answer the question.

Chris looked at Cappy. "She was all right, wasn't she? What happened? Tell me!"

Sonya lowered her hand to rest on Cappy's arm. "She was fine, Christina. They all just gave her a rough time."

"And she gave them one too!"

"Now, please, Capriella," Sonya said softly. "Don't get upset. Let's just enjoy our dinner. In a few weeks, we'll have the gym ready, and Alaina can play as often as she likes. And yes, Christina—" Sonya gave Chris a wink—"she shoots even better than she dribbles!"

Chris wanted to smile, but she couldn't. She wanted to finish her steak. She couldn't bring herself to pick up her fork. It was probably for the best. She wasn't sure if she could keep down the steak she had already eaten.

✲✲✲

Too much Chicken Oscar and ever-building concern irritated Erin's stomach as she walked with Scott and Chris across Kimberley Street. The night had been pleasant enough: good food, good company, a nice after-dinner visit with Ben and his family. Chris seemed to enjoy herself, especially when she and Benny pushed Tonka trucks around the dry macaroni "quarry" Benny had built in front of the crackling fire. Chris had seemed delighted as Benny's Tonka dump truck hauled Sonya's bulk variety macaroni from Chris's "loading dock" to the "quarry pile." As the trucks hauled their loads, Benny carefully explained the inner workings of his enterprise with four-year-old precision. Their laughter reached the depths of Erin's soul, warming her, quieting her. But now, as she climbed the porch steps and walked through her front door, her soul trembled with dread.

Chris stopped smiling over an hour ago. Her face had grown pale, somber, her eyes heavy and dull.

And Scott. Had he said one word to Chris the entire night? Maybe, but Erin didn't think so.

Inside the house, Scott finally spoke. "Good night, Chris," he said without looking at her. He pulled Erin toward the stairs.

Hesitating, Erin turned to Chris, who had walked into the kitchen to pour herself a glass of water.

"Good night, you guys," Chris said softly.

Scott again pulled; Erin said to Chris, "Are you coming upstairs?"

Turning to lean against the kitchen counter, Chris gave no reply, didn't even glance up.

Scott pulled—Erin gave him a harsh glare. Then softened. "Go on up," she said, her voice almost a whisper, "I'll be right there."

He stood and looked at her.

"Go on." She tried to smile as she leaned in to give him a quick kiss.

Scott turned and stomped up the stairs.

The tension in Erin's stomach burned. She took a few steps closer to Chris. "How was your steak?"

Chris stared at the water glass in her hand, then mumbled, "Fine."

Erin moved another step closer. "I'm, um . . . I'm sorry about not telling you about Alaina. I didn't think it was important. Not at the time."

Chris's teeth clenched; the muscles in her jaw rippled until she pressed open her lips to speak. "It's okay."

"I can't wait until they get the gym finished."

"Erin . . ."

She waited. Barely breathed.

"Please don't hate me."

A laugh bubbled up inside her. She didn't let it surface.

"But . . ."

She waited.

"I'm sorry, Rinny, but I need a drink."

The words fell over Erin with the weight of an iron blanket. A part of her wanted to lash out in anger. The rest of her wanted to burst into tears. She drew in a deep, silent breath, then asked, simply, "Why?"

Chris stared at the floor. "I can't take this."

"Take what?"

Her gaze lifted for a second, then again fell to the floor.

"It's late. Aren't you tired? Why don't we just go on upstairs? Get a good night's sleep."

Chris turned to look out the darkened kitchen window.

Erin bit into her lower lip. *Take it slow* . . . seeped into her thoughts. *Lord, help me.* "Hey. Chris, don't worry about Scott. He's just a little overprotective of me."

Chris quickly turned around. "Don't say that, Rin. He's great. This . . . This isn't about Scott."

"He's being so stupid."

"Stop it. No he's not. Don't say that. He loves you."

The anger in Chris's eyes surprised Erin. Almost frightened her. She didn't know what to say.

Chris pushed away from the counter and emptied her water glass into the sink.

A sudden thought startled Erin. *Go with her, or she'll go alone. If she goes alone, she may never return.* Fear coursed through her. *Oh, Lord God, help me to know what to do!*

Another thought startled her even more. Shocked her. Then warmed her. She raised her head, tilted it a bit, then smirked at Chris. "Okay. We can go. I know a quiet place. And, um . . . maybe you'll let me beat you at a game of pool? I haven't played in years."

Chris quickly looked at Erin; her mouth fell open as her eyes narrowed.

"Give me one minute to go up and talk to my loving husband." Another smirk. "Wait right here. You hear me?"

Chris slowly nodded.

Erin hurried upstairs, then sat on the bed beside Scott. She looked him in the eye. "Sweetheart," she said softly, "I need you to trust me. I know you're upset."

"I'm not upset." He stared straight ahead.

"Good. Please go on to bed. Chris and I are going out for a little bit. We'll be back in about an hour. All right?"

"I'm not upset."

She let her smile show. "I love you when you fib." She leaned in to kiss his cheek.

"One hour, right?"

"One hour."

"All right. Take my car."

She turned his face to kiss his lips. "Please go to bed, baby. You've got a big day tomorrow."

"I always have big days."

"I know you do, my poor, sweet baby." She kissed him again, then eased herself off the bed. "I'll be home soon." She headed for the stairs.

"Be careful, love."

Erin heard the words and turned to say, "I will," before descending the stairs. She said, "Ready?" to Chris, then grabbed her jacket, snatched the keys to Scott's Mustang, and drove Chris to a place called Dandy's Northtowne Pub and Grille.

✯✯✯

"Now this is a wild-n-crazy place."

"Well, it's probably not as happenin' as Barney's, but it'll have to do."

A laugh. "It's fine, Rin. Besides." Chris leaned over to gently pat Erin's stomach. "We can't have you takin' in too much excitement."

Erin glared playfully at her.

Of all the bars in the area, Erin knew Dandy's was all right. The cooks threw together a tempting burger and served a variety of three-egg omelets any time day or night. Erin could get a fresh-brewed cup of decaf coffee, a frosty mug of root beer, or a tall iced tea with lemon.

And tonight, Chris could get a shot of Jack Daniel's.

Sipping her Seven-Up, Erin tried not to watch as Chris downed her first shot of the whiskey, signaled for another, then signaled for yet another as the second shot went down. After the third shot, Chris struggled to swallow. *Well, serves you right,* Erin thought as she stirred the ice in her glass with her finger.

Chris thanked the bartender, slipped him a twenty-dollar bill, then picked up her bottle of Coors Light and drew in a long drink.

Their eyes met for a second. Chris swallowed the beer, then gave Erin a small, embarrassed smile.

Erin returned it.

They begged five dollars' worth of quarters from the bartender, claimed a vacant pool table, took off their jackets, then chose their cue sticks and chalked them up.

Laughing, small-talking, kidding each other and sipping their drinks, they played game after game. Chris would win, then Erin. Best of three became best of seven. Then best of eleven. Then they stopped keeping score all together.

The bar was full of people talking, laughing, drinking, watching the basketball game; everything played out peacefully, everyone simply hanging out, enjoying the night. Chris and Erin finished another game, saw the weariness in the other's eyes, and decided to call it a night. Close by, at the pool table next to them, three men suddenly roared with laughter at their fellow pool player, who obviously blew an easy shot.

Erin looked, but paid the men no mind. She grabbed her jacket and started to work her way around them toward the front door.

A second later, loud curses exploded around her. From the corner of her eye she saw one man pushing another, then felt the pushed man fall into her. Her feet tangled, and she felt herself flying until everything exploded in sparks and stars, in blinding white light. As she fell, she instinctively wrapped her hands around her belly to protect her precious little one. But then her head smacked against the floor. For a few seconds, she hung in that place where light and dark collide, all breath lost, time and space suspended. A few seconds later, breathing, taking stock, she started to smile.

She heard Chris's frantic voice calling her name, felt Chris's hands gently touching her shoulders, supporting her, pushing the hair out of her eyes. She looked up at Chris and laughed.

"Are you all right? Rinny? Are you okay?"

Seeing the sheer terror in Chris's eyes, the concern, Erin blinked away stars and laughed again. "I think so." The floor was hard, her head throbbed, her dignity had been obliterated, but she wasn't hurt.

"Are you sure?"

She was. "I'm fine, Chris."

"Just stay still a second. Make sure. Catch your breath."

Raucous laughter suddenly ripped through the room. The man who had done the pushing stood beside Erin laughing hysterically at the entire spectacle.

Embarrassed, Erin started to push herself up from the floor, felt a little dizzy, then jumped at the sound of a loud crack, violent curses, shouting. Through her dizziness she tried to look, had to blink to clear her head.

Shouting filled the room. More cursing.

She blinked again, then almost fell back to the floor, her strength ripped away by what she saw.

Dear . . . God! No!

Chris McIntyre was killing the man who had laughed at Erin. On the floor, almost hidden behind him, she held a broken pool stick in her hands, against the man's throat, buried into his throat. The man had turned purple, was gasping, "Help—m–me!"

His friends just stood and gaped. Nobody moved.

Erin staggered forward, staring at Chris, staring into her eyes. The sight terrified her. She stopped and gasped.

Chris in the desert. Khaki-camouflaged booney hat on her head. Such beautiful laughing eyes. Dark, dark brown, reflecting every hint of light. Revealing eyes. Erin could see into Chris's soul, looking into those eyes.

Right now, Erin could see into hell.

Never. Never before. Not even on TV. In a movie. At a game. At a fight. Kids fought all the time in Kimberley Square. Portland's Outer Northeast was gangland. Kids killed each other over there. But never had Erin seen this depth of anger. Rage. Worse than rage. Pure, concentrated fury. Intense hatred. Overpowering, consuming hatred.

Nausea hit her so quickly, she gagged.

Chris was killing the man. She was half his size. Sitting behind him, her knee in his back, the stick buried into his throat—she would kill him. The man had one hand under the stick, pushing it forward just enough to force in gasps of air, his other hand slapped at Chris's face, clawed at her fingers; she held on. Chris was not going to stop until this man was dead.

Erin moved in quickly, knelt beside her, started to speak softly, then more loudly. "Chris? Chris, no! Focus. Let him go. Stop this. Let him go."

Nothing.

The man's bulging eyes rolled toward Erin. "Help—stop—!" he gasped. He cursed and pushed again, clawed, and kicked.

Erin glanced up at the man's friends. They stayed back, watching, gaping.

Panic shot through her as she turned back to Chris. Tiny drops of sweat lined Chris's forehead. Erin lifted her hand and touched the back of Chris's neck. The muscles felt like stone.

Her eyes . . .

Slowly, carefully, Erin lifted her right hand and covered Chris's eyes. Completely.

Instantly. Chris relaxed. Her rage seemed to burn itself out. Erin stared, unbelieving, completely amazed.

The man pushed the stick out of his throat and rolled away, drawing in loud gulps of air between rasping coughs and ragged pants.

Her hand still covering Chris's eyes, Erin glanced up at the bartender, then around the room. "Please," she said. "Nothing's hurt.

It's over." She looked at the man's friends. "We're leaving. Okay? We're leaving." She turned to the man who was rubbing his neck. "You may want to pack some ice on that." She ignored his vicious look, ignored his friend's bursts of laughter. She turned to Chris, moved in close beside her, lowered her voice. "Chris? It's all right. It's okay." She slowly pulled her hand away, then turned Chris's face to look directly into her eyes.

Night and day. East and west. Two extremes—two distant extremes. Rage, such intense hatred, was now complete terror. Confusion. Overwhelming horror.

Blinking deeply, Chris looked at Erin, slowly focused.

"It's all right, Chris."

More blinking. "R–Rinny?"

"It's all right."

Chris looked down at the broken pool stick in her hand. Quickly glanced around the crowded room. And began to tremble. Her shoulders shook so hard Erin rubbed them. All color drained from her face.

"Come on." Erin pulled her up slowly. "Let's go home."

Declining the bartender's offer of assistance, she pushed Chris to the door. Chris dropped the stick as she walked, stumbled, regained her footing, walked. They made it outside.

Darkness, cold, light rain falling. Ten feet from Scott's car, Chris suddenly came alive. With a violent shake, she pulled herself out of Erin's arms and leaned over the hood of the car.

Erin stood there, irritation sweeping through her, concern, overpowering sadness. Her head throbbed. She lifted her hand to Chris's shoulder.

"Leave me alone."

Fine. She walked around to the driver's side of the car, popped the locks, opened the door, and crawled in. She sat, trembling, breathing deeply, waiting for Chris to get in. She gently rubbed her belly, then reached up to pull the hair away from her forehead. She turned on the car's interior light and leaned forward to look into the rearview mirror.

There, on the corner of her forehead, a nice little knot had already formed.

Great.

Chris slowly got into the car. Quietly pulled the door closed. They didn't look at each other or say a word all the way back to Kimberley.

ELEVEN

FIRST OUT OF THE CAR, Chris slammed the door behind her. First up the porch steps, she pushed through the old wooden door so quickly it smacked against the wall. The door's window rattled, but didn't shatter. Grateful for that, Erin slowly followed, hoping Scott was unconscious in bed. She didn't like thinking that way, but right now she didn't like any of her thoughts.

She walked into the house and quietly closed the door behind her. Turned around and looked up, and saw Scott standing directly in front of her, a shocked look on his face. Shock immediately transformed into concern—he must have noticed the knot on Erin's forehead—then into anger. "What happened to you? Are you all right?"

Erin could not keep her exasperation out of her tone. "Yes, darling, I'm fine."

"What's this?" He pushed Erin's hair away from the bruise.

She pulled her head away before he got a good look. "It's nothing, Scott. Please." She looked him in the eye. "It's just a bump. I bumped my head."

His voice climbed an octave. "Bumped your head? How?"

"This isn't important right now. I need to go upstairs and talk to Chris."

"To Chris? I think you need to stay right here and talk to me, Erin. What's going on? What happened? How did you—?"

"Scott." Erin's eyes fell closed as she desperately tried to control the turmoil racing through her. "Please, sweetheart." She reached up and caressed his cheek. "Please . . ."

His jaw clenched as his teeth ground.

"Give me a few minutes. Just a few minutes. I need to talk to Chris. I know you're upset, and that's all right. I don't blame you. But please—"

"Did she hit you?"

Erin's control shattered. "What? No, Scott!"

"Did she push you down? What did she do?"

For a second, eyes pinched shut, Erin felt her own teeth grinding. "Nothing, Scott. Chris did not do anything to me."

"Where did you go? Has she been drinking?"

"Guys."

Startled, Erin quickly looked toward the stairs, saw Chris standing halfway down.

"Please don't do this . . . because of me. I'm out of here, Scott. I'll be gone as soon as I pack my stuff."

"No!" Erin wanted to scream. "Chris?"

"I'm sorry, Rinny. Can't say I didn't try, huh? Scott . . . I'm really sorry." Chris turned and walked back up the stairs.

Erin felt her husband's arms around her and was glad. She would have fallen if he hadn't caught her.

For a long moment they looked at each other.

"Erin . . ."

"I have to talk to her, Scott."

"I know." He moved in close to gently nuzzle her cheek. "Go ahead." He stepped back. "Are you sure you're all right? Let me look into your eyes."

"Just a bump, I promise."

He gazed deeply into her eyes, felt her entire head, palpating, again studied her eyes, then pulled her close and kissed her forehead. After a deep sigh, he whispered, "Go." He released her and moved away.

Erin hurried to the stairs, but stopped to look back.

Scott stood in the middle of the living room, his back to her.

Heartsick, Erin hurried up the stairs and down the hall, then peeked inside the door of Chris's room. She whispered a silent prayer, let out a deep breath, then moved in slowly, cautiously, to sit beside

Chris on the bed. Glancing around the room, her heart slowed with relief. Chris had not started to pack. Yet.

She let another long, deep breath calm her. Slowly turned her head.

Chris sat with her elbows on her knees, her face in her hands. Erin bit into her lower lip to keep from crying.

"Some night, huh."

A laugh spurted out of her. "You could say that."

Chris looked up. "Are you sure you're all right? Are you okay? Really?"

She waited, then told the truth. "No. Right now, I'm horrible."

Chris's eyes widened. "Is it the baby?"

"My baby is fine, Chris. I'm fine. I'm not hurt; I told you that. But I feel terrible right now."

Chris turned her head away. "Don't, Rin. Not about me. I'm not worth it. This shouldn't be about me anyway. You're the one who got hurt."

Erin sighed in frustration.

"Like walking into an ambush."

"It was just an accident."

"I should have seen it coming."

"What? Don't think like that. You couldn't have known. Let's just forget it. Okay?"

Chris studied her hands. Spread her fingers wide. "What a . . . jerk that guy was." She clenched her hands into fists. "What a royal jerk."

"Just forget it. Please? Can you forget it? Forget everything. Let's sleep. I'm exhausted."

"Rin—" Chris tightened; she drew in a deep breath that quivered.

Erin waited; her heart almost slowed to a stop.

"I am so sorry . . . about what happened."

Gently, "You have nothing to be sorry for."

"I wanted to kill him." Chris turned her head to look Erin in the eye. "I wanted to kill 'im dead."

Erin pressed her lips into a smile as she studied Chris's face. Those eyes. Her smile faded. She hated what she saw. Such weariness.

"He really could've hurt you," was a whisper.

"But he didn't. Besides, I never did learn how to fall gracefully." She tried to laugh. "I'm fine. Do you hear me? It's over. Don't think about it anymore. It was just a freak thing."

"I wish I could have stopped it."

"Come on, don't." Erin stood, then turned and offered Chris her hand. "Come on. Jump into your jammies. Let's call it a night." She stood there, hand out, waiting.

Chris looked down, then whispered, "I can't, Rinny. I can't let this go."

"Why? Chris, it was nothing! A stupid accident!"

"Nothing? Erin, you're lucky you weren't really hurt! And I just stood there!"

"What are you talking about? Neither of us saw it coming!"

"No!" Chris jumped up and stepped away. "I heard them arguing. I didn't anticipate it! I let you walk right into it!"

Erin's eyes narrowed in amazement. "What? Will you stop? There was no way to anticipate what was going to happen!"

Turning, Chris struggled for words. "No, Rin. You don't . . . you don't understand. I can't—"

Erin waited.

Chris headed for the closet, grabbed her clothes off the hangers, and started throwing them on the bed. Two sweatshirts. A pair of jeans.

"No. Chris!"

"I can't stay here."

"Yes, you can."

"No, I can't, Erin!"

"Why not? Tell me why!"

"I just can't."

Erin moved in and grabbed Chris's arm. "Don't do this. Please. Not now. Not tonight."

Chris pulled her arm away and stormed to the dresser. She tugged a drawer open. Out came underwear, bras, socks. Everything ended up on the bed.

Tears welled in Erin's eyes. She couldn't stop them.

Chris turned—and froze. The last sock landed on the pile. All was still. She looked at Erin; her mouth fell open.

Erin held her breath and forced away her tears. Silence filled the room. She studied the pile of clothes on the bed. "This can wait until later. Can't it? I'm tired, aren't you?"

Chris reached for her backpack and tossed it on the bed. She started stuffing her clothes into it.

Erin moved closer. "Chris? Please. Don't do this now. Just forget tonight. Forget it ever happened. We're both tired. Let's get a good night's sleep."

Growling, almost laughing, Chris mumbled, "Forget it. Right."

"Come on, leave this! Push it all to the floor!"

"NO!"

Erin's breath caught in her throat as she flinched back.

Chris looked up, the anger in her eyes instantly giving way to regret.

"Please, Chris." Erin couldn't think of anything else to say. She could only repeat the word. "Please."

Chris turned away.

"I need you to stay."

That brought her around quickly. "Don't say that, Erin."

"Why not? It's true."

"No it's not."

"Why won't you let me—?"

"Don't say it!"

"Let me say it, Chris. Please. I want you to stay. I mean it. Stay here at Kimberley. Live here. I love you, Chris, and I don't want you to leave."

Chris almost fell as her knees gave out. She turned quickly and leaned over the dresser, locking her arms out in front of her. Her voice shook. "Erin . . . please, don't say that."

"We're friends. Aren't we? Why can't I tell you how I feel?"

"I don't . . . I don't want to hear this!"

"Why not? Can you tell me why?"

"I don't . . ." A pause. "I don't want you to care about me."

"Why? Please tell me why!"

Silence.

"You did once. Didn't you?"

"We were friends. For a while."

"Then what. I saw your big secret?" Erin winced, instantly regretting her words.

Chris let out a grunt of disgust and pushed herself away from the dresser.

"I'm sorry, Chris. I didn't mean to say that."

"Yes, you did."

"No, I didn't. I'm just tired. And you're frustrating." Erin smiled, hoping Chris would smile too.

Chris did not smile. She grabbed her brush off the dresser and turned to stuff it into her pack.

Desperation rose so quickly inside her, Erin almost choked on it. She took a step closer, slowly working her way around the bed to where Chris stood. "Don't do this! Please, Chris. I can't—"

Chris stopped and looked up.

"I can't let you leave here."

"You're kidding, right?"

"Do you . . . Chris, do you know why I left Ticket? That day? At the Dustoff?"

Chris's eyes flared as she growled the words, "No, Erin. Don't drag that up."

"Do you know why I left Ticket and ran to you? I left a critical patient without care. Did I suddenly get the urge to run a hundred-yard dash? Did I suddenly need the exercise?"

Struggling to breathe, Chris said, "Don't do this to me, Erin! Please."

"Do what? Please tell me what I'm doing that's so wrong!"

"Don't push me!"

"Why am I pushing you?"

"Stop this! Leave me alone!"

"Is that what you really want? Is it? To be alone?"

Chris sat on the bed and closed her eyes.

"You don't want to be alone. I know you. You're afraid to be alone. You won't ever admit it, but I know you are. You are so empty inside. You don't show it. You never will. But I see it. Chris, I see it." Erin had to swallow. "And . . . you know? Chris?" Her voice shook. "Knowing you're so empty inside . . . frightens me more . . . than the thought of what happened to your back."

Chris cursed. Softly. Clearly. Without another word, she stood and turned to continue packing.

Erin stood there, helpless to stop her. Strength gone, hope fading, she slowly turned and started for the door. She stopped after two steps and turned back around. "Listen to me, Chris. Hear me. No matter what you think, you could not have prevented what happened tonight. And you know what else? It's not your fault Teddy died. Or that I was shot. And, no, you could not have stopped that man from killing Travis. I know you don't believe me, and I am so sorry about that. But it's true. Believe me or don't believe me, hear me or don't hear me, it doesn't matter. That's the truth. And you can't change the truth." She softened. "Chris, I want to love you. I mean it. With all my heart. But I can't love you if you won't let me."

Chris stepped around the bed to grab a sock that had fallen. When she stuffed it in the backpack, she zipped the pack up and lowered it to the floor. She glared at Erin. "You don't even know me. You know nothing about me. And you don't want to know. I don't *want* you to know. It was a mistake for me to come here."

Erin gave voice to a sudden thought. "You think something's going to happen to me, don't you? That's it, isn't it? You're afraid to care about me. You're afraid . . . because you think something might happen to me!"

Chris's face softened. "Erin, come on."

"No, listen to me! Nothing is going to happen to me! You won't lose me! And I don't want to lose you!"

Another trembling glare. Erin knew the walls were up, and high. But she never expected the words, "Just like tonight, huh."

Her eyes closed. Her head throbbed. What could she say? It was just a "freak" thing?

Chris turned away. "Thanks for everything. I mean it. Thank Sonya for me too. And tell Scott . . . tell Scott I'm sorry. "

"So you're leaving? Just like that?"

"It's better this way."

"For who? You? What about me?"

"What about you."

Astonishment swept through her. "What about our trip? I thought we were supposed to go back together. What about that?"

"Sorry."

"Sorry? That's it?" Patience lost, Erin moved toward Chris. Too fast. Too close. "Look at me!" She grabbed Chris's arm and tried to turn her.

Chris turned. But the instant Erin touched her, she threw out her arm to break Erin's grip. The back of her hand hit the bruise on the side of Erin's forehead.

Erin fell away, stunned by the pain, tears flooding her eyes. She turned and stumbled toward the door. She closed her eyes for a second, then said, trembling, "If you're leaving . . . tonight . . . alone . . . be careful. And this time? Please? At least say good-bye."

She left the room without looking back.

★★★

AGONY COURSED THOUGH HER. HER own words, spoken out of rage, out of fear, had inflicted pain. She didn't care. She looked up. Scott stood in front of her in the hallway, his eyes burning with emotion.

Sudden loud crashes startled her, violent curses, things hitting the wall in Chris's room. Stepping forward, Scott's eyes narrowed. Erin put both hands on his chest, then gently pushed him backward into their bedroom. "Let her be," she said softly. "Just let her be."

She pushed him back the entire way to their bed; they both sat down, waiting, listening.

Scott circled his arm around her shoulders. She leaned into his warmth, then melted into his embrace. Closed her eyes. Ignored the vicious sounds still coming from the next room. Ignored the person making those sounds. She had failed. There was nothing more she could do. Weary to her soul, all she wanted to do was sleep.

She wanted to weep, but tears wouldn't fall. She wanted to pray. She couldn't force two words together in her heart. She felt Scott's tension, heard the anger in his breaths. She sat there, in his arms, and waited.

$$\star\star\star$$

EVERYTHING LAY ON THE FLOOR. Her clothes. Her backpack. Two drawers were missing from the dresser. She spotted them by the door. One was shattered. The wall above them sported nasty gashes.

Did she do this?

She stood there, breathing hard, trembling, heart thumping; sweat dripped down her cheek.

She did this.

She hit Erin.

She hurt Erin. Again.

She fell to the floor and wept uncontrollably.

$$\star\star\star$$

TEN MINUTES SHE LAY THERE. Too long. She should have been long gone by now. She slowly pushed herself up. Her shoulder felt sore. Stiff. Too long on the hard floor. Her head reeled. Exhaustion flooded her. She needed to leave. She wanted to lie back down on the floor, sleep, and never wake up.

She remembered everything. And knew she somehow had to make it down the hall to Erin's room. She had no idea what she would say. She would somehow try to apologize. Try to make things right. Before she left and never came back.

She made it to Erin and Scott's room. The door was open; she didn't look inside. Knocked softly on the door frame. Her heart pounded like a drum. Which was good. It was the only way she could tell for certain she was still alive.

✷✷✷

THE KNOCK WAS SO SOFT, Erin barely heard it. She met her husband's gaze. Scott drew in a long, deep breath. Erin pushed herself out of his arms.

They shared another look.

She tried to smile. "Just . . . another few minutes? Please?"

Scott let out a breath of soft laughter. He leaned over, gently kissed her on her lips, pulled away, barely smiled, then slowly stood and walked to the door.

She couldn't hear what he said to Chris as he passed through the open door, but Chris smiled weakly, then gave him an embarrassed look. Scott headed downstairs; Chris hesitated, looked at Erin, then stepped into the room and closed the door behind her. She leaned against the door and slid all the way down to the floor. She sat there, feet outstretched; her head fell back against the door.

They sat in silence for a while.

Until, just a whisper, "Rin . . . please forgive me."

Erin smiled faintly. She didn't let it fade. She said, simply, "Done."

Chris's eyes softened. "How can you say that?"

"Easy."

"Tell me how."

For a moment, Erin savored what she was about to say. "Because . . . I love you."

Chris closed her eyes and thumped her head against the door. "Why, Rin? Why do you . . . ?"

Erin waited a long while before saying, "Love you?" She looked away and almost laughed. "You know? I don't honestly know."

Chris smiled, though it trembled and seemed to drain what little strength she had left. Her eyes remained closed. She remained quiet.

After a long, uneasy silence, a tear dripped down her cheek. "Rinny, I am so sorry . . . about everything."

Erin spoke the words as gently as she knew how. "You don't ever have to say you're sorry to me, Chris. Don't ever be sorry."

"But I am."

"I know."

"Rin . . . I can't—"

She barely breathed, waiting, desperately trying to stay patient. Desperately trying to ignore her building headache. She barely heard Chris's next whispered words.

"I'm spent, Rinny."

She carefully slid off the bed and lowered herself to the floor, then moved in slowly, as close to Chris as she dared. "Please don't say that. You're just tired. It's all right."

Chris shook her head against the door. "No, Rin. It's over."

All breath slipped from Erin's lungs. She couldn't say a word.

"I just want it all to end."

There were no words. Erin had no reply. And what Chris whispered next almost tore her heart in two.

"I am so ready. I just want . . . to die."

She laughed. The sound of it startled her. But she couldn't stop. She smiled as Chris turned and looked at her, as stunned and startled as Erin was. Erin spoke the words the Lord gave her, to go along with the laugh. Simple words. "Okay, Chris. Tonight, you can die."

Chris's mouth fell open; Erin could tell the woman was not breathing. She smiled and gently reached up to wipe away one of the tears falling down Chris's face.

"Listen to me. Tonight, you can die. It's time." She had to pause; her heart pumped so hard her voice shook.

Chris's whispered word barely left her lips. "What?"

Erin blinked her own tears away. "Chris, you say you're ready to die; I want you to die. I want you to give up your old life, to die to your past. And tonight, right now, start a new life. It's time, Chris. It's time for you to give up the pain and the guilt and the shame, all the bad memories. Give it all up. Give it away. To God."

Chris looked lost. Confused. "Why would He want to help me?"

Erin smiled. "Ahh, Chris. Why? Because He loves you. So very much. He can take your pain; He can change your heart. He can make you a new person."

"No." Chris shook her head. "He wouldn't do that for me."

"He'll do it for whoever asks Him to."

"No!" Chris choked back a sob. "Rinny, He's God! How can I even think of asking Him anything? I'm nothing! I'm less than nothing. I'm hideous to Him!"

Erin stared at Chris. "No! No, you're not! Don't say that! Don't even think that! He *loves* you."

"No." Chris covered her face with her hand.

"Are you saying the Bible is a lie?"

She quickly looked up. "No, Rinny, not at all!"

"Yes, Chris, that's exactly what you're saying. You're saying that God doesn't love you, when the Bible, God's Holy Word, clearly says He does."

A pause. "But how . . . ? No, Rinny. How could He . . . ?"

Erin bit her lip and waited for her thoughts to clear. "He knows you, Chris. He knew you before the beginning of time. He made you; He formed you in your mother's womb."

A weak grunt of disgust. "Then He wasted His time. And mine."

Ignoring the comment, she quickly said, "He allowed us to meet."

Chris blinked.

"I know He loves you because He . . . gave you to me. To love."

Her bottom lip started to shake.

"I've heard you talk about Isabella. I know you love her. And I know you love Raymond. Do you know Raymond is praying for you? Probably right now. It's probably his prayers that are giving me what little strength I have left right now." Erin tried to smile. "Chris, think about the people who love you. Raymond, Sid, Travis, me . . . Why do you think we love you? Why do you think I love you?"

She only shook her head.

"Because there's life inside you that you haven't lived yet. There's hope burning inside of you that you haven't tasted yet. I see that life. I see that hope. And I need to help you find it."

Tears dripped down Chris's face.

"That life, that hope, is God, Christ Jesus His Son. He is Life. He is Hope. He is Truth. And He is Love."

Chris's eyes pinched shut.

"Do you want Him to take your pain?"

A sniff. "He won't take it away."

"I know you don't really believe that; you're just saying that. So let me ask it this way. Do you want to get rid of your pain?"

She let out a desperate breath as her head fell back against the door. "Oh, Rin . . . I've lived with it so long."

"I know you have. And it's time to die to it. Right now. Tonight."

"But how?" She looked at Erin with eyes reflecting pure exhaustion. She struggled to swallow. "It never goes away. I can't keep it away. I see it; it's there . . . constantly."

"I know, Chris. And . . . God knows."

"He doesn't care."

"Yes, He does. He cares more than you will ever know."

"How can He? After everything I've done? After everything that's happened?"

"He's been with you. Through everything you've been through. He has felt your pain. He knows your fear. Chris, He knows. He wants you to trust Him."

Chris blinked deeply, as if she couldn't focus. "How can I trust Him, Rinny?" Her voice broke. "You say He loves me, yet . . . You say He's been with me, but after everything . . ."

"No matter what. No matter what's happened."

"Travis trusted Him, and he's dead. Because of me."

"Chris, I could slap you!" Erin gave her a smile. "Please . . . please, try to understand. I don't know why, we cannot know why things happen as they do. God's ways . . . they're so much higher than our ways. We cannot know His plan, or why things, terrible things, happen. He just asks us to trust Him."

"No . . ."

"Travis trusted God. And he prayed for you; I know he did. He probably prayed that God would use him to reach you. I know Travis loved you. And I know you loved him."

Chris's eyes pinched shut as she cried.

"Please, Chris. I don't know why he was killed. But God didn't take him from you. God wasn't punishing you."

A tiny whisper. "I could've really loved him, Rinny."

Erin fought desperately against her tears. "I know, Chris." She wiped them from her eyes, only to have them flood again. "I know. I'm so sorry." She struggled for words, but there were none.

Chris slowly lifted her head; her dark eyes reached Erin's, focused. Her lips trembled, but no words were spoken.

They sat in silence, weeping, searching each other's eyes. Then Chris slowly leaned forward, closer . . . Erin pulled her in and held her close. "I can't even imagine what you're feeling," she said, "but please hear me. Know it. Feel it. Deep in your heart. From that first day . . . Chris, our friendship always meant so much to me. These last five years, I've missed you."

Chris sobbed against Erin's shoulder.

"But I know, Chris, I'm amazed to know . . . that God loves you so much more than I do. He wants to hold you, closer than I ever could. If you'll let Him."

Seconds played out in heart-wrenching silence. Until the words, "I . . . can't."

"Don't be afraid of Him."

"Rinny, I . . . I don't know how."

"Just let Him in. Like you let me."

"I don't . . . Rinny, I can't. Travis . . ."

Erin begged her Lord for words to say. He didn't disappoint. "He's not lost, Chris. Travis is not lost. He's in heaven. Right now. And he will always love you."

A breath of a whisper. "Oh, Rinny . . . Heaven's for him. And for you."

"For you too, silly."

"No."

"Yes."

"No, Rin! I don't—!" Chris pushed herself away and growled the words, "I don't deserve to go to heaven!"

"You think I do?"

"You never killed a man! You never cursed God!"

"What? Are you kidding? I've never killed anyone, true, but I have never been a saint. I'm a sinner, just like you. I still am! But He forgives."

"Not like me, Rinny."

"Sin is sin, Chris."

"But I've killed two men!"

"Sin—is—sin. And the Lord Jesus' blood covers it *all*."

Chris shivered as if the words electrified her.

"What? What's wrong?"

No reply.

"Chris?"

Still no reply.

"What do you know about Jesus? What have you heard?"

"Nothing, Rin." Chris's face fell hard with anger as she swiped her sleeve across her wet cheeks.

"Nothing? You've never heard about how He died for our sins on the cross?"

"Stop it! Don't say it! Please!" Chris turned her entire body away.

"What? Easy, Chris, it's all right. Please. Tell me what you're thinking."

"I can't."

"Yes, you can. Please."

"I'm too tired to talk about this, Rin."

"Me too, but this can't wait. Not anymore."

"I can't."

"Travis talked to you about God, didn't he?"

Chris leaned her shoulder against the door and pulled her knees up to her chest.

Erin slid a little to her left to be able to see into Chris's face. "What did he tell you? About God."

Chris let out a disgusted grunt. "That He *loves* me."

"What did he tell you about Jesus?"

"That He died."

"That's right. Jesus died on the cross."

"Rinny . . ." The word washed away on a sob. "I can't talk about this."

"Why not? It's all right, whatever you're thinking. Whatever you think you can't say, it's all right. Please, say it."

"Rinny . . ."

"Let me help you. Let the Lord Jesus help you."

Chris's sobs intensified, the anguish tore at Erin's heart. A long moment passed.

"I wanted to know Him . . ."

The words haunted Erin, sounded too much like the voice of Chris's dreams. The little girl's wail. She waited for more, but there was no more. She gently asked, "When, Chris? When you were young?"

"Mrs. Anderson came out to pick me up, to take me to church. Easter Sunday. Dad said I could go."

Erin forced breath into her lungs.

"He said I could go, but he changed his mind. He wouldn't let me go. I was so mad."

She bit into her lower lip.

"Oh, God, Rinny . . . I can't . . . I can't tell you this. Not now. I'm too tired. I can't."

"Please . . ." She slowly, so very gently, reached her hand up and rubbed Chris's shoulder. "Please tell me. Don't keep it in any longer."

Chris turned to look at her; Erin saw pure misery in her eyes. "There was a play," Chris said softly, "That Sunday night. An Easter play. Mrs. Anderson told me it was about Jesus. I really wanted to go. Dad said I could." She turned her face away.

"He changed his mind."

"I was so mad. We really argued about it. I knew I was in trouble as soon as I yelled at him, but I couldn't stop." She sniffed and wiped her face on the shoulder of her shirt.

"He hit you."

A small breath of weary laughter. "I hit *him*." Chris slowly shook her head and blinked her swollen eyes deeply, trying to keep them open. "I was so stupid. I deserved everything I got that night."

"No you did not."

"All I wanted . . . Rin . . . all I wanted was to go to church and see a play . . . about Jesus."

"Oh, Chris . . ."

"Don't, Rinny. It doesn't matter. Not anymore."

"Your life is at stake, Chris! Your eternal soul!"

"Doesn't matter."

"Stop that! It matters to me! When will you see that?"

"It shouldn't, Erin. When will you see that?"

"I do not believe you!"

"All I wanted to do was go see a stupid play! About Jesus!" Chris sniffed deeply. "I wanted to, but it all blew up in my face. I spent a week in the hospital. Ended up in foster care. Dad spent six months in jail. Just because I wanted to see a stupid play!"

Erin's teeth clenched. She had to force herself to calm down. "That was then, Chris."

"I've lived with it all my life."

"So, let it go."

A laugh. "Right. Just let it go. You have no idea how many times I've tried."

"Okay, well, then, live with it. Carry it around like you've been carrying it around for . . . how long? When did this happen?"

Chris's eyes fell closed. "I was fifteen."

The words kicked away Erin's breath. *Dear Lord. Only fifteen . . .*

Sudden movement—Chris started to pull her feet under her so she could stand.

Erin reached out and grabbed her by the shoulders, then pushed her back down to the floor.

"Let me go, Rin. I've gotta get out of here."

"No. You're not going anywhere."

"Let me go, Rinny!" Chris's hands slapped at her.

"I am not letting you go."

Louder now, more desperate, "Stop this, Erin! Please! Let go!"

"No."

"I gotta leave! I can't—!"

"You're not going anywhere."

Chris tried to push away. "Rinny, I can't . . . I can't stay here!"

"You must."

A curse. "Let me go!" Another curse. "Please! I can't—!" Chris struggled and pushed, but Erin would not let go. She fell against Erin's shoulder and sobbed. "Please . . . Rinny . . ."

"Where would you go?"

"Away."

"And do what?"

"End it."

Yes. Erin knew this would be Chris's answer even as she asked the question. Chris was strong, so strong, all these years, holding on, surviving the dreams, the pain. She found reasons to go on, lived to serve others. Pulled people from danger, from the very brink of death; she saved lives, but then, in the name of war and self-defense, she took two lives.

And now, with her grief and her guilt, her shame, her rage, the unbearable pain of remembering, Chris was truly spent. Tonight, she would have to end it, or it would kill her. She would not survive the night unless she opened her heart and let go.

"Please—please—please," Erin said aloud, a prayer to her Lord, "Chris, *you* let go. Let go of everything. Do it right now. Don't wait another second."

"Rinny . . ." A whimper. "Stop this."

"No. Listen to me. Do it. Let go."

A vicious curse. "I can't, Rinny!"

"Ask God to help you. Let yourself trust Him. Just try."

A trembling pause. A breath. "I . . . I just want it to end."

"It will. Reach out to Him. Give it all to Him. Let Him take it. Everything."

"He's too big."

"He loves you."

"I can't."

"I can't do it for you, Chris. If I could, believe me, I would. You have to do this. Let Him love you. Talk to Him. Like you're talking to me."

A sniff. "Will He hear me?" Chris slowly pushed herself out of Erin's arms. "Will He really hear . . . *me*?"

Erin let out a small laugh. "Yes. Absolutely. He'll hear you."

Chris struggled to keep her eyes open, her head up. "Are you sure, Rinny?"

"Yes. He'll hear you. Tell Him what you want Him to do."

A moment passed. A long moment. A long, silent, trembling moment. Almost a full minute. Chris slowly drew in a deep and terribly ragged breath, held it a second, then let it out in a rush with the words, "Oh, please, God! Jesus! Help me!"

She fell forward but Erin caught her, gently guided her in, leaned her back to cradle her like a newborn, a very large newborn. Erin's breath burst out in sobs of gratitude, of relief, of complete exhaustion . . . of pure and simple joy.

TWELVE

TAILBONE SCREAMING IN AGONY, LEGS asleep, head throbbing, eyes burning . . . heart basking in joy . . . Chris sleeping in her arms . . . Erin drew in a deep, full breath and opened herself to the moment, wanting to capture the moment to remember for all time. But still, her tailbone was not going to last much longer.

She crooked her neck once more to look into Chris's face. Out. Completely. Nose running, cheeks red and wet with tears, eyelids swollen, mouth open, breaths deep and steady.

Tailbone.

"Scott?" Not more than a whisper, she hoped her precious husband sat just outside their bedroom door.

The door cracked open an inch.

"Erin?"

He did. Erin smiled.

The door thudded into Chris's back.

"We're sort of blocking things, but I need you in here to help me."

"Are you all right?"

Erin laughed. "Yes, sweetheart, I'm fine. And so's Chris. She's not leaving, if you're still holding out hope."

"Actually, I didn't think she would."

"That's 'cause you're a smart man."

"Not smart enough to figure out how I'm going to get in there with you blocking the door."

"Push us."

"You're kidding."

"No I'm not. We'll slide on the floor. Push the door open."

A laugh.

"I can't move, Scott. Neither can Chris."

"Are you sure you're all right?"

"If you ask me that one more time, you're sleeping on the couch."

"I'll take that as a yes."

Erin laughed.

"All right, hold on."

I am, she thought, smiling, looking down at the load in her arms. *And I'm never letting go. Ever.*

Scott pushed on the door and, sure enough, Chris and Erin slid a few inches across the hardwood floor. Again Erin laughed; it sounded like a childish giggle.

"Almost there."

"This is fun."

"Just don't get a splinter in your behind."

"Always concerned for my safety."

"Well, you are my one and only."

"Oh, darling, you say the sweetest things."

"And you're havin' my baby."

She heard the words just behind her ear, turned, and saw the brown-haired head of her husband poked through the door. "Can you get through?"

"No problemo, señorita."

He appeared to her left, in close, suddenly kissing her earlobe and cheek, gently turning her face so he could kiss her lips. "Mmm. You taste good. Salty. Like a hot pretzel."

"Could you be serious for a second?"

"Hmm. What did you do to her?"

"She sort of did it to herself."

"She's really out."

"Unconscious."

"Yes. We know these things. We're medical professionals."

"Just help me get her up."

Scott gave his wife a smile. "Tell you what, just stay still. I'll get her up. When you're free of her, slide away from the door. I'll carry her to her room."

"Watch your back."

"Lift with the knees, right?"

It took some finagling, but Scott soon lifted Chris into his arms and carried her down the hall to her bed. Erin walked slowly behind them, rubbing her bottom and wincing at the pins and needles electrifying her feet and legs. Adoration for her husband filled her heart as she watched him carry her friend, an unspeakable love she didn't even know she was capable of feeling.

Such love.

Thank You, Lord Jesus, for this beautiful, perfect man. I love him so much. And . . . I love You.

"Watch your step in here. There's a mess."

Understatement. Erin's eyes widened in amazement. Scattered wood from shattered drawers, clothes strewn about, huge gouges on the wall by the door. She looked at Scott sheepishly.

"Nothing a little putty won't fix. Grab the blankets."

Erin quickly pulled the covers back; Scott eased Chris down onto the bed with such gentleness Erin gave him a smile. He centered Chris's head on the pillow, then carefully brushed the hair from her forehead with his fingers. "Wow. She is *really* out."

Erin pulled off Chris's shoes and felt her feet. They were warm. "We should get her jeans off, at least. She'll be more comfortable that way. Her blouse should be all right to sleep in."

With considerate, professional efficiency, a minute later they had her tucked warm and safe under the covers.

Erin gently washed Chris's face with a cool, wet washcloth. Scott picked up the worst of the mess, kicking shards of wood into the corner, out of the way. When both finished their tasks, Erin stood by the bed; Scott moved in to stand beside her. They looked at each other for a second, then at Chris.

"I think she'll be fine," Erin said in a whisper.

"I know she will," Scott whispered in reply. "I know these things. I'm a doctor."

Erin turned to nuzzle his neck, in his tickly spot, just under his ear.

With one sudden, graceful move, Scott swept her up into his arms as she squealed with delight, then carried her out of the room, down the hall, into their bedroom, letting her flip off all lights as they passed. He lowered her ever so gently onto the middle of their bed, stopped to look deeply into her eyes.

"I love you, Doctor Mathis," was barely a whisper.

Scott's reply left Erin breathless; his powerful, passionate kiss flooded her entire universe.

✯✯✯

"SWEETHEART?" JUST A WHISPER. "ARE you awake?"

She let an outgoing breath carry a sleepy hum.

"Sonya's on the phone. Wants to know if you and Chris are up for a visit later."

She forced one eye to peek open.

"Much later." Her husband scrunched his face into a grimace. "I'll tell her maybe. Later."

"Mm-hmm. Thank you, dear."

"Go back to sleep."

"Mmm." And she did.

"Sweetheart?" Just a whisper. "Are you awake?"

Erin let out a gravelly groan. "Didn't you just ask me that?"

"Well, yes. Two hours ago."

Another peek. "What time is it?"

"Eleven-something. Give or take."

She forced both eyes to open. "I should probably get up."

"Nah. It's Saturday, it's raining, and you're entitled. Sleep."

"Is that an order, doctor?"

Scott crossed his arms and leaned against the bedroom door frame. "Do you need me to write a prescription?"

She smiled. "I need to get up."

"What did I just say? No you don't."

"Your daughter is lying on my bladder."

"Oh." Scott winced. "But don't you mean, my son?"

She gave him a smirk. "We'll just have to wait and see, now won't we." She pushed herself up to sit on the bed. "Have you checked on Chris?"

"She's still out."

Erin smiled. Returned from the bathroom. Slept for another hour.

Just after noon, finally up and ready for the day, she peeked in at Chris. Smiled at what she saw. Thanked her Lord for His mercy. And His love. Took a long, hot shower. Ate a late breakfast. Cleaned up her dishes, called her mother, moseyed over to the clinic to cuddle with her husband, supervised his insurance paperwork for a few minutes, then returned, upstairs, to peek in at Chris. Again, she thanked her Lord.

Again, she smiled.

✯✯✯

"AND SHE'S STILL ASLEEP?"

The story had been told completely abridged, condensed into short headlines, yet Sonya seemed to hang on every word. Erin smiled as she bit into one of Sonya's orange-cranberry muffins. Slathered with butter, warmed slightly in the microwave, the confection melted in her mouth.

"She's going to be all right, isn't she?"

Erin swallowed. "Yes. I'm sure of it. We still have some ground to cover, mostly the entire gospel." She smiled. "But I know she's more open now than she's ever been in her life."

"Oh, thank You, Jesus."

Erin smiled. *You can say that again.*

"Do you think she may want to stay for a while longer? Maybe even permanently?"

Erin slowly lifted her glass of milk and drew in a long drink. She swallowed. Then sighed. "I sure hope so, Sonya. I sure hope so."

"We could really use her help when we get the gym finished. It looks like Bettema may not be able to spend time with the kids like she first thought. They're really upping her hours at the airport."

"I can't believe she's getting married."

"Her time with us may be shorter than any of us know."

"You think Mason will take that job in San Diego?"

"Yes, I do. He's a fair-weather lad. Needs sunshine and palm trees."

Reminded Erin of her own fair-weather lad.

"If Christina wants to stay, Erin, she has a home here. I want you to know that."

Her eyes flooded with tears. "You have no idea how much that means to me."

"Well, now, I think I do," Sonya said, with a grin and a nod. "But I'm just the messenger here. Benjamin wants her to stay too. Said he'd put her on the payroll just as soon as she gives the word."

Erin's eyes closed as her heart swelled with gratitude.

"We love you too, sweetheart," Sonya said softly, moving closer to grasp Erin's hand in her own.

Unable to speak, Erin leaned in and kissed Sonya Connelly on the cheek.

✯✯✯

SHE COULDN'T HELP STARING. THE sight before her was so tender.

Hours had passed. She stood just inside Chris's room, leaning against the wall, just watching, waiting. She was in no hurry at all.

On the bed, wrapped up in Erin's grandmother's old quilt, Chris slept.

Verses from the Word filtered through Erin's thoughts. She closed her eyes and let them flow. *Peace I leave with you, My peace I give to you* . . . John chapter 14, verse 27. *Rest in the LORD, and wait patiently for Him* . . . Psalm 37, verse 7.

Rest.

Chris was resting. Resting in the peace of God. Literally. After all the years, all the pain, all the nightmares that had fragmented her nights and terrified her heart, Chris slept. She didn't dream. She didn't cry out. She didn't toss in the bed or repeat the word, *No, no, no.*

Since the last time Erin peeked in on her, Chris had rolled over onto her right side; the entire side of her face was buried in the soft pillow. Slow, steady breaths hushed in and out.

I cried to the LORD with my voice, and He heard me from His holy hill. I lay down and slept; I awoke, for the LORD sustained me. I will not be afraid . . . Psalm 3, verses 4–6.

Erin smiled. Basked in gratitude. She slowly pushed herself away from the wall, gave her sleeping friend one last smile, then left the room for her own bed. It was late. Again. She laughed to herself and shook her head. Unwrapped the fleecy robe from around her shoulders, kicked off her slippers, quietly lifted back the covers on her side of her bed, quietly crawled in beside her sleeping husband.

When you lie down, you will not be afraid; Yes, you will lie down and your sleep will be sweet . . . Proverbs chapter 3, verse 24.

She smiled.

Come to Me, all you who labor and are heavy laden, and I will give you rest . . . Matthew 11, verse 28.

Dearest Lord Jesus . . . thank You. Thank You so much.

She snuggled up beside Scott and drifted off to sleep.

✯✯✯

A NOISE WOKE HER. THAT all too familiar sound . . . water flushing. She barely smiled, then felt her husband still snuggled up beside her. Her eyes popped open. She lifted her head to see what time it was. The clock radio on Scott's side of the bed beamed the numbers: 2:57.

Well, well, well. It's about time.

She leaned over to kiss her snoozing hubby on the nose and laughed when he mumbled something incoherent. "Just sleep, my love," she breathed. She heard muted footsteps moving down the hall. Quietly pushed herself out of bed.

Wrapping her robe around her, she shoved her feet into her slippers and padded slowly into the hallway. Darkness surrounded her, but as long as electricity flowed, the city's darkness was never complete. She stopped at Chris's open door and peeked inside. Chris sat on the edge of the bed. She watched her for another second, then whispered, "Hey there, sleepyhead."

Chris looked up. Looked surprised. "Hey."

"Are you . . . ?" Erin couldn't find the word to complete her question.

"I don't know," Chris replied.

Erin stepped into the room. "Are you okay?"

"Rinny?"

"Yes?" She moved another step closer.

"What time is it?"

"Almost three." Mixed in with her concern, she felt laughter building in her heart. "But that's not the question you should be asking."

Through the gray night, she saw confusion on Chris's face.

"You should be asking, 'What *day* is it?'"

A long pause. "Oh, Rinny . . . Please don't tell me . . ."

Erin started to smile. "What."

"Aww, please don't tell me I slept . . ."

"Almost twenty-six hours?"

Chris growled. "I told you not to tell me that."

Erin laughed. "Sorry."

"Well . . ." A long, deep breath. ". . . that would explain why I feel so weird, now wouldn't it." The breath whooshed out. "Is it really Sunday?"

"Saturday wasn't all that exciting anyway. It rained. Sonya stopped by. Nothing major."

"Oh, man." Chris hid her face in her hands.

"How do you feel? Are you okay?" She moved a step closer.

"I feel really stupid right now." Chris uncovered her eyes and slid over on the bed.

Erin sat beside her. They sat for a while in silence.

"How did I . . . ? Rinny? How did I get into bed?"

"Scott carried you."

Chris groaned. "That was *not* what I wanted to hear."

Erin laughed, but kept silent about whom else Scott carried to bed that night.

"And Sonya came over."

"Yep. Brought more muffins. I bet . . ." She turned to look at Chris. "I bet you're just a wee bit hungry."

"I'm just a wee bit . . . embarrassed."

"Don't be. I'm glad you slept so long. You didn't dream or anything."

She seemed to consider that.

"I did have to stop Scott from setting up an IV on you. I didn't think it was necessary."

Chris let out a burst of laughter.

"I'm just kidding."

"I bet the thought did cross his mind."

"Oh, no. Never." But Erin seriously doubted her words.

The silence lingered.

Erin's voice barely broke it. "You have a lifetime of sleep to catch up on. You need the rest."

Chris looked at Erin, her eyes soft. "Why do you put up with me? No. Wait. Don't answer that."

Erin laughed.

"How are *you* feeling?" Chris asked. "How's your head? Does it hurt?"

"Nah. It's okay."

She reached over. "Do you mind?" She gently felt Erin's forehead. Then winced. "Sore?"

"A little."

She pulled her hand away. "Nice little knot."

"Right on top of the other one. The eternal one." Erin rolled her eyes, then hoped Chris didn't see.

Chris reached over again. "Is that what this is?" Her hand gently palpated the entire right side of Erin's head. "Last time I did this, it felt like you packed a softball in there. Yep. It's still there, a little bit. Either that or you just have a lopsided head."

"Hmm. I never thought of that."

Chris lowered her hand. "We could shave your head and find out."

Erin growled, then smiled. "Come on, let's go get some breakfast."

"Aren't you going back to bed?"

"Are you?"

"Um, I don't think so."

"Well, then, neither am I. Besides, I slept most of Saturday too."

"Ahh, now the truth comes out."

And Erin laughed.

✯✯✯

CHRIS SAVORED A SWEET-TANGY ORANGE and cranberry muffin, warm from the microwave and dripping with butter, as Erin fixed them both a cup of Earl Grey tea with a little sugar and cream. The microwave bell dinged. Chris's second muffin was ready.

Erin carried it to the table. "I must have eaten ten of these in the past few days."

"Sure are good." Chris wiped her mouth with a napkin. "Smell good too."

"I bet you could eat ten right now. Aren't you starving?" Erin turned back to the counter to carry over the tea.

"A little."

She carefully placed Chris's mug on the table, then her own beside it. "Did you drink a big glass of water yet?" She sat at the table next to Chris.

"Yes, mum, as soon as I got up."

"Don't want you getting dehydrated."

"You should have another muffin." Chris scooped up her own and took a big bite.

"Oh, I shouldn't. One is plenty for me."

"Don't want you getting emaciated," she said, chewing through a wry grin.

Erin smiled, then made a face. "Somehow, I don't think that will be a problem."

Eating and talking, sipping tea and soaking in the quiet of the early-morning hour, Chris knew Erin would soon want to discuss more serious things. She would want to talk about their fight. About God. Chris tried to stay upbeat, focused on the present moment, yet in her uneasiness, the conversation dragged. Long silences fell between short exchanges of small talk. Finished with breakfast, the silence grew increasingly uncomfortable; Chris grew increasingly uncomfortable. Her breathing became shallow. Intensified. She stared at the last few drops of tea remaining in her mug and desperately wanted to escape.

"You want another cup of tea?"

She looked up and tried to smile. "No. Thanks."

Erin hesitated. Then said, "You want to move over to the couch? Where it's more comfortable?"

After a second, Chris nodded.

She left her mug on the table and moseyed to the living room. Erin turned on the lamps on the end tables at both ends of the couch. The warm glow softened the early-morning chill. Then she reached inside one of the end tables and pulled out a Bible, casually left it out on the end table.

Hugging a throw pillow, pulling one leg up under her, Chris sat on the love seat and let out a deep breath as three words filtered through her thoughts. *Here it comes.*

Erin sat across from her on the couch, then kicked up her feet on the coffee table between them. Slouched comfortably. Looked comfortable.

It was a petty question. But Chris asked it anyway. "Think you're gonna need that?" She used her eyes to point to the Bible.

Erin's face softened. "I'm hoping so."

Silence again fell, lingered; Chris struggled with the moment, with what she knew was to come. She drew in another deep breath. Let it out slowly. "I'm not sure, Erin," she said, forcing strength into her voice, "that I really want to talk right now."

Silent and still, Erin waited.

A nervous laugh spurted through Chris's lips. "Well, I'm not sure about anything right now." She was sure she wanted to crawl into a hole and disappear. Other than that? She had no idea. "I guess, mainly, Erin, I'm not sure about what happened. I mean, like I said, I'm not sure about anything."

Erin waited. Silent. If nothing else, she was patient.

"Ahh, man, Rinny . . ." *Just say something, Chris.* "I am really sorry about going ballistic on you. When was it? Two nights ago? I was completely out of hand. I'm sorry."

"I really wish you'd quit saying that."

"What else am I supposed to say?"

"Do you remember our conversation that night?"

Chris tried to remember it. "I know I hit you."

"Besides that." Erin smiled. It faded quickly. "Do you remember what we talked about after that? On the floor in my room?"

"I think. Some of it, anyway." Chris forced her way back through the swirl of murky thoughts in her brain. She didn't like what she saw. "I know I ran my mouth off way too much."

"Why? Because you told me the truth? Because you told me about your past?"

"The past is better left alone, Rin."

"But yours has never left you alone."

Chris looked up, surprised.

"Has it?"

Erin had a way of laying the truth bare. Chris pressed her lips into a firm line. "Nope, I guess not."

"Until the other night."

Wasn't that true? Just what happened the other night? She studied the fringes of the pillow she hugged close to her chest. "I . . . let it go, huh?"

"Yes, you did. Do you remember what you said?"

Chris sighed deeply. "I, um . . . no, not really."

"You cried out to God. You finally pulled down a few of those walls around your heart, you cried out to God . . . then you fell asleep and slept for twenty-six hours."

Chris smiled. Then laughed.

"How do you feel? Can you tell me?"

There was no other way to describe it. "Weird."

Erin waited.

No, that wasn't true. Another word worked equally well. "Alive."

"Funny you'd say that, because the other night, you actually . . . died."

"Oh, yeah. I remember that." Chris pulled a fuzzy off the pillow and rolled it between her fingers. "You wanted me to die."

"It was your only hope."

"Did I?" She looked at Erin.

"I don't know; you tell me. Do you feel different?"

"I feel . . . weird."

Erin let out a small laugh.

What really did happen that night? "I cried out to God?"

"Yep."

"And He heard me."

Erin gave her a warm smile. "He sure did."

Chris slowly shook her head. "It's too much, Rinny."

"What is?"

"Talking about God. Talking to God."

"He listens. He wants us to talk to Him."

"I know, but how can I? How can someone like me just . . . talk to God?"

Erin sat up in the couch. "He knows what you're thinking. So why wouldn't He want to hear what you have to say?"

Maybe it was time for Chris to lay out a little truth of her own. "I'm . . . nothing, Rinny."

"Not to Him. Not to me, either."

Ouch. "No, Rin, I mean . . . I know we're friends. You put up with me." *Why, I'll never know.* She allowed herself to laugh. Once. Just a breath. "But God doesn't have to put up with me. He has much better things to do."

"See, I'm glad I got this out. Saves me having to get up right now."

Chris watched Erin lean over to the end table and retrieve her Bible. "Don't, Rin."

Erin looked up at her. "Don't what?"

"Look. I know God is love and all that. Okay? He loves a lot of people."

"He just doesn't love you."

"I think He's made that perfectly clear. At least He has to me. Look, Erin, I really don't want to talk about this." Chris started to push herself up from the love seat.

"If you get up, I'm gonna smack you."

She froze. Her eyes bulged.

"If you even think about walking out of this conversation, I'm gonna . . . Well, I don't know what I'm gonna do, but it won't be pretty."

She could only stare.

A faint smile softened Erin's face. "You are so wrong, Chris. That way of thinking died with your past. I know you've been through a lot. But this is a brand-new moment for you, and I'm not gonna let you ruin it."

Chris sighed deeply and slouched back again.

"Okay?"

"Yeah. I guess."

"Fine. So sit there and listen to me. Please. Chris, I'm not kidding. You listen."

What other choice did she have? "All right, I'm listening!"

It took only a second for Erin to find the place in her Bible; she said the words softly, read every word carefully. "'In this the love of God was manifested toward us, that God has sent His only Son into the world, that we might live through Him. In this is love, not that we loved God, but that He loved us.'" She looked at Chris. "His love is not for a privileged few. It's for everyone. You, me . . . for anyone who calls on His name. Just like you did the other night."

Her voice carried every word straight to Chris's soul. God loved us . . . sent His only Son . . . that we might live . . . One word escaped Chris's tangled thoughts. "Jesus."

The word tasted strange on her tongue. Sounded vile to her ears. She couldn't look at Erin. Seconds ticked off in the awkwardness of the moment. Many seconds. Erin stayed quiet.

Just tell her the truth. You owe her that. Lay it out there, and let her decide if she still wants to care.

"He's my problem, Rinny." Too late to turn back now. "All my life, He's been my problem. The reason everything went haywire."

No lightning bolts. No earthquakes. Chris glanced at Erin. Saw in her eyes the struggle to comprehend.

"I mean, don't get me wrong. I know He's the key to knowing God. I know that. But yet . . ."

"You wanted to go to the play."

Chris heard the words. Her heart slammed to a stop.

"You wanted to learn about Jesus, but your dad wouldn't let you. And all the years since, you've been afraid to try again."

She could only stare.

"Am I close?"

She blinked. Let out the breath that had frozen in her lungs. Swallowed. Said, "You, Mrs. Mathis, should be a shrink."

Barely a smile. "Nah. I've got enough to worry about."

Chris had to look away. At the pattern on the curtains. At the fringe on the pillow. "Pretty crazy, huh."

"Not crazy at all. Considering . . ."

"Association anxiety. Toward the most important figure in the universe."

"I'd say you know more about the Lord Jesus than you care to admit."

Chris drew in a deep breath. "Well, I know He's God. That He died for my sins. That He loves me. That He gave me ... you." She turned to meet Erin's gaze. Yet still had to quickly look away. "I just don't understand ... why ..." She growled when the words wouldn't come. "Things could have been so different. I guess I just don't understand why it all went down like it did." Disgust swept through her. "And then, hey. Don't I go and kill someone. Not once, but twice."

"God will forgive any sin."

"Even murder?"

"You did not murder those men, Chris. You killed them because you had to. You saved lives by doing it. Including mine. You defended yourself."

"Yeah, yeah, Rinny. I know. But it doesn't change the fact that two men are dead because of me. I killed them. Maybe it *was* murder. Maybe I didn't have to kill them."

"God will forgive any sin. No matter how we label it."

She shook her head. Enough was enough.

"Jesus looked upon those who were killing Him and said, 'Father, forgive them.' Is your sin worse than theirs?"

Her mouth fell open. "He said that?"

"Yep, it's recorded right here." Erin lifted her Bible for emphasis.

"He died ... ugly too. Man." A shudder tore through her just thinking about it.

"You're one of the few people who may have even an inkling of what He went through before He was crucified."

Chris looked at Erin. Saw dismay on her face. Yet, what she said? Why would she say that?

"I'm sorry, Chris. I shouldn't have—"

"Why would I know what He ...?"

The question hung in the air between them for a second.

"He was beaten too, Chris. Before He was crucified. Pilate found no fault in Him, but he still ordered it. He thought it would satisfy the crowd. Obviously it didn't."

Oh, God ... It wasn't possible.

He was God, wasn't He? Why didn't He stop them? Why did He let them?

But hadn't she heard that? So long ago? Jesus wasn't just crucified, He was beaten and spit upon. Demeaned in every way. Didn't He die ... because He wanted to? Didn't He take it all ... because of love?

Erin's face blurred as tears filled Chris's eyes. Erin was so right. It was time. Right now. After everything, all the mess, all the hurt, all the shame, it was finally time to hear the truth. "Rinny," Chris said as she wiped her eyes, "you'd better tell me. You'd better tell me ... everything." She sniffed. "Please, Rinny. Tell me about ... Jesus."

A long silence fell as Erin opened her Bible. Then she did exactly what Chris asked. She told Chris everything. They talked for over two hours.

Chris soaked in every word, but had a hard time believing. It all seemed too amazing.

But Erin had an answer for that. "You're right, Chris. It is."

"It's too wonderful." Chris slowly shook her head. "How can it be true?"

"It's the only thing in this universe that is."

Chris considered her words. Then looked up and said, "Tell me again, Rinny, please? Tell me about Easter."

"'He is not here; for He is risen, as He said. Come, see the place where the Lord lay.'" Erin paused a moment, seemed to savor the words. "That's what the angel told the women who came to the tomb. They were so sad. They watched their Lord die. They believed in Him. Trusted Him. And now He was dead."

"But why did He have to die?"

"His death gives us life. Remember? He became our sacrifice. For our sins."

"But why did He have to die like that? Why did He let them—?"

"He was beaten and nailed to the cross, and He willingly hung there and died. He allowed them to kill Him . . . because He loved them. Because He loves us. Because He loves you. Chris, He did it all . . . for you."

Too wonderful. Could she even dare to believe it? She closed her eyes.

"He died willingly, completely obeying His Father's will. Even though He never sinned, He paid the price for our sins; He paid the price we should have paid."

Slowly opening her eyes, she thought about that. "Jesus died, but on Easter . . . He was brought back to life again."

"Three days after He died, God reached down and breathed life back into his lungs. And then He took Him by the hand and raised Him to life again. That's when He appeared to Mary."

"And He's alive."

"He's here with us right now."

Too amazing.

"He wants you to trust Him, Chris. He wants so much to love you."

Chris looked at Erin. Knew in her heart, it was time to lay the truth bare. "I think . . . Rinny . . . I think I want to let Him."

Erin's eyes filled with tears. "Tell Him," she said, her voice shaking.

Chris tensed. Did she dare speak even a word to God? To His Son? To Jesus?

"Do you know the first thing the angels said to the women at the tomb? When they saw the stone rolled away and their Lord's body gone?"

She shook her head.

"'Do not be afraid.'"

Sounded easy. She tried. Yet . . . "I can't, Rin." She held her breath to stop the tears. "I'm afraid."

"I know," Erin said, so gently.

"I can't help it. This is too much for me."

"It's okay. Be honest with Him. Tell Him exactly how you feel."

"How can I tell Him what I can't even figure out myself?"

"'Do not be afraid.'"

"Rin, I—"

"'Come, see the place where the Lord lay.'"

"It's not that easy."

"'Come to Me, all you who labor and are heavy laden, and I will give you rest.'"

"Rin."

"You read the words, Chris. I'm not making this up."

"I know."

"Do you want to read them again?"

"No."

"Tell Him. It is easy. It's that easy."

No, it isn't, Rinny! Oh, God . . . help me!

Erin quickly leaned over to the coffee table and grabbed her Bible. Sighing loudly, yet playfully, she plopped the book down on her lap, turned the pages, found the place, turned the book over, plopped it back down on the coffee table in front of Chris, leaned way over to put her finger on the page, and said, "These are Jesus' own words. They come straight from Him. Read."

"Come on, Rin—"

"Read. And hurry. I can't stay this way much longer."

Chris surrendered with a laugh, then leaned forward and read the words Erin pointed to. "'Peace I leave with you, My peace I give to you; not as the world gives do I give to you.'" She paused, staring at the words, then continued reading the words slower, wanting to absorb the sound and feel and meaning of every word. "'Let not your heart be troubled, neither let it be afraid.'"

"Don't be afraid, Chris."

It was too much. She closed her eyes.

"You've been afraid too long."

And started to cry.

"He's here. Just try to tell Him how you feel." Erin left the couch and moved to the love seat to sit beside her. "Tell Him, Chris."

So many tears, all the years, tears mixed with pain, with rage. Yet now, as Chris sobbed, she couldn't force them back, couldn't stem their flow. These weren't tears of misery. These were tears of hope. Maybe, just maybe, this was the truth. If anyone would know, Erin would. The Bible was true. It spoke of Truth. Of Jesus. All He did in love. So that all would believe. And live.

It was time. Too wonderful, too amazing, yet she would believe. She swiped at her tears and slowly whispered the words, "Jesus . . . I want to know You. I don't want to be afraid of You. Please . . . hear me."

Beside her, Erin whispered, "He hears you," as she gently put her hand on Chris's shoulder.

A simple touch, yet warmth spread quickly through her. A simple touch of friendship, of love. *Oh, God, thank You . . . for Rinny . . . for . . . her love. She never gave up on me!*

Such love. Too amazing to believe. Yet, Chris prayed. She didn't know how to pray; she stumbled over words and said nothing for quite a while. But she didn't stop. She tried to give up every deepest, hidden part to Jesus. Tried to give up even the deepest, most horrifying memory she had locked so tightly away. She pulled down every single wall around her heart she had worked so hard to construct. And none of it hurt. None of it seemed crazy. She had hungered for this moment her entire life and didn't even know it. Filled with the moment, overwhelmed by it, she let everything go, gave everything to Jesus.

She heard Erin softly weeping, whispering, praying. Felt the warmth of her touch continue to radiate through her.

God . . . Jesus, please. Forgive me. I've been so stupid thinking You didn't care. Forgive me for everything. Forgive me for hurting Erin, so many times. Thank You for this moment.

The moment swelled. Something expanded inside her, deep inside her, in the deepest reaches of her being, in the darkest, most terrifying places of her soul . . . brilliant light. All through her. A billion rays of the most brilliant, colorful light.

Filled by it, then panicked by it, she jumped up and backed away from the couch. Stopped. Looked at Erin. Couldn't breathe. Couldn't think.

"Chris? What is it?" Erin stood and reached for her. "Are you all right?"

The words garbled in Chris's brain. She grabbed at her shirt, pulled it out, away from her chest, hoping that would release the bind on her lungs, would allow air to enter. It didn't help. Overwhelmed, she ran to the front door, unlocked it, threw it open, and ran outside.

On the porch, the cool morning air stunned her. Then slowly refreshed her. She breathed again and again as her mind slowly started to work. The air tasted so sweet; each breath washed through her. Calmed her. Filled her completely.

A hand touched her shoulder. She heard her name spoken softly, with concern. She turned. Blinked deeply. Slowly started to smile.

Erin looked terrible; her face was splotchy from crying, her eyes swollen with tears, flooded with worry.

"I . . . really . . . don't know what just happened," Chris said, "but . . . I know something definitely just happened."

Erin's smile slowly overtook her entire face.

"I mean . . . whatever just happened, it's for real."

Her smile widened as she nodded.

"Can you tell me? Rinny? Can you tell me exactly what just happened?"

She reached up to wipe her eyes. "Believe what I'm saying to you, Chris. It is for real. All the sin, I mean *all the sin* you've *ever* committed has just been completely forgiven, and completely forgotten. Forever. The very essence of the Lord Jesus Christ, the Son of Almighty God, has moved into your heart and is, right now, at this very second, setting up shop. He's moving in, Chris, and He'll be a permanent resident within you until the day we see Him face-to-face."

Chris gave Erin a long look. Tried to process all she just said. Then said one word. "Okay."

Erin broke into laughter.

"I mean . . . it had to be something like that."

Still she laughed.

"I mean . . ."

She restrained herself long enough to look Chris in the eye.

"I mean, well, I don't know what I mean." Chris started to laugh. "I have no idea why He'd want to do anything for me but . . . I like it."

Erin pulled Chris into a tender embrace. "I like it too, lady," she said, her voice shaking. "I like it too."

THIRTEEN

The long, hot shower steamed up the bathroom mirror. Chris wiped it with a towel, then stared at her reflection.

I'm different. I feel it. I think I still look the same, but I certainly don't feel the same.

She squirted toothpaste on her toothbrush and went to work brushing her teeth. She stopped mid-swish. *Do I look different?* Her hair hung in wet ropes. Steam slowly overtook the mirror. *Too bad.* She continued brushing. *It'd be nice to look different.*

Finished spitting, she wiped her face with the towel and ran it again over the steamy mirror. *Jesus? Am I different? Are You . . . really inside me?* She looked at the mirror, expecting an answer.

It came in the form of the huge smile that burst across her face. *Wow. What was that?*

When she smiled like that, she definitely looked different.

Think I like it. She smiled again. *Thank You so much, Jesus.*

She brushed out her hair, puffed a little powder on her nose and cheeks, then gathered up her things and headed for her room. In a little over an hour, she would walk across the street with Erin and Scott to the Kimberley Street Community Church.

She closed her bedroom door and sat on the bed. Her stomach fluttered with nervousness. *You know I've never been to church, Jesus. Please don't let me mess up. They'll tell me when I should stand and sit and all that, won't they? Oh, I'll need some money . . .* She jumped off the bed and reached for her bag. *How much should I . . . ?*

Calm descended over her like a blanket. She pulled in a deep breath, but held it as pain sliced through her side. Ever-present, yet fading. She let the breath out slowly, then sat again on the bed.

"Jesus . . ." Barely a whisper. "Lord, this feels so weird, just talking to You. But I know You hear me. Thank You." She let her eyes fall closed. "I'm afraid again. No big surprise, huh? But I'm afraid because something always happens. But I'm not going to worry about it. Okay? I'm going to trust You. Please help me trust You. Please don't let anything happen . . . to her. Please, God. If anything happens to her, I don't think . . . well, You know. And please help Scott. I know he's dealing with me being here. I don't want to cause him any grief. Please help everything be all right. Please don't let anything happen. Thank You. I mean it."

Her eyes popped open. "Oh, and, um . . . Lord? I'm only wondering about this because it's all I brought and Erin said it was but . . . is it really okay to wear jeans to church?"

✯✯✯

THANK YOU, FATHER. OH, THANK YOU THANK YOU THANK YOU.

All morning the words rang sweetly through Erin's soul. *And thank You again, Lord Jesus. Thank You so much! I was a fool to doubt You. I knew You wanted me to go to Colorado! I'm witnessing the result of Your faithfulness. Of my own obedience! Even though I doubted. It's too much! Thank You!*

They sat together around the huge dining room table at Ben and Sonya's house, enjoying the afterglow of a grand Sunday afternoon dinner. Ben and Sonya, Andy and Sarah, Amanda and Benny, Bettema and Mason, her boyfriend. Cappy. Isaiah and his wife, Emily. Erin and Scott. And Chris.

Erin watched Chris, had been watching her most of the morning, saw her smiling, then laughing as she talked with Bettema. The laughter captured her entire face, beamed out her eyes like lasers, dimpled her cheeks, exposed silver fillings in her back teeth.

Thank You, Christ Jesus, my Lord and my God.

Erin held her breath. She didn't want to cry. Not again. Even happy tears could sometimes be a pain. Especially with everyone watching. She stood quickly and gathered up a few plates. She would sneak into the kitchen and cry there if she needed to. Then at least no one would know.

It was a good plan. Until Cappy followed her right in, laughed, and handed Erin a tissue.

Standing beside the refrigerator, trying to hide behind it, frantically wiping her eyes and nose, she heard Sonya's voice. "Christina, please tell us all that you'll stay. Be a part of our work here at Kimberley."

Her blood turned cold. She lowered her head, straining to hear Chris's response.

"Got a lot of work yet to do on the gym," she heard Isaiah say. "Sure could use the help."

"I could use another hand in the computer lab," she heard Bettema say.

She heard Chris's voice. "Tee, I don't know the first thing about computers." But what else did she hear in those words? She closed her eyes. *Please, Lord.*

"We'll need a coach for our new team."

Ben's voice. Erin wondered, *What new team?*

His voice again. "Next fall we'll be the home of the Kimberley Angels. City league twelve-and-under girls' basketball. Whaddaya say, Chris?"

Erin could not breathe. Eyes still closed, she reached out blindly and leaned over the counter to steady herself.

The pause lasted forever.

Then, "No. I don't think so. Thanks, everyone. I mean it. I really appreciate it. But I have to go back. I don't belong here."

Erin's heart dropped to the floor; her knees almost buckled. She pinched her eyes shut and forced back a groan. She heard Chris's voice again.

"Not without my rain jacket. Man! I've never seen so much rain. And my skis. I hear Timberline's the best. The lodge sounds awesome. I'll need my clothes, and my books, and . . ." A long pause. "You can open your eyes now, Rinny."

Her eyes flew open. She heard bursts of squelched laughter.

"And you better breathe too. You're looking a little . . . sickly."

Her lips firmed into a restrained grin. She slowly pushed herself away from the counter and turned to look at Chris. "Sickly?"

Everyone stood there, goofy smiles on their faces, holding back their laughter.

"Well . . ." Chris's head tilted.

"Sickly, huh. Hmm. Well, in that case . . . you can do the dishes!" Erin grabbed a hand towel and threw it at Chris's face. "I'm going to read the children a story. How would you like that, Amanda? Benny?"

The Connelly children squealed with joy and ran for their storybooks stuffed inside the wicker basket by the front window.

"Excuse me, please." Glaring playfully at Chris, Erin pushed her way through the crowd, walked purposely toward Ben's recliner, backed herself into it, sat with gusto, then immediately pulled the handle to recline oh-so-comfortably in the big chair. She pulled the giggling children onto her lap, tickled their ribs, then let Benny choose the first book. She began to read with exaggerated dramatic flair.

Behind her, she heard Bettema's voice. "Well, sorry, Chris, but we've gotta go. I've got to get ready for my class at church tonight." And Cappy's voice. "And I've gotta help her." And Mason's voice. "See ya later, Chris! Take care, everyone!"

Erin only laughed, squeezed the little tykes on her lap into two sideways hugs, and continued with their story.

✯✯✯

"TOMORROW? WHY DO YOU HAVE to leave so soon?"

"Chris needs her stuff, Scott. And to check out of her work. The sooner we go, the sooner we'll be home." Erin savored the sound of that last word as she pulled socks out of her bedroom dresser.

"She's gonna stay over with Cappy, right?"

Erin frowned at her husband. "Did you think she was going to stay here?"

"Well . . . no. But I wouldn't put it past you."

She didn't like the feeling zipping through her at that moment. She jammed the socks into her overnight bag, then turned to her dresser to pull out underwear and bras.

"Look. I just don't understand why you have to go back with her. I'm sorry, Erin, but can't she go back alone? Just get her stuff and come back?"

"Sweetheart, come on." After jamming her load into the bag, she glanced up. "Do you hear yourself?"

Scott's face darkened even more. "Yeah. I hear myself." He rolled off the bed and stood beside Erin. "When will you be back?" He reached out to touch her silky pajama top.

Erin allowed herself to be pulled into his embrace. "At least a week."

He pushed her to arm's length, his eyes wide. "A week?"

"Yes, baby. Maybe longer. We're going to finish our trip. Remember what I told you? We're going down the coast, then across through Tahoe."

"You're still going to go through with that? In the middle of winter?"

"We'll be all right. Chris is used to driving in snow." Erin watched the struggle play out in his eyes.

Scott let out a growl, then pulled Erin against him. "I'm not trying to make this difficult for you, Erin, but I just don't understand . . ."

His words faded as Erin started to laugh.

"Oh, man. Did somebody just hit a rewind button? We already did have this conversation, didn't we?"

"Yes, sweetheart, I think we did."

"I *am* trying to make this difficult for you, aren't I? Again."

Erin kissed his cheek, then his earlobe. "I understand, baby." She blew warm breath in his ear. "Really, I do."

"You do? Because I don't."

"I know. It's all right."

"I just get so crazy." He turned his head to look in her eyes. "I worry about you. I miss you when you're gone."

"I know you do. I miss you too."

"Besides, when do I ever get to go anywhere? All I do is work day and night, healing the sick, caring for the injured ... the infirmed ..."

They both laughed, until their eyes fell closed, their lips touched, their hearts melted together.

"I'm sorry, Erin."

"Don't be."

"Please be careful. Promise me."

"I promise."

"Come home quickly. And call me this time."

"I will."

"Promise me."

"I promise."

⭐⭐⭐

"YOU KNOW, THAT WAS A dirty trick. I can't believe they don't have a dishwasher."

Erin held her breath and bit her lower lip to keep from laughing.

"Ben should buy his wife a dishwasher. Every wife needs a dishwasher."

The laughter could not be restrained. She let it out, then turned her head to watch northwestern Oregon pass by as they cruised toward Astoria for a full trip down US Highway 101 and the magnificent Oregon Coast. On the way to Colorado, for the second time in two weeks. But this time, Erin Mathis was having the time of her life.

"Especially with that brood. I think I got dishpan hands. Look how dry they are!"

Another laugh. Two weeks. How could so much happen in only two weeks? She closed her eyes as her heart whispered, *Thank You, Lord Jesus. Thank You so much.*

"Oh, just laugh, lady. Go ahead. Make fun of me." Chris faked a pout.

But just who played the dirty trick on whom? Did Chris realize she had taken years off Erin's life with her little "trick" about leaving? She heard a gentle voice inside her whisper, *Sneaky maybe, but not dirty. Right, Erin?*

Grinning to herself, she answered, *Not exactly, Lord. We did have lasagna with garlic bread. All that burnt-on marinara, all that buttery mess . . .*

In her heart, she heard laughter.

Chris McIntyre was not laughing; that fake pout still worked her bottom lip.

Until the beach. Chris couldn't force that pout to stay put; her face broke into a huge grin that stayed there the entire next hour as they walked the beach and searched for sand dollars and laughed and talked and waded in the surf.

Later that night, in a small motel on the southern Oregon Coast, Erin told Chris about the Bible. Every word inspired and preserved by the Holy Spirit of God. Together they read Genesis chapter one. And John, up to chapter four.

The next night, over a pepperoni and mushroom pizza, Erin told Chris about the Holy Spirit. Our Comforter, our Helper, our Peace. Living as close as our own heart, filling us with the very presence of Jesus Christ, transforming us into the very image of God. Together they read John chapters 14–16. Chris was amazed.

The night after that, in central Utah, Erin told Chris about heaven, about eternity, about opening her mind to the realities of God. The reward for trusting their hearts to Him. For Chris, peace was reward enough. Heaven was simply beyond her wildest imagination.

The next afternoon, Chris steered the Explorer into the San Juan Search and Rescue station's parking lot. One quick last stop to get her gear. And to say good-bye.

They walked through the back door and down the hall toward Sid's office. He met them with hugs and laughter, then summoned all available hands to the main office. Loud, joyous noise filled the room. Chris's face blushed bright pink.

Mack was back. But not for long. They all wanted to know why. Erin leaned against the wall and listened, watched; a bit of sadness tugged at her.

Chris had found peace. And a new work that needed to be done. She would help out at an inner-city community center, and be close to some old and very dear friends.

Carla Crawley almost started to cry on the spot. She threw her arms around Chris, slapped a huge hug on her, and said, "We'll miss you, Chris. We surely will."

Chris glanced at Erin, appeared to grimace, then returned Carla's hug.

"You know she's right, don't you?" Liz Caswell said as she stepped closer to Chris. "We're gonna miss you around here."

Chris's eyes filled with tears. "I'm gonna miss you all too."

"Keep in touch, you hear me, girl?" Liz pulled Chris into a close hug.

"I will. I promise."

"We haven't finished our game yet. To five hundred, remember?"

Over Liz's shoulder, Chris looked at Erin. "Come on up to Portland. I know the perfect place where we can play."

Liz pulled away. "I may just have to do that. One of these days."

★★★

ERIN AGAIN HELD ON FOR dear life. Chris maneuvered her Explorer up the road leading straight for the mountain. The truck bucked and slipped sideways in the snow; Erin held her breath most of the way.

"Guess we should've chained up, huh."

"I thought we were forgetting something." Erin's voice shook just a bit. "I can't believe you made this trip every day!"

"Yeah." Chris flashed her a grin. "I'm gonna miss it!" She downshifted and spun the Explorer more straight ahead than sideways.

"Hope you're hungry, Rinny. Last time Raymond brought steaks, he also brought six different kinds of salads, French bread, a case of Pepsi, and three pies his wife baked."

Erin smiled. She was hungry. "He really looks out for you—" The words abruptly ended when her teeth smacked together. "Do you have to hit all the bumps?"

"Just the big ones," came the reply.

How could she travel this every day? Erin wondered. *Hah. What will her commute be like now? Down the stairs and across the street?*

"Yeah, Raymond's the best. His wife too. Once we build a fire, you can clean some potatoes while I fire up the barbeque. Sound like a plan?"

"Sounds like a great plan." She smiled at Chris as the Explorer cleared the last hundred meters to the clearing at Chris's cabin. She laughed. "I can't believe he's closing the diner to—!" The words stuck in her throat—she choked on a gasp of horror.

Deep, raw, unimaginable horror. Before them, complete and utter destruction.

A tornado passed through? Erin blinked. The pile of firewood on the front porch lay scattered everywhere. Chris's camping gear? A tent, a sleeping bag, a Coleman camp stove—everything Chris kept in the small storage shed beside the cabin—broken, torn, smashed, scattered.

The Explorer rolled to a stop, then started drifting backward before Chris stomped on the brake. She sat, brake to the floor, staring, gaping.

They slowly forced themselves out of the truck, then very cautiously moved closer to the cabin. Chris's face was filled with horror. "Who . . . Chris, who would do this?"

Her voice was hollow. "I don't know."

"Should we . . . should we call someone? The police?"

Chris didn't seem to hear. She gazed at her ruined camping gear, then slowly moved toward the stairs. Almost stumbled. Climbed the few stairs in slow motion.

Erin followed; Chris pushed the door of the cabin open and let out a soft groan. Erin looked over Chris's shoulder. Whatever destroyed the outside of the cabin completely destroyed the inside. Everything lay in ruins.

Chris walked inside. Erin forced herself to follow. Slowly, she reached up to lay a hand on Chris's shoulder. "Why . . . ? Why would anyone . . . ?"

Chris moved forward, staring, her face reflecting heartbreaking misery.

The windows were gone; a cold breeze blew in across shredded curtains. Her couch had been pulled away from the wall and slashed, the pillows obliterated, fabric ripped to shreds. Her coffee table lay on its side by the bookcase, which still stood, though two of the shelves and everything on them lay strewn across the floor. Smashed. Torn. Broken dishes lay everywhere. Silverware. Her cache door hung precariously by one hinge, the food inside splashed over every wall. Over every flat surface, dust—pancake mix? Everywhere. Her books. Trinkets from Alaska. Her collection of shot glasses. Smashed. Glass glittered on every inch of the floor.

Erin moved closer and again touched Chris's shoulder. "Are you okay?"

Chris pulled away from the touch. "I'm gonna check the bedroom," she said, the words straining her throat.

Chris walked away as Erin slowly turned, surveying the mess. She couldn't move, she couldn't speak; mouth gaping, she stared.

A terrible noise—a struggle—in the bedroom—a scream! "Erin! Run! Ru—!" A gasping cry sliced through the words.

Erin whirled around. A man—a giant of a man—behind Chris, pushed her through the doorway. Blood poured from his nose, dripped off his chin. Rage—pure hatred—contorted his features. He had Chris by the back of her neck. She struggled, reaching behind to pry open his grip. She groaned, "Ruuunnn—" until the man squeezed her neck and the word was cut off by a sharp breath, a face drawn with unbearable agony.

Too stunned to move, Erin stared; Chris signaled with her eyes: *Run!*

Another man. Younger. Behind them. At the bedroom doorway. Moving closer.

Chris screamed, "Rinny! Ru—!" Again cut off by a cry, a gasp.

Two words burst through Erin's mind. *GET HELP!* She turned to run outside, to get to the radio in Chris's truck, but before she reached the door, another hulk of a man stepped in front of her. With a menacing grin, he grabbed her and spun her around, twisting her right arm up behind her shoulder blades. She let out a shriek that was smothered by a cold, clammy hand.

"Shhh . . ." Breath tickled her ear. "Just take it easy . . ."

Her arm separating from her shoulder, the pain turned her knees to liquid. She gasped, tears prickling her eyes.

"Set her down here, Rich."

The youngest man had turned upright one of Chris's bar stools. Pushed toward it, she went, then sat in it, praying the pressure on her shoulder would ease, that soon she would wake up—all of this just a dream.

The young man in front of her dangled a bootlace from one of Chris's Sorrells in Erin's face. "Tie her up with this. If she gets it in her head to run again, she'll have to take the stool with her. Got it?"

The hand came down from her mouth as the hulk behind her laughed and grabbed the lace. He pulled Erin's arms behind her and tied her wrists to the stool back.

She didn't care. She watched Chris. Watched the tall man leading her by the neck toward the couch, his fingers gouging deeply into the sides of her neck, throwing her into the couch, walking around behind it, then grabbing her again . . . Erin watched, nearing hysteria.

Chris's eyes were squeezed shut; her mouth hung open, frozen in a silent scream. She reached up, behind her, struggled to slap away the hand, the grip. Her movement only increased the pressure, the agony.

Erin shivered, felt the bootlace bite into her wrists. Felt her focus funnel down to only . . . Chris. So lean and strong. The man's huge hand gripped so severely, his fingers grinding, gouging deeply into Chris's neck muscles. Erin's medical training kicked in. Three layers of muscle protect nerve cords leading to the cervical plexus, nerves leading to arms, hands, fingers, the phrenic nerve leading to the diaphragm—*suffocation*—muscles protect cervical vertebrae—*paralysis* . . . He would paralyze her! He would kill her!

"Nooo!" The word wrenched Erin's throat. "No! Please, stop!" She met the younger man's eyes. "Make him stop! Please!" She looked back at Chris, saw her struggling to push herself up from the couch.

The man narrowed his eyes Chris's direction. "Go on, Del. Let her up."

"Aww, come on, Matty! Let me kill her. She almost broke my nose!"

"Not yet. Soon."

Hope and terror collided; Erin's stomach lurched.

The man released Chris with a rage of protest and one last vicious squeeze. Cursing, he leaned against the wall behind the couch, then pulled his arm up and swiped at the blood under his nose with the sleeve of his jacket. Another curse. He lit a cigarette.

Erin's eyes fixed on Chris. The men watched her as well. She pushed herself up from the couch just enough to sit. Head down, eyes closed, she slowly lifted a trembling hand to rub the back of her neck.

Erin's voice, her one word, shook. "Chris?"

"No, no. Please. Just be quiet now." The younger man turned to stand between Erin and Chris, his eyes taking in every bit of Erin's face and chest. "Just be quiet."

Erin glared at him.

"Is she secure, Rich?"

Another tug on the bootlace. "Yep. As tight as I can make it."

"Leave her alone," came from across the room, Chris's breathless voice.

"Chris?" Erin leaned her head around the younger man, trying to see.

He stepped closer, blocking her view. "Shhh ... " He gazed at Erin's face. His eyes softened. His hand reached up to touch her hair. "Hmm. So pretty."

Erin pulled her head back.

From across the room—a sudden burst—Chris shouting, "Don't touch her!" She jumped up from the couch, but the tall man yanked her back down. Erin's teeth clenched. Her heart hammered her chest.

"Now, now." The man in front of Erin gave her a smile, then slowly lowered his hand. "Let's all just calm down a minute. Del, let 'er go. Let's all get to know each other first." He finally backed up a few steps, then turned to Chris.

Erin glanced at her, then closed her eyes, struggling against the rope around her wrists, the ache in her shoulder, the panic in her belly. Silent screams of prayer ripped through her soul.

"Of course, we were expecting *Chris* ..." The young man spun again to face Erin. "But we weren't expecting you. How nice of you to join us."

She looked at him, felt her upper lip quiver as her teeth clenched. "And you are ... ?"

She only glared.

"Come on now, don't be shy."

She forced her teeth to part. A small breath. "Erin."

"Erin? Okay. Nice to meet you, Erin. Welcome to our little homecoming party." Quiet laugher filtered out of the three men. "Me?" The man's blue eyes widened. "I'm Matt. Behind you is Rich. Behind *Chris*—" he spoke the name as if it tasted vile on his tongue—"is Del. Say hello, gentlemen."

A grumble from Del. Another quiet laugh from Rich.

Erin again had to force her teeth to part. Matt reached up to run the back of his fingers down her cheek. She pulled her head away before he could touch her.

He laughed, then turned and crossed the cabin to sit in Chris's glider rocker, the only piece of furniture in the cabin that hadn't been damaged in some way. He made himself comfortable. "We are so pleased to finally meet you . . . *Chris.*"

Erin shuddered. Fear was fading. Replacing it, pure rage. She watched Chris, never took her eyes off her.

Matt rocked in the chair and glared at Chris. He spoke to her as if she was a filthy, worthless creature. "Christina McIntyre. Big hero. Kills the bad guy. Saves the day."

Erin needed to see Chris's eyes, but Chris's head hung too low. *Please, dear Lord, put an end to this. Please help us . . . protect us.*

Chris started to lift her head, but stopped. She raised her eyes to look at the man sitting in front of her, rocking. She said nothing.

The man spoke again, the man named Matt. "Don't you know who we are, Chris? Haven't you figured it out yet?"

She lowered her eyes and blinked deeply. Erin heard a faint, "No."

"My brother didn't tell you about us? About how we were going to meet him? At the cabin?"

Erin flinched as sudden awareness, then a flood of terror, poured into Chris's eyes.

"Yes, *Christina*, the man you killed was my brother."

And the man behind Chris jumped forward and grabbed her again, his fingers crushing the back of her neck.

Chris melted into the pain. She tried to lift her hands but now seemed unable to reach above her shoulders.

Erin convulsed with empathy. She started to scream out, to beg the man, but sobs choked her words, her air, then a hand suddenly covered her mouth, pinched her nose shut. Panic bolted through her.

"You SHUT UP!" Matt stood and pointed his finger at Erin. "I might let you go, if you shut up and do what you're told."

Rich spoke up. "You sure, Matty? I can take care of her right now."

Erin pushed her head back only to feel it pushed forward. Nothing to breathe, nowhere to go, panic reached the farthest corners of her being—she heard Chris scream, "Nooo! Don't—!"

"All right!" Matt shouted, "Guys, not yet. Let 'em, go."

Neither man made any effort to comply.

"Do it! Now!" Matt's face tinted pink. "Let them go!"

His voice filled Erin with . . . *hope?* Slowly, Rich was first to obey. His hand came down. Erin coughed and gulped in the air.

"Del! Not yet, man! LET HER GO!"

Del flicked his cigarette into the corner of the room, then leaned over Chris's struggling form and said, loud enough for Erin to hear, "He was my best friend, Chris. You killed my *best friend.*" With one final clench, he released her.

Erin sat completely paralyzed. Barely breathing, she couldn't think or move.

Facedown on the ruined couch, Chris did not move. Erin wanted to scream her name, to run over and help her. She pulled and twisted her wrists, frantically trying to break free. She couldn't move.

Matt walked over to where the coffee table lay on its side by the bookshelf. Reaching around it, he pulled out a big book from the bottom shelf. Chris's scrapbook. He crossed the room and sat again in the rocker, crossed his legs to hold the book in his lap, then slowly, casually, opened the book and browsed through the pages.

Del lit another cigarette.

Chris moved her hand.

Erin's heart resumed its scream. *Please! Chris! Come on . . . you're doing it! Push up! Move. Please, dear God, help her. Please help her!*

Chris moved. Slowly, agonizingly slow, she pushed herself up. Sitting in the mess of her couch, she trembled and pulled air in through a mouth that hung open. Was blinded by eyelids she could not force up. Sitting. A small cough. Nothing else.

Tears dripped down Erin's cheeks. She closed her eyes and they poured, heavy and quick. She blinked them away. Was repulsed to hear Del's voice.

A low growl. He leaned over the couch and blew cigarette smoke directly into Chris's right ear. "I'm gonna break your puny neck, Chris. You'll be dead before I throw you to the floor."

"Now, now," Matt said lightly as he leafed through the book on his lap. "Not yet, man. Let's talk a little. With our new friends."

Del leaned back against the wall and drew in another long drag of his cigarette.

A thought burst through Erin. *Raymond! He's on his way! Oh, God! Please!*

"So, tell me, Chris McIntyre," Matt said. "How's it feel being a hero?"

Chris didn't move. She still hadn't opened her eyes.

Erin stared at her. Trembled, ached, pleaded, prayed, screamed for her. The bootlace was stretching. Her shoulders ached from pulling. Her wrists were cut and burned like fire. But she could almost slip her right hand through. She glanced at Rich. He watched Chris, oblivious. *Thank You, Lord. Please keep on . . . Lead us out of here.*

"Aww, come on, Chris. Don't have anything to say?" Matt waited for a second. "Come on! You're a hero! Aren't you? You killed the bad guy. It's just too bad you didn't do it . . . before he killed your friend." And he laughed.

Chris opened her eyes.

"Sorry to hear about that. He sounded like such a pillar in this community." Another laugh. "You know, my brother always was a little bit . . . handy with a knife."

All three men laughed heartily. Chris's eyes fell closed. She didn't move.

Matt continued browsing the scrapbook. "Tell me about yourself, Chris. How long have you been working here in the beautiful San Juans?"

Her response was slow. Almost whispered. "Three years."

"What'd you do before that?"

"Look. This is between you and me." Chris leaned forward. "Let her go, and I'll answer your questions."

"Not a chance."

"Let her go! This has nothing to do with her!"

"Maybe not, but that doesn't matter anymore now, does it?" Matt pressed his lips into a smirk.

Chris let out a quiet curse. Erin felt her heart rip apart. "It's okay, Chris," she said softly.

"Shut up over there," came quickly from Matt. "If I want to hear anything from you, I'll let you know."

Erin's teeth ached as she ground them viciously.

"So, Chris, where were we? Ahh, yes. I asked you a question. What did you do before you came to work here in the beautiful San Juans?" Matt again turned his attention to the scrapbook on his lap, turned a page, then discovered the answer to his own question. His foot hit the floor as he sat up suddenly and drew the book closer.

Erin watched him. A thin breath of hope again fluttered through her.

Eyes bulging, Matt stared at the book. At each picture. Slowly. Taking it all in.

Erin knew what was in that scrapbook; she had looked at it herself, just over a week ago.

Del was losing patience. "Come on, Matt. Let's do it and get outta here."

Rich was inclined to agree. "Yeah. Let's have us a little fun—"

"Shut up."

The words were so sudden and pointed, everyone in the room gazed at Matt.

Chris blinked deeply, trying to focus.

Matt said softly, "Army. Fort Sam." He looked up. "You were a medic."

A few seconds passed. Chris said, simply, "Yes."

"Landstuhl. How long were you in Germany?"

Faintly, "Two years."

"And Alaska?"

"Yes."

"How long?"

"Three years."

"And then?"

Chris was silent. She raised her eyes, so slowly, and looked at Erin.

Erin wanted to weep. Chris's eyes were empty, dulled by pain Erin could only imagine. She softened her gaze and tried to give Chris a strengthening look as her heart whispered, *Just hang on, Chris. Try not to be afraid* . . . Suddenly infuriated, she wrenched on the lace pinning her wrists. It stretched a tiny bit more.

"Desert Storm."

Matt's voice was soft, quiet, strangely changed. Erin sensed a faint hint of admiration in his tone.

Chris turned her eyes but not her head to look at him. "Yes."

"Where?"

She seemed to consider her response. "Everywhere."

"You moved a lot?"

"Yes."

"Around Kuwait?"

"More west."

"Hmm. Following . . . ?"

"Hundred and first. Fourth Brigade."

"You were out by Rafha then."

"At the end, yes."

Matt looked at Chris. And almost smiled. "I was there," he said softly. "Well, not actually in the desert. In the gulf, on the USS *Saipan.*" He grunted a laugh, then slowly shook his head. "Twenty thousand Marines, and all we did was float around. Mail and cargo. Mine sweeps. Amphibious rehearsals. Just so old 'Insane' could concentrate his forces."

"He did," Chris said.

"Diversion." The word dripped with disgust.

"Worked like solid gold."

And Del was fed up. "Come on, Matt! This is crazy! Let's do what we came to do!"

Matt looked up with sudden confusion in his eyes.

"Who cares who she is!" Del slammed his fist on the top of the couch. "She killed Wayne!"

Chris's eyes pinched shut.

Matt quickly stood, holding the scrapbook with one hand tightly against his chest. "Shut up, Del! Wayne—!"

Silence. Ear-ringing silence.

Matt glanced at Chris, then at Del, and said, quietly now, "Wayne didn't need to kill that guy."

Rich shouted, "What? Matt? Are you—?"

"Shut up, Rich!" Matt glared at Chris. "That night. Was your friend armed?"

Chris scowled. "Why would he be armed?"

"Did he carry a weapon? Yes or no!"

"We never carry weapons."

"Why were you there? At the cabin, that night."

"I was just checking supplies."

"What does that mean?"

Chris looked down and swallowed hard.

Erin watched, completely breathless.

"Check the radio, blankets, food cache—"

"For what?"

"For whatever!"

"How long would it have taken you?"

Chris lifted her eyes again and frowned.

"How long!"

"Five minutes!"

"And then what?"

"And then nothing."

"What does *that* mean?"

"I would have left," Chris said, raising her voice. "It wasn't like I was going to spend the night or anything."

"So . . . that was it?"

"Yeah. That was it."

"He was there! Why did you barge on in?"

She laughed. Then winced. She lifted her hand to rub her neck, but couldn't, not very far. Obviously frustrated, she blurted, "I didn't know anyone was there."

"How could you not have known?" Matt shouted.

"It's not like he waved a bright orange flag at me! There was no smoke from the stove, no lights, no movement—!"

"Where was his snowmobile?"

"I don't know."

"You didn't see his tracks?"

"Sure, I saw tracks. I just figured—"

"You went right on in."

A growl. "Didn't think to knock."

Del flicked his cigarette away and moved in to lean over the back of the couch.

Erin pulled desperately on the lace around her wrists.

"What'd he do?" Matt said to Chris.

She blinked but said nothing.

"What did he do?"

"What's it matter, Matt?" Rich shouted, moving closer, "She killed him!"

Matt ignored him. Or tried to. He asked Chris again, "What'd he do?"

"He hit me," came with a cold glare.

"How. With his fist?"

"With a piece of firewood."

Erin winced.

"Then what happened?"

"You know? You're a smart Marine. You should've read the police report."

No, Chris . . . hold on. Erin flinched as Del lifted his hand, as the bootlace sliced deeper into her skin.

"Tell me what happened, Chris."

A change. Her name. Spoken with . . . *respect?* Erin's heart soared with hope.

"We waited," Chris said.

"For us."

"Yes."

"Your friend got there first."

Barely a whisper. "Yes."

Matt again sat in the chair, then lowered the scrapbook down to his lap. Slowly, he flipped the next page and studied it.

Rich and Del exchanged an angry glance before Rich shouted, "Matt? What are you doing?"

The young man ignored both of them. Leafed through the pages. "How many combat missions?"

Chris looked up, confusion narrowing her eyes. "Combat missions?"

"Yeah. Combat missions."

Glancing at Erin, Chris swallowed, then looked down. "One."

Matt laughed. "One?"

Chris scowled.

"Now here I thought you saw a lot of action."

"Are we still talking combat? In a war that lasted one hundred hours?"

Matt's eyebrows lifted as he nodded. "Okay. I get your point. So, then, how many other missions did you run?"

"Our total medevac mission count since our arrival at King Fahd in August? Is that what you want to know?"

"Don't you remember?"

"Sixteen. Five stupid accidents, three cases of severe sunburn, three cases of dehydration, two dumb-heads with self-inflicted gun-shot wounds, two cases of severe diarrhea, and one scorpion bite. Does that answer your question?"

Matt let out a burst of laughter. "Are you serious?"

Chris glanced at Erin.

Erin's lips trembled as she tried to smile.

"Did anybody die?" Matt asked.

Chris's teeth clenched for a second. She blinked, but didn't answer.

"Did you lose anyone . . . close to you . . . during the war?"

She pulled in a deep breath. "Yes."

"Really? You actually lost someone you knew?"

Chris gave him a vicious look.

"Who?"

"Our crew chief."

"You lost your crew chief?"

"Isn't that what I said?"

"What was his name?"

"Why do you care?"

Erin bit her lower lip.

Matt's eyes hardened. "Say his name."

Chris lifted her head without revealing the pain it caused. "Edward Theodore Brisbaine. Staff Sergeant. U.S. Army."

Keep it up, Chris, Erin thought, *You're doing it. Just hang in there a little longer.*

Matt was silent; his gaze fell to the floor.

"Teddy," was a whisper as Chris's eyes closed.

Matt returned to the scrapbook, turned the page, and saw a sight that startled him. He turned to Erin. "You were there? Is this you?"

Chris responded before Erin could breathe. "U.S. Army trauma nurse. First Lieutenant Erin Grayson. We were Fourth Brigade's Wild Card. Medevac Huey Twelve-oh-seven. Ticket to Paradise."

Matt stared at Chris, his eyes again wide. "That was your ride?" His voice carried childlike wonder. "You called your Huey 'Ticket to Paradise'?"

"Fitting." Chris gave him a smirk. "Wouldn't you say?"

Del and Rich frowned at each other, ready to see an end to the entire conversation.

"Did you medevac any Marines?" Matt asked.

"Before we moved west, yes," Chris said. "We took a few to the support hospital."

Matt turned to Erin. "Do you remember that?"

"Yes," Erin said quickly. "One of the Marines cried like a baby when Chris stuck him with the IV needle."

Matt glanced at Chris and hesitated a few seconds before laughing. "Do you remember . . . who?"

She swallowed, then lowered her head and slowly lifted her hand to rub the back of her neck. "Couple of dumb-butts from First Division. They were packing a homemade potato launcher with explosives when it went off . . . prematurely." She slowly rubbed her eyes, then lowered her hand, but did not look up.

Matt smiled. Then laughed. Then grew deadly serious. "First Division. They were the ones who took back Khafji."

"With a little help from the Air Force," Chris said.

Matt lifted his hand and started to protest, but stopped. Then shook his head. "Yeah. As long as they were bombing the enemy and not our own guys."

Chris softened her eyes and gave Matt a small smile.

"Were those guys you hauled out . . . hurt bad?" he asked.

"Nah. It was a little bomb."

"How'd your crew chief buy it?"

Chris hesitated, glanced up at Erin, then at Matt. The word shook. "Sniper."

Matt frowned so hard his entire face bore it. "You took fire? When?"

"Second day of the ground war. On our one and only 'combat mission.'"

"How? What happened? Who took him out?"

"She did," Erin said quickly. "Teddy was hit; I was hit—"

Matt turned quickly and looked at her. "You were hit?"

"In the head, yes. Left a serious dent in my Kevlar."

"Are you serious? Who got you out?"

Erin looked at Chris. "She did."

Matt turned. And stared at Chris.

Del was done with it. "Come on, Matty! You're breakin' my heart here!" He leaned over the couch. "Wayne is dead. Remember? He's dead! And this little hero killed him! Now I'm gonna kill her!" He reached down and grabbed Chris again by the neck, his fingers squeezing.

"NO!" Matt jumped out of the rocker. "Del, no!"

"I'll give you a *ticket to paradise*, you little—"

Matt drew a pistol from under his jacket. He aimed it at Del. "Let her go. Del? I mean it!"

Del looked up, surprise flickering in his eyes. "This is what we came to do, Matty."

"No. We're leaving. Let her go."

Del stared for a second, then laughed. And squeezed. Chris fell limp in his grip, her arms hanging from her sides as she barely sat on the edge of the couch.

Erin whimpered and pulled. One quick twist, it would be over; Del would break Chris's neck. Erin looked into his eyes and instantly knew it. "Make him stop, Matt, please!"

Matt turned his gun on Erin, steadied it, pointed it directly into her face.

Erin's heart seized.

"Nooo . . ." came weakly from Chris.

Matt swung the gun back at Del. Pulled the trigger.

Slammed by the percussion, Erin screamed as Del hit the wall and fell backward, gasping, cursing; Chris fell forward to the floor as Rich assaulted Matt with everything he had. Matt was younger, smaller. Rich was enraged. They fought for the gun. Cursed and swore. Fists flew. And connected.

With a ragged cry, the lace tearing into her wrists, Erin pulled herself free and jumped off the stool.

The gun exploded again.

Stunned by the blast, she fell against the bookcase, breath and time suspended. Blinked. Matt was down, bleeding. Rich pushed himself up off the floor, holding the gun. Chris was moving, lifting! The huge couch teetered, then landed on Del, crushing breath out of him in an audible *whoosh*.

Chris fell, then tried to crawl toward the coffee table. She stopped, pointed to the leg of the couch, then fell again. Erin rushed to her as Chris whispered, "Table . . . pull it—"

Erin pushed the coffee table against the bottom of the couch, wedging it under the upended leg as Del shouted violent curses.

Matt was down and bleeding severely from a hole in the middle of his chest. Chris had already moved in beside him. The sight paralyzed Erin.

Arterial bleeding. Matt was going to die.

"Rinny . . . help me!"

Erin blinked, looked at Rich. Standing beside her, he held the gun loosely in his right hand. He stared at Matt, eyes wide with disbelief, mouth gaping with horror.

"Rinny!"

She moved in beside Chris and gently touched her shoulder.

"No, help me!" Chris had grabbed a throw pillow and mashed it into the hole in Matt's chest. "Take it!" Her voice was only a gasp, barely audible over Del's rants and curses.

Erin pushed herself around Chris to Matt's other side and pressed firmly on the ragged pillow. The young man's eyes were wide with terror. Chris had fallen beside him, her face close to his right ear.

Matt coughed and gasped, "Please—help me—I'm—!"

"Don't talk. Be still." Chris spoke directly into his ear.

He tried to turn his head, coughed again. "I'm—I'm sorry, Chris. Please—"

Erin could not breathe.

"My broth—didn't—he didn't have—to kill—"

"Don't! Please!" Chris reached for Matt's hand.

"I'm sorry . . . s—sorry . . . Chris . . ."

Tears flooded Erin's eyes. Blood saturated the pillow; her pressure was having little effect.

"You're . . . gonna die, Matt." Chris's voice shook. "We can't stop it."

"I—I know."

"In Saudi. Did you pray?"

Another cough. A whisper. "Yeah."

"Pray now. Tell God you're sorry. Like you told me. He'll forgive you too."

Oh . . . Lord God . . . swept through Erin's soul as her jaw slowly dropped.

"No . . . time . . ."

"Yes! Matt!" Wincing, Chris reached up and slapped the young man's cheek. His eyes flew open. "He'll hear you! Listen to me! He heard me. Just the other night. He heard me, Matt. Tell Him!"

An anguished pause. "I'm . . . afraid."

"No doubt. So was I. But tell *Him*, not me."

Matt started to weep. But between coughs and jagged breaths, he whimpered the words, "God . . . Jesus . . . hear me. I don't . . . wanna die." Again he coughed. Blood spilled through his lips.

Silence fell through the cabin. Erin saw movement to her left, looked—Del had forced his way out from under the couch and stood holding his left shoulder, blood seeping through his fingers, eyes wide, listening.

Matt whispered, "God . . . I'm sorry."

"Ask Him . . . to forgive you . . . for everything," Chris said into his ear.

"God, please . . . forgive me. I'm s–sorry . . . I mean it, God— please . . . my brother . . . shouldn't have . . . I'm so sorry . . ."

Chris whispered, "He heard you . . ." then collapsed and slowly rolled onto her back, almost unconscious.

"Nooo . . ." slipped through Erin's lips.

A faint hiss. "Thank You, Jesusss . . . Thank you . . . Chrissss . . ." And the young man did not draw in another breath.

"My . . . God."

Erin looked up at Rich, saw the horror, the wonder in his eyes. Saw the gun he still held in his hand. She moved in close to Chris, gently lifted her head and shoulders from the floor, and cradled her. Only then did she glance up at Del. The fury in his eyes chilled her.

"What in the . . . ? Rich? What happened?" he shouted.

Rich struggled for words. His lips shook. "It just—it just went off! We were fighting . . . and it just went off!"

Del let out a savage growl. He reached awkwardly inside his jacket and pulled out his own pistol. Aimed it at Chris. It shook in his hand.

Erin's heart slammed to a stop. She threw herself over Chris, feeling the pressure on her abdomen, terror electrifying her blood. She waited, whimpering, "Please . . ." Praying, *Please . . . dear God.*

"Get away from her," Dell said, his voice low and loud. "Right now. Or I'll kill you both with one shot."

She didn't move. Waited. Trembling. Praying.

"Let's just get out of here, Del," Rich said.

"No."

"Come on! Matt's dead! It's over!"

Erin heard vicious curses. Glanced up, then gasped. Del had turned his gun on Rich. The two men stood face-to-face, each with his gun raised, aimed at the other's head.

"We came here to kill her. That's why we're here!"

"No. It's over, man. Let's just go."

"You wanna go? Go!" Del's face hardened into stone. "I should kill you."

Rich blinked. Then slowly lowered his gun.

A long, loud, guttural scream tore out of Del's throat. His gun swung back around.

Erin froze. A bullet from that gun would hit her between her eyes.

A click. Del pulled the hammer back.

Erin waited, trembling, not breathing, not blinking.

"Del, don't do this," Rich said.

Nothing. Silence.

"It's over, man! It's over!"

Silence.

The gun started to shake in Del's hand. Staring at the barrel, Erin saw it slowly raise just an inch. Del pulled the trigger. The gun exploded. Again and again and again.

Erin's eyes pinched shut; she pushed against Chris.

Silence.

Ringing dulled her ears, yet she heard Chris's weak, terrified, "Rinny! Rinny!"

A click. Another click.

Slowly, barely, Erin looked up, peeked up from over Chris. Another click. Del was still pulling the empty gun's trigger.

Silence.

A quiet curse.

Del lowered the gun slowly, then tucked it into the back waistband of his jeans. He gave Erin a long, steady look. Turned to Matt. His stony face cracked. After a long, deep breath, he walked over to his young friend, knelt beside him, grabbed his right hand, then the shoulder of his jacket, and pulled him up and over his own shoulder, in a fireman's carry.

He stared down at Chris. Unblinking. Then, gritting his teeth, he turned and left the cabin.

Rich gave Erin a look. Glanced at Chris. Then turned and left as well.

Chris and Erin lay on the floor of Chris's cabin, trembling, alone.

She waited. Listening. A truck started up in the distance. Its tires crunched down the snow-packed road in front of the cabin. Listening . . . until she couldn't hear it anymore.

They were gone. Still, she waited.

"Rinny . . ."

Her heart melted inside her. "Shhh, it's okay, Chris."

"Are you . . . ? Rin, are you . . . okay?"

"Yes. Just be still."

"You sure? Rinny?" Chris's eyes barely opened.

"Yes, I'm fine. Stay still." With her right hand, Erin gently swept Chris's hair back, examined the sides of Chris's neck.

Swelling . . . already it was awful. Two large, deep, dark red contusions were spreading rapidly, were fiery hot to the touch. She had to move quickly. Gently easing Chris to the floor, she ran for the bedroom, grabbed a towel and two of Chris's fleece blankets, then ran outside for snow and ice.

She packed the snow around the back and sides of Chris's neck, then held her down as she struggled against the shock and the cold. Erin cried as she gently wrapped Chris in the blankets; her tears fell, mixing with blood that dripped from her wrists.

She tried to pray. Lowered herself to lie beside Chris, gently hushed her. "Shhh, don't be afraid. It's over. You're gonna be all right. Shhh . . ."

Shivering overtook both of them. Erin cried. Again tried to pray. Tried to think—

Looked up. Heard something. A truck?

Breath froze in her throat. *Oh, Lord . . . no . . . please!* She waited. Listened. Heard the truck park. Heard the door slam. Heard a voice.

"Chris?"

She blinked.

"Chrissy? Are you all right?"

Raymond!

Erin rubbed her eyes . . . Raymond Gordon stood in the doorway, but he took one look at Erin and rushed back out to his truck. A moment later, she heard his voice working a radio, calling Colorado's State Police, calling . . . for help.

Erin lowered her head against Chris's shoulder and cried.

FOURTEEN

THE WORD WAS SO SOFT and quiet, Erin barely heard it. But she heard it. She leaned in closer over the bed and smiled. "I'm here, Chris. Right here."

The word was repeated. "Rin?"

"I'm here."

Chris blinked open very heavy eyelids. But she couldn't keep them open.

"It's all right. Sleep. You're safe. Can you feel my hand? Please say you can. I'm squeezing it . . . Can you feel it?"

Chris smiled. Feeble, faint, but still a smile. And whispered, "Yeah."

"You can?"

And Chris squeezed. Erin felt it. Her head fell forward in an uncontrollable rush of relief. She closed her eyes and laughed. Only temporary paralysis, no lingering signs of permanent damage.

A breath of a whisper. "Are you okay?"

She blinked back tears. "Yes, Chris, I'm fine."

Chris pushed her eyes open. "What's . . . What's on your . . . ?" She struggled to lift her head, to raise Erin's hand. She tried, but couldn't.

"Hey, don't move yet, okay? It's just a few bandages. It's nothing."

Chris's eyes fell closed. "Major bandages. Pulled yourself free . . ."

Erin barely laughed. "Yeah."

"Oh, Rinny . . . please tell me. Tell me the truth. Are you sure . . . you're okay?"

"Yes. Chris? Right now? I'm great. Being here, hearing your voice . . ."

"Your . . ." Chris's eyes opened. "Your baby?"

"Will have a very exciting story to tell her grandchildren someday."

"You . . . sure?"

"I wasn't hurt, Chris. They didn't hurt me."

Chris finally relaxed. "Thank You, God," was just a whisper. Then she tensed. "Rinny, did you tell . . . Scott?"

"Just relax, will you? Go back to sleep. And don't worry."

"Did you call him?"

"He's on his way here. Ben and Sonya too."

Chris's eyes widened. "I'm sorry, Rinny."

"Don't be. It's all right. Just sleep. I'll be here. I'm not leaving you."

Chris let out a long breath. And relaxed. Her tiny smile remained for quite some time, even after she fell asleep.

✯✯✯

IT SNOWED AS THEY STOOD in the cabin. Tiny flakes blew in on the breeze.

Ben Connelly held up the remnant of a candleholder. "How about this?"

Chris turned her entire body to look. The stupid foam collar around her neck made her feel like the Michelin Man's wife. But she smiled anyway. And said, "Toss it."

She heard a laugh. Turned again. Saw Erin's silly grin.

It was kind of funny. The entire corner of her cabin was piled high with tossed items, junk now, just a pile of junk. Treasures she once valued, now nothing but a mess in the corner. Sid would have his work cut out for him when he brought the district's one-ton truck up later to haul everything out to the dump.

Poor guy.

"Shot glass from Germany?"

Chris slowly turned to look at Sonya. "Toss it."

And Sonya tossed. The glass clanked and *tinked*, but didn't break.

Chris let out a laugh. "Wow. Unbreakable."

"Maybe you should keep it," Erin said, teasing.

"Nah. Don't think I'll need it." Chris enjoyed Erin's smile, but her heart clenched—Scott Mathis definitely was not smiling. Chris looked away. She heard his voice.

"Um, what about this book? *Track of the Cat, An Anna Pigeon Mystery.* It's just a little bit ripped."

She slowly lifted her eyes to look at him.

"It may be . . . fixable." He gave her a lopsided grin.

"Toss it," Chris said, allowing a smile to soften her eyes.

Erin giggled again. Chris turned to find out what was so funny this time.

But Erin was suddenly next to her, lifting her arms, wrapping Chris in a gentle embrace.

Chris didn't know how to give hugs. Or how to receive them. She never had. But she learned quickly. She simply did what Erin did, and held on. Closing her eyes, for that moment, she felt more alive than she had ever felt in her life.

Thank You, Lord Jesus. It's too wonderful. Too amazing. Just . . . like You.

She slowly pulled away. And blushed with embarrassment. And laughed. And swiped at her eyes. "Come on, guys. Let's get out of here. I've got everything I need." She looked at Erin, smiled, and said, "Let's go home."

A Sample from the Sequel to
Wounded Healer by Donna Fleisher:
Warrior's Heart

ONE

WEARINESS REACHED INSIDE HIM, MORE deeply than ever before. He wanted to sleep. Needed to sleep. Yet sleep would not come. He wouldn't allow it. Stupid, irrational fear. He honestly believed if he closed his eyes, he'd wake up to discover his life had all been a dream. A cruel dream. He didn't deserve the life he lived. Didn't deserve the love of the beautiful woman who lay sleeping beside him. If he slept, he'd wake up and it would all be gone.

Tears filled his burning eyes as he lay beside her, facing her, listening to the soft hush of breaths filtering in and out, as soft as baby's breaths. In the orange hint of flickering light reaching her from the single lit candle on the nightstand, she was so beautiful, her face perfect in every way, her lips full and soft. Her hair . . . he gently lifted away a stray strand from her forehead; his breath caught as the backs of his fingers brushed her forehead. Her skin felt warm, soft, so very soft. He wanted to scream, to shout for the entire world to hear, *Oh, Erin! How I love you! Oh, you are my sweet and priceless treasure!*

And the babe she carried, the wonder of life growing with each new heartbeat inside her, cell upon cell forming exponentially. All so perfect.

Scott Mathis didn't deserve such perfection. Such priceless gifts. His eyes pinched shut; a tear fell to his pillow. *Lord, I cannot begin to thank You. You've given me so much, so much that I don't deserve.*

Grace.

So much grace. So much love. Thank You, Father. Lord Jesus, thank You.

Sleep.

No! His eyes flew open.

No. Not now. Later. Maybe. Right now he needed to see her. Hear her soft breaths. Watch her as she slept. The way he watched her that night. No, it was almost morning by the time she returned to bed. So early, that morning. She eased into bed beside him, while he pretended to sleep. She lay quietly, yet he could tell she did not sleep. Not until distant sunlight lit the morning sky. He turned then to face her, to watch her as she slept.

Lord, just when I think I'm starting to understand . . . I can't let it go.

Chris came home drunk that night. Only a few weeks ago. The memory hung in Scott's mind.

Chris returned well after midnight. Unable to sleep, Scott tossed in the bed until heard the car pull away. Heard the front door downstairs close. He strained to hear what his wife and Chris talked about in the living room below.

It wasn't right to listen in on their conversation. But none of it was right. Nothing he felt about Chris McIntyre was right. If he had his way, he'd erase even the memory of the woman from everywhere, everything. He rued the day she was born. The day she met Erin.

"I can't take it, Rinny." Chris's voice, quiet yet clear. She was drunk. "Being here. I don't belong here."

She was so right.

"Where *do* you belong?" Erin had asked. Scott heard nothing more, until Erin said, "You belong here. With me."

Oh, no, she didn't! She didn't then, and she doesn't now. Scott's eyes clenched. *Forgive me, Lord!*

Erin's voice. "Where do you belong, Chris? Tell me."

Chris's response. "Nowhere."

"That's a very lonely place."

"It's safe there," Chris had said. "Safe . . . for you."

What did *that* mean? What did any of it mean?

"Maybe I don't want to be safe." Scott almost leaped out of bed that night, hearing those words from his wife. And on this night, as Erin slept so peacefully beside him, he wanted to rant and scream and kick. Oh, to turn back time!

But then Erin went on. "I'm perfectly safe around you. You saved my life."

He crept to the stairwell then, sat on the upper step, barely breathing, listening.

"I did not. I'm why you got shot."

His heart slammed to a stop at Chris's admission.

"I shoulda listened to Teddy," Chris went on to say, "and left that dumb ring."

Erin never wanted to talk about that day during Operation Desert Storm. No, that wasn't true. Scott didn't wanted to listen to any more. He didn't wanted to know, to fully realize, how close he came to never holding Erin Grayson Mathis in his arms.

But . . . leaving a ring. What ring?

"What would that have done?" Erin had asked.

"Saved Teddy's life."

Was Chris responsible for this man's death?

"It shoulda been me, Rin."

Yes. It should have been.

God, please . . . Tears burned his eyes. *Please forgive me.*

"Don't say that." Erin snapped the words.

"It was stupid."

He stopped listening then. None of it made sense. All of it infuriated him. But then Chris started to cry. Such desperate crying. Then her shout of, "NO!"

Scott gripped the stairwell handle, keeping himself from running down the stairs and throwing Chris out the front door.

"It's okay, Chris . . ."

How many times did Erin say those words that night? It's okay. It's okay, Chris. It's okay, Scott.

No, Erin. It's not. He reached now to lift a stand of hair away from her forehead. *Lord, I'm sorry. But none of this is okay. I'm going to find out what happened. Don't I have that right?*

His hand trembled. He rubbed his eyes.

Lord, I'm gonna find out. And if I don't like what I hear, then, I'm gonna throw Chris out. I don't care what anyone says. If she in any way endangers my wife or my child, I'll drive her back to Colorado myself. His stomach burned. He pinched the bridge of his nose.

A soft hum, soft as the faintest whisper, carried on his wife's gentle breath.

Oh, Erin. God. I'm sorry. Please help me do what's right. Please help me understand.

✶✶✶

IT WAS HIS FIFTH TRIP that morning past the Kimberley Street Community church. This time, instead of trying to see through the brightly-lit basement windows, he looked the other direction, across the street, allowing his drunken gaze to follow each house, each bush and tree, each pathetic white picket fence. Why did people insist on pretty little white fences? Did they actually think a fence like that would stop someone from walking across their precious yard? Would it stop him if he wanted to break into that house?

He slowed the car to a crawl. Grinned. There, parked in front of a white picket fence, sat that shiny dark green Mustang. Even in the dreariness of the steel gray morning, the metallic flakes in the paint sparkled. The rain still beaded up and rolled off. Perfect wax job.

He glanced up at the house. Saw two doors. Must be a duplex. Saw writing on one of the doors, yet couldn't focus his eyes to read. No matter. He didn't care.

What he cared about was behind him. Back in that big, beautiful church. Two women. Soon, very soon, he would walk right in, seeking shelter from the storm. He'd walk right up to them. Say hello. Then finish it. He'd finish everything. Bang, bang, bang.

Soon. Very soon. He was running out of gas. And money. And time.

He stomped the car's accelerator and sped off down the street.

✯✯✯

ALL DAY. HEAVY, DARK CLOUDS. Torrential rain. Sustained winds, violent gusts.

This stinking storm will never end. None of this will end.

Scott's stomach churned; he wished he'd thought to pack Erin's Rolaids in the glove compartment.

Don't be stupid. The day's almost done. Let it go.

Scott jerked the Blazer over to the curb. *If I don't do this now, I'll never be able to let it go. Right here, right now.* He shoved the gear shift into park, reached for the key, and shut down the Blazer's engine. He stared at the dash. Didn't look at his passenger.

A long moment of silence passed between them. When he spoke, his voice sounded gruff to his own ears. He didn't care. "Chris, I'm sorry about this. But we've got to talk."

He didn't look at her. Wasn't surprised when she said nothing.

"I am really sorry. I mean it. I don't want this to come out wrong. I don't want you to think I'm mad, or that I don't like you. I'm not mad. And I'm trying to like you. But we've got to talk. Today was fine, but I can't work with you until I find out what happened ... that day ... when Erin was shot."

Silence fell, thick and black. He almost welcomed the roar of the wind, the smattering of rain beating the truck. Still, he didn't look at her. "I'm trying to deal with all this. About you being here. About all that's happened. I'm trying to understand. But it's too hard. There are too many unanswered questions. Questions Erin can't—or won't—answer. I know she loves you—that the two of you are friends, and that's okay. But I'm her husband and I have a right to know exactly what happened ... so that I can prevent anything else from happening."

Oh, that didn't come out right. Please help me, Lord.

He forced himself to relax. "Chris, I've been praying about this, and I am trying to trust the Lord, but I need to know the truth. And I need to hear it from you."

He tightened his trembling hands into fists and pulled them under his jacket. Then slowly, he turned his head and studied the woman sitting beside him.

Her face had paled to a deathly white. Her eyes stared at the glove box door. Her teeth were clenched.

Scott pushed himself back into his seat and laid his head back. "I'm sorry. Please believe me. I know this is hard for you. And I know ... you know ... this is hard for me." He waited. And was pleased to hear her voice.

"I know. Don't be sorry." The words were soft. Broken.

Erin's words. For a second, Scott wanted to cry. *Help me, Lord. Please. Forgive me. I'm so sorry.*

They sat in silence for another long moment.

He pulled in a deep breath. "So, will you to tell me what happened that day? During the war? I do know ... you saved Erin's life."

He could barely hear her voice over the pelting rain. "I didn't exactly save her life."

Didn't exactly? "All right, well, would she or wouldn't she be here today if it wasn't for what you did that day?"

Another long moment of silence fell. Until, "I guess she wouldn't be here."

"So you did save her life."

"Sort of."

Just what did that mean? Scott cleared his throat to conceal his growl. "Was it ... Chris, did you do something ... that put Erin's life in danger to begin with?"

Another long pause. He didn't think she would respond. He turned his head to look at her.

"Yeah." Her expression didn't change. "Sort of."

He jerked his eyes back to the Blazer's dash. *I knew it. I knew it, Lord!* "What. Did you disobey an order or something?" He waited.

"I guess you could say that."

"You disobeyed a direct order, and Ben wanted to give you a medal?"

"It wasn't like that. There was no direct order."

"Who told you not to do what you did?" Scott glared at Chris.

She swallowed deeply. Seemed to be struggling with her reply. Finally, she said one word. "Erin."

Scott's eyes bulged. "Erin?"

"Yeah. She told me not to . . . do what I did."

"And she was your immediate supervisor, right? She was an officer, and you were an enlisted person. Right?"

Chris's upper lip pulled into a sneer. "Right."

"She gave you an order, and you disobeyed it."

"Yeah. That's exactly what happened."

"What did you do? It involved a ring, didn't it?"

Her eyes slowly found his. Reflected pure misery. "Yes. I went after the ring when I should have just left it."

"What ring?"

"Archie's wedding ring. It was sewn into his boot. They had to cut off his boot to get his foot out of the Humvee."

"And this man, Teddy, who was killed. Who was he?"

"Our crew chief."

"Why did he die?"

Chris looked out her side window. "Because I didn't obey an order."

No. Scott drew in a sharp, deep breath. "Don't lie to me, Chris. I need you to tell me the truth."

She glared at him. "I'm *not* lying to you, Scott. You're asking what happened that day, and I'm telling you."

"No. There's more to it. Ben wanted to give you a—"

"So what! Ben wanted to give me a medal. Ben wasn't there, okay? Only Erin was there. Erin and Teddy and Angelo . . . and Teddy died because I didn't listen. Erin got shot and almost died. Okay? That's the truth. I'm sorry, but that's the truth."

He wanted to punch something. Anything. Chris. *Lord! Help me!* "All right, look." He forced his anger down. "I know Erin loves you. She wouldn't love you if you were careless and caused that man's death. Or if you were the reason she almost died. If it was your fault that Teddy died, Ben wouldn't have wanted to give you a medal. He would have thrown you in the brig. So. Stop wasting my time and tell me the truth."

Chris reached for the Blazer's door handle.

"Don't you dare run out on this! That's what you do. You run. Well, you can't run from this, not if you want to stay here. If you run . . . I'm gonna chase you. You are not leaving Kimberley. Do you understand me, Chris? You can't. I know that. And besides." Scott softened his voice. "If you leave, Erin will kill me. And we can't have that, now can we?" He tried to smile.

Chris didn't turn to see his smile.

"Ahh, Chris. God knows I'm trying to understand. And He knows how sorry I am to be doing this."

"Stop being sorry, Scott. Like you said. You have every right to know the truth."

Long, stormy silence fell over them.

"Why did Ben want to give you a medal?"

Chris's voice barely carried. "Because I killed an Iraqi soldier."

"The one who shot Erin?"

"Yes. I had to kill him before he threw the grenade. It woulda gone boom. Woulda blown up the precious supply route. And all of us. That's why Ben was so determined to give me a Star."

"Why wouldn't you take it?"

A harsh glare. "That's my business, Scott. And none of yours."

He wanted to slap her hard across the mouth. His stomach heaved at the thought. *Oh, Lord, I'm out of control.*

The silence worked to calm him. He only worried about breathing. In and out. Slowly. *Help me, Lord Jesus.*

All that time, Chris said nothing. She stared out her side window.

So many questions bombarded his mind. So many angry, cruel questions. Sorting through them, he was startled to hear Chris's voice.

"What are you afraid of, Scott? Just say it."

He couldn't believe he heard the words.

"You're afraid I'm going to hurt Erin. You know I could never . . . that I would never allow myself to come between you two. That's not what has you so terrified. You're afraid I'm going to hurt her. Or physically, somehow, get her hurt. Aren't you?"

Scott swallowed. He couldn't think of one thing to say.

"Will you believe me if I tell you that's what has me terrified too? I've hurt her so many times before. I don't know why. It just seems like . . . things always happen to those . . . I love." Chris glanced away. "You've just got to know, Scott . . . I would never do anything to hurt Erin. Or your baby. Or . . . you. I'd rather die. I mean it. I would leave . . . before I let anything hurt either of you."

Scott sat in silence, gazing into the darkest, saddest eyes he had ever seen.

"I should just leave here. I am so sorry about all the hurt I've caused you."

"No. No." He couldn't say anything more. His head shook. "No."

"I will leave, Scott. If you want me to leave, I will. In a heartbeat."

"No. Chris, that's not what I want. You can't leave."

"Erin and I will still be friends. We'll always be friends. I'll just go back to Colorado. Get my old job back. I like it there. I have friends there."

Her eyes told a different story.

"I'll leave today. Take me home. I'll be gone in an hour."

"Stop it."

"It's what you want, isn't it? You want me to leave, don't you?"

"No. I don't. You can't leave, Chris."

"Stop saying that. I can leave. And I will."

"No! Stop it!" Scott's fists thumped the steering wheel. "Listen to me, Chris. You've got to understand what I'm saying here! There is no way I want you to leave. You must stay here. And I'm serious. If you leave, I'll track you down myself and haul you right back. Do you hear me?"

Chris looked away.

"This isn't about me wanting you to leave. I don't want you to leave. It's just . . . if you're going to stay, there's a few things I need to understand. There's a few things . . . I need you to understand." He stared at the steering wheel and drew in a deep breath, hesitant to press on. But he had to press on. He had come too far. He needed to finish saying what needed to be said.

"Chris, I love my wife. I'll do anything I have to do to protect her. Anything. You need to understand that. She's accused me several times of being overprotective. Well, I'm sorry about that, but, then again, I'm not. I'd rather be overprotective, if it means saving her from harm."

Chris didn't make a sound.

"She's carrying our child. My child. The last thing in the world Erin needs right now is stress. And this past month . . . I'm sorry, but because of you, this past month, there has been nothing but stress in her life. That must stop." Scott paused to let those three words sink in. "For her own health, and for the safety of our child, at least until she delivers, she must rest and keep up her strength. That means there must not be any more stress. No more trips to Dandy's. No more trips to Colorado. No more sleepless nights or careless, stupid decisions. The other morning, when I saw her at Isaiah's, Chris, that almost made me insane. I know she only went there because of you. If you hadn't gone, she wouldn't have gone either."

Chris's face turned hard. Her eyes cold.

"I'm sorry about all this. But I need you to understand what I'm saying. Do you understand what I'm saying?"

She nodded. Then her lips parted. "Yes."

"You're not still drinking, are you?" He let out an exasperated growl, then briskly rubbed his face, ran his fingers through his hair. "I'm sorry. That was uncalled for."

"No, it wasn't."

"Yes." He sighed deeply as his hands came down. "Yes, it was. I had no right to say that." He stared at the rain coursing down the windshield. Watched the rivers of rain . . . and had no idea what to say next. Maybe there was nothing left to say. "I'm sorry about all of this, Chris."

She rubbed her eyes and nose. Her voice still barely carried. "If you say that one more time, I'm gonna punch you."

He laughed quietly. Then slowly reached for the Blazer's door handle. "Listen. I've got to get some air. Will you give me a few minutes to sort all this out?" Scott sighed, then pushed himself out of the Blazer into the gusty rain. *Lord God . . .* swept through his heart as he walked aimlessly across the street and down the flooded sidewalk. *Lord, I'm so sorry.*

✯ ✯ ✯

ANOTHER SWALLOW. AND ANOTHER. NAUSEA coursed through her belly, but if she stayed calm, maybe she could swallow it down.

Breathe. Just breathe. Oh, Jesus, help me.

Scott had every right. She couldn't blame him at all. She knew this moment would come. And yet, hearing his words, his concern. . .

Breathe. And swallow. She laid her head back. Closed her eyes. Her entire body trembled.

It was all true. Everything he said. He loved his wife. It was that simple. Erin was so fortunate to have such a loving husband. And he was not being overprotective. *No, Lord, not at all. Erin thinks he is, but it's only because she's making excuses . . . for me. Blaming Scott for my mistakes. My carelessness.*

Breathe.

How could I have been so stupid? Oh, Lord, everything he said was true. I disobeyed a direct order. Got Teddy killed. If I just would have left that stupid ring, Erin would not have been shot. . .

Quiet and still, Erin suddenly lay on that bed again, on board the *Mercy*, her forehead cut, her eyes almost swollen shut, her entire face bruised, unconscious. . .

Chris violently rubbed her eyes as they filled with tears. *No, God, please! Lord, I can't . . . I can't take any more of this.*

Tears smeared across her face as she rubbed—she jumped when Scott opened the driver's side door of the Blazer and climbed in. Wiped her face with her wet sleeve and quickly sat up, embarrassment flaming her already burning cheeks.

"Whew! I am so ready for this storm to be done with!" Scott pulled the door closed against the gusts of wind forcing its way inside. "Enough is enough!" He slowly turned to look at her.

Chris felt her lips tremble as she glanced at him and tried to press them into a smile.

His face softened. He looked away. It took a few seconds for him to speak. "I don't know about you, but I don't think I can be of any help to anyone right now. We've been out here long enough anyway. Let's call it a day."

They still had at least three more people on their list to visit. Yet . . . yes. She wouldn't be very helpful either.

Scott started the Blazer and pulled a U-turn back toward Kimberley Street.

Chris sat quietly, not wanting to speak, not wanting to cry any more.

She only breathed. And swallowed down the bile in her throat.

✷ ✷ ✷

HE HAD PAID GOOD MONEY for it. It fit in the palm of his hand, a perfect fit, as if it had been made just for him. Small, black, long smooth barrel. A classic .38 caliber revolver. Six bullets fit into the cylinder. But today he had only put in three. Three bullets were all he needed.

He had come to Portland for this one reason. He told Del he would finish what they had started that night in McIntyre's cabin. But he wasn't a cold-blooded murderer. Sometimes he saw that look in Del's eyes. Del could kill a man. Outright.

If I don't do it, Del will. He will kill both women. Then track me down and kill me too.

But still, here to finish the job, Rich knew he couldn't go through with it. Not outright. He would leave it to chance. Test the fates. If there was a God, he'd leave it in His hands.

He would play a little Russian Roulette. Three bullets in his .38. He would spin the cylinder and pull the trigger. Three times. And see who died.

But what if he killed one of the women, and not the other? No, that wouldn't do. Yet, maybe, if he only killed the one he knew best, Erin, beautiful Erin, then maybe McIntyre would really suffer for killing Wayne. And Matt. She'd know how it felt to have a friend die—

No. Wait. McIntyre did not kill Matt.

I did. I killed Matt.

He drew a bottle of gin to his lips and sloshed a huge gulp into his mouth. Let it burn. . .

Yeah. Face it. Del's right. About everything. This is for you, Wayne. All for you. I'm so sorry about killing Matty. I didn't mean it.

Three bullets. That's all I need. Let's get it on. Spin the cylinder, pull the trigger . . . and let's see who gets dead.

✫✫✫

IN THE CORNER OF THE church basement, at her improvised first aid station, Erin ever-so-gently dabbed a spot of Neosporin onto the small carpet burn on Jimmy Thurman's elbow. "Easy now," she said softly, as the little boy squirmed. "Nothing to it. You'll be good as new in just another . . . second."

Chasing Benny and Jason, Jimmy had tripped on his over-sized high tops and crashed to the floor. Except for the nice raspberry, he'd conquered the fall without a trace. But the abrasion had to burn.

Erin unwrapped a Bugs Bunny Band-Aid and carefully stuck it to the boy's elbow. "Leave this on until it stops stinging, all right?"

His big dark eyes glimmered with unshed tears. "Yes, Miss Erin."

She pulled off her rubber gloves, tossed them on the table, then pulled the little boy into a monstrous bear hug. "And why don't you tighten those shoe laces, you goofy dude? Before you fall again."

Jimmy pulled away, his new front teeth shining against his dark skin. "Can't tie 'em, Miss Erin. That's not how yer 'posed to wear 'em!" He pulled away and ran across the room to find Benny and Jason, high-tops clomping.

Erin laughed, watching him go. Until the basement's back door was pulled open with such force . . . wind and rain blew a man inside. Her husband. Erin stood and moved toward him. "Hey, stranger. How was your day?" she asked him. She saw a strange look in his eyes. "Are you all right?"

"Hi, love." He moved in to kiss her lips.

His face was so wet, after the kiss Erin wiped her nose and cheek with her sleeve.

"I need to talk to you, sweetheart." His voice carried a hint of tension. "I . . . I need to ask you some things."

"What are you talking about? What's wrong?"

"Nothing's wrong." He pulled off his jacket and ran his hand down his face. "I talked to Chris, and now I need to finally get some answers from you."

Erin backed up a step. "What? Where is she?"

His face hardened. "I don't know. Last I saw her, she was heading home."

Erin's teeth clenched. "Stay right here. I'll be back." She didn't turn around as she ran across the basement to the stairs leading to the church's front doors. She ran up the stairs, pushed the heavy door open, ran down the stairs—Chris was halfway across Kimberley Street, heading for home. "Chris!"

She stopped and turned around.

Wind whipped fat raindrops into Erin's ears. She had run out without a jacket, without thinking. She didn't really care. "Wait!"

Chris's eyes hardened. Anger saturated her voice. "What are you doing? Are you crazy?"

Already the rain had soaked Erin's sweatshirt, had flattened her hair against her head. It ran down her face, into her eyes. She had to almost shout above the wind. "Where are you going?"

Chris shouted too. "Where do you think I'm going? Home!"

"Why? What happened?"

"Nothing happened." She almost spat the words. "Go back inside!"

"No! Chris, tell me what happened! What did he say to you?"

"Who? Scott?"

"Yes! What did he say?"

"He didn't say anything to me! Erin, stop this and go back inside!"

She couldn't move. Couldn't speak. She could only stare, blinking as the rain stung her eyes.

⋆⋆⋆

WHO WAS THAT, WALKING ACROSS the street, right in front of his car? Walked like a woman. A woman in a hurry. Where did she come from?

He tried to blink away his drunkenness.

Another woman suddenly burst through the front doors of the church. Ran down the stairs. Yelled at the first woman. The first woman turned around.

He blinked.

McIntyre. It was Chris McIntyre! He couldn't believe his eyes! And then, could it be? Could the second woman be . . . ?

Yes.

A breath of glee slipped out his lips as he tossed the bottle of gin to the floor and grabbed the pistol from the passenger seat. Holding it, he caressed the cool metal, the smoothness of the long barrel, the firmness of the black rubber grip. He used his thumb to flick off the safety. Pulled it up to look at it. Popped open the cylinder. Counted his three bullets.

What better time. He couldn't believe his luck! There they stood. Right there in the street. Right there in front of him.

They were going to make this easy for him! Laughter rumbled up from deep in his chest. He cranked down his window, then cursed as the storm blew into his car. Cursed the storm. He was so ready to see an end to it all.

Today. Right now. What better time.

We want to hear from you. Please send your comments about this book to us in care of zreview@zondervan.com. Thank you.

ZONDERVAN™

GRAND RAPIDS, MICHIGAN 49530 USA

WWW.ZONDERVAN.COM